The Color of Secrets

The
Color of Secrets
LINDSAY ASHFORD

LAKE UNION
PUBLISHING

Text copyright © 2015 Lindsay Ashford
All rights reserved.

Published by Lake Union Publishing, Seattle

www.apub.com

Amazon, the Amazon logo, and Lake Union Publishing are trademarks of Amazon.com, Inc., or its affiliates.

ISBN-13: 9781477828434
ISBN-10: 1477828435

Cover design by Connie Gabbert

Library of Congress Control Number: 2014955245

Printed in the United States of America

In memory of my grandmother, Evelyn Mary Groom

Prologue

The photograph still startles me, even though I've looked at it a dozen times since it landed on the doormat. An elderly white woman with her arm around a beautiful black girl. The magazine has put us on its front cover with the line: "Mixed Blessings—Rhiannon's White Family."

The article is to help publicize her new show. I understand that, of course, but I was worried when she told me about it. Afraid of what she would say about me. She knows only the bare bones of what happened because I didn't want to tell her. That was a terrible mistake.

I wondered if she would tell them that my stubborn silence almost proved deadly. Thankfully she told them the truth, but not all of it. She painted me much better than I am.

And the real story? That will never be told. Not by me, anyway. Some things are too painful to put into words.

Will he tell her?

He stares out at me from the inside pages of the magazine. It's a picture of the two of us, taken that summer of 1943. There was a time when I couldn't have looked at it. Even now I'm fighting back tears. But Rhiannon smiles at me as I turn the page over. I can hear her voice, as clear as if she was standing next to me. Don't cry, *she says.* Look at you and Granddad: you were happy, weren't you, in the end?

It's a question she has never really asked me. Perhaps she doesn't need to. Perhaps she thinks she knows the answer.

Part One

EVA

Chapter 1

Eva sensed what was coming before she saw it. She could feel it through the soles of her boots. Catching her breath, she tasted smoke in the air. She heard the rumble of the wheels. It was the rhythm of carriages, not the usual clatter of coal wagons. Wiping her forehead with the cuff of her jacket, she leaned forward on the handle of her spade.

The other women had heard it too. Shovels, rakes, and pick-axes were cast aside as they shaded their eyes against the sun. Some pulled off their hats and scarves, trying to fluff up hair gone limp with perspiration in the unexpected heat of an English summer morning.

As the train slowed to a crawl, eager heads leaned through the windows. They were wearing squashed-up caps the color of sand. Some were blowing kisses. A cargo of men, carriage after carriage of them. About to pile out here. In this town.

The women started cheering, waving, but Eva's hands never left the wooden shaft of her spade. She couldn't do it. Couldn't bring herself to smile at the faces gliding by. The sight of so many men in uniform triggered a dull ache below her ribs. She was searching each passing carriage, as if she might spot Eddie's face among these American soldiers.

Idiot.

She made herself stop, look away.

He's not coming home because you don't want him to.

The words dropped into her head, as clear and brutal as a telegram. Was it true? Had she done it by some sort of telepathy? Jinxed him?

A loud wolf whistle cut through the engine's noise. One of the older women was wiggling her well-upholstered behind at the men hanging out of the carriages, sending a peal of raucous laughter down the line. Something flew through the air and landed a few feet from where Eva was standing. A brown tube, like the inside of a toilet paper roll. A little scuffle broke out. The winner was a woman whose head looked too big for her body, swollen with rows of curlers crammed inside a workman's cap. She waved the tube in the air and it rattled. Then she cupped her hand around her mouth and yelled at the passing carriage.

"What is it?"

"M&M's! Candy!" the men shouted back.

Eva felt a trickle of saliva run beneath her tongue. Funny how the very thought of sweets did that to her now. And these Americans were throwing them from trains. She swallowed and reached for her spade, trying to think about something else. But not Eddie. She mustn't think about Eddie.

"Want some?"

Eva looked over her shoulder. "Me?"

"Yes, you!" The woman held out her hand, revealing a perfect little disk the same vivid yellow as the curlers poking out of her cap. "Plenty more where these came from, eh?"

Eva hesitated. The woman's smile was conspiratorial, the implication obvious.

"What's the matter? They're not poisonous!"

Eva felt something shift in her stomach. It had been hours since breakfast. She stretched out her hand. "Thank you . . ."

"Iris."

Eva nodded. She popped the sweet into her mouth. As her tongue brought it up against the roof of her mouth, the candy shell disintegrated, releasing the long-forgotten taste of chocolate. She tried to hold it there, but she could feel it melting away, dissolving so fast that she just had to swallow.

"Mmm . . . sex-starved Yanks! Yes, please!" Iris arched her eyebrows and cocked her head at the train. "Thirteen carriages so far—and there must be about sixty or seventy in each one. That's . . ." Her look of concentration vanished as the last carriage rolled into view. "See that lot coming now," she said. "At the back?"

Eva followed her gaze, her eyes temporarily blinded by the sun glancing off the windows.

"Look at their faces . . ." There was a breathless curiosity in her voice, like a kid seeing someone naked for the first time. "You know what *they* are, don't you?"

~

Inside the last carriage one of the soldiers was fast asleep, a beam of light falling on the sweep of skin between his collar and his jawbone, making it glow like tortoiseshell. Bill was dreaming of home. Of New Orleans. Of slipping nickels in the drugstore jukebox on a slow afternoon. The first few beats of "Drum Boogie" making milkshake glasses wobble on the counter as the girls came shimmying out of the kitchen for a jive.

They were there in the kit bag at his feet, the drugstore girls, members of the grainy gallery of faces smiling out from between the tissue-thin pages of a US Army–issue Bible: Alice, Pearl, and Cora-Mae in Genesis; his mother and sister in Psalms; and Rita

5

Hayworth in Revelation. Only Rita was in color. A glossy head-and-shoulders ripped out of *Billboard* magazine.

"Wake up, man!" Someone was shouting in his ear. "This is it! End of the line!"

Opening his eyes, Bill saw the back of Jimmy's head as he turned away, scrambling for a space at the open window. He jumped to his feet and plunged into the tangle of uniforms until he felt a rush of smoke-tainted air on his face. He glimpsed dirty factory chimneys, a mud-colored canal. And then he saw what all the fuss was about.

"What kind of place *is* this?" He craned his neck, holding on to his cap. "They've got *women* working on the railroad!"

"Jeez!" Jimmy was standing on tiptoe, trying to get a better look. "What are they doing?"

"Laying track, looks like."

"No way!" Jimmy gave a low whistle. "No wonder they need *us*. Hey, Bill—look! They're waving at us!"

"Well, they sure have pretty smiles." Bill scanned the line of women in caps, donkey jackets, and wide-legged trousers, a wry grin on his face. "But hey, you seeing what I see?"

"What?" Jimmy yelled back, struggling to make himself heard over the clapping and cheering.

"No colored faces—not a single one!"

Jimmy stuck his head out farther, his knuckles tight as drum skin as he clutched his cap. "Holy Moses," he groaned. "What we gonna do for girls?"

~

Eva tried not to stare as the train emptied the final group of GIs onto the platform. Other than in films, only once had she seen a person with skin the color of the men in this last carriage. He had come to the house selling brushes. She must have been about eight or nine years old. Her mother was busy in the kitchen and had called out to her when the bell rang. Eva had let out a scream when she saw his face, thinking it was someone in a mask. He looked like a forgotten apple, wrapped and tucked away for Christmas in a dark corner of the larder and unearthed, brown and wrinkled, long after it should have been eaten.

At the sound of her scream Eva's mother had come running from the kitchen. She had a tea towel in her hand, which she flicked at the man like a whip, catching his ear. She shouted abuse at him as he backed away, staggering with the weight of the brushes he carried on his back. Eva could still remember the look in his eyes, a wariness tinged with resignation, as if this sort of treatment was no more than he expected. And she had felt an odd mixture of fear and shame at the sight of her mother lashing out at someone who, for all his strangeness, looked very, very old.

The men now spilling out of the train were quite different from the man her mother had driven away. Young. Confident. Smart in their beige uniforms. As she watched, one soldier broke into a little jive, his shoulders and hips swinging this way and that in a fluid, mesmerizing motion. His friends laughed and clapped and clicked their fingers till a sergeant bustled up and put them in line. They were still smiling as they marched off. They looked like people who knew how to have fun.

Eva picked up her shovel. A wisp of auburn hair, damp with perspiration, trailed beneath the collar of her jacket. Suddenly self-conscious, she tucked it in before slicing into the dry, gritty soil at her feet. What they would make of her, in these baggy workman's clothes, hair stuffed inside a cap and sweat beading her face, she couldn't imagine. Would they even be able to tell she was a woman?

In daylight hours she was a strange, sexless creature who dressed like a man and did a man's work. And in the evenings, like a species of vampire, she turned back into a woman again.

Or, more truthfully, a person who wore a skirt instead of trousers, shoes instead of boots. A person who had a child to look after. With a jolt of alarm she realized she no longer *felt* like a woman. She plunged the spade into the ground, scattering crumbs of earth all over herself.

"Eva? You okay?"

The speaker of these words had her hair bundled up in a sort of turban—a scarf of faded leopard-print silk wound around her head and tucked in at the back. There were a couple of pea-sized moth holes above her left eye.

"Cathy! I thought you were on the night shift."

"I was. They called me in, though. One or two shirkers, apparently: not sure if it's the weather or the Yanks!"

"Did you see them? I lost count of the carriages." Eva smiled. "Hundreds of them, all in those very . . ."

"*Tight*-fitting uniforms?" Cathy's eyebrows slid upward and disappeared under her turban. "You can't really picture them doing anything energetic in those, can you? Imagine how long they'd last doing this!" She swept her hand, palm up, toward the piles of earth the women had dug up. "Anyway, how are things? You coping?"

"Sort of." Eva looked away. Cathy Garner was the only person on the rail gang she'd had a proper conversation with in the two weeks since she'd started; the only person who knew anything about her. "David seems to have settled in at the nursery. I still feel guilty every time I leave him there, but I think it's . . ." She couldn't say it. Felt ashamed to admit that somehow it was easier to face things, working on the railway, than sitting at home all day with her son.

"I know," Cathy nodded. "It's hard to tell yourself it's for the best when they're clinging on to you and crying. I remember how it was when Mikey was that age. But you have to have something to take your mind off things." Cathy reached for Eva's arm. "Come on. Don't know about you, but I'm starving."

~

The smell of cabbage and mutton had seeped into the walls of the station canteen. No matter what was on the menu, the sour odor hung in the air, making Eva feel slightly ill as she walked in. But she was always hungry. All the women on the rail gang were. Too hungry to care about the smell, the chipped crockery, and the stains on the tablecloths.

"It's Sardine Pancakes or Sour-Sweet Cabbage with Sausage Meat Cakes," Eva read aloud from the blackboard over the serving hatch. "Followed by Mock Mashed Banana."

"Ugh—not sardines!" Cathy grabbed a tray and peered up at the menu. "And what on earth is Mock Mashed Banana? Sounds absolutely disgusting!"

"Parsnips and powdered milk, probably," Eva grimaced. "Don't know why they bother. I'd rather have them as they are with the main course."

"Me too!" Cathy slid her tray along the metal runway. As the sausage meat cakes landed on her plate, she gave Eva a sideways look. "Someone said the Yanks were throwing sweets from the train. Did you manage to grab any?"

Eva huffed out a laugh. "I've never been much good at catching. They were shared round, though. I'd forgotten how good chocolate tastes."

"Chocolate? Wow! I thought it'd be gum or something."

"No. They were like Smarties—remember them?"

"You lucky beggar! How many did you get?"

"Just the one."

"Good. I won't have to kill you for not saving me some, then."

They took their trays to a table near the window overlooking the platform, which was deserted now that the GIs had gone. For a couple of minutes they ate in companionable silence. One of the things Eva liked about Cathy was that she never asked about

Eddie. Other people she met—the old man in the corner shop, the women at David's nursery—would start or finish most conversations with: "Any news?" They meant well. Of course they did. And she would put on the brave smile that felt so false and shake her head.

But Cathy was different. When they'd first met, Eva had told her she was married with an eighteen-month-old son whose father was missing, presumed dead. And since that first day Cathy had never mentioned him. Not once. Perhaps it was because she knew how it felt. Eva didn't know what had happened to Cathy's husband, only that he had died soon after the war started. An unspoken pact had developed between them: they would talk about pretty much anything other than their men.

"Look at my nails," Cathy said as she reached for the salt. "You'd never think I used to work in the beauty department at Beatties, would you?"

"Well, they're no worse than mine!" Eva splayed out her fingers. "Do you miss it? What you did before?"

"Not really." Cathy shrugged. "It was . . . well, I don't know: I never felt I was doing anything particularly *useful*." She swallowed a mouthful of sausage. "Did you have a job before this one?"

"I worked in a library when I left school."

"Did you like it? Forgive me for saying so, but you don't exactly fit the image."

"Don't I?" Eva grinned. "Well I suppose I was a bit subversive. I almost got fired in my first week."

"What did you do?"

"I put a book about birth control in the Romance section."

Cathy spluttered as she swallowed. "Seriously?"

Eva nodded. "It was called *What Every Mother and Girl Should Know*. It arrived in the post one morning, and I thought it ought to go somewhere prominent. I got into terrible trouble with the head librarian; her brother was the Roman Catholic bishop of Birmingham—"

A screech from the next table made them both look around.

"Is it true? Are they long? And hairy?" It was Iris, the woman who had shared the sweets. She was clutching her sides, tears of laughter streaming down her face.

"How the hell should I know? I don't go round putting my hand down men's trousers!" The woman who'd spoken was someone Eva hadn't seen before. She had ferociously plucked eyebrows, a grin splitting her face. She paused, making sure she had the full attention of the women sitting around the table. "My dad told me. Tails like monkeys, apparently. This Yank came round the Air Raid Patrols last week, telling them what to do if they came across a colored GI. Be polite but not too friendly—that's what he said— because they howl at night and cut folks up when they get mad. And their tails start to twitch when it gets dark."

Iris and her friends could hardly contain themselves. Their food lay uneaten on their plates as they struggled to suppress their hysterics.

Eva and Cathy exchanged glances.

"I saw them coming out of the station," Cathy whispered. "Did you?"

Eva nodded, staring at her half-finished lunch. She could feel the color rising up her throat to her face, her skin burning.

"Eva? Are you all right?"

"I'm fine. Food's a bit hot, that's all—should have waited till it cooled down." How could she explain it to Cathy, the feelings those stupid words had stirred up? Since David's birth she had felt as raw as an oyster building a pearl around a piece of grit. Thoughtless people, staring into the pram, their smiles frozen when they saw the face peeping over the blanket. And he would reach out to them, the way babies do, but no one wanted to touch him.

She wanted to shake Iris's friend until her teeth rattled, wanted to shove a plate of Mock Mashed Banana right into that spiteful, grinning face. She stared at the dirty marks on the tablecloth, dug her fork mechanically into the congealing mess on her plate.

"There's a dance at the Civic on Saturday. Fancy coming?"

Eva looked up, blinking. Cathy had untucked the ends of her turban and made them stick up like rabbit's ears. It was impossible not to smile. "I don't know," Eva said. "I haven't been dancing since I don't know when."

"Good. That makes two of us."

"Well . . . I'd have to find a babysitter."

"Won't your mum do it? How about your sister—she's old enough, isn't she?"

"Old enough to babysit, yes; old enough for boys as well. If she finds out there's a dance on, I won't see her for dust."

"Well, my neighbor's offered to sit with Mikey—I'm sure she wouldn't mind looking after another one."

"Do I detect a whiff of determination here?" Eva rolled her eyes. "Okay, I'll ask my mum. On one condition, though."

"What?"

"No ditching me for the first American with a bar of chocolate and a packet of ciggies."

Chapter 2

Eva sat on the double bed in her best underwear—the cream silk camisole and knickers her mother had fashioned from an old nightdress for her nineteenth birthday. She hadn't even been able to try them on at the time as she was eight months pregnant. *You can save them, can't you*, her mother had said with a conspiratorial smile.

She stared out of the window at the jumble of slate roofs stretching into the distance. On the horizon the square tower of St. Peter's Church was silhouetted against the orange evening sky. She poked her head through the open sash, sniffing the air. A wisp of acrid smoke from Goodyear's tire factory floated over the narrow back gardens, mixing with the smell of boiling tripe from next door's kitchen. She caught sight of a group of women filing through a garden gate into the street beyond. They were chattering and giggling, all dressed up for a night out.

She had been saving her underwear for Eddie. For his first leave after David was born. She had planned it all in her head. She would have lost the baby fat by then. Mum would take David off somewhere and they would have a romantic evening in, just the two of them.

She ran her finger over the lace border of the camisole. It hadn't happened. He'd taken one look at the livid birthmark on his son's face and recoiled in horror. After that she hadn't wanted him anywhere near her.

She glanced at his photo on the dressing table. So smart in his navy uniform. Now his smile seemed to accuse her. "I shouldn't be going, should I?" Though she whispered the words, her voice sounded loud in the quiet bedroom.

"Shouldn't be going?" Eva's sister darted into the room and jumped onto the bed beside her. Her black hair was piled high on her head and her face was almost unrecognizable.

"Since when did you start wearing lipstick?" Eva didn't know whether to laugh or cry at the vampish look Dilys had managed to contrive. "And who did you pinch that mascara from?"

"Didn't pinch it from anyone—it's soot from the chimney mixed with Vaseline! Looks good, doesn't it? And I found the lipstick in one of Mum's old handbags—but that's not all . . ." She danced around the bed, rippling her fingers under Eva's nose.

"Nail varnish as well! Dil?"

"Got it from a girl from school who works in Woolworth's," Dilys trilled. "It's not really nail varnish. They call it *Ladder Stop*."

"Let's see it."

"You don't believe me?" Dilys bounded out of the room and reappeared with a small, white-capped bottle, which she tossed onto the bed.

Eva picked it up and examined the label.

"See! Told you, didn't I? Did you think I'd been with a Yank or something?" Dilys folded her arms, a smug look on her face. "You can have some if you want, but you'd better get ready first."

Eva glanced at Eddie in the silver frame, at herself clutching him with one hand and her wedding bouquet with the other. Part of her wanted to break free. To blot out that hopeful, hopeless image. But Eddie's voice was whispering in her head. *How could you? What if you meet someone?*

"Come on, Sis!" Dilys grabbed Eva's hands. "Eddie wouldn't want you to be staying in all the time feeling miserable, would he?"

Eva swallowed hard and slid off the bed. "I suppose it won't hurt to go for an hour or so—but no moaning when I say it's time to leave, okay? And wipe some of that lipstick off, for God's sake."

Dilys gave a theatrical sigh. "Must I really? It's such a *waste.*"

"Well, I'd rather see it on a bit of paper chucked in the bin than smeared over some boy's collar!"

"Spoilsport!" Dilys dodged out of the way as Eva swiped at her. "Hurry up! You're not even dressed!"

"That's because I don't know what on earth I'm going to wear. You do realize I haven't been anywhere apart from the cinema since David was born? I don't think any of this stuff's going to fit me."

Eva's body had not gone back to its prebaby shape. Her hips were wider and her breasts fuller. The only thing she had a chance of wriggling into was a blue woolen shift dress that had been hanging neglected in the wardrobe since before she was married. There was a short boxy jacket that went with it.

She was trying them on when her mother walked into the bedroom. Eva saw her reflection in the long mirror. She was standing in the doorway, rubbing her wedding ring. It was something she did often. A habit she seemed to have acquired since being widowed. As if to remind herself she hadn't always been alone. She had been married for twenty years when Eva's father died. If he had lived, they would have been celebrating their silver wedding anniversary this year. What did it feel like, Eva wondered, to spend that long living with a man? The longest she and Eddie had lived together without a break was ten days.

She tugged at the hem of her jacket, glancing at her reflection. She had never called herself a widow—despite the long, long months without any news. The word felt as awkward as her suit.

"Don't bother with the blackout boards," her mother said. "I'll put them up later. You go and enjoy yourself. Got your gas mask and your torch?"

Eva nodded, watching her mother tuck a pile of clean, folded baby clothes into the chest of drawers. Had she imagined it, or had there been a sharpness in the way she'd said the word *enjoy*? Mum had never encouraged her to go out in the evenings. It wasn't the fear of German bombs. Not any longer. It was as if Eddie's absence had forged a bond that hadn't existed before Eva's marriage. They would listen to the wireless together or sit reading in companionable silence, Eva with a book and her mother with the newspaper; two women alone but not lonely, with Dilys and David at the center of their universe.

In the years before the war they had not been close—not as close as Eva had been to her father, anyway. When he was alive, Eva had often found herself wishing her mother had been a little kinder, a little less sharp. Had they been happy? She wasn't sure. And what was it like for her mother now? Would she want another man if chance should bring one, or had she cast off that part of herself with the handful of earth she'd thrown on Dad's coffin?

As Eva glanced back at the mirror she caught the reflected black-and-white image of Eddie's face. She thought of how he had devoured her on their wedding night. For both of them it had been the first time. She had been nervous, hoping to take things slowly. He'd tried—for all of thirty seconds. He'd said sorry, that he couldn't help himself. She wondered if he'd been afraid it was going to be his one and only time. Was that how he'd felt when he went off to war? That if he died now, at least he would not die a virgin? Was that why he'd been so keen to get married?

"Come on, Eva!" Dilys called her from the landing, hiding her made-up face from her mother. "You must be ready by now!"

Eva didn't feel ready. Under the jacket her dress was unzipped. She couldn't do it all the way up. She told herself she'd be all right as long as she kept the jacket on.

"See you later, Mum." She caught a trace of Devon Violets as she brushed her mother's cheek with her lips. For some reason she couldn't explain the scent set off a feeling of unease, which shifted into nervousness about the evening ahead. She had forgotten how to do this. How to be in a crowd. How to be with men.

She tiptoed across to David's cot and gazed at his sleeping face. The birthmark had almost gone now. Two years, the doctor had said. At the time she hadn't believed him. It was impossible to imagine that the ugly, blood-colored blob the size of an egg could simply disappear. She stroked the pale-pink patch on his cheek before bending down and kissing him softly.

"Hurry up!" Dilys hissed. "Cathy's at the door!"

Eva's jacket swished against the bars of the cot. David stirred, murmuring something in his sleep, but his mother was already halfway down the stairs.

Chapter 3

"You coming?" Jimmy flicked Bill's cap with his fingers, knocking it sideways. "Don't want to miss the passion wagon!"

"*Passion* wagon?" Bill repositioned the cap, frowning at his reflection in the tiny square of mirror on the wall between the bunks. "No chance in this one-horse town!"

"Ah, but we're not going to Bridgnorth tonight," Jimmy tapped the side of his nose. "They're taking us to Wolverhampton. Remember? That place we got off the train."

Bill swung around, his arms folded. "Wolverhampton? But that's a *white* town . . ."

"Not tonight." Jimmy chuckled. "I was in the guardhouse when they dropped off the invitation."

"What invitation?"

"From the Royal Netherlands Regiment. There's a dance in honor of Queen Wilhelmina."

"Queen *who*?" One of Bill's eyebrows jerked toward his cap.

"Wil-hel-mina. Dutch Queen. It's her birthday or something. All Allied troops within ten miles of their camp are invited."

Bill sniffed. "So we're going to some barracks in the middle of nowhere? Sounds even worse than Bridgnorth!"

"No, you got it all wrong." Jimmy shook his head. "It's at the Civic—biggest dance hall in town! I tell you, man, there'll be more girls than you can handle!"

"Is that a fact?" Bill's eyes narrowed. "And who do you reckon they'll go for? A bunch of Dutch fellas, three white Yankee companies—or us? Try thinking like a white girl, Jimmy."

Later the two men jumped out of a US Army truck and stood for a moment on the pavement, taking in the unfamiliar surroundings. The mellow stone of St. Peter's Church glowed in the light of the sinking sun. In its shadow were knots of women, laughing and chattering as they moved past empty market stalls. Across the square was the Civic Hall, its Doric pillars towering over the heads of the khaki-clad soldiers filing through the doors.

"Don't look now," Jimmy said, as the company of black GIs set off across the square, "but I think we're being followed."

Bill could hear barely suppressed giggles and loud shushing noises over his left shoulder. As the others marched ahead, he signaled to Jimmy and they sidestepped out of the line, slipping behind one of the market stalls.

"Here they come," Bill whispered. Both craned their necks as far as they could without being noticed.

"Stop staring at their backsides!" A woman with sparse brown hair regimented into a stiff marcel wave nudged the younger one walking beside her. The rest of the group of women started giggling.

"I can't help it!" The girl's round cheeks reddened as she tried to get the words out. "I only want to see their tails!"

"Don't be stupid! It's not dark yet!"

"Well, it soon will be . . ." the girl trailed off, clapping her hand to her mouth and snorting.

The two men stared wordlessly at each other as the women disappeared from view.

"What did I tell you?" Bill said through clenched teeth. "We're headed for a goddamn circus!"

"Come on, man!" Jimmy coaxed. "They're not all like that! Remember that sassy blonde with the sandwiches at Liverpool docks? She couldn't take her eyes off you—and it wasn't your ass she was looking at."

Bill grunted.

"Come on!" Jimmy shoved him forward. "We've got to go in there anyway—there'll be worse trouble if they think we've skipped the line."

Once inside, the men were shepherded to a corner of the dance hall, to the right of the stage. From that position it would be impossible to see the band when the music started up. There were plenty of women in the room—Jimmy had not been wrong about that.

Bill watched the men around him. Hungry looks were accompanied by whispered expressions of desire. The words he caught were mostly too crude to repeat. He stared at the floor between his feet. What was the point of looking?

"Hey, man! Get a load of her!" Jimmy poked him in the ribs. When Bill failed to respond, his friend grabbed him by the chin, jerking his head upward. "The one with the tight blouse . . . Man, I swear if I get up close to her, those buttons are going to pop right off!"

"Dream on, Jimmy," Bill grunted as he pulled away. But as he did so, something caught his eye. A flash of long red hair. As he focused in, she turned to the woman beside her. Now he could see her in profile. He blinked. It was Rita Hayworth, come to life.

As if she'd stepped out from between the pages of Revelation and followed him here.

~

The dance floor was a sea of khaki and blue, the odd flowered dress making the only splash of color. About half of the women were in uniform, most of the others wearing drab two-pieces cut in military styles from old coats or curtains.

"This was what I wore on my first date with Eddie," Eva whispered as she and Cathy fox-trotted across the floor. She was beginning to feel hot in the woolen jacket and wished she could take it off. "Seems like such a long time ago," she went on, "doesn't seem real, sometimes, but—" She stopped short as Dilys danced past, clutching a Dutch soldier like a trophy. She'd left her sister near the entrance to the dance floor with a group of her school friends. She was going to have to keep a very close eye on her.

"Is that why you don't wear a ring?" Cathy, facing the other way, hadn't spotted Dilys.

"No," Eva said, watching her sister move across the room, "I started taking it off for work because the spade handle was giving me a callus, and now I hardly ever remember to put it back on again. I suppose it looks bad, but it's not deliberate."

"Don't worry. If people want to think badly of you, they'll do it anyway—they don't need an excuse. Anyway, I know how you feel—about it all seeming unreal, I mean: next Christmas I'll have been a widow for longer than I was married." She pressed her lips together, draining them of their color. "I look at Stuart's photo sometimes and I think, that's all there is. The only thing I've got to remember him by. Apart from Mikey." Her eyes were bright with unshed tears. "He's the image of his dad."

"You've never talked about him," Eva began. "I've always been afraid to ask . . ."

"I suppose I just find it easier not to when all the girls are around." Cathy pushed a stray lock of dark-brown hair from her eyes. "Like I said the other day, work helps. I tend to shut everything to do with home out of my mind."

As they drifted across the dance floor, Eva tried to do the same. Thinking about Eddie stirred up an unsettling mix of emotions. The fear and the worry were shot through with guilt. She had never cried for him; never missed him the way Cathy so obviously missed Stuart. Was that because they had had so little time together? Or because she had been so angry at the way he had been with David? There was also a third reason: one she hardly dared put into words. That she was fearful, not for him, but for herself. Afraid of what it would be like if he did come back.

"He was killed at Dunkirk." Cathy's voice cut across her thoughts, all the more startling for its matter-of-fact tone. "It was the day before Mikey's birthday. He was only three. When I told him, he asked me if his dad would be able to send his present from heaven."

"Oh, Cathy," Eva began, "I'm sorry, I should never have—"

"No, it's okay," Cathy said quickly. "Sometimes it helps to talk about it. Funny, though, isn't it, how you can feel even more lonely in a great big place like this?"

The band struck up another number. "Do you want sit down?" Eva glanced toward the side of the hall, where men in uniform were craning their necks on the lookout for partners. Dilys was still on the dance floor, holding hands now with the soldier from Holland, who looked way too old for her.

"No, let's keep dancing." Cathy hooked her arm through Eva's. "I shouldn't have started talking about Stuart—you of all people don't need to hear me wallowing in it. Come on, let's have some fun!"

"All right, ladies and gentlemen," the MC boomed, "it's time for something a little different! Can I have all the gentlemen—and

I mean *all* the gentlemen—making a circle in the center of the floor, please!"

There was a rumble of chairs and feet as the men at the margins of the room rushed forward.

"Come on, now, spread out," the MC called. "Make a big circle, facing outward—and ladies, I'd like you to make another circle round the outside."

"I think we're about to be paired off," Eva hissed. "Are you sure you—"

"Now, ladies," the MC cut in, "I don't want any of you sitting this one out! Let's give a special welcome to our visitors!" He gestured to the men standing awkwardly in the center of the room. "From Holland!" A forest of hands waved as the women cheered. "And from the US of A!"

It was then that Eva noticed the black soldiers. She hadn't seen any of them on the dance floor. Now, while their white compatriots waved for all they were worth at the cheers and whistles, the black GIs simply raised their hands to chest height in a halfhearted gesture, as if they were embarrassed at being recognized, Eva thought.

Suddenly the band struck up and the MC was barking out instructions.

"I haven't got a clue what this one is." Cathy giggled over her shoulder as the women and the men marched past each other, forming two giant wheels turning in opposite directions.

Eva's mind was not on what her feet were doing. She was scanning the circles, searching for Dilys, worried that she might have sneaked off somewhere with the Dutchman. So preoccupied was she that when the music stopped and a pair of muscular arms grabbed her from behind she let out a little squeal of shock.

"Don't worry, lady, I don't bite!"

It was a voice from a movie. An American voice. His hands were on her shoulders. She could feel their warmth through the fabric of her jacket. As she twisted around, he released her. She saw only the uniform at first because her eyes were level with his chest. And then she looked up.

"Good evening, ma'am."

His lips slid into a wide smile. Lips the color of bonfire toffee, just a shade darker than his face. With a hint of pink at their inner edges. His eyes, above sweeping cheekbones, were a deep, fathomless brown, almost black. They crinkled at the edges with his smile.

Suddenly aware that her mouth was open, she clamped it shut.

He made a sort of bow, his eyes fixed on her face, not running the length of her body the way some men's did when they encountered a woman. Then he held out his hand. A giant's hand to match his height. The palm was pink. She stared at it for a moment, fleetingly aware that she hadn't known this; hadn't noticed it with the old man who'd come to the house selling brushes. And at the same time something was bubbling up inside her, a mixture of fear and wonder. Slowly, nervously, she held out her hand to him.

Their fingers had barely touched when the music struck up again and the MC's voice barked out more instructions. Before she could register the words, he was whisking her off in a promenade, his arm tight around her waist. She could smell his uniform, a scent of warm wool and something spicy, like oranges spiked with cloves. As they spun together, she felt her feet leaving the ground. It was an odd sensation, feeling a man's arms around her after so long. She tensed, thinking of Eddie. The scent of this man was so different from that old, familiar smell of sweat mixed with cigarettes. As they danced, she felt the heat of him through her clothes and the bubble of fear turned into something else, a long-forgotten sensation that surged beneath the silk against her skin.

"And release your partner!" The MC's voice rose above the music. "That's right, ladies and gentlemen—back into your circles, please! Here we go again!"

She wasn't sure how, but he managed to get around to the very same position, opposite her in the men's circle, a second time. As they danced, she felt his hands travel from her shoulders, down her spine, coming to rest halfway down her back. That rush again. She broke away as the rhythm of the music changed, diving back into the anonymous crowd of women in the outer circle. But she had underestimated his determination. She danced with only one other man before he caught her again.

"Can I have a proper dance with you? After this, I mean?" Because of the volume of the music, his mouth was very close to her ear, his lips brushing against it. She gazed at him, fascinated by the velvety brown of his skin. His eyes were hypnotic, daring her to say yes.

"I . . . I'll have to sit the next one out." She looked over her shoulder, searching for Cathy. "It's so hot in here—I could do with a drink." She needed to find Dilys. She glanced back at him. His eyelids were lowered, the spell broken. She hoped she hadn't hurt his feelings. She wanted to say that she'd be glad to dance with him later, but she held back, unsure whether she should be encouraging him.

A woman pushed past them—a woman she recognized from the rail gang—arm in arm with another GI. He was white. Childhood images crowded her mind. Not the brush seller this time, but skipping with a rope in the playground, singing words that made nine-year-old girls snigger with ignorant mischief: *She likes coffee, she likes tea, she likes sitting on a black man's knee . . .* You had to jump with the beat. The rope would go faster and faster. And if you tripped on those last few words, they would point at you and fall about laughing.

"Can I get you something? There's beer if you like it; not much else, I don't guess. Maybe some lemonade?"

She took a breath, gave a single nod of her head. Like she was giving herself permission. "A shandy would be lovely."

"A shandy?" A puzzled, lopsided smile. It made his face puppy-dog cute.

"Half-and-half." She smiled. "Beer mixed with lemonade. Can I meet you by the bar in a minute? I have to find my friend—and my sister."

"Sure," he shrugged. "Will they drink shandy?"

"Oh, you don't have to . . ."

He held up his hand. "It's not a problem. I'll come find you."

As he turned away, she caught sight of Dilys clapping enthusiastically near the stage. Cathy was standing next to her. Eva made her way through the crowd as the band struck up the opening bars of another number. Before she reached them, she saw Dilys turn away, led back onto the dance floor by the same Dutch soldier who had partnered her before. As Eva made eye contact with Cathy, she felt a hand on her shoulder.

"Can I have this dance?" Twisting her head, she saw blue eyes beneath an RAF cap. The edges of the mouth formed a familiar, lascivious smile. He was the other man who had stopped in front of her at the crucial moment during that last dance. And his arm had brushed against her breast—*accidentally-on-purpose,* she thought—as they joined hands for the promenade. Now it felt as if he was looking right through her clothes to her lace-trimmed underwear. She shifted uncomfortably and glanced back at Cathy, who was coming toward them.

"I'm sorry." Eva gave the airman a hard stare. "I'm sitting this one out—and I've promised the next dance to someone else."

"Oh, all right." The airman was totally unfazed by her reply. His gaze switched to Cathy, who was beside her now. "How about your friend?"

Cathy glanced at Eva, whose eyes said yes, go ahead, he's all yours if you want him.

"Watch his hands," Eva whispered as he led Cathy away. "Wave if you need rescuing!"

As they disappeared, Eva caught sight of her other dance partner coming across the room with a tray of glasses. It was like watching a giant crossing an undulating ocean. He was head and shoulders taller than the majority of the men in the room. The unhealthy pallor of the underfed civilians made his smooth brown skin all the more striking. He walked very erect, very dignified, as if his mission was of the utmost importance. He was looking for her; hadn't spotted her yet. She could disappear if she wanted to. *Did* she want to? She tugged at the hem of her jacket. Then, as if some invisible wire was pulling it, her arm rose over her head and waved.

~

"I never asked your name," he began as he set the glasses down on the table. "I'm Bill. Bill Willis—pleased to meet you." He held out his hand once again and this time she shook it properly, smiling self-consciously.

"Eva. Eva Melrose." She slid her fingers around the stem of her glass so that he wouldn't see the nails, stubby and broken from digging out tracks.

"You live round here?"

She nodded.

"Guess you come here all the time."

"I don't, actually." Eva shrugged. "This is the first time I've been here since . . ." she hesitated, wondering how much she should tell him. "Since the war started."

"Really?" He raised his eyebrows.

She nodded. Safer to let him think that. *Safer?* She took a large gulp of shandy.

"Well." He smiled. "The way they dance over here sure don't make it easy for a guy. Getting round that line to you was harder than a game of Chase the Queen."

She felt a blush rising up her neck. "What's that?"

"Oh, just a card game we play back home—takes a lot of concentration."

"And where is that? Home, I mean."

There was a sudden eruption of laughter from a group of men gathered near the stage. Bill glanced over his shoulder before replying.

She frowned at the unfamiliar word. "Nwoorlins?"

"You heard of it? It's in Louisiana."

"I don't think so. How do you spell it?"

She laughed when he reeled off the letters. "New Orleans! Stupid me—it sounds so different with an American accent."

"Sounds real fancy the way you say it," he chuckled.

"What's it like? Is it nice?"

He pursed his lips. "That depends."

"On what?" She wondered where his smile had gone. His eyes had a troubled look now, darting from side to side as he drank his beer.

He shook his head. "Guess it'd take some explaining. They call it the Big Easy. Easy place to make a living." He blew out a breath. As he set his glass down, the music changed to a faster rhythm. Instantly his fingers took it up, rippling over the lacquered surface of the table. "Could we dance to this?" That eagerness was back in his eyes. It was contagious. Moments later they were bouncing across the floor, his hand squeezing her waist. She could feel his breath on her cheek as he moved, sure of each step, his body fused to hers.

"You're a very good dancer." She wasn't sure if he could hear her above the music.

"You think so?" He gave her a curious look, as if weighing her up. Then he smiled, setting off that surge in her stomach again. She fought down the feeling. I'm only dancing, she told herself. Nothing wrong with that.

Suddenly all the lights went out. There was a loud "ooh" from the crowd. Eva felt Bill's fingers tighten around her waist, pulling her to him, as the MC's voice rang out in the darkness: "Don't panic, ladies and gents! It's not an air raid—just the Blackout Stroll, specially requested by our hosts, the Royal Netherlands Regiment!"

With a rush of panic Eva thought of Dilys. In the excitement of dancing she had forgotten all about her. Where was she? What was she doing?

"What on earth's the Blackout Stroll?" Eva heard a familiar-sounding voice somewhere to her right. It sounded like Cathy. She opened her mouth to call out but before any words came she felt Bill's hand glide up her back. His fingers were stroking the bare skin at the base of her neck.

"Can I kiss you?" The scent of him engulfed her as his mouth found her ear. She felt the slight graze of stubble as his chin moved across hers. As their lips met, a current of heat shot down her body, as if she were melting. She felt the tip of his tongue sliding into her mouth, tasting her. And his hands cupped her face so gently, as if she were something delicate and expensive that might break. The irony of this made it all the more delicious. She pressed her fingers into his back, feeling the muscle beneath the fabric of his shirt, drawing him closer, closer.

But it was over in seconds. The lights snapped on to reveal couples in clinches all over the dance floor. She looked into his eyes, shamefaced, awkward. What had she done? He was smiling, but she looked away. Looked for Cathy. Looked for Dilys. But all she could see was a tangle of bodies and unfamiliar faces.

"Hey, Bud!" An American voice boomed from a few feet away. "Yes, you!"

A white soldier sauntered over to them, hands on his hips. He was shorter than Bill but much heavier. "You better make the most of that while you're in Britain, boy," he said in a languid, menacing voice. "'Cause by God, if you was in Texas, you wouldn't be doing it!"

Bill let go of Eva, squaring up to the man. "Well, we're not *in* Texas," he said, his eyes narrowing, "so why don't you do like the British do?"

The punch sent Bill staggering backward into Eva's arms. She felt her legs buckle as she caught him. Somehow he managed to spring up from his back foot, saving her from falling underneath him. But as she lurched sideways, the strain on her tight blue dress was too much. The stitching ripped from the waist to the hem.

Chapter 4

Eva was half kneeling, half crouching on the floor. She heard shouts as two Dutch soldiers grabbed the white GI and frog-marched him off the floor. Where had Cathy and Dilys gone? Bill was bent over her, cradling her shoulders. A mottled graze marred the skin beneath his left eye.

"Are you all right, honey?" he said. "Did I hurt you?"

"Never mind about me!" Eva forced a smile. "You're the one who got hit—are *you* all right?"

"Oh, I'm fine," Bill closed his eyes for a second. Eva was not sure if he was in pain or trying to summon some inner strength.

"Let me help you up." He started to lift her.

"No!" she whispered. "I . . . it's my . . ." she faltered. "Could you lend me your jacket?"

"Sure," he said, taking it off and placing it around her shoulders.

"Thanks." She slid the jacket down, knotting the arms around her waist. She caught the puzzled look on Bill's face as he helped her to her feet. "Could we go outside? I think I could do with some air."

"Me too," he replied, taking her arm before shouldering his way through the crowd.

He pushed open the two sets of blacked-out glass doors and led her out into the twilight.

"Are you sure you're okay?" she asked.

"Uh-huh." There was no edge to his voice; nothing to convey what he really felt about what had happened. They stood there in uneasy silence. In the gathering darkness it was difficult to make out the expression on his face.

"I'm sorry," she whispered.

"Sorry for what?" He sounded gruff now, almost angry.

"For what happened in there. It was disgraceful. That idiot punching you like that . . ."

"Oh, it's nothing to get riled up about," he said. "It's what I've come to expect from the likes of him."

"But he's a soldier." Eva frowned. "He's an American . . ."

"Sure he is." Bill gave a low, sardonic chuckle. "A *white* American. And this is a *white* town."

"What do you mean?"

She heard him sigh. "Colored guys like me, we don't usually get to come here. Far as Uncle Sam's concerned, it's for white GIs only. We get taken to a little town called Bridgnorth, about ten, fifteen miles from here for Rest and Relaxation, as they call it—the kind of place that's too small for us to cause any trouble. We only came here tonight 'cause it's a special occasion."

"You mean they separate the whites and the . . ." she broke off, uncomfortable with the word he had used to describe himself, the same word Iris had used in the station canteen.

"Yes, ma'am. Separate barracks, separate jobs, separate dances—the works!"

Eva suddenly remembered the train. Carriage after carriage of white soldiers, then Iris pointing at the one bringing up the rear: *See that lot at the back? Look at their faces!*

"You're shivering," Bill's voice cut across her thoughts. "Do you want my jacket around your shoulders?" His hands went to her waist, untying the knot she had made with the arms. "What was this for? Are your legs cold?"

"No. It was my dress . . . when we fell on the floor." She stopped, too embarrassed to explain. As he draped the jacket over her, he pulled her to him, his lips hungry.

"I . . ." She hesitated again. *I what?* The touch of his lips and hands made her heart flip with excitement. What should she tell him? That she was married? Why, when she didn't even know if it was true any longer?

She let sensation wash over her, her stomach contracting as he pressed against her. Out here, in the dark, what they were doing somehow felt less wrong. But in there, on the dance floor she had betrayed Eddie in the most public way possible. Through that single, reckless act she had crossed a line in her marriage. And in doing so she had caused this man actual, physical harm.

Dilys's words crept into her head. *Did you think I'd been with a Yank?* She had spat them out, full of contempt, as if going with an American was little better than being a prostitute. What would Dilys make of this, Eva wondered?

She clung to Bill in the growing darkness, her head against his chest. Closing her eyes, she breathed in his scent. The pulsing heat low down in her belly told her just how much she wanted him. She was stunned, shocked by the chemistry between them. What *was* it about him?

She tried to remember how it had been with Eddie. It had been exciting, yes, at the beginning, but in a different way. She had been excited about getting married. About having a baby. About having someone older to rely on instead of being the one everyone else depended on. But kissing Eddie had never made her feel this way.

"I love this," Bill said, stroking her hair. "You're so pretty!"

Eva smiled inside. He made her *feel* pretty—in spite of her ripped dress and her rough hands with their chipped nails.

"I feel like I need to pinch myself," he said. "I never kissed a girl like you before."

Eva found this hard to believe. He was so striking. He must have had plenty of girls after him back home. She frowned, trying to remember what the thug on the dance floor had said. Something about making the most of it in Britain.

"What did that lout mean?" she asked. "You know, when he was ranting on about Texas?"

Bill's head was resting against her neck. She felt the muscles of his jaw tense. "Where I come from, we have these stupid laws," he said. "Depends what state you live in, but in the South, most places colored folks and white folks don't mix. It's not allowed."

"Don't mix? You mean like this?" She traced his lips with her finger.

"Uh-huh." He took her finger in his mouth. "Crazy, I know," he mumbled.

"I didn't know it was like that. How can they do that?"

"They think we're inferior to them. That's the top and bottom of it," he said, caressing her cheek. "Same in the army. We don't get to fight, don't get to handle weapons; all we're here for is to cook for them, clean up after them, that kind of thing."

"Is that what you do? Cook, I mean?"

He went quiet for a moment. "That's not what I wanted to do. I wanted to fight."

She thought of Eddie then, wondered what he would say in response. Eddie *hadn't* wanted to fight. His father had been mustard-gassed in 1916 and returned from the war a shadow of the man he'd once been. He'd died when Eddie was ten years old, too weak to withstand the bronchitis that plagued him each winter. No wonder Eddie had dreaded being called up.

"Have you lost anyone, Eva?" Bill's question sliced through her thoughts like a knife. Had he guessed? Was she that easy to read? She was framing some vague response when the sound of giggling floated across the square from the gloomy recesses of the shop fronts. Eva's breath caught in her throat. Dilys! Where was she? And what had she been doing all this time?

She pulled away from Bill's arms. "I've got to find my sister! I was supposed to be keeping an eye on her . . ." She stumbled down the steps, fumbling in her bag for her torch, calling Dilys's name.

"Hey, wait a minute!" She could hear his footsteps behind her as she ran toward the shops, past the ghostly market stalls. "Let me help you!" A needle-thin beam of light fell on the metal framework of the stall in front of her. "Whoa!" he said as he caught up to her. "How do you know she's not back inside, dancing?"

"I looked for her when the lights went on and she wasn't there," Eva groaned. "She's only fifteen and she was with one of those Dutch soldiers!" She bit her lip as the beam of her own torch, dimmed by the brown paper wrapped over its end, caught a flash of bare legs in one of the shop doorways.

They walked the length of the row of shops—the groans, whispers, and giggles punctuated by shouts of abuse as her torch beam settled on one couple after another. Dilys was not there.

"Come on," Bill said, "let's go back inside—she'll be in there, you betcha."

It was hard to adjust to the brightness of the lights as they pushed open the inner doors. Bill hung back as Eva headed into the crowd.

"Where have you been?" Eva jumped as she heard her friend's voice. There was a mischievous grin on Cathy's face as she glanced at the pale-khaki jacket around Eva's shoulders.

"Oh, don't ask!" Eva cast a nervous smile. "I've been trying to find Dilys. And anyway," she said, eyebrows arching, "what happened to you? You disappeared during the Blackout Stroll."

"I went to look for Dilys too: I needed an excuse to ditch that RAF chap. Hands everywhere—like Christopher Columbus discovering America!" Cathy rolled her eyes. "Anyway, I found her in that little alcove behind the cloakroom. She's over there now."

Eva followed Cathy's gaze and spotted Dilys waltzing toward the stage. Her partner was the same Dutch soldier as before.

"Cathy, they weren't . . ."

"Don't worry! They were just necking. The minute Dilys clapped eyes on me, she turned bright red and shot back onto the dance floor."

"Thanks, Cathy. I should never have gone outside."

Cathy's mouth framed the beginning of a question, but Eva felt a sudden rush of cold air against the back of her legs. Someone had opened the doors behind her. Her hand shot to her behind as she remembered her torn dress. She stepped backward and sideways into the sheltering shadow of the wall, pulling Bill's jacket off her shoulders and knotting it around her waist again. Cathy followed, a look of amused confusion on her face. Before Eva could explain, she heard someone shout Bill's name.

"Hey man, you okay?"

She saw another black GI, shorter than Bill and with small, darting eyes, pushing his way through the knots of people at the edge of the dance floor.

~

"I heard about what happened." Jimmy peered into Bill's face, taking in the graze beneath his eye.

"And where were you when I needed you?" Bill dug his friend in the ribs and grunted a laugh.

"Getting to know a young lady," Jimmy replied coyly. He glanced toward the door. "Don't worry—she's gone home. And in case you're wondering, no one saw us. What were you thinking of, man? If you want to get past first base without getting flattened, you'd better do your smooching in the dark!"

Bill's expression told him to button his lip.

The music faded out and couples began filing past them, heading for the door. Over the babble of voices the MC bid everyone good night. Where was Eva? Bill craned his neck, looking over the heads for that distinctive long red hair.

"Wait for me a minute, will you?"

Jimmy gave him a sideways look. "You be careful, now!"

~

Eva was glancing distractedly about the room when she spotted Bill coming toward them. He stopped when he caught sight of Cathy. She bit her lip. What should she do? She didn't want him to leave. Not without saying good-bye. She smiled at him, angling her head, trying to communicate without drawing attention to them both. She saw him glance at the people on either side of her before stepping forward.

"Good evening, ma'am." He addressed Cathy first, with the same small bow he had given Eva earlier. "Would you excuse me? There's something I need to ask your friend." He leaned in close to Eva. "Can I walk you home?"

Eva felt his breath on her face. It set her skin on fire, the blush spreading all the way down to the neckline of her dress. She glanced at Cathy, whose eyes were like saucers. "Well," she said, "I'm with my friend . . . and my sister. We're all walking back together and . . ." She hesitated, embarrassed to be having this conversation in front of Cathy.

"I don't mind," Bill replied. "I'll walk you all home."

Before she could respond, she heard another voice call his name. It was the man Eva had seen before. His friend. He was coming toward them. He stopped when he was still a few feet away from where they stood, cupping his hand around his mouth.

"Come on, man! You're gonna miss the wagon!"

"Could you wait just a second?" Bill said to the women. "I'll be back, I promise."

He strode over to his friend. Eva couldn't hear what he said, but she could see the expression on the other man's face. With a frown, a shrug, and a shake of the head, Bill's friend turned away.

"Wow!" Cathy whispered. "Where did you find him?"

Eva just looked at her, tongue-tied. "I . . . I . . . is it okay?" she stuttered. "For him to walk us home, I mean?"

Cathy nodded. "Fine by me."

Bill was coming back. "What do you say?" He looked from Eva to Cathy.

"Are you sure?" Eva asked. "Won't you be late getting back to your camp?"

"It's not a problem. I'll wait for you outside, okay?"

He was halfway to the door, swallowed up in the crush of people leaving, when Dilys came bouncing up to them, hand in hand with her Dutch soldier.

"This is Anton," she said, looking smug. "He's from Holland: Maastricht." She rolled the name of the city off her tongue and through her teeth like a purring tiger.

Eva held out her hand. He didn't look any younger, up close. She wondered if he had any idea her sister was only just out of school.

"Guess what," Dilys said, beaming, "he's going to give us all a lift home!"

"Oh . . ." Eva looked at Cathy. "But we were going to walk . . ."

"Oh no! Who wants to walk when you can travel in style?" Dilys grabbed Anton's arm. "He's a driver! Gets to swank about in all the posh cars, don't you, darling?"

Eva winced. Anton was gazing adoringly at her sister.

"So this is what we'll do," Dilys went on before Eva could get a word in. "Anton's going to take his boss to the barracks and then come back for us—we'll only have to wait for about a quarter of an hour—"

"But Dilys," Eva cut in, "won't he get into trouble?"

"'Course not!" Dilys laughed. "Don't be such a spoilsport!"

Eva scanned the crowd of people by the door. Bill wasn't among them. She took her sister by the hand and gave her a speaking look. Reluctantly, Dilys let go of her soldier and allowed herself to be taken to one side.

"Listen, Dil," Eva whispered, "I'll meet you outside in a minute, but I've just got to go and say good night to someone."

"Mmm!" Dilys wiggled her eyebrows and cast about for a likely candidate. "Who is he, then?"

"Just mind your own business and leave me alone for five minutes, will you?" Eva hissed. "If you don't, I'll tell Mum all about you know who!" She cocked her head at Anton.

"Okay, keep your hair on!" Dilys flounced back to her man. "You'd better come with us," she said to Cathy. "Don't want to be a wallflower, do you?"

Eva rolled her eyes, mouthing "sorry" to Cathy, who shrugged and smiled before following Dilys and Anton out of the side entrance to the hall, which opened onto the street, not the square. This, presumably, was where Anton's car was parked. Eva hoped Dilys wouldn't be able to see her from there.

She needn't have worried. There was no moon. It was now pitch-black outside. She had to call Bill's name to find him.

"Look, it's all right—I don't want to get you into trouble," he said when she explained what had happened. "Just promise me something, though, will you?"

"What?" She was suddenly aware of the sounds around her, of all the couples thronging the square, making reluctant, steamy farewells.

"Meet me next Saturday night, seven o'clock right here. We could go to the movies and I'll take you for something to eat."

"Next Saturday night?" The sound of her voice echoing his unnerved her. She nuzzled his chest, searching for the right words.

"Well? What d'you say?"

His eagerness shot her through with guilt. Would it be so terrible to say yes? A distant voice inside her head said that it would. That to take this any further would be as wrong as the punch that had felled him half an hour since. But she didn't want to listen.

"Well, if the answer's no," he said wryly, "I'm going to have to give you this." She felt him rummaging inside his jacket, which still hung from her waist. He found her hand and pressed something thin and hard and flat into it. "Here," he said, "ransom for my jacket. I'd let you keep it, but I think someone back at camp might notice."

"What is it?"

"It's candy: a Hershey bar. Do you have them over here?"

Eva lifted it to her nose. The scent of it seeped through the wrapper. "Well, now, I *was* going to say yes to that date . . . but if it means I have to give this back, well . . ."

He grabbed her and kissed her, but she wriggled free.

"I've got to go," she whispered, untying the jacket and hooking it over his arm. "I'll see you next week."

"Do we have a date, then? Really?"

"Yes." She squeezed his arm. "We've got a date."

Chapter 5

"It's Curried Carrots or Spam Hash." A woman in a hairnet bobbed up from nowhere, heaving a pile of plates onto the counter as Eva and Cathy arrived with their trays. "You're lucky to get a choice on a Monday."

"What about the pudding?" Cathy looked hopefully at the board above the hatch.

"Eggless Sponge with Mock Cream."

"I can hardly wait," Cathy muttered as the woman receded into the steaming kitchen.

"Never mind." Eva pulled something from her pocket and slipped it under Cathy's plate. "Have this—it'll help take the taste away."

Cathy's eyes widened as her fingers found it. "It's not . . ." She looked over her shoulder. "Eva," she hissed, "where'd you get this?" Her head tilted as Eva busied herself collecting cutlery. "Was it that Yank at the dance? It was, wasn't it?"

"It might have been," Eva bit her lip to stop herself from smiling. "Sorry it's not very much, but I gave a bit to David and a bit to Mum. I've been trying to ration myself, but it's not easy!"

Halfway through the meal Cathy leaned forward and whispered, "I daren't ask what you did to deserve a whole bar of chocolate!"

This brought on a spasm of coughing from Eva, who had been about to swallow a mouthful of curry. The look on Cathy's face reminded her of her old headmistress.

"I only kissed him!" She hissed, reaching for water and gulping it down.

"And?"

"And what?"

"What about next time?"

"Who said anything about a next time?" Eva glanced over her shoulder. "I suppose the gossips are having a field day."

"It's okay, you know," Cathy said. "You don't have to feel guilty about it."

"Don't I?" Eva mumbled, still staring at her plate. "I've promised to meet him next Saturday night and I feel as guilty as hell. If I knew how to get hold of him, I'd call it off." She prodded the congealing remains of her lunch with her fork.

"But you want to see him?"

Eva made a face. "Is it that obvious?"

"I could tell as soon as I saw you. Your eyes are all . . . you know . . . and you've hardly stopped smiling all morning—I mean, how can anyone *smile* when they're eating Curried Carrots?"

Eva gave a helpless shrug. "It's like he pressed some switch I can't turn off. I've been playing the whole thing back in my head. Over and over. I can't sleep for thinking about it." With a sigh she pushed her plate away. "I know it's wrong, but I'm desperate to see him again."

"So do it." Cathy's voice was matter-of-fact.

"*You* wouldn't, though, would you? If you were me?"

"But I'm not you. I can't feel what you're feeling and I can't say what I'd do if I did.

Anyway, if I *was* to meet someone, I could go ahead and do pretty much what I liked, but you—you're in an impossible situation."

Eva traced a stain on the tablecloth with her finger. "I thought I was coping with it, though, Cathy. I was coming to work, looking after David, staying in with my mum most nights, just the odd trip to the pictures now and then. And I was okay. I didn't sit there every night wishing I was out dancing or whatever. I'd got to a point where, secretly, I thought I didn't really need a man at all. And then what happens? One night out and wham!"

"What's his name, this Yank?"

"Bill. Bill Willis."

"*William* Willis? His parents must have had a sense of humor!"

"Well, yes—I suppose it must be short for William. He didn't say."

Cathy smiled. "Too busy kissing, I suppose?"

Eva grunted. "We talked about all kinds of things, actually! Where he comes from, what it's like at his camp, his thoughts about the war and . . ." she broke off, rubbing her finger around and around the greasy mark. "God, what must I sound like?"

"Worrying about Eddie's not going to help, is it?" Cathy said gently. "How long since you heard anything?"

"Fifteen months since his last letter. Three weeks after that I got the telegram about his ship going down." Eva raked her fingers through the tendrils of hair that had worked free from her cap. "Sometimes I have this nightmare that I'm with him on the ship and we're trapped in a locked room with water pouring under the door. And when I wake up, I think for a second that he's there in the bed beside me." Her eyes pooled with tears and she swallowed hard. "Then I see David, fast asleep in his cot and it hits me. He's never even going to remember Eddie. He's never going to know what it's like to have a dad."

"I know," Cathy squeezed her arm. "Mikey has no memory of Stuart. It's hard. It seems so unfair."

"But it's different for you, Cathy."

"Why?"

Eva's finger stopped its relentless circling and she looked up. "You really loved Stuart, didn't you?"

"Didn't you love Eddie?"

Eva hesitated. "I don't know. That's what makes it so awful. When he left, we . . . we weren't exactly on good terms."

Cathy shook her head. "I'm sorry—I shouldn't have asked. Tell me to mind my own business."

"No, it's okay. It's just that I've . . . well, I've never come out and said it to anyone before."

"How long were you together?"

She blinked once, twice, before replying. "Two years when he went missing. But we spent a lot of that time apart." Eva's eyes darted to a patch of wall above Cathy's head. "We got married on a special license a week after my old house was bombed. We were both eighteen and we'd only been seeing each other for a few months. Eddie lost his mother and sister in the bombing and I . . . I lost my dad." She pressed her lips together until they disappeared.

"I'm sorry," Cathy whispered. "Listen, you don't have to . . ."

"I do." Eva nodded slowly and deliberately, still staring at the wall. "I do." She took a long breath. "We had to move here, to Wolverhampton. Eddie had just joined the navy and expected to be sent abroad straightaway. It was all so . . ." she paused again, tears prickling the back of her eyes.

Cathy waited, silent now.

"My life just changed overnight. Before we were bombed—before the war—I had the job in the library in Coventry. Dad was a signalman on the railway. Mum was at home, and Dilys was at school. We felt lucky because Dad was in a reserved occupation." She took another breath. "When we lost him, I was suddenly the one in charge. Mum wasn't in a fit state to do anything. For the first time in my life I had to behave like a grown-up. And getting married seemed a grown-up thing to do. Eddie and I just clung to each other. We were both in shock about the bombing, and Eddie was terrified of going to war."

"How long did you have together before he left?"

"He was posted to the south coast two days after the wedding." A fleeting, wistful look that was not quite a smile crossed her face. "I used to live for the times he came home on leave. Mum bought us a double bed as a wedding present. I remember going to sleep that first night thinking that if I had a baby, it would be lovely for Mum; that it was the only thing in the world that might help her get over Dad." She gave a slight shake of her head. "It didn't happen that quickly for us, though. I got pregnant on our first anniversary, when Eddie came home on leave."

"Didn't he want a baby?"

"No, it wasn't that: he was thrilled about it, actually." Eva paused, looking directly at Cathy now. "But David didn't look like other babies: he was born with a big strawberry birthmark on his cheek. The doctor said it would disappear—which it nearly has— but Eddie hated it." She closed her eyes for a second. "I'll never forget the look in his eyes when he saw David that first time. He tried to hide what he felt, of course, but he didn't fool anyone. He wouldn't hold him, wouldn't come with me when I took him to the shops or the park. I don't think he could face the idea that he'd created something less than perfect."

Cathy bit her lip. "That must have been unbearable."

"Yes, it was: as if he'd stuck a knife into me." She crossed her arms over her chest, rubbing them as if she was cold. "It wasn't only him: I used to get it from other people too. They'd stop when they saw the pram and lean in, and then they'd tut under their breath and give me pitying looks." Eva unfolded her arms, pushed her plate aside, and unwrapped a piece of chocolate. "I despised them for being so ignorant. But I despised Eddie more for not being able to love his own flesh and blood."

Cathy nodded. "Remember last week when Iris Stokes and Betty Pelham were coming out with all that rubbish about colored men?"

"What about it?"

"Is that why you got so worked up? Because of the way people reacted to David?"

Eva huffed out a breath. "Was it that obvious?"

"You do realize you're going to get that all the time—if you start dating Bill, I mean."

"I know." Eva broke the chocolate in half and pushed a piece across the table. "You didn't see what happened to him at the dance, did you?"

Cathy's face clouded when she heard about the confrontation.

"If I refuse to see Bill just because of what others might think, that makes me as bad as them, doesn't it?" Eva's eyes flashed rebellion.

"Just as long as you can handle it."

"Well, I'll find out next Saturday, won't I?" Eva screwed up the foil from the chocolate into a tiny ball.

"I don't know—tall, dark, and handsome and a Hershey bar in his pocket—what more could a girl ask for?" Cathy leaned back in her chair. "Will you tell him about Eddie?"

Eva shook her head. "Not yet." She looked away, aware that the very thought of seeing him again was making her blush. "This probably sounds terrible, but when he kissed me, all of a sudden I wasn't David's mother or Eddie's wife anymore. I was just . . . me."

"It doesn't sound *terrible*." Cathy smiled. "It sounds fantastic."

Chapter 6

"Hey, come and look at this!"

Jimmy was emptying leftovers into the pig bin when Bill called him over. The cookhouse was deserted except for the two of them. He followed Bill past the stores and out into the yard where empty milk churns stood glinting in rows, waiting for collection. Bill dived behind them, pulling out a rusty bicycle with the tattered remains of a wicker basket strung from the handlebars.

Jimmy's mouth fell open. "Where in hell did you get that old wreck?"

"From the farmer up the road," Bill grinned. "Best bargain I ever had—all he wanted for it was a pack of Lucky Strikes and some nylons for his old lady."

"Man, you were robbed!" Jimmy shook his head, chuckling.

"Well, I know it's kind of rusty, but I'll fix it up just fine, you'll see." Bill knelt down, inspecting the chain. "Got a couple of days before I'm going to need it, so . . ."

"Oh, I get it!" Jimmy snorted. "Boy, is she gonna be impressed when you come rolling up on that!"

"Think I'm stupid or what?" Bill stood up, giving him a shove. "I'm not going to let her see it, am I? But how the hell else am I supposed to get to Wolverhampton and back on a Saturday night?"

"Well, you got imagination. I'll give you that!"

"How about you?" Bill shot his friend a knowing glance. "I thought you might want to be hitching a ride on the handle-bars . . . ?"

"Oh, didn't I tell you?" Jimmy smirked back. "My girl's daddy, he's some big-shot factory owner. She reckons on taking one of his cars, so she can meet me in Bridgnorth."

"No kidding?" Bill let out a low whistle.

"Can I help it if women find me irresistible?" Jimmy batted his eyelashes.

"Come on, lover boy." Bill grinned. "Stop bragging and help me fix this little beauty."

~

Eva could hear snatches of familiar melodies as people went into the dance hall. There was a cold wind blowing across the market-place, and she pulled her coat up around her neck. *He's going to stand me up*, she thought, *and wouldn't that just serve me right?*

She glanced at a couple in uniform who were laughing as they came up the steps in front of her. The man looked a bit like Eddie. Same stocky build, same deep chuckle. It brought back memories of her wedding night. He had made her laugh as she stood awk-wardly in a corner of the room, tickling her into submission when she refused to get undressed with the light on. The memory was as sharp and painful as a nettle sting. She thrust her hands into her coat pockets, digging her nails into the palms as she clenched her fists.

"Hi, honey! Am I late or are you early?"

The sight of him made her blood surge. Eva's eyes darted left and right, unable to stop checking for hostile stares. One or two heads turned as he wrapped his arms around her. It gave her a feeling that she couldn't quite explain: a mixture of fear and defiance that was strangely intoxicating.

"You're out of breath," she said. "Have you been running?"

"No, not running," he laughed, coughing as he caught his breath. "Just don't ask me how I got here." He smiled as he took her arm. "I might die of embarrassment if you make me explain. Come on, let's go eat!"

It took them a while to find the restaurant. She had picked the smallest, most out-of-the-way place she could think of.

"Well, it ain't the Ritz," he chuckled as he helped her off with her coat, "but what the heck—I'm hungry as a bear: let's see what's on the menu."

She could tell he wasn't impressed, although he tried to sound enthusiastic.

"I'm sorry," she said. "I know it's not very exciting—nearly everything's rationed, that's the trouble."

"It's okay." He shrugged. "We've been trained for this."

Eva looked at him, mystified.

"Take a peek." Arching his eyebrows, he took a slim booklet from his jacket pocket.

"*A Short Guide to Great Britain*," she read aloud, looking at the eagle crest on the front cover. She opened it and a broad smile spread across her face. "'The British have movies, which they call cinemas,'" she read, "'but the great place of recreation is the pub. Stop and think before you sound off about lukewarm beer or cold boiled potatoes or the way English cigarettes taste. If you are invited to a British person's house, never criticize the food . . .'"

"Oh, don't stop." He grinned. "You haven't got to the best bit."

She laughed, turning the page. "'Don't try to tell them America won the last war,'" she continued. "'Never criticize the king or queen. If British civilians look dowdy and badly dressed, it is not because they do not like good clothes or know how to wear them. All clothing is rationed.'" She clapped her hand to her mouth, suddenly remembering her dress at the dance. "Oh no!" She giggled. "I'm surprised you want anything to do with me after reading this!"

She passed the booklet back to him. Something was handwritten on the back cover. She glimpsed the last four letters of his last name as he clamped his hand over it.

"What's the matter?"

He made a face. "My name—my first name—I don't use it."

"What is it?"

He smiled and shook his head. "Just call me Bill, okay?" His eyes held hers. They were such a deep brown: so dark it was hard to tell where the irises ended and the pupils began. She carried on watching him as he gave the order to the waitress.

"Tell me about where you come from," she said. "It's in the South, isn't it?"

He nodded. "It's way down south, not far from the Gulf coast."

"What did you do there? For a job, I mean?"

He shrugged. "Nothing special. I worked in a drugstore."

"A chemist's?"

He laughed. "No—strange name, I suppose: sells more milkshakes than drugs."

"Did you like it?"

"Hell, no. It's just a job."

"So what do you like?" She studied his face. "What's your favorite thing in the whole world?"

"Music," he replied without a second's hesitation.

"Do you play an instrument?"

"Well, no—not unless you count a comb and paper or a tin can you beat with a spoon . . ." he trailed off with a shrug. "When I was a kid, we didn't have any real musical instruments, but we were pretty good at what you might call improvisation. Most nights we'd be out on the porch with family or neighbors, and someone would tap out a beat with their feet or sing a line of a song and, before you knew it, everyone would be up and dancing."

Eva smiled, trying to picture the child that he had once been. "It sounds very sociable," she said, "not like here—it's hardly ever warm enough to sit outside in the evenings."

"Is that so?" He huffed out a laugh. "Well, sometimes it's too darn hot where I come from: too hot to dance or do just about anything—even at night." He leaned closer, his chin propped on his hand. "Anyway, how about you? What do you love best?"

David's name sprang automatically to her lips, but she closed her mouth just in time to stop herself saying it. She laughed to cover her confusion. "Oh, I don't know—books, films, chocolate . . ."

"What's your favorite movie?"

Gone with the Wind was what she would have replied if anyone else had been asking. But she checked herself once again. What would Bill think of a girl whose favorite film was about the spoiled white daughter of a slave owner?

The waitress saved her by plunking two steaming plates of minced beef and onions in front of them. Distracted by the unfamiliar food, Bill was easily drawn into a safer topic of conversation. They were halfway through the meal when she caught sight of something out of the corner of her eye that made her flinch.

"What is it?" Bill had seen her face change.

"Oh nothing—just a draft or something."

He followed her eyes, catching sight of a pale-khaki cap disappearing around the corner of the street opposite.

"Oh, I get it," he said, nodding his head slowly. "Is that why you brought me to this funny little place?"

Eva stared at the table. "I just didn't want a repeat performance of last Saturday," she said, "so I thought it'd be better to choose somewhere, you know, off the beaten track."

"Hey," he said, reaching across to take her hand, "I'm a big fella—I can take care of myself." He stroked her arm, touching the spot where a ray of the setting sun had turned the white flesh pink. "But I sure appreciate your concern." He scooped up some food on his fork, moving it slowly and deliberately toward her mouth. "Come on," he said, "let's finish this up and go catch a movie." He smiled. "No lights, no trouble."

~

The newsreel was showing as Bill and Eva fumbled their way to a pair of empty seats. As the screen flashed with the explosions of torpedoed U-boats, she felt his arm slide around her shoulders. She glanced at the people in the seats in front and to the sides. Lots of uniforms. But difficult to tell Britons from Americans in this artificial twilight, let alone black from white.

Her attention was drawn back to the screen, not by the images but the words. A British soldier was delivering a message to his wife and child back home. Eva felt a stab of guilt as the camera panned along a line of other men, all desperate to speak to their wives, mothers, or sweethearts.

She glanced at Bill. He was gazing at the screen, his eyes betraying no emotion. *Had he left anyone behind in New Orleans?*

The signature tune of the newsreel blared out as the program ended and suddenly Bill's lips were on her neck, setting her skin on fire. In her mind the images of homesick soldiers and U-boats whirled together and dissolved like sugar in a teacup. *This is all there is,* she thought, as their lips met in the darkness. *This is now, and now is all that matters.*

By the time they looked at the screen again, it was filled with more images of fighting men.

"What did you say this is?" Bill whispered, squeezing her shoulder as they settled back into their seats.

"*For Whom the Bell Tolls*," she said, her mouth brushing his ear. "Ingrid Bergman and Gary . . ." she never finished the sentence. As they clung to each other in the flickering light, she heard gunshots and explosions, the fake sounds of a distant, re-created war. And in that moment she buried Eddie in a deep recess of her mind. Now he was as unreal to her as the figures on the screen.

"Guess we'll just have to go see it again next week," Bill grinned as they emerged from the gloom of the cinema to the deeper darkness of the street. "Looked pretty good, the little bit I saw!" He chuckled, squeezing her waist as they walked along the pavement.

"What do you mean, next week?" she said coyly, wondering where she was going to tell her mother she was going on yet another Saturday night.

"Oh, so you've had enough of me already?" He wheeled her around to face him. But he was smiling. She could see his mouth and his eyes, disembodied, almost, in the blacked-out night. He looked so eager, so confident that she would not turn him down. *Was this how he acted with girls back home*, she wondered, *or had the war made him this way?*

"It's not that I don't want to," she said, reaching up to stroke the back of his head. "But it's not always that easy to get away." She paused. How could she explain? What reason could she give for not being free to do exactly as she liked outside working hours? For a fleeting moment she thought about telling him the truth. But that would ruin everything. He wouldn't want her then, would he? Not if he knew she was somebody's wife, somebody's mother.

"Oh, I get it," he said, the smile disappearing. She looked at him in alarm. Had he read it in her face, guessed what she was hiding? "It's your folks, I guess," he went on. "You're scared of what they'll say if they find out you're dating a black fella."

"No, of course it's not that!" She almost told him then, so unbearable was it that he should think that was the reason. But she checked herself, burying her head in his jacket as his words struck home. It was the perfect excuse. It would give her time. She would tell him eventually, but not yet.

"Well, you're not completely wrong," she began. "I don't really know what my mother would say. I haven't told her about you. She thinks I'm meeting some of the girls from work tonight." She looked up into his eyes. "Actually, I'm more worried about my sister than my mum. She can be a real sneak. Blackmail is her specialty."

"Hmm." Bill cupped her chin in his hand. "Sounds like we got ourselves a problem then, huh?"

She nodded.

"But wait a minute." He shifted his hands to her shoulders. "Didn't you say she was with some Dutch guy at the dance?"

"Yes—the one who took us all home."

"Will she want to see him again?"

"Going on the fact that every other sentence she utters has his name in it, I'd say yes. Why? What of it?"

"Well, you said she's only fifteen years old, so it sounds to me like you got her over a barrel," Bill replied. "If you really want to see me, all you have to do is blackmail her back—just tell her you'll spill the beans about her unless she puts up an alibi for you seeing me."

"You mean get her to say she's going out with me, so I can meet you instead?"

"It's perfect, don't you think?" Bill chuckled. "That way she gets to see her fella too."

Eva struggled for an answer, frantically trying to work out the implications of what he was suggesting. "It might not be as easy as you think," she said at last.

"What's the problem?"

"Well, I don't know if I can trust her."

"Why not? What can she say without blowing it with the Dutch guy?"

"It's not what she might say, it's what she might *do* that worries me." Eva frowned. "She's very . . . advanced for her age, Bill. I'm worried she might . . . you know."

"Hmm." He grunted. "I hear what you're saying." He hugged her to him. "In that case you and I are just going to have to play chaperone."

"You mean go out with Dilys and . . . ?"

"Yep—better a foursome than nothing at all." He took her arm and led her toward the market square.

"I don't know if I can handle going on double dates with my kid sister."

"We don't have to hang out with them all the time—just go to the same places, keep an eye on them, like you were doing last week."

The strains of dance music drifted from the Civic Hall.

"Shall we go in?" He took her by the waist, waltzing her across the pavement.

"And see you get beaten to a pulp?" She tried to pull him the other way.

The music changed to a faster beat.

"Hold on," he said. "I have a better idea!" Scooping her up in his arms, he ran across the marketplace toward the squat silhouette of the public air-raid shelter.

Chapter 7

As he ran down the steps, he held her so tight she felt dizzy.

"Bill! What are you doing?" Her voice sounded strange in the air-raid shelter, shrill and echoey. Suddenly she felt scared.

"Sorry, honey: hope I didn't shake you up!" He lowered her to the ground, fishing in his pockets for the torch. He found a hook and hung it up, the thin beam giving the gray walls an eerie glow. Through the open door Eva could still hear the dance band at the Civic.

"What—" Before she could get the words out, he had grabbed her, clasping her right hand in his while his left hand slid around her waist.

"Okay, this is what you do," he smiled, moving her hand in time to the music. "Watch my feet: right foot forward, left heel up . . . and back!"

"What *is* this?" She laughed as he spun her around.

"Well, it sure ain't the fox-trot!" he said, watching her face as he took both her hands and slid her between his legs. "I don't think it has a name," he said, catching his breath as she emerged, openmouthed and speechless. "Not a proper one, I mean. But folks in Louisiana call it the jitterbug."

She squealed as he jerked her off the ground so that her legs straddled his waist. "Bill! This is crazy!"

"Don't you like it? I'll stop if you want me to."

"No!" She squealed again as her head tipped back, her hair brushing the floor. This was not like dancing. More like . . . She gasped for breath. Was that his plan? To get her down here, in the air-raid shelter and soften her up for . . .

"Hold tight!" With a whoop of delight he scooped her up and threw her over his left shoulder, turning deftly to spin her around as her feet touched the ground. The music faded and she clung to him, breathless. The sound of applause drifted from the dance hall and a slower number started up.

"Guess you deserve a little rest," he said, stroking her hair as they began to sway gently in the torchlight, "although I reckon you held up pretty well for a first-timer."

"Is that supposed to be a compliment?" She gave him a wry smile.

"Why yes, ma'am," he said, sliding his hand along her shoulder to squeeze her arm. "Hey, where'd you get muscles like that?"

"You jealous?" She smiled. "They come courtesy of Great Western Railways."

He stopped moving and held her at arm's length. "You're not one of those girls I saw laying track at the railroad station?"

She nodded, wondering what was going through his mind. He looked indignant, almost angry.

"Why?" He frowned. "Did they *make* you do it?"

"No." She laughed. "They didn't make me. I could have done something else—if I'd wanted to."

"Well, pardon me for sounding dumb," he said, "but why would you choose a job like that? I mean, where I come from that's the kind of thing they make colored folks do—the *men*, that is, not the women!"

Eva took a breath and sat down on one of the wooden benches stacked against the walls of the shelter. "It's a long story," she said.

"Well, I've got time if you have." He settled down next to her, curiosity furrowing his forehead.

"My father worked on the railway," she said, biting her lip. "He was a signalman. He died a couple of years ago. Our house was bombed and . . ."

"Gee, I shouldn't have asked." He drew in his breath and looked at the ground.

"No, it's okay." She swallowed hard, wondering if she would ever be able to talk about it without getting a lump in her throat. "We had to move here, to a new house, and it was too far from the place I used to work. And anyway, my old job—in a library—suddenly seemed pretty useless. They said they needed women to do men's jobs. I thought it'd be good to work on the railway, like Dad did. I suppose it makes me feel he's still around, somehow."

He took her hand and she stared at the wall, thinking of all the things she couldn't tell him. Like how marrying Eddie had been a kind of antidote to losing Dad. And how she'd cried every morning the first week on the rail gang. Cried for Dad, cried for Eddie, and cried for David, handed over bewildered and frightened to the uniformed women at the nursery.

She felt his fingers stroking hers, and she turned to look at him. "I bet you miss your family, don't you?" she said. "Being so far from home, I mean."

"I guess," he nodded. "At least, I miss my mom and my kid sister. Never knew my father."

"Oh." Eva hesitated. "Is he . . . ?"

"No, he's not dead," Bill said quickly. "Well, I don't know that for a fact, but I don't think he is. Last Mom heard, he was living in Chicago."

She looked into his eyes. The words had come out casually. *Too casually*, she thought. "It must have been hard for you," she said, "growing up without a dad."

He shrugged. "What you've never had you don't miss." But there was a flicker of something behind the defiant gaze. He was holding something back, just as she had been.

He took her in his arms again, kissing her neck and moving his hand slowly down her back. She arched her spine, pressing against him, her body aching for him. If he tried to take things further now, in the private gloom of the shelter, would she have the will to resist? She felt his fingers slipping under her blouse.

"Bill," she whispered, "I . . ."

He pulled away. "I'm sorry: I thought . . ."

There was an awkward silence. *What did he think?* Eva wondered. That she was easy? Was that how all Americans saw English girls? Theirs for a bar of chocolate and a meal out? She wanted to reach for his hand, kiss him again. But if she did that now, what sort of message would she be giving?

The music came to her rescue. Striking up suddenly after what must have been the interval, it was another American number she didn't recognize. In an instant Bill was on his feet.

"Do you know this?" He pulled her up. "It's 'Drum Boogie'!" he beamed at her puzzled face. "Come on, let's dance!"

~

Dilys came creeping into Eva's room as she was getting undressed that night. Their reflections were captured in the dressing table mirror—one redhead, one brunette—so different they looked like strangers, not sisters.

"Where have you been?" Dilys hissed. "I thought you were going to the pictures!"

"Shush! You'll wake David!" Eva glared at her sister and glanced across at the cot where the child lay with his arms stretched out above his head like a sunbather.

"Did you go to the Civic? You did, didn't you?"

Eva could hear the envy in Dilys's voice. "No, I didn't actually," she said, pulling on her nightdress.

"Well, you've been somewhere—I can tell." Dilys's eyes narrowed. "*Fee-fi-fo-fum*—I smell something American!" She grabbed Eva's bag and emptied it onto the bed. "Oh, what's this?" she snatched up a slim, square packet wrapped in cellophane and waved it in the air.

"You little . . . !" Eva tried to grab it back, but Dilys leapt onto the bed, holding it out of reach.

"Nylons! Oh Eva! Whatever would Eddie say?"

Eva snatched the packet from Dilys, landing her a sharp slap on the arm with her other hand. "Don't you dare come in here poking your nose into what's none of your damn business!"

There was a whimper from the cot.

"Now look what you've done!" Eva reached through the bars, stroking David's hair until he closed his eyes again.

"I'm sorry," Dilys whispered, peering anxiously at the cot. "I'm just jealous, that's all. I really wanted to see Anton tonight. I'm sure he was at the dance—with someone else." Her lip wobbled and a tear splashed onto the bedspread.

"Oh Dil!" Eva slid across the bed and put her arm around her sister's heaving shoulders. "Look, I'm sorry—I shouldn't have lashed out at you like that. Come on, please don't cry."

"But it's not fair!" Dilys wiped her streaming nose on the back of her hand. "He's going to find someone else—I know he is!"

"Here," Eva pulled her handkerchief from the jumble of things on the bed. "Blow your nose, cheer up, and listen."

~

Bill coaxed the ancient bike up the hill to the barracks. It was after midnight and the country lane was spookily quiet, no sound apart from the odd rustle of an animal in the hedgerow on either side of him.

He almost rode straight into the Bentley. It was parked at the entrance to a field, its black bodywork blending seamlessly with the shadow of a tree.

It was the noise coming from inside that alerted him. The steady, rhythmic creaking of the leather upholstery and a low, unmistakable moaning. He stopped dead in the middle of the lane, not sure what to do. What if it was an officer? He couldn't risk being seen sneaking past on the bike, on his way home from forbidden territory.

"Bill!"

"What in hell . . ." The sound of his name hissed from the car window made him jump.

"It's me—Jimmy—you mutt!"

"Jeez, man, what are you doing? Damn near scared me to death!"

Jimmy laughed, buttoning up his shirt. "What's it look like?" He jerked his head toward the backseat. "Me and Philippa's been getting acquainted."

Bill heard muffled giggling and the sound of a zipper being pulled up.

"We got kinda bored of Bridgnorth," Jimmy said, leaning out of the window. "So Philippa offered to take me for a drive. She's a real beauty, ain't she?"

"You talking about the lady or the car?" Bill said drily.

"You son of a . . ." Jimmy chuckled, taking a swipe at his friend's head and missing. He jerked his thumb at the bike. "You been all the way to Wolverhampton on that thing?"

"Yes, sir!"

"Man, you gonna have blisters on your ass the size of melons! Hope she was worth it."

Bill's mouth clamped shut.

"Well?" Jimmy persisted. "Was she?"

"Unlike you," Bill hissed, "I don't feel the need to share the details of my private life!"

"Shame," Jimmy said. "Thought we might compare notes . . ."

"In your dreams!" Bill turned away, pointing the handles of the bicycle back toward the road.

"Hey, man, don't go!" Jimmy called after him. "Just give me a minute to say good-bye to Philippa and I'll walk back up the hill with you. I want to know your secret!"

"What secret?"

"How you spent a whole night in a white town without getting seven shades of shit beat out of you. Where'd you go to—the cemetery?"

Bill kept on walking as Jimmy disappeared back inside the car to bid his girl a lingering farewell. He'd almost reached the brow of the hill when he heard the car's engine hum into life. Glancing over his shoulder, he saw the Bentley ease out of the muddy track and onto the road. The moon came out from behind a cloud, falling on the girl's face as she leaned out of the window to blow Jimmy a kiss. It could have been a child's face.

"Is she old enough to drive?" Bill asked when Jimmy caught up with him.

"Hell, I don't know." Jimmy grinned. "How old do you have to be in this country? But she sure knows what she's doing—in the front seat and the back!" He gave Bill a sly look. "Come on, tell me: you make out or what?"

"Like I said, it's none of your goddamn business!"

"I hope you're not telling me you went all that way for nothing?"

Bill stared at the road ahead, refusing to rise to the bait.

"You gonna see her again?"

"Yes I am, if you must know," Bill replied, a smile playing at the corners of his mouth. "I'm taking her out next Sunday afternoon. How about you? Are you and Philippa planning to go for another *drive*?" He gave Jimmy a sideways look. "You'd better watch out, man—I don't think her daddy's going to be too impressed if he catches your black ass on his shiny leather seats!"

"Makes it more of a thrill, though, doesn't it?" Jimmy whispered as they crept past the dozing guard at the entrance to the camp. "Doing it with a white girl, I mean."

Bill stopped dead and gave his friend a long, hard stare. "You say that," he said, raising his hand to touch the fading bruise beneath his eye, "and you're no better than the son of a bitch who gave me this!"

~

Eva and Dilys sat in the shade of the wooden bus shelter, waiting.

"I think that must be him," Dilys said, jumping to her feet at the sound of a car engine. She ran along the pavement, waving furiously when the car came into view.

Eva watched as the Dutch soldier leapt out and swung her sister into the air in a tight embrace. In daylight he looked a little younger, perhaps twenty-two or twenty-three. Still far too old for Dilys, though. She wondered if he would think so, too, when he saw Dilys without the makeup she'd plastered on for the dance.

Out of the corner of her eye she caught sight of Bill coming around the corner on foot. As she went to hug him, she saw Dilys wheel around, staring at them both with undisguised curiosity.

"You can put your eyes back in now," Eva said, turning to her sister after giving Bill a long, slow kiss. Eva had not lied to Dilys about Bill—she had simply let her make her own assumptions about the giver of the nylons. Her sister had not mentioned Eddie since that initial gibe and seemed happy that Eva was getting out.

The look of shock on Dilys's face now gave her an odd feeling—the same feeling she'd had when people outside the Civic Hall had turned to look at Bill hugging her on the steps. It was like wearing clothes without underwear on a hot day—rather daring but very liberating.

She smiled as Dilys turned, openmouthed, to Anton. Anton didn't seem to notice her sister's reaction. He stepped forward and offered Bill his hand.

"Congratulations," he said in his slightly accented English.

"What for?" Bill towered over him, looking down at the blond Dutchman with a bemused smile.

"Sicily," Anton replied. "Without your people the Allies would never have taken it."

"I guess not," Bill said. "Unfortunately I didn't have much to do with it."

Eva saw his eyes cloud and wondered what he was thinking. "Come on," she said, steering him toward a farm gate, "Let's go for a walk."

The sun beat down on them as they strolled through a field waist-high with wheat. "When do I get you to myself?" Bill whispered, his lips brushing her ear.

"I don't know," she whispered back. "Do you think we can trust them?"

"I doubt it." Bill grinned. "But I have an idea. Call your sister over."

As Dilys drew level with them, Bill produced a bottle of Coca-Cola from his kit bag.

"Dilys," he said, passing her the bottle, "that sure is a pretty name—where does it come from?"

"It's . . . er . . . Welsh." Dilys glanced at the unfamiliar label, then at Eva, a nervous smile on her lips. "My mum's side of the family comes from Wales. We've got an aunt and an uncle and a cousin there. We used to go to their farm for holidays, didn't we, Eva?"

Eva nodded, wondering what Bill was up to.

"Is that so?" Bill gave Dilys a disarming grin. "Well, you try some of that. See what you think. Don't worry—it's not alcohol. Now, I just want a little word with your boyfriend."

He led Anton a few yards along the path, and Eva saw him take something else from his kit bag. It glinted as the sun caught it, but she couldn't make out what it was. After a brief conversation the two men walked back over and Anton took Dilys's arm.

"Let's go and see what's down there," he said, pointing to a stream that wound along the boundary of the field.

"What did you say to him?" Eva hissed as they strolled off.

"I showed him these," Bill said, pulling a pair of field glasses from his pocket. "I told him he could take her as far as the stream, but you'd be taking a peek at what they were up to every five minutes." He chuckled as he passed them to her. "If that doesn't put him off, well . . ."

"My, aren't you clever . . ." She took hold of his lapels, pulling him close. "You even managed to win Dilys over—she was so busy drinking that stuff, she didn't say a word. What was it?"

"Don't you have it over here?" he murmured, nibbling her ear. "Gee, that's too bad." His hands slid from her head to her shoulders and down her back. She could feel the heat of them through the thin fabric of her dress as his fingers traced a slow, spiraling path down her spine. Then he knelt on the ground, kissing her bare ankles, her calves, her knees. She felt her legs buckle, and in a moment she was lying beside him, the pale stalks of wheat splaying out around their bodies.

His fingers were on the buttons of her dress now, tugging at the fabric as his mouth slid down her neck. She could feel his breath on her skin as he paused, and glancing down she saw that he was gazing at her breasts above the low, lacy edge of her bra. The look in his eyes was so strange, like a child the first time he sees snow.

"Is this okay?" he whispered, his hands sliding around to undo the hooks.

She wasn't sure if he was asking her or himself. She stroked his head, her skin on fire as his tongue slid between her breasts. Her heart was beating so fast she was sure he must be able to hear it. Now her dress was down past her waist. With a delicious flick of his tongue across her belly, he raised himself up and moved his body onto hers.

"Bill, I . . ." she faltered.

He froze for a second and rolled onto the ground. "You don't want to," he said, sucking in his lips as he stared at the sky.

"It's just . . ."

"I know." His voice was a gruff whisper. "It's because I'm black."

"No! It's not that!" She closed her eyes and drew in her breath, tugging the fabric of her dress together to cover herself. *Oh God*, she thought, *what am I going to do?* She wanted him so much she felt a physical ache where his lips had touched her body. Should she let him make love to her? Would that be such a wicked thing to do? More wicked than letting him think that she despised him? After a silence that seemed to last forever, she propped herself up on one elbow and slid her hand under his neck.

"It's not you," she whispered, drawing him close. "I'm just worried about Dilys and Anton catching us." It wasn't a complete lie.

"Is that all?" He reached for the field glasses, and Eva watched his mouth slide into a smile. "Well," he said, "I don't think they're going to be too bothered about what we're up to right now . . ."

Eva almost snatched the binoculars from his hand. "They're not . . . !"

"Don't worry—they're just necking."

She flopped down with relief. Closing her eyes, she could hear nothing but the sweet, distant call of skylarks. The scent of earth and ripening wheat mingled with the scent of him. *This is all there is . . .* The words echoed in her mind. Without opening her eyes, she let go of her dress, allowing it to slide away from her breasts. She undid the rest of the buttons. The fabric slithered to the ground as she leaned across to undo his. She took off all his clothes, her hands working slowly and deliberately. For a moment they lay still, marveling at the strangeness of their limbs intertwined.

"You sure?" he whispered.

"Yes," she said, shutting out the nagging voices in her head as her fingers slid down the smooth slope of his chest. "I'm sure."

He cupped her breasts in his hands, kissing them before moving down her body. She had never known kisses like these. His breath and the flicker of his tongue made her shiver and cry out with delight. She felt his hand move across her leg to where his jacket lay, heard the rustle of cellophane. And then in one swift movement he was on top of her and inside her. She clung to him, oblivious of the coarse stalks of wheat rasping her naked back as she writhed beneath him. Her eyes were shut tight, but as she climaxed a rainbow of color exploded inside her head. She heard him moan with pleasure, felt him shudder and then settle against her breasts, his skin as wet as hers.

When she opened her eyes, all she could see was the sky, clear and blue, stretching endlessly above them. She felt as if he had turned her body inside out, found her soul and set it free.

Chapter 8
September 1943

A cold wind tugged at Eva's jacket as she picked her way past a line of women queuing for tangerines. The name of the fruit, scrawled on a makeshift cardboard sign, conjured the smell of the night before. As they had danced together by torchlight, the spiced orange scent of him had rubbed into her skin. She'd asked him how he always managed to smell so delicious. He had hung his head, embarrassed by the compliment. He seemed to have no vanity; no idea how good-looking he was. After much coaxing he had confessed that the scent of oranges came from a bottle of oil he used on his hair. All his friends used it, he said, because it made their hair look more European.

Then he had stroked her long auburn curls and told her they had drawn him to her that first night at the Civic Hall. "I thought you looked like Rita Hayworth." He smiled. "But when I got a bit closer, I realized you're even prettier than she is."

Eva smiled at the memory of it. To anyone else it would sound like a lame attempt at flattery, but the way he'd said it, his eyes misty with longing, had made her feel very special. She forgot about her rough hands and her aching back when she was with him. She didn't care about having to skulk about town, hiding in the darkness of the cinema; didn't feel the slightest bit envious, waving Dilys off for a dance at the Civic Hall while she waited for Bill on the steps of the air-raid shelter.

Last week he had surprised her. Coming out of the station after work she'd spotted him waiting for her by the ticket office. She'd dropped her head, fumbling in her bag, telling the others she'd forgotten something. Ten minutes later they were making love, urgent and frantic on a bed of soft grass behind the railway embankment. They had been so desperate for each other that neither had remembered the army-issue condoms in his pocket.

As she hurried along the street, she caught her breath, her head reeling at the memory of it. She tried to put it from her mind, panic-stricken at the risk they had taken. She told herself that she would be all right; that it had taken her a whole year to get pregnant with David. But she knew in her heart that if things were different, she would be savoring it like a delicious secret, the possibility of Bill's baby growing inside her.

She thrust her hands into her pockets and felt the hard edges of a little bottle of Southern Comfort. He had given it to her last night. "Something to keep you warm on that goddamn railroad," he'd whispered, as they held each other, hidden from prying eyes. He'd slipped it into her bag along with a tin of peaches smuggled out of the cookhouse stores. Her mother had stopped raising her eyebrows when such goodies appeared on the table.

Sometimes, when they were sitting by the wireless in the evening listening to the news, Eva would catch a pensive look in her eyes. She never mentioned Eddie now. Had she heard some gossip? It was as if her mother knew what was going on but chose to keep silent. If that was the case, she was grateful for it.

Glancing across the street she saw a newspaper boy blowing on his hands. On a board by his feet were scrawled the words: "ITALY SURRENDERS!" She quickened her pace, remembering a news report that had sent a chill down her spine two nights ago: "Now there is new hope," the voice from the wireless had crackled, "for all those wives and sweethearts of the seventy thousand British, Commonwealth, and American servicemen held as prisoners of war in Italian concentration camps."

New hope. She thrust her hands deeper into her pockets. The words made her feel like a traitor. What about those other women? Had they spent months, years, wondering whether their men were dead or alive? And what were those POWs going to find when they came home?

Her head suddenly filled with an image of a weary-looking Eddie walking down the street toward the house. Was it possible? Could he have been taken prisoner? Surely someone would know if that had happened? Weren't the enemy bound by some international treaty to inform the Allies of those held in internment camps?

"Eva!" Cathy's voice, calling from across the street, brought her back to the present. She was waving, a tangerine clutched in her hand.

"I've been queuing since seven o'clock for these," she said breathlessly as she caught up with Eva. "Did you get any?"

"No, but Mum and Dilys were going to try—I hope they're not too late."

Cathy stopped as they passed by the newsstand and rummaged in her bag. "I must get a paper—isn't it fantastic news about Italy?"

Eva murmured a reply, the words at odds with what she felt inside.

"They say it'll be France next." Cathy glanced up as she located her purse. "I suppose that's where Bill's lot are headed."

Eva shrugged, not trusting herself to speak. She knew, of course, that Bill would have to leave sometime. But it was something neither of them ever mentioned. It was as if they were living their days in a kind of enchantment that could be broken by a few forbidden words.

Eva kept her eyes fixed on the pavement as they neared the entrance to the railway. Inside the station there was no chance to talk. The other rail gangers were crowded into the women's lavatories, changing into their heavy work boots, all chattering at the tops of their voices. It was a raucous mix of exclamations about Italy and gossip about what they'd been up to the night before. Eva and Cathy changed in silence and filed outside to collect their spades.

By eleven o'clock a sudden shower had turned the stretch of track the women were working on to a quagmire. The rain stung Eva's face, and she stopped digging for a moment, rubbing her raw fingers to warm them up.

"Is it tea break yet?" Cathy groaned.

"Half an hour to go," Eva said. "Here." She fished in her pocket for the little bottle. "Have a swig of this to keep you going—but don't tell the others, they'll all want some!"

Cathy's eyebrows arched as she read the label. "Did Bill give you this? No wonder you're nuts about him," she laughed, bending as if to dig and taking a crafty sip from the bottle. As she straightened up, her expression changed. "Have you told him about David?"

"Not yet," Eva said, looking at the ground. Cathy had touched a raw nerve. Ever since her first date with Bill, she'd felt guilty about this denial of her child's existence. Felt guilty about the Saturday nights and Sunday afternoons when she left him with her mother. She could justify it if he was asleep when she went out, but last time he'd still been awake, peering at her curiously through the bars of the cot as she did her hair. It wasn't fair, she knew that. He was too young to understand why she no longer spent every moment of her free time with him. It would be so much better if she could take Bill home. She took a breath. "I'm going to tell him on Saturday: I'm going to tell him everything."

Cathy nodded, raising the bottle to her lips for another sly nip.

"And if he asks me, I'll go with him. To America. When the war ends."

Cathy nearly choked as she swallowed. "Are you crazy?" Glancing at the women nearby, she lowered her voice. "I mean, even if he's okay about David, who's to say he's still going to be around when the war's over? Who's to say any of us are?"

"I know, I know," Eva hissed, "but I can't help it! He's so . . ." she trailed off, crossing her arms over her chest, her hands gripping the fabric of her jacket. "He makes me feel *alive*."

"I hear what you're saying," Cathy replied. "You've been having the best time of your life—having some fun after months and months of just existing from one day to the next. But that's all it's supposed to be: a bit of fun. Everyone knows that."

Eva shook her head. "It's *more* than that, Cathy. I had no idea what it felt like—being in love, I mean—until he walked into my life."

"But don't you see," Cathy pleaded, "it doesn't matter if he's the most wonderful man who ever walked this earth, sooner or later he's going to disappear from here and he might never come back. You've got to think about that—otherwise he's going to end up breaking your heart."

"But it's not like he's a normal soldier." Eva's voice had a defiant edge. "He told me the colored GIs aren't allowed to fight: he just does the cooking."

"But he'll still be there, won't he? Go wherever they go? He could just as easily get a bomb dropped on him in the kitchen as anywhere else."

"Don't say that!"

"I've got to say it," Cathy sighed, "because it's true. Do you know what Stuart did in the army?"

Eva shook her head.

"He was a mechanic. Mended trucks. Not exactly high-risk, I didn't think when he told me. But he got killed waiting for a boat at Dunkirk. In the end it didn't matter what job he had—he was just stuck there with all the rest of them."

"God, I'm sorry, Cathy. Really I am." Eva dug her spade into the muddy ground. "I know how it must sound." She shook her head. "A part of my brain—the sensible, logical part—tells me that you're right to warn me off; that he'll be gone soon and . . ." She kicked the pile of earth at her feet. "But I can't allow myself to believe it. I just can't."

~

At eleven thirty the women trooped into the canteen. They hunched over steaming mugs of tea, warming their numb fingers as they drank. Iris Stokes, who had taken to staining her lips with beetroot juice since the GIs arrived, pulled a magazine from her pocket.

"Read us the agony column, Iris," Betty Pelham shouted from the other end of the table. "I could do with a laugh!"

Iris frowned and flicked through the pages. "All right," she said, casting her eyes up and down. "Listen to this one: 'Dear Leonora, my husband is a prisoner of war and I became so lonely and depressed without him. Then I met two Allied officers who took me out and really cheered me up. The friendships soon developed into something much more serious. Now I realize that I am going to have a baby, and I don't know which of the two is the father . . .'"

Iris paused as gasps and titters rose from around the table. "'I have just heard,'" she read on, "'that my husband, who is sick and wounded, is about to be repatriated, and I do not know how to tell him. What shall I do?'"

"Poor bugger!" Betty grunted. "Fancy coming home to that!"

"What's Leonora say?" another voice piped up.

"She says: 'Dear Mrs. X, I appreciate your problems of being lonely and depressed, but how a woman could do such a thing with two men is beyond my comprehension . . .'"

This brought screeches of laughter.

"Do you want to hear this or not?"

The women went quiet and Iris picked up the magazine again. "'The main thing to do is to avoid hurting him, isn't it?'" she read. "'I advise you, as soon as you know he has reached the country, to write to the matron of the hospital or the commander of the next camp to which he is sent, tell them the whole truth and ask how you can arrange some way of not seeing him until your condition is not apparent. Wait until his health is better before you tell him the truth. It might be the finish of everything if he knew it now.'"

"What good's that going to do?" Betty demanded. "She's still going to have to explain the poor little bastard away, isn't she?"

"Not if she gets it adopted," Iris said, a superior smirk distorting her puce lips.

"I think she should keep it," Eva said quietly.

The others looked at her.

"Oh yes," Iris sneered, "and get thrown out on the streets when her husband gets back? Fine mess she'd be in then, wouldn't she?"

Six pairs of eyes flicked from Iris to Eva, who rose to her feet. "Come on," she said. "Tea break's over."

~

The following Saturday Eva, Dilys, and Anton were sitting in their usual seats at the Savoy cinema. *Jane Eyre* had started more than half an hour ago and even the most passionate couples had paused to watch Orson Welles running into Joan Fontaine's blazing bedroom. But Eva wasn't looking at the screen. The seat beside her was empty and every few seconds she glanced toward the red exit sign.

"Don't worry," Dilys whispered. "He'll be here soon!"

But Bill didn't come. Eva tried to concentrate on the film, a host of possibilities running through her mind. What if his camp had suddenly moved to another part of the country? How would he have been able to let her know? He could have sent her a letter, but what if he hadn't had time to write? How could she find out where he was?

Then another nagging voice started up. What if he was tired of her? What if he had decided life was too short to stick to just one girl? All the presents he'd given her—the nylons, the chocolate, the fruit, and the whiskey—how many girls would give their eyeteeth for those things, especially when the giver was so gorgeous?

Her fingers were on the straps of her handbag, pulling distractedly at them. There was a package inside it for him. She had felt so uneasy about his generosity and wanted to give him something in return. He had laughed when she asked if there was anything he needed, grabbing her around the waist and giving her a long, lingering kiss. "This is all I need," he'd whispered, "nothing else." But she had persisted, and in the end he had told her the one thing he really would like was a book.

"Well, that's easy," she'd replied. "What sort of thing do you like?"

He had looked away, then, and muttered something she couldn't catch. When she'd prompted him, he said, "You choose. You're the expert, aren't you? Working in a library and all." Then the penny had dropped. He'd hinted at a childhood where money was short. *Were books as unattainable as musical instruments?* If so, this was something she could remedy. Her books were among the few possessions to have survived the bombing. Stashed under her bed in wooden boxes, they had been better protected than almost anything else in the house.

It had been a difficult decision, choosing the right book for him. In the end she had gone for *Three Men in a Boat*, because it was funny and involved a journey through a very English landscape. Then, when she was wrapping it up, she had slipped in a slim volume of love poems in case he was in any doubt about the strength of her feelings.

Now the hard edges of the parcel pressed against her legs through the fabric of the bag on her lap. She felt terribly alone, sitting there with an offering so tender, so personal, when he was somewhere else. *With* someone else.

When the film ended, she stayed in her seat as everyone else got to their feet.

"Come on," Dilys said. "He could be waiting outside—maybe they wouldn't let him in."

"Why wouldn't they? We've been coming here every week for the past three months!"

"Oh, I don't know," Dilys shrugged. "He could have got into a fight or something—you know what it's like when the two of you are out together. Some people take offense, don't they?"

"But *I* wasn't with him, was I?" Eva hissed. "Why would anyone pick a fight with him if he was on his own?"

"Don't ask me!" Dilys grabbed Eva's arm and pulled her to her feet. "Come on, you're not going to solve anything by staying here, are you?"

Eva allowed herself to be pushed forward by the throng of people leaving the cinema. Outside a gust of wind blew a pile of brittle leaves against her legs. A few of them caught on her stockings. "Damn," she said, snagging them as she pulled the leaves off. She gulped as she felt tears threaten. Where was he? Why hadn't he come? Through blurred eyes she saw a figure running across the street.

"Eva!" He ran up to her, his face beaded with perspiration. "I'm so sorry! I couldn't get here any sooner—it's Jimmy," he paused to catch his breath, "he's been arrested!"

"What?" Eva blinked. "What's happened?"

"You know that girl he was seeing?"

She nodded.

"She's pregnant," Bill gasped, "and she's telling everyone he raped her!"

"Raped her?" Eva echoed. "But it's not true, is it?"

"Absolutely not true." Bill grasped her hands, panic in his eyes. "But when her folks found out she'd been seeing a black guy, they just hit the roof. Her daddy's a powerful man, Eva. He says Jimmy's going to hang for what he's done."

Chapter 9
OCTOBER 1943

They met in the cinema again the following Saturday, but neither of them watched the film. Leaving Anton and Dilys in their seats, they crept to the back and sat on the floor with their backs against the wall, talking in whispers.

"They've taken Jimmy to the glasshouse," Bill said, tugging distractedly at the lapel of his jacket.

"What?" Eva stared at him, uncomprehending.

"Some old prison miles away from here. A place called Shepton Mallet. US Army's taken it over." He sniffed. "Guess they're keeping him there till they decide what to do with him."

"What do you mean?" Eva peered at his face in the darkness.

"Well, it's a straight choice, isn't it?" Bill hissed. "They'll either hang him or shoot him!" He gave a deep sigh that was almost a sob, and people on the back row turned to shush them.

"But how can they do that?" Eva whispered, taking his hand. "That girl's lying! Can't you tell them that?"

"God knows I've tried, but nobody listens." He drew in a breath, shaking his head. "You don't know what it's like. We're *nothing* in their eyes. If a white girl says it happened one way and a colored guy says another, who do you think they're going to believe?"

Eva fell silent. The memory of the soldier who had felled Bill with a punch that first night at the Civic Hall came flooding back. If that was what they did to a black man just for *dancing* with a white girl . . . She reached out, pulling him to her. His head sank onto her shoulder, and she sat rocking him to and fro, his tears seeping through her woolen sweater.

Like David, she thought. How could she possibly tell him now?

～

At work on Monday the trumped-up rape case was the talk of the station canteen. Although the girl's name had never been mentioned in the newspaper reports, it was being bandied about by some of the women on the rail gang. Betty Pelham had let it drop that her sister was Philippa's parents' housekeeper.

"You should see the house," she said, a lump of sausage on its way to her mouth. "I had a sneaky look once when they were away on holiday. It's got three bathrooms, a billiard room, and this enormous glass aviary full of parrots and things. And you should see the cars they've got! Two Bentleys and a Rolls-Royce Silver Ghost."

The others gaped as she stuffed the food into her mouth, agog for more juicy gossip.

"It wouldn't be anywhere round here, then," Eva said, her heart beating faster as she tried to sound casual. "I suppose it's in Finchfield. Or Tettenhall."

"No, it isn't." The sound of the words was distorted by Betty speaking with her mouth full, so eager was she to correct her. "It's up on Goldthorn Hill. A big black-and-white place right at the top: Rookery House, it's called."

～

It took Eva nearly an hour to walk to the mock-Tudor pile on the hill. She set off first thing on Saturday morning, pushing David in his pram. There was a cold wind, but by the time she got to the top, she could feel the perspiration running down her temples. She stopped when she caught sight of the place. It was surrounded by a thick stone wall with a castellated top. Even standing on tiptoe, she couldn't see over it. She followed the wall around a corner and came upon a pair of huge wrought-iron gates. She peered through and glimpsed a red-tiled veranda and a black-painted door with polished carriage lamps on either side of it.

She watched and waited for a while, but there was no sign of life. There was a whimper from the pram. David was stirring in his sleep. He'd be awake soon and hungry, probably. She wondered what to do. Suddenly she saw a flash of color behind the laurel bushes fringing the house and the end of a broom pushing leaves into a pile.

"Excuse me!" She tried not to shout, not wanting to wake David. "Hello!" She tried again. The broom disappeared and a thin old man in a tweed jacket came ambling toward her.

"What do you want?" He peered through the iron gates.

"I'm a friend of Philippa's," she said, trotting it out just as she had planned. She was amazed at how confident her voice sounded. "Is she in?"

"No she isn't," the man said, raising an eyebrow as he caught sight of the pram. "They've gone away."

"Gone . . ." Eva's voice faltered. She swallowed in an effort to clear her throat. "When will they be back?"

"They didn't say." There was a superior look on his face. "Two weeks, maybe three. Do you want to leave a message?"

"No," she said, turning away. "No message."

~

That night Eva and Bill sat in the air-raid shelter just holding each other in the dark, listening to the music coming from the dance hall.

"I thought if I could just talk to her," Eva said, "I could maybe change her mind. Get her to tell the truth. I felt so stupid when he said she'd gone away."

Bill sighed as he stroked her hair. "You took one hell of a risk. No telling what could have happened if her old man had been home."

"I didn't think about that. I just wanted to *do* something. You said they wouldn't listen to you, so I thought . . ."

"I know, I know," he whispered, "and I appreciate what you tried to do. But folks like that—rich, powerful folks—there's no way you're gonna change their mind. Not even if you're the same color as they are."

In the gloom of the shelter she touched his face, half expecting to feel tears on his skin. But she sensed he was beyond that now, as if he had resigned himself to Jimmy's fate. He had given her so much, and now she felt she had failed him. Moving closer, she kissed him, her lips lingering on his, longing to blot out his misery.

"I've been reading that book you gave me," he said when they drew apart. "It's beautiful."

"Really?" The beam of his torch, suspended from the ceiling, caught her puzzled face. Of all the words she might have chosen to describe *Three Men in a Boat*, "beautiful" would not have occurred to her.

"I mean the love poems, not the novel—I haven't read that yet."

"Oh," she smiled. "I'm glad you liked them. Which was your favorite?"

"That's hard to say." He ran his finger along her jawline, cupping her chin in his hand. "The sonnets by Shakespeare—well, they're amazing, of course, and that one about the flea—John Donne, was it?—that made me smile. But the one I like best?" He paused, pursing his lips. "Well, it's a little bit strange: I'm not sure anyone else would choose it. It's called 'A Sanskrit Proverb'—about the crocodile. Do you remember it?"

Eva's look of puzzlement deepened. "Yes, I do: *Love is a crocodile on the river of desire . . .*"

"That's the one."

"Are you serious?" Eva reached up for the torch, batting it with her hand so that the beam fell on his face. "Why that one?"

"Because love is a risk, isn't it? Like the guy says, life is dangerous enough, but falling in love is like swimming in a river full of crocodiles." He leaned toward her, snapped his jaws, and chuckled as he went to kiss her.

"Is that what you really think?" She turned away, hurt that he was making light of it.

"Don't you?" He cupped her chin in his hand again, turning her back to face him. "Don't you think that loving somebody is dangerous?"

"Like Jimmy and Philippa, you mean?"

He shook his head. "That wasn't love."

"You don't think he loved her?"

"I know so. He told me."

A silence descended. Another question hung in the air, with an unspoken answer.

And what about you? The words beat a tattoo inside her head as she leaned forward to kiss him. She was afraid to ask, afraid to know the answer.

Chapter 10

Three weeks later Eva's mother was preparing a birthday tea for Dilys. Eva was helping, although the last thing she was in the mood for was a celebration.

Jimmy's execution the day before had knocked the war off the front page of the *Express & Star*. Eva watched her mother push aside the mound of bread she had sliced to pick up the paper. The headline screamed at her: "HISTORIC HANGING FOR GI RAPIST."

"Have you read this?" Without looking up, her mother began to read aloud: "'An American serviceman was hanged yesterday at Shepton Mallet prison in Somerset for raping a sixteen-year-old Wolverhampton girl . . .'" She tutted under her breath. "'It is the first time that a man has been hanged for the crime of rape in Britain.'" She continued, "'The soldier—a colored man from the Quartermaster Corps based near Bridgnorth—was executed under US Army jurisdiction.'"

Eva sat motionless, staring at the knife she had just dipped in a jar of fish paste.

"They say she's pregnant." Her mother glanced up from the paper, clearly expecting a reaction to this bit of gossip. Eva kept her head down. "Imagine what it's going to be like for that poor child," her mother went on. "They won't let her keep it, that's for certain. But who's going to want it? She'll never find anyone to adopt it." This was followed by a heavy sigh. "I suppose it'll end up in a home." The knife rattled against the jar of fish paste as her mother dug it in. "Won't it?"

"I'll just go and check the cake," Eva mumbled, dashing toward the kitchen.

~

The small front room was filled with people, all glad to get out of the biting October wind. It was a noisy mix of neighbors and friends, some clutching presents and others with rations to donate for the party. Cathy arrived last with a large tin of pineapple chunks, which brought cheers from the other guests.

Dilys made a grand entrance, swanning into the room with Anton on her arm.

"Don't look so shocked!" she whispered to Eva. "I'm sixteen now—I can do what I like!"

"Never mind me!" Eva hissed back. "How are you going to explain him to Mum?"

An awkward few minutes followed, during which their mother shot speaking glances at Eva. *Better to go along with the pretense that this was a new romance,* Eva thought. Otherwise her mother might start asking what her daughters had really been up to on all those long Sunday walks.

While Anton was working his charm on her mother, Dilys started opening her presents. It was an interesting assortment: "A pair of shoes, three pairs of silk stockings, a brooch, half a dozen grapefruit, and two Hershey bars! I didn't do too badly, did I?"

Dilys laughed. "Did Bill get you these?" she whispered, picking up one of the bars of chocolate, peeling back the paper and taking a big bite.

"Dil! You're supposed to be saving them! What about all this food?" Eva waved her hand at the table.

"It's only one bite!" Dilys grinned, stuffing the chocolate back into its wrapper. "Anyway, I've got to keep my strength up." Eva shot her a worried glance, but her sister was too busy examining her presents to notice. "I'm starting my training next week," she said, without looking up.

"What training?"

"I've signed up for the Auxiliary Territorial Service," Dilys said. "Didn't I tell you? I've been planning it for ages."

Eva stared at her sister. "Does Mum know?"

"I haven't told her yet—thought I'd wait till after the party."

"Oh, Dil . . ." Eva bit her lip.

"Listen," Dilys said, "I'm sorry if it's a bit of a shock, but I can't go on like this." She fingered the rhinestone pin in the shape of a *D* that Anton had given her for her birthday. "*You* might not mind skulking about, hiding from people, but *I* do. The ATS camp is just down the road from Anton's barracks. We can be together—*really* together." Her expression was one Eva remembered her using as a child when she was trying to wheedle something out of their father. "You do understand, don't you?"

"Well, yes . . . but you're so—"

"You mustn't breathe a word of this to Mum," Dilys cut in, glancing over her shoulder, "but Anton's asked me to marry him! He wants me to go back to Holland with him when the war's over!"

"What?" Eva's jaw dropped. A jumble of words rushed through her head, but she felt numb, paralyzed. A thin cry from the room above broke the spell. "That's David," she said, "the noise must have woken him up." She made for the door, glad of an excuse to get away. For the first time in her life she had looked at her sister and felt jealous.

Eva scooped David up in her arms, rocking him in an effort to comfort him. "Nanna gone?" he lisped, pointing to the door. "Dilly gone?"

"They're downstairs, sweetheart," she said. "We'll go and see them in a minute. Let's just change you first." She laid him on the bed and rolled down his rompers. He kicked his legs as she did it.

"Want Dilly! Want Nanna!" he cried.

Eva shushed him, wondering what Bill would think if he could see her now. She tried to imagine David calling his name, following him around the way he trailed after Dilys and her mother. Calling Bill "Dad." It frightened her, knowing how desperately she wanted it, because right here, right now, it seemed utterly impossible.

As she undressed her son, she found herself thinking about the baby Philippa was carrying, a baby who would never see his or her father. The injustice of Jimmy's execution had shocked her to the core. *The Americans are supposed to be our friends,* she thought. *They're supposed to be just like us.*

She remembered what Bill had told her about Louisiana, about the demeaning laws that kept black people away from whites. What would it be like for the child she was carrying to grow up in a place like that—a country whose laws allowed a black man to be hanged for doing nothing worse than what she and Bill had been doing? Could they ever be a family in a country like that?

There was a knock at the bedroom door. "Can I come in?" Cathy's head appeared. She sat down on the bed, making faces at David until he stopped kicking and started to giggle.

"How's Bill?" Cathy's smile vanished as she looked up. "I saw the paper."

"I don't really know," Eva said. "I haven't seen him since last Saturday."

"He must be going through hell."

Eva nodded. "You'd never guess it, though." She stopped trying to pull one of David's socks over his wriggling toes and gave a deep sigh. "He's so hard to read. When Jimmy was arrested, he was in a terrible state. But the past couple of weeks he's been really calm." She stared at the sock in her hand. "Unnaturally calm, really. It was his birthday last week—his twenty-first—and he didn't even tell me. But then he sent a note to the station asking for a date with me, even though he knew Jimmy was going to be . . ." She stroked the soft, plump skin above David's toes.

"Sounds like it hasn't really sunk in yet."

"He's asked me to book a table at the best restaurant in town. Says he wants to give Jimmy a good send-off."

"Grief comes out in strange ways, sometimes." Cathy brought her face close to David's and he grabbed at her hair. "I remember when we got the news about Stuart, it took a long time for me to accept that he was never coming home. People used to say how well I was coping, but about two months after the funeral it suddenly hit me. I just broke down in tears one morning while I was peeling the potatoes. I was counting them out, and I thought *this is it*: we're never going to need any more potatoes than this for Sunday dinner ever again, because he's not coming back." She pulled a silver bangle from her wrist and gave it to David to play with. "Bill's really going to need you," she said, "more than he probably realizes at the moment."

Eva raised herself on her elbows. "I want to be there for him. Of course I do. But . . ." she trailed off, searching for a way of saying what she dreaded putting into words.

"Don't tell me you're breaking it off with him? After everything you—"

"Oh, God, no!" Eva cut her short. "It's not that!" She turned her anguished face away from Cathy. She couldn't, mustn't tell her. Mustn't tell anyone.

"It's Dilys," she lied, her eyes fixed on the bedspread.

"What's wrong with her?" Cathy asked. "She looked absolutely on top of the world five minutes ago."

"Yes, she is," Eva said. "Anton's proposed to her, apparently. She's joining the ATS so she can move out and spend more time with him. So that's why I'm not going to be much use to Bill," she went on. "I don't even know if I'll be able to see him when Dilys isn't around to give me an alibi."

Cathy laughed. "Cunning little minx! I hope she knows what she's letting herself in for!" She put her hand on Eva's shoulder. "Hey," she said, "don't worry about seeing Bill—you can use me as an excuse if you want to. And if your Mum gets fed up with babysitting, you can always bring this little chap round to me for the night." She tickled David, making him giggle again.

Eva felt shamed by Cathy's generosity. "No, I couldn't possibly ask you to look after him—I feel bad enough leaving him at home."

"Why not? I'd enjoy it." She leaned across the bed and gave Eva a shove. "I know I'm a boring old has-been, but that doesn't mean I don't want anyone else to have any fun!"

"Is that how you see yourself, Cathy? Seriously, I mean: you don't feel you want to . . . you know . . . meet someone else?"

Cathy sighed and ruffled David's hair. "I don't know. I'm just scared, I guess. Remember that sleazy so-and-so at the dance? The one with the wandering hands?"

Eva nodded. "But you can't let one bad experience put you off men for life."

"I know. And I look at you sometimes and think, yes, go for it! Be happy while you've got the chance. But then I look at Stuart's photo and . . . well, I just can't. I can't imagine being that way with anybody else."

"I wish it had been that way with Eddie and me," Eva said quietly.

"You gave him everything you could," Cathy said. "You made him happy."

"Did I? He wasn't happy about David."

"He would have got over that. He just didn't have the chance." Cathy reached out and stroked the pale pink patch on the little boy's cheek. "David's his legacy to the world. That's the gift you gave him: don't sell yourself so short."

Eva closed her eyes tight. She had never cried for Eddie. To do so now would be the worst kind of hypocrisy, because the tears she was fighting back were for herself.

~

It was cold and dark when Eva and Dilys left the house that night. Anton was waiting in the car at the end of the street, ready to whisk them into town. Eva asked to be dropped off at the usual place. Telling Dilys about Bill's strange request would have prompted too many awkward questions.

When she found her way to the restaurant, Bill was already waiting outside. He greeted her with a smile and a hug. There was no hint of what yesterday had meant to him: of the anguish of sitting in front of a clock watching the minutes of his friend's life ticking away.

The restaurant was crowded, mostly with white Americans and their girlfriends. Few local people could afford the prices the Victoria charged. There was a lot of pointing and whispering, but to Eva's relief no one actually came up to the table to challenge them.

"This sounds pretty good, for Britain!" Bill laughed as he scanned the menu. "Now, what will you have?" Before she could answer, he pulled a piece of paper from his jacket pocket and passed it to her across the table. "Thought we could go see these guys after this," he said. "Go on—read it!"

He's talking too much, she thought, frowning as she unfolded the flyer. *He's acting as though he didn't have a care in the world.*

"'Civic Hall, Wolverhampton,'" she read aloud. "'Anglo-American Ball. By public demand—return of that Dynamic Colored Personality, Stanley Carter and His All-Colored Harlem Hot Club Dance Band, featuring Vic Brown—the colored Bing Crosby . . .'"

"Sounds perfect, don't you think?"

"Well, yes . . . but do you *really* want to go dancing?" She frowned, trying to work out what was going on inside his head.

"Are you kidding?" Bill smiled broadly. "You know how I love to dance—and anyway, it's what Jimmy would have wanted. Back home we believe in enjoying ourselves when we have a funeral. Just because there isn't going to *be* a funeral doesn't mean we can't pretend . . ." His voice faltered and almost broke. But before Eva could say or do anything, he was on his feet, helping her out of her chair. "Come on," he said, "let's skip dinner and get over there!"

"Are you sure this is a good idea?" Eva whispered as they made their way past the shadowy recesses of shops where cigarettes glowed and hushed voices could be heard in the darkness.

"Why not?" Bill quickened his pace, almost pulling her along.

"You saw what it was like in the restaurant," she said, catching her breath. "It's going to be worse if people see us dancing." She clamped her mouth shut. She had almost said: "Especially with Jimmy all over the news."

"You worry too much," Bill replied. "Like I said, it's perfect: an all-black band and a black singer. What white guy's going to have the nerve to lay a finger on me with them on the stage?"

He was right. The singer soon spotted that he was the only black man on the dance floor and called him up onstage to shake his hand. From then on it was as if a bit of Vic Brown's stardust had rubbed off on Bill and Eva. As they jitterbugged and jived around the room, the spotlight followed them, daring any trouble to follow in its wake. There were white American soldiers in the room, but she saw them only as a blur of color as Bill spun her around. And as the light caught his face, she could see that it was transformed. For the first time since Jimmy's arrest, he looked happy, carefree.

"Can we have a rest now?" Eva gasped as she flopped into a chair and took a gulp of shandy. "I thought I was going to end up on the ceiling during that last one!"

Bill laughed. "You're as light as a feather, that's why. Don't think I ever had a partner I could lift so easily."

Eva's face clouded at his words and she bent over her drink to avoid his eyes.

"Hey, what did I say? It was supposed to be a compliment!"

"Oh, nothing." She took another swallow of her drink. "Come on," she said, taking his hand. "It's a slow one—I think I can just about manage that." As they danced, she buried her head in his jacket. If she told him what was on her mind that brave smile of his would wither like a blossom after frost. Despite his best efforts not to show it, she knew he was still raw with the pain of Jimmy's death.

She felt his hands slip down around her waist. It wouldn't be long before he worked it out for himself. And then what?

She closed her eyes, concentrating on the music. Vic Brown had a voice like melting chocolate. He was singing about love, of course, about a love that was too hot not to cool down. The words of the song sent shards of ice through her stomach.

Chapter 11
LATE FEBRUARY 1944

A flurry of snow was falling on the railway line, turning the forlorn-looking trucks a dazzling white. The women were shoveling it away where it had drifted, clearing the line for incoming trains. Cathy Garner glanced around as she paused to shake snow from her cap. Betty Pelham's big round face had turned red with a combination of the cold and the effort of digging. Iris Stokes had taken off her gloves to examine the chilblains on her fingers. And Eva . . . what was Eva doing?

Eva was doubled over, clutching her stomach. Cathy dropped her spade. As she ran across the tracks, she saw that her friend's face was as white as the snow clinging to her hair.

"Eva—what's the matter?"

Eva gasped in answer and reached out, hands flailing.

Cathy grabbed her around the waist as her friend swayed toward her. "Come on, let's get you inside!" She guided her over to the toolshed.

Betty Pelham was following them. "Shall I get the nurse?" she asked. "Or is she just faking it?"

"Yes, get the nurse!" Cathy hissed. "Can't you see how pale she's gone?"

Eva slumped back on a wooden bench, oblivious of a huge cobweb that attached itself to her hair and hung down one side of her head like a tattered veil.

"Eva, what is it? Please, tell me!"

"I . . . it's nothing," Eva whispered, taking a breath. "I'm just tired, that's all."

"Well, it doesn't look like nothing!" Cathy put her hand to Eva's face. "You're as cold as ice! Have you got any of that stuff Bill gave you?"

Eva shook her head.

"Well, you need something inside you. Did you have any breakfast?"

"I didn't really feel like anything," Eva mumbled.

"No wonder you look so pale, you daft thing! Fancy not eating in this weather!"

A woman in a Red Cross uniform appeared in the doorway with Betty following in her wake. "Thank you, Mrs. Pelham," the nurse said as Betty parked herself down on a pile of sacks. "You can get back to work now." As the door closed, she shook the snow from her cape and gave Eva a long, hard look. "Now, what seems to be the matter?" She addressed this question to Cathy. "Not idle-itis, I hope!"

"It's all right," Eva said, lurching from the bench. "I'm fine, really." She took a step toward the door, but her legs crumpled. Cathy grabbed her as she collapsed onto the dusty floor.

~

Half an hour later Eva was lying unconscious on a couch in the stationmaster's office. The nurse had unbuttoned the shapeless gray donkey jacket and was pressing down on Eva's stomach. Cathy stood silently beside her, holding Eva's hand.

"About five months gone, I'd say," the nurse pronounced. "Married, is she?" She lifted Eva's left arm, which hung limply from the side of the couch, examining the fingers. "Hmm," she grunted, "I thought as much!"

"She *is* married," Cathy said. "She doesn't wear her ring at work because it gives her calluses."

"Really?" The nurse raised an eyebrow. "And is the husband home or away?"

"Home," Cathy lied. "He works at Goodyear's."

"Well, he's a foolish man, letting his wife do this kind of work in her condition." The nurse pulled down Eva's lower eyelids, peering at the skin beneath. "Anemic too. No wonder she passed out. She needs to see a doctor."

Eva came around suddenly, sitting bolt upright and staring at the unfamiliar surroundings.

"It's okay," Cathy said, squeezing her hand. "You passed out."

"Congratulations, young lady," the nurse said with a grim smile. "Did you realize you are expecting?"

Eva looked from Cathy to the nurse and back again, wide-eyed with alarm.

"It's all right," Cathy said. "I don't suppose you've even told Eddie yet, have you?" She made an anguished face behind the nurse's back. "Shall I take her to the canteen?" she said quickly. "Get her something to eat and then take her to the doctor's?"

"Well, she definitely needs some food inside her," the nurse muttered. "Are we strong enough to walk now?"

"Yes, I'm fine," Eva said. She slid one leg off the couch, desperate to get away.

"Let me help you." Cathy took Eva's arm as she stood up. "Come on: lean on me if you need to."

When they got to the canteen, the other rail gangers were already there.

"Oh no," Cathy said, glancing at her watch, "it's tea break."

"She all right?" Betty Pelham yelled over her shoulder.

"Yes, she's fine now," Cathy called back. "Skipped breakfast, that's all."

"Oh, really?" Iris Stokes piped up. "Are you sure that's *all* it is?" She smiled slyly at the others. "I saw her dancing with a Yank at the Civic: a *colored* one!"

Cathy felt Eva's grip tighten on her arm. "So what?" she shouted back before Eva could react. "I saw *you* with one of those Italian POWs from Moseley Farm: necking at a bus stop in broad daylight!"

All eyes shot from Eva to Iris.

"Dirty bitch!" Betty Pelham was on her feet. A gob of spittle flew across the table, landing on the sleeve of Iris's jacket. A deafening volley of abuse followed Iris as she leapt to her feet and ran to the door.

Cathy sat Eva down at the far end of the canteen while she went to beg something more substantial than a hot mug of tea from the woman at the serving hatch.

"Here you are," she said, returning with a slab of bread-and-butter pudding. "Now, eat up! We're not moving until you've finished it."

Cathy sat in silence as Eva ate, watching the color slowly return to her cheeks. "Why didn't you tell me?" she whispered, as Eva pushed the empty plate aside.

Eva stared silently at the table.

"Does Bill know?"

She shook her head.

"But hasn't he . . . *noticed* anything?"

Eva gave a short, humorless chuckle. "He thinks it's all those Hershey bars." She lifted her teacup, her hand shaking.

"Why have you kept it to yourself all this time? You know you can trust me. I could have helped you."

"Helped me? How?" Eva made a small, strangled sound that was a cross between a laugh and a sob. "Do you know when I found out? It was the night before Bill's best friend was hanged for getting a white girl pregnant." She shook her head. "And my mother never stops going on about how dreadful life's going to be for Jimmy's baby: it'd just about kill her if she knew I was in the same boat!"

"So what were you going to do?" Cathy whispered. "Did you really think you could go on hiding it for much longer?"

Eva stared blankly at the wall in front of her. "I don't know," she murmured, her lips moving but her face expressionless. "I wanted to tell you. But that would have made it . . . real."

"But it *is* real!" Cathy gasped. "You've got to tell him, Eva: it's his baby and he needs to know. He must have realized it could happen."

"I *want* to tell him," Eva said. "So many times I've nearly said something . . . but I'm afraid to."

"Why? I mean, it's not like Jimmy, is it?" Cathy dropped her voice. "Nobody's going to try to say he raped you."

"It's not that," Eva said. "Don't you see? If I tell him I'm pregnant, I'm going to have to tell him everything. About David, about Eddie."

"You mean you haven't—"

"No!" Eva reached for her tea, cradling the mug in both hands. "I was going to tell him the night Jimmy was arrested. I thought I'd wait, give him time to get back on an even keel. But now there's a baby . . ."

"I see," Cathy nodded. "You're afraid that if he finds out you've lied to him, he'll leave you?"

Eva closed her eyes. "I didn't *lie* to him: I just didn't tell him the whole truth."

Cathy reached across the table, laying her hand on Eva's arm. "But the fact is he's going to have to leave you anyway," she said gently. "It could happen any day: you know that."

"Of course I do, but . . ." she faltered.

"But what?"

"I can't let myself believe it. I can't imagine life without him, Cathy."

"Do you love him? You said you were *in* love, but that's not the same, really, is it?"

Eva buried her face in her hands. "Yes," she mumbled, "I do."

"And does he love you?"

A few seconds' silence, then: "I don't know."

"There's only one way to find out, then, isn't there? Before it's too late, I mean."

Eva looked up, her face marked red where her fingers had pressed against it. "What are you saying?"

"Well," Cathy replied, "if he really loves you, it won't matter about the past, will it?" She paused, studying Eva's face. "And if he doesn't, then you've still got time to decide what to do."

~

Eva got out of Anton's car and picked her way by torchlight across the treacherous frozen slush the snow had left in its wake. She was early. And with the weather, Bill would probably be late. Making her way down the steps of the air-raid shelter, she settled down to wait on one of the wooden benches. As she did so, she felt a familiar fluttering in her belly. She caught her breath, suddenly realizing what it was, that odd sensation like the wings of a butterfly caught inside someone's hand. That first, fragile movement had thrilled her when she was pregnant with David. Now she felt numbed by the reality of what was happening to her body.

The beam of another torch danced on the walls of the shelter, making her jump. "Hi, honey, what are you doing in here?" Bill's voice echoed in the empty space. "I thought you'd stood me up," he laughed, taking her in his arms and squeezing her tight. She felt as limp and lifeless as a rag doll, incapable of hugging him back.

"Hey, what's wrong?" He hung the light on the hook on the wall so that he could see her face. "What is it?" he repeated. "You look like you've seen a ghost!"

"Bill, I . . ." she faltered. "There's . . . something I've got to tell you."

He blew out a breath. "I had a feeling this was coming."

His words threw her. The carefully rehearsed speech went out of her head.

Bill raised his hands to her shoulders, holding her there as he searched her face. "You're going to have a baby, right?"

Eva blinked. "How did you know?"

"Honey, I'm not blind!" He sighed, pulling her to him. "Don't you think I've noticed how you've changed the past few weeks?"

"But I thought that you thought . . ."

"The candy?" He grunted. "That was just my way of passing it off, I guess. Pretending it wasn't real." He reached across and put his hand on her stomach. His face was a mixture of fear and fascination. "Sweet Jesus, what do we do now?"

Eva closed her eyes, panic rising like bile. "You don't understand. There's . . . something else." She felt for his hand, clutching it tightly in both of hers. "It's something I should have told you a long time ago." She opened her eyes and looked straight into his. "I already have a child, Bill." Her mouth trembled as she spoke. "A little boy. His name's David and he's two years old."

Bill blinked at her, the skin between his eyebrows furrowing as her words sunk in.

"And I'm . . ." she swallowed hard. "I'm married, sort of."

"What?" He whipped his hand from her grip. "What the hell does that mean? You're either married or you ain't!"

"No, you don't understand," she gasped, running after him as he paced the floor. "Eddie—my husband—his boat was torpedoed off Singapore . . ."

He stopped dead as he reached the door, his back to her. "Is he alive?" The brick-lined walls threw back a menacing echo.

"No! I . . . I don't know. He . . . he's missing." She put her hand on his arm, but he shrugged it off.

"Missing?" he shouted, his voice bouncing back at her from all directions. "Missing?" He backed away from her, his eyes full of loathing. "You *lied* to me! All that crap about your mother not approving of a black boyfriend! Just a bunch of goddamn lies!" He spat out a curse and ran from her, up the steps and out into the cold white night.

She clung to the frame of the door, paralyzed, listening to the sound of his footsteps fading away. "What did you expect?" she whispered. Her voice sounded ghostly. She felt utterly alone. This was how it was going to be: just her. And David. And the baby. Her fingers tightened on the rough wood. She felt sick, dizzy. A gust of wind blew down the steps, ruffling the snow. It carried with it a mocking snatch of music from the dance hall. Dilys and Anton were in there. But the thought of going to find them, trying to lie about Bill's absence, was more than she could bear. Pulling the collar of her coat up around her ears, she took a deep breath in and another out, counting to four in her head, trying to blot out everything but the business of how to get herself home.

Bill's torch was still hanging from the hook on the wall. Mechanically she walked over and unhooked it. "He'll want this back," she said, staring at it, knowing that she was talking nonsense, but talking all the same to keep herself from breaking down. She shone it at the doorway and saw snowflakes in the beam of light. Pulling her collar tighter, she propelled herself out of the shelter. *Go to the bus stop. Get David from Cathy's.* She repeated the words like a mantra as she stumbled across the square.

The bus stop was deserted. She waited for what seemed like hours, willing a bus to come. The snow had stopped, but it was as cold as ever. She could no longer feel her toes and standing for so long was beginning to make her feel breathless. She shone the torch at the buildings around her, looking for somewhere to sit within sight of the stop. There was a low wall outside the magistrates' court. It was covered in snow, but she could scrape it off. As she turned, her foot slipped. She waved her arms wildly, struggling to keep her balance, but she felt herself falling.

"Jeez!" Bill gasped as he grabbed her under the arms just in time to stop her from hitting the pavement.

"You . . . you came back," she stuttered, her teeth chattering as much from shock as from the cold.

"Yeah," he mumbled, looking away. "You'd better watch out—you haven't just got yourself to think about anymore!" He carried her over to the wall and sat her down. "Guess I shouldn't have stormed off like that." His voice was edgy, defensive. "I just want to know why you lied to me, Eva."

"Because I wanted you," she whispered. "And I thought you wouldn't want me if you knew the truth."

"Wanted me for what?" His voice sounded very loud in the silent, snow-muffled street. "For candy? For nylons?" He stared pointedly at her stomach. "By God, you sure got more than you bargained for, didn't you!"

Hot tears coursed down her pale cheeks. "Is that what you think of me? Really?" She rose unsteadily to her feet. "Because if you do, that makes me nothing more than . . . than a prostitute! And a bloody cheap one at that!" She ran blindly down the dark street, not caring if she lost her footing.

"Eva! Wait!" She heard his footsteps crunching after her. "Please! I'm sorry—I didn't mean it!" He caught up with her, catching her arm and nearly pulling them both over. "I want you," he said, hugging her to him, "and I want the baby." He stroked the snowflakes from her hair. "Listen, honey, I don't care if you're married or not: I'm not running out on my kid the way my daddy ran out on me."

Chapter 12

Bill couldn't sleep. He lay on his back on the hard bunk bed, staring into the darkness, turning the endless possibilities over in his mind. It was hopeless. How could he offer Eva and the baby any kind of future when he didn't know if he had one himself?

The next morning he sought out the chaplain, one of the few white men in the US Army he felt he could trust. Father Corrigan had battled in vain to get Bill's evidence heard at Jimmy's court martial and had been with Jimmy the day he was hanged.

Bill hesitated outside the door. A tangle of emotions held him back. Guilt, shame, anger, and frustration. Fear too, although he hated to admit it, even to himself. He took a deep breath and knocked.

The chaplain smiled at the sight of him. "Good morning, Wilbur," he said. "How are you doing?"

Later on, Bill wasn't sure if it was the smile or hearing the name his mother always called him by that did it, but his carefully prepared speech went right out the window. Everything came out in a jumble.

"Hold on a minute, son," the priest said, putting up a hand to stop him. "Just sit down, will you?" Bill bit his lip and did as he was told. "Here," Father Corrigan proffered a pack of Lucky Strikes. "Have one of these."

There were three cigarette butts in the ashtray by the time Bill had finished explaining. "You see, Father," he said, "I can't marry her, because she's still married. And even if I could, where would we go? There's nowhere in Louisiana we could live, a black man with a white woman."

"If she was single," the chaplain said, stroking his chin, "would you have asked her to marry you by now?"

Bill frowned and looked away. "Hell, I don't know. Like I said, marriages like that never happen where I come from—you know that."

"You don't have to go back to Louisiana, though, do you? You could settle anywhere when the war's over. What's to stop you from going north? New York, Illinois—someplace where it's legal."

Bill sighed and stared at the ceiling. "When the war's over?" He shook his head. "When the war's over, I could be dead—what's the use of planning anything for the future?"

Father Corrigan shook his head. "You're twenty-one years old, Wilbur—how can you talk about dying?"

Bill jumped to his feet and strode over to the window, hiding his face. "Because of Jimmy!" The hoarseness in his voice betrayed him. "Jimmy was only six months older than me and look what happened to him! Never got near no front line, did he?" He paused, staring at the groups of soldiers walking past in the yard outside. "I've just got this feeling inside, Father," he whispered. "Jimmy never lived to see his baby, and I don't believe I'm going to live to see mine."

Father Corrigan walked over to where Bill stood and put both hands on his shoulders. "You can't think like that," he said, looking him straight in the eyes. "You've got to see beyond this war—for the sake of your own sanity, as well as for your girlfriend and the baby."

"I want to—but I just can't." Bill buried his face in his hands. "What am I going to do?"

The chaplain frowned. "Well, you can't send Eva to the States, that's for sure—not until she has proof that she's a widow—and that might not happen till the war's over. But there is something you can do."

"What?"

"You can get the Red Cross to send the baby over." He smiled at Bill's shocked expression. "Don't worry—you won't be the first to do it. There've been at least a dozen American soldiers who've done it already—white men, admittedly, but there's no reason why you can't do it too."

"What, you mean the baby goes without the mother?"

"Yes. The cases I've heard about have all involved married women who've had affairs with GIs and faced a straight choice between keeping the baby or hanging on to their husbands. Once the baby's weaned, it's taken across the Atlantic by a Red Cross nurse on the first available boat."

Bill stared at him, incredulous. "But what happens on the other side?"

"The father's relatives take care of it—usually the grandmother."

Bill grunted. "I couldn't do that! Can you imagine what would happen to my mom if she took in a child half-black and half-white?"

"Haven't you got relatives anywhere else?"

Bill scratched his chin. "Well, there's my aunt Millie in Chicago . . ." He frowned. "But wait a minute—who says Eva's gonna let the baby go?"

"Well, she might not," the chaplain replied. "All I'm saying is if you want to do the right thing by the baby and you're worried you might not survive the war, this is the only way of making sure he or she is provided for."

Bill's eyes narrowed as he weighed the priest's words. "Guess you're right," he said at last. "Seems like it's the only way."

He lay awake for a second night, going over and over it in his head; planning the letter he would write to his aunt and the one he would also have to write to his mother and sister. By the time the first hint of daybreak lightened the sky beyond his window, he had worked most of it out—even down to the amount of money he would need to send to Chicago each month to provide for the baby for as long as the war went on.

What he could not work out was the part about Eva. If she agreed to the plan—which was by no means certain—would she go to Chicago when the war ended? Would she be willing to leave her family behind and start a new life in a new country? Of course, she would have to bring her other child, her little boy. Bill tried to imagine what that would be like: the two of them walking up Michigan Avenue, a white woman and a black man with a white child and a brown baby. In New Orleans he'd be lynched, no question. Was it really going to be so very different in Chicago?

A ray of sunlight fell on the pillow. He pulled his gray army blanket over his head and shut his eyes tight.

~

It was a whole week before Bill could face telling Eva what Father Corrigan had suggested. He chose his moment carefully. He took her for lunch at the quiet little backstreet restaurant they'd been to on their first proper date. Better than telling her when they were alone, he thought, less chance of another painful scene.

"Send the baby to America? Without me?"

Bill had underestimated the effect his words would have. If he had pulled out a gun and fired it at the ceiling, Eva couldn't have looked more stunned, more outraged. The forkful of mashed potato that had been on its way to her lips clattered onto the plate.

"I know it's going to be tough." Bill reached across the table and took her hand. "But I don't see what else we can do." He tried to explain what the chaplain had said, but Eva was having none of it.

"You seriously expect me to send our baby across the Atlantic with some stranger?" This was not whispered. The woman on the till turned to look as she stood up. "I thought you cared about me! About both of us!" Throwing down her napkin, she dodged the approaching waiter and made for the door.

All Bill could see were the eyes turned on him. The waiter, the cashier, and the other couples in the room. Their hostility paralyzed him. For those few crucial seconds it was as if he was back in New Orleans, in a room full of rednecks and horribly alone. He looked away, at the space Eva had vacated. Jimmy's desperate, pleading face hovered over the chair, crying out in terror, begging him for help.

Bill fixed his eyes on the crumbs of toast on the tablecloth, his head pounding. He needed to get outside. Talk to Eva. He glanced at the door. People had stopped staring now. He could do it. He could get out. As he rose to his feet, he caught sight of Eva through the window. She was half running, half walking down the street toward a waiting bus.

~

Eva didn't see Bill chasing after her, didn't spot him trying and failing to grab the metal pole of the double-decker as he sprinted along the pavement. She was sitting at the front, behind the driver, her face hidden from the other passengers. When the conductor came to take her fare, she held out the money without looking up.

Half an hour later she was sitting at Cathy's kitchen table, a sodden handkerchief clutched in her hand. She had managed to keep it all inside until Cathy opened the front door. Then it had come rushing out in jumbled, sobbed sentences.

"How could he . . . *suggest* such a thing?" she sniffed, as Cathy poured hot water into the teapot.

"Probably because he's scared," Cathy replied without looking up.

"Scared? Of what?"

"Of everything." Cathy set the pot on the table and sat down opposite Eva. "He's suddenly realized what he's done. He's going to be a father. That's scary enough for a man who's not even married." She passed Eva the milk jug. "And he's about to go to war. Ever since he arrived in this country he's known that he could wake up one morning and find out he's off to France or Holland or goodness knows where. You said yourself he thinks he's going to die."

Eva stared into her teacup. "But he's *not* going to, Cathy. I just know he's not."

Cathy gave a guarded smile. "Well, I hope you're right, but you've got to try to see it from his point of view. He's just trying to make sure you don't get left to bring up the baby on your own."

Eva huffed out a breath. "I'd rather do that than send it halfway across the world to be brought up by someone I've never even met!"

"But think about it for a minute," Cathy said. "How can you provide for David and the baby with no man to support you? Especially if your Mum throws you out—which sounds pretty likely, from what you've said."

"Oh, I don't know," Eva shrugged. "I'd get another job, I suppose. I'd manage somehow."

"How are you going to get a job with a baby to look after?" Cathy sat back in her chair, her arms folded. "It's all very well now, with the war work and the WVS nurseries, but what do you think's going to happen when it's over and all the men come back? There won't be nearly as many jobs going then, will there?"

"You sound as if you're on his side!"

"No, of course I'm not—I'm just trying to warn you what it's going to be like. I know how hard it is trying to survive on a widow's pension. If it wasn't for my job, I don't know how I'd make ends meet. I'm just hoping to goodness I can keep working until Michael's old enough to leave school and bring some money in."

"So what are you saying? That I should give the baby up? Send it away before it even knows who I am?" Eva's eyes were bright with unshed tears.

"It'd probably only be for a short time," Cathy said. "When the war's over and you can prove you're a widow, you and Bill can marry and you'll move to America." She paused. "He has said he'll marry you, hasn't he?"

"Not in so many words, no." She brought her cup to her mouth, swallowing tea that was still too hot. "He won't talk about it because he's convinced himself he's not going to survive."

"Is that the real reason?"

Eva shied away from Cathy's frank gaze. "I . . . don't know."

"All the more reason to send the baby to his relatives, then, I'd say," Cathy replied.

Eva frowned. "Why?"

"Well, he's bound to feel different when the war's over, isn't he? It's hard for him now: there's too much pressure. But if he gets back to the States and the baby's there waiting for him—well, he'd have to be pretty inhuman not to want you there too."

~

It was dark when Eva left. David was asleep in the pram, and she wheeled him along the few silent streets that separated Cathy's home from her own. She turned up the alley that ran along the side of the house and shone her torch into the yard, easing the pram into the narrow space by the door. As she backed into the kitchen, light streamed out. Pulling the pram inside, she turned quickly to shut the door.

Her mother was sitting at the table, her arms folded on the green chintz cloth. There was no one else in the room and no sound of the wireless. Eva wondered what was wrong.

"Mum?" She went across to her, shrugging her arms out of her coat. "What's up?"

"You weren't with *Cathy* this afternoon, were you?" she hissed.

"Yes I was—I left her house ten minutes ago!" Eva could feel her heart thumping against her ribs.

"You haven't been there *all* afternoon, though, have you?"

"What are you saying?" Eva clutched the back of a chair.

"I got it out of Dilys. She told me you were seeing a *Yank.*" Her mother stood up as she spat out the word. "As if that wasn't bad enough! I followed you from Cathy's—you little slut!" She lashed out at Eva with the back of her hand. Eva dodged sideways and her mother lost her balance, knocking over a chair that clattered onto the floor in front of her. Seizing this chance to escape, Eva pushed open the door and heaved the pram out.

"Where d'you think you're going?"

"Away from here!" Eva shouted over her shoulder. She paused for a split second, fumbling in her bag for her torch.

"Don't you dare run away from me, you little madam!"

Eva lurched forward, the torch abandoned, so desperate was she to get away. The pram bumped against the walls of the alley. She couldn't trust herself to defend what she had with Bill. Not without letting on about the baby. *My God,* she thought, as she stumbled off the pavement into the road, *she'd bloody well kill me if I told her.*

"Eva! Come back here!"

LINDSAY ASHFORD

She heard the door slam shut, footsteps echoing up the alley. Eva quickened her pace. As she crossed the road, she heard a car. No lights. It must be in the next street. She bumped the pram up the curb and turned the corner, heading back toward Cathy's house. Her teeth were rattling. She was shivering and sweating at the same time. There was a sudden screech of brakes. Silence. Then a chilling sound echoed through the street. A man shouting. Crying out for help.

Chapter 13

Cathy's arm was wrapped around Eva's shoulders. She lifted a glass of brandy to her friend's mouth, but Eva was shaking too much to drink it. "Come on," she whispered, "take a deep breath."

She glanced across at David, who had slept through all the frantic activity going on around him. Ambulance men, the police, and that grim-faced doctor. All of them had gone now. Cathy felt numb. Useless. What on earth could she say to Eva to calm her down?

"It's . . . my . . ." Eva's teeth knocked together as she tried to speak.

"Don't try to talk," Cathy said gently. "Just drink that up—it'll make you feel better."

"But it's . . . all . . . m . . . my . . . fault!" She clutched the brandy glass to her chest, the liquid slopping over the sides and soaking into her woolen scarf.

"No!" Cathy breathed, "You know that's not true!"

Eva nodded her head. Up and down, up and down, as if unable to stop.

"She . . . f . . . followed . . . me." Her teeth chattered like rattling bones. "She . . . s . . . saw . . . him!"

"Oh, God, no!" Cathy gasped as it sank in.

"We . . . had . . ." Eva faltered, tears brimming her eyes.

"A row?"

Eva nodded again, took a gulp of brandy.

"You walked out and she was coming after you?"

Eva shut her eyes tight. "Dilys!" she whimpered. "How—"

"You can't," Cathy broke in. "You mustn't. Dilys doesn't need to know."

Eva's eyes snapped open. She stared at Cathy, uncomprehending.

"Of course, she has to know that your mum is . . ." Cathy bit her lip, unable to say the awful word. "But please, Eva, don't tell her what you've just told me. The two of you are going to need each other more than ever now." She hesitated, not wanting to spell it out. *God*, she thought, *Dilys would never forgive her. Never in a million years.*

~

Three days later the ice and snow had all gone, giving way to torrential rain. Cathy paused outside Eva's house. She shivered, feeling the dampness around her neck where the rain had penetrated her overcoat. She knew it wasn't going to be easy, trying to persuade Eva to get on with the funeral arrangements. Yesterday her friend had just sat in a chair staring into space, giving monosyllabic answers to everything Cathy said.

As she raised her hand to knock, the door swung open. Eva stood there, dressed as if for a special occasion, her cheeks rouged and her hair swept up in a bun.

"I was upstairs and I saw you coming," she said, taking Cathy's dripping coat. "What do you think? Will this do for Friday? I haven't really got anything black."

"You look very smart," Cathy said, trying to conceal her surprise at the change in her. "Do you want to borrow my black hat?"

Eva nodded. "If you're sure you don't mind."

"Of course I don't: I can wear a headscarf." She followed Eva into the kitchen and saw a pad and pencil lying on the table. "Now," she said, "tell me what you need doing."

"Well," Eva began, "I've ordered the flowers and I've sent a telegram to my aunt and uncle in Wales . . ." Her voice broke and tears trickled down her cheeks, leaving pale tracks in the rouge. "I'm sorry." She pulled out a clean, folded handkerchief and dabbed at her face. "I promised myself I wouldn't do that today."

"Hey, don't apologize!" Cathy put her arm around Eva's shoulder and gave her a squeeze. "It's better to let it out than bottle it all up—believe me, I know."

"Well I won't do it again," Eva sniffed. "I can't—there's too much to do."

"But you don't have to do it all on your own." Cathy took the pad, scanning the list. "Have you told Bill yet?"

Eva shook her head. "I can't face it, Cathy. I feel so . . ." She twisted the ends of her handkerchief into tight spirals.

"And Dilys?" Cathy frowned. "You haven't said anything, have you?"

Eva shook her head quickly and looked away. "She's going away, you know. They're sending her to the south coast."

"Oh Eva—that's awful! You're going to be all on your own!"

"Serves me bloody well right, doesn't it?" There was a faraway look in Eva's eyes, but her fingers were working away, smoothing out the screwed-up ends of the handkerchief, then twisting them up again.

"You can't go on blaming yourself for this!" Cathy put her hand on her friend's arm. "It was an accident—a terrible accident. It wasn't your fault."

"Of course it was my fault!" Eva's voice was an agonized whisper. "If I'd killed her with my own hands, I couldn't be more guilty!"

"No, Eva!" Cathy pleaded, "You mustn't talk like that!"

"Why not? It's what Dilys would say if she knew the truth."

"You must never, never tell her. Promise me you won't—for her sake as well as yours. She's only a kid, for God's sake. Life's going to be tough enough for her, being sent off down south with no friends or family! Promise me, Eva?"

Eva looked at her with big, frightened eyes. She nodded slowly. "And *you* won't tell anyone?"

Cathy's hand crisscrossed her chest. "I'll never tell a living soul."

~

Nearly every pew was full, and nobody noticed when Cathy crept in at the back ten minutes after the funeral service had started. She could just see the back of Eva's head through the sea of heads in front of her, the auburn hair coiled into a neat bun beneath the borrowed hat. The sight of her made Cathy feel utterly wretched. With all Eva was going through, how on earth was she going to tell her what she'd just found out?

When the service was over, Cathy stepped out of the pew to follow the rest of the congregation to the graveside. She had seen Eva go past, arm in arm with Dilys, her features hidden by the black net veil of the hat. Behind her was a tall woman with gray hair and skin the pale-brown of hazelnuts. She was carrying David, who had fallen asleep. Beside her was a short, stout man with white hair and a weather-beaten face. *This must be the aunt and uncle from Wales*, Cathy thought.

As the pews emptied, she tried to get nearer to Eva. It was difficult to squeeze past people without pushing, but eventually she managed to find a space just behind her. Eva's shoulders were rigid in her military-style jacket. Its length concealed her bump completely. *She must be nearly six months, now,* Cathy thought, *but no one would ever have guessed.*

When the coffin was lowered into the ground, Dilys crumpled. She looked so grown-up in her ATS uniform, but her tears suddenly revealed the child inside the woman's shell. She clung to Eva, who put a protective arm around her. Cathy could hear her whispering reassuring words. However was she managing to stay so strong?

Eva stumbled slightly as she bent to scoop up some earth to throw on the coffin. Instinctively Cathy put out a hand to help her. But it wasn't needed. Eva steadied herself and walked in a slow, dignified manner to the funeral car waiting by the railings.

By the time Cathy got to the house, it was crammed full of people eating fish paste sandwiches and jam tarts. She hurried into the kitchen to help make cups of tea and found Eva about to carry a heavily laden tray into the front room.

"Here, let me take that," she said.

Eva shot her a grateful smile.

"I bet you're worn out, aren't you? You should sit down—you mustn't overdo it."

"It's better if I keep busy," Eva whispered, glancing at her aunt, who was over by the sink, filling the kettle and chatting with Dilys. "If I sit down, I'll just start crying again, I know I will." She took in a breath. "As soon as everyone's gone, Anton's going to drive me over to see Bill. I really need to . . ." She paused, seeing the look on her friend's face. "What is it? Cathy? Why are you looking at me like that?"

"Come into the hall," Cathy said quietly. She pushed the door open with her foot and glanced up the stairs before setting the tray down. "Bill came looking for you this morning. He was in a hurry." She saw the agitation in Eva's eyes. "They were all getting on a train, heading for some new camp down south: he didn't know where."

"What?" Eva's face had turned deathly pale.

"He said he'd write as soon as he gets there and you . . ." Cathy never finished the sentence. Eva slumped against the hall table, sending the tray of sandwiches crashing to the floor. Cathy caught her as she fell, bracing herself against the banister rail to stop herself from falling too.

The noise brought Eva's aunt rushing out of the kitchen with Dilys following behind.

"She's okay," Cathy gasped, as they both ran to help. "Just worn out, I think."

"Fetch some brandy, Dilys!" The aunt bent over, cradling Eva's head. "Dai!" she shouted. "Where are you?"

Eva's uncle emerged from the front room, a half-eaten sandwich in his hand. "Good God!" He dropped the sandwich on the floor when he caught sight of Eva. "Is she sick, Rhiannon?"

"Come and help us get her upstairs!"

Then Anton appeared. He scooped Eva up and carried her up to the bedroom, where he was promptly shooed out by Aunt Rhiannon. Before Cathy could stop her, she was unbuttoning Eva's jacket.

"Iesu mawr!"

"What?" Dilys appeared at the door with the brandy bottle. She ran to the bed and saw what her aunt had seen: a gaping skirt zipper held together at the waist by a thin strip of elastic pulled so tight it had left a red imprint in Eva's belly.

Rhiannon took the bottle from Dilys and unscrewed the top. Turning to Cathy, she said, "How many months?"

"About six, I think."

"You knew?" Dilys gasped. "Why didn't you tell me? How could you have let her carry on doing that terrible job?"

"Shut up, Dilys!" Rhiannon hissed as Eva's eyelids fluttered. "It's not her fault!" Turning to Cathy again, she whispered, "Who's the father?"

At that moment Eva opened her eyes wide, staring at the ceiling. "His name's Bill," she murmured. "He's an American. And he's gone." She reached out and touched her aunt's arm. "I'm sorry." A tear ran down her cheek and splashed on the faded pink eiderdown. Rubbing her wet face with the back of her hand, she looked at Dilys. "I was going to tell you," she said softly. "Honest."

Rhiannon took Eva's hand in both of hers. "You can't stay here on your own, *cariad*. Not with that little lad to look after. You're coming home with me and your uncle Dai." She glanced at Dilys, then at Cathy, as if daring them to challenge this decree.

Eva looked broken, defeated, as if the last bit of fight left in her had ebbed away. She nodded slowly, a faraway look in her eyes.

"Fetch a sandwich for her, would you, *bach*?" Rhiannon said to Cathy. "And then we'll need to pack a suitcase."

Chapter 14

Eva lay on a blanket on the grass, drowsy in the afternoon sun. The only sound was the bleating of the sheep on the hill behind her and the odd whistle from Uncle Dai to his dogs. David had gone with them, running through the grass, his legs pink and chubby in the new boots Aunt Rhiannon had bought him.

He was so happy here on the farm, and she knew it should make her happy to see him thriving. But every time she closed her eyes, the ghosts were waiting. Mum glowering at her across the kitchen table, spitting out those awful words. Eddie with that disappointed look he'd had when he first set eyes on David. And Bill. Not a ghost. Not yet, at least. But every time he floated into her head, his eyes were full of anger, the way they'd been that night in the air-raid shelter. She tried to blot the picture out with better memories, like lying beside him in the cornfield on that hot August afternoon. But the images were growing fainter every day, like snapshots bleached by the sun.

She felt a sudden, sharp kick under her ribs and caught her breath. She moved her hand to the spot, feeling the tiny elbow or foot or whatever it was as it jabbed her again. She wanted to cry and laugh at the same time. It was as if Bill was saying *I'm still here—don't you dare forget about me!*

As if she ever could. Lying in bed at night, listening to the strange calls of owls and foxes, she would try to imagine where he was, what he was doing, and whether he was thinking of her and the baby. And she would play back that last meeting in the café over and over again. If only they hadn't argued. If only she hadn't run out on him. If only her mother hadn't seen them. If only . . .

"Eva!" Her aunt was half running across the farmyard, waving something in her hand.

"What is it?" Eva propped herself up on one elbow.

"A letter—with a US Army postmark!" Rhiannon was breathless with excitement. "Cathy sent it with a pile of mail."

Eva tore it open. The date at the top was March 13: three days after her mother's funeral. The handwriting was small and sloped at an odd angle across the page, as if it had been done in a hurry. Her hand was trembling as she shaded her eyes against the sun.

"My darling Eva," he had written, *"I tried to find you at the railroad and your friend told me what had happened. I was so sorry to hear about your mother. You must be going through a terrible time right now and I wish I was there to help you through . . ."*

Eva caught her breath, tears welling in her eyes. The words blurred and swam on the paper. She swallowed hard and they came back into focus.

We have been moved to a new camp in the south of England, near a town called Newbury. I tried to get a 24-hour pass to come see you, but all leave has been canceled. They won't tell us what's happening, but it's pretty clear that we're about to start some big operation.

I know how you feel about sending our baby to the States, but please think about it. My aunt Millie lives in Chicago, where there's no law against black and white people being together.

She raised five kids of her own and I've written her to ask if she would take care of ours for the time being. What do you say, honey? I think it would be for the best.

I don't know how long we're going to be here, so if I don't hear from you, I'll write again from the next place we go. I miss you so much. I'll never forget the time we had together. I guess those crocodiles swam too fast for us, didn't they?

Take care of yourself and the baby.

With love,

Bill

Eva pressed the letter to her chest. She could feel the thud of her heart through the thin fabric of her smock and her mouth was as dry as the mud caking her boots. What was he saying? It was all about the baby, wasn't it? No mention of her going to the States. No words of hope for a future together.

"Does he say where he is?" Rhiannon sank down on the blanket next to her.

Eva took a breath. "Near Newbury, but he could have gone somewhere else by now." It sounded to her like someone else's voice. Rational, composed, unnaturally calm. "If only I'd known earlier," she went on, "I could have gone down there and found him, talked to him."

"What? Go chasing off on a train in your state of health? I don't think so!" Rhiannon reached over to pat her shoulder. "And anyway," she went on, "do you really think it would have done any good, seeing him again? I thought he . . . well, you know," she said awkwardly.

"You thought he'd . . . abandoned me?" Eva was looking straight ahead as she said this, unable to meet her aunt's gaze. "Well, he hasn't. He didn't *want* to leave me. Didn't have any choice in the matter, that's all."

Rhiannon picked up the envelope from where Eva had dropped it on the blanket. "He's addressed it to E. Melrose. No Miss or Mrs. Does he know that you're married with a child?"

Eva swallowed hard. "He didn't at first, but he does now." She turned away, pulling at tufts of grass. How could she tell her aunt about Bill? It was hard enough for her to cope with the fact that there was an illegitimate baby on the way. How would she react if she knew its father was a colored man? And that her sister-in-law would still be alive if she hadn't spotted Eva walking out with him?

Eva brushed the fallen grass off the blanket. Somewhere behind her a sheep called to its lamb. A buzzard soared overhead on silent wings. It was so peaceful here. So safe.

Rhiannon squeezed her arm. "Don't talk about him if it's too painful. You're with us now." She smoothed the white apron that covered her dress, then stretched out her legs. "You know, it's a long time since I've seen Dai looking as happy as he has these last few weeks. Having young David around has been a real tonic for us both, with Trefor away so long."

"I'm glad," Eva replied, thinking how ironic it was that she had Trefor to thank for this unconditional welcome. Her horrible cousin, who had made childhood holidays in Devil's Bridge an utter misery with his endless spiteful tricks. And now he was in Italy, no doubt taking the role of conquering hero beyond all reasonable expectations. *God help them,* she thought.

"Do you feel up to sorting through the rest of the letters?" Rhiannon asked. "There are quite a few addressed to your mother— I'll open them if you'd rather . . ."

"No, it's all right," Eva said. "I've got to face it sooner or later." She shifted her weight onto her knees and, with an effort, rose to her feet. Tucking Bill's letter into the pocket of her smock, she walked purposefully toward the farmhouse, determined to get through the next half hour without crying.

~

Eva wrote half a dozen letters to Bill over the next few weeks, but none of them could be posted. The farm was so remote that deliveries only came once a week. She tried not to get excited when the ancient postman wheeled his bike into the farmyard on Tuesday mornings. But every time he came, the sense of anticipation followed by crushing disappointment grew stronger. How could she write to Bill if she didn't know where he was?

On the last day of May there was a letter from Dilys. Her neat, round handwriting sent a pang of guilt through Eva's heart. That big, awful lie was like a concrete wall between them. If they hadn't been parted so soon after their mother's death, Eva doubted she could have kept up the pretense. She knew Cathy had been right. That it was better for Dilys not to know why their mother had been chasing her across the street in the dark. But to Eva it still felt like a betrayal.

Dilys was with an anti-aircraft battery of the Royal Artillery, learning to track enemy planes and direct the gunners' fire. It sounded terribly dangerous, but the tone of the letter was cheerful enough. She warned Eva not to worry if she didn't hear from her for a while because a lot of the Allied forces' mail was going astray with all the movement going on. *Perhaps that was why there was nothing from Bill*, Eva thought.

The next day she wrote back to Dilys. It was a difficult letter to write. She tried to make it lighthearted, but as she began describing the advantages of life on the farm, she was only too aware of how miserable that might make her sister feel. In the end she settled for a few short lines. Then she composed a much longer letter to Cathy:

"I feel as if I've been wrapped in cotton wool and packed away in a drawer," she wrote. "It's so quiet in this part of Wales, it's hard to believe there's a war on. We can't even get the wireless up here in the mountains. The only news we have is from the paper, which comes once a week with the post. I'm not complaining, though, because the food is fantastic. It's as if rationing didn't exist. We have eggs every day, and there are huge slabs of bacon hanging up on hooks in the kitchen. At breakfast time Uncle Dai just slices great thick pieces off and we eat it with homemade bread."

She paused for a moment, glancing out of the window. "David is putting on weight at last," she went on. "He's starting to talk a lot now. Sometimes he asks where Nanna and Dilys have gone, which is upsetting. Often he talks in Welsh. It's funny to hear him come out with things I don't understand. He knows there's a baby coming, but I don't think he grasps what it really means." She hesitated before writing the next line. Cathy was the only person in the world she could confide in, and she felt an overwhelming need to unburden herself. "I'm due in three weeks and I still haven't told my aunt the whole truth about Bill," she wrote. "It's partly because I'm afraid of what she'll say and partly because I don't want to upset her. It's going to be a terrible shock. I don't think she and Uncle Dai have ever seen a black person—not even in a film, because the nearest cinema is in Aberystwyth, which is miles away.

"Bill said in his letter that he'd tried to get a pass to come and see me. But even if I could find a way of letting him know where I am, he'd use up all his leave just finding this place. I've got no idea where he is now, and I sometimes wonder if I'll ever see him again."

Perhaps you never will, a voice whispered somewhere in her head. She bit the end of her pen, panic swirling in her stomach.

"I feel so useless," she went on, her fingers slippery with perspiration. "I've asked if I can help on the farm—milk the cows or something—but they won't let me do a thing. It gives me too much time to think and that's bad. I miss work and I miss you. I wish I could talk to you. I hope that once the baby's born, I might be able to come back, for a visit at least (if they haven't thrown me out, that is). Can't plan much further ahead than that at the moment.

"Thanks for collecting the mail. Please keep sending it on. I'm sure there'll be something from Bill soon."

As she wrote the last sentence, she willed it to be true. She couldn't stop torturing herself with thoughts of him going out in some new town, dancing with other girls the way he'd danced with her.

She stuffed the letter into an envelope and grabbed her knitting needles, forcing herself to concentrate on the fancy pattern for a matinee jacket her aunt had bought on her monthly ride into Aberystwyth. Eva had not been allowed to go with her. "Too risky," Rhiannon had said. "All those potholes in the road. You stay here where it's safe."

~

Eva's only excursions from the farm were to attend chapel on Sundays. On the fourth of June she was there, as usual, after a hot, dusty ride down the farm track and along the narrow, winding lane that led down the valley.

David had leaned over the sides of the cart to grab at the wildflowers sprouting from the hedgerows, and now he was sitting underneath the pew, poking the stems of campions and dandelions through the buttonholes of his jacket.

The service was conducted entirely in Welsh, which Eva was struggling to master. Her attention often wandered, and she would find herself studying the rapt faces of the other members of the congregation instead of listening to the sermon. One thing that had surprised her on her first visit to the tiny chapel was the way people stared. Her auburn hair and freckles and David's blond curls made them objects of curiosity. Like her uncle and aunt, most of the congregation had dark, almost olive skin, tanned nut-brown by the summer sun. The younger ones all had jet-black hair, and if she hadn't known they were Welsh, Eva would have taken them for Italians or Spaniards.

As they left the chapel that Sunday there was a strange stillness in the air, as if the world had paused to take a breath. Although the heat was overpowering, Eva shivered as she walked through the door. She blinked as the sun's blinding light hit her eyes. Bill's face flashed in front of her, his eyes wide and frightened. "Where are you?" she murmured, as the image disappeared. "Where have they sent you?"

~

That same Sunday Cathy was at home in Wolverhampton listening to a news broadcast. One of the war correspondents was on board a sealed troopship with forces that were about to stage an invasion of occupied France.

"All contact with the shore has ended," the reporter said, his voice edgy with the drama he was about to witness. "No one may come aboard. No one may go ashore. In navy jargon, all of us aboard the ship are sealed. We're sealed because we've been told the answers. The answers to the questions that the whole world has been asking for two years and more. Where. And how. And when.

"The troops swarmed up the rope ladders last night. Strong, healthy, formidable men, many of them going into battle for the first time. As you walk along the decks, men are reading or sleeping or talking in small clusters. Across the water we can hear the jazz from a minesweeper's gramophone . . ."

Cathy clicked off the set. It was so horribly familiar. Like Dunkirk all over again. Reaching up to the mantelpiece she took down Stuart's photograph. "Please, God," she said. "Not again. Not this time."

~

Eva was in the farmyard when the postman arrived two days later. She saw him from a distance, pushing his bike up the hill. The bike was almost as ancient as he was, but there was something different about the way he was moving. He was pushing with one hand and waving something in the other: the newspaper, by the look of it. As he wheeled the bike over the rutted mud, he panted for breath, thrusting the paper into Eva's hand.

"D-day!" he gasped. "They've landed in France!"

As Eva unrolled it, the headlines jumped out at her: "Waves of Khaki on the Beaches: British and Americans in D-Day Invasion." She dropped the paper as if it were red-hot.

"What is it? What's happened?" Her aunt came, scooping the paper up from the dusty yard.

The postman opened his mouth, but before he could get the words out, Eva doubled over, crying out in pain.

"Eva!" Rhiannon shouted something in Welsh, which sent the old man hurtling off, bumping along the track with his mail sack flying out behind him.

~

It was all over long before the midwife arrived. Rhiannon had never delivered a baby before but had brought enough lambs into the world not to be fazed by it. She was as calm and steady as a rock until she cut the cord and the newborn girl began to wail. Tears streamed down her face as she wrapped the tiny body in a towel. She dabbed water on the baby's face and wiped the mop of hair, which was slicked down like sealskin.

"*Duw, Duw,*" she muttered, laying her in Eva's arms. "Dark hair like Dilys! And such beautiful skin! Anyone would think she'd been sunbathing in there!"

Eva looked at her baby through a film of tears. Puzzled indigo eyes stared up at her. The hair was beginning to dry into tiny ringlets around a face the color of cinnamon. She was perfect. Beautiful.

Glancing up nervously at her aunt, Eva saw that she was staring transfixed at the pair of them, a radiant smile on her face. How could she not notice? Surely it was as plain as day that this baby's father couldn't be a white man? Eva looked at the child again. Her skin was the same color as the people in the chapel—the ones she had thought looked Italian or Spanish. And her aunt had never seen a black person. Suddenly Eva understood. It simply would not occur to Rhiannon because it was outside her experience. But she was going to have to tell her. This was too big a secret to remain hidden for long. If her aunt didn't suspect, it wouldn't be long before someone else told her.

"Have you chosen a name yet?" Rhiannon sounded fit to burst with excitement.

"Well," Eva said, as the baby turned her head and began nuzzling her neck, "I thought I'd call her Louisa. Louisa Ann, after Louisiana, where Bill comes from."

Her aunt nodded. "Louisa. That's a pretty name. I thought you might decide to call her after your mam."

"I will," Eva replied, her voice wobbling with emotion. "Louisa Ann Mary." It didn't sound right. One name too many. But she must include her mother's name. Fresh tears welled in her eyes. "Bill never told me his mother's name," she murmured. *And what would your mother have made of that?* A sudden wail from the baby drowned out the sinister whispering in her head.

"Oh, she's hungry." Rhiannon smiled. "You give your daughter a feed, and I'll go and tell Dai and David the good news—that little lad's going to be so excited when he finds out he's got a baby sister!"

"Please," Eva said, holding out her hand to her aunt. "Don't go yet."

"What's wrong, *cariad*? Are you in pain?"

"No, it's not that." She took a breath. "There's something I've got to tell you."

Chapter 15

A letter was lying on the mat when Cathy got home from work. Recognizing Eva's handwriting, she ripped it open.

"A girl!" She ran into the kitchen, spreading the pages out on the table.

She was two weeks early, but she wasn't a bad weight: six pounds three ounces. I would have written sooner, but life here has been pretty difficult these past few weeks. My uncle Dai had a stroke three days after Louisa was born. He was shearing the sheep when it happened, and the doctor said it was overwork that caused it. But I can't stop thinking that it was my fault.

I hadn't told them about Bill. Louisa was born so quickly I hadn't got around to it. My aunt delivered her, but even then she didn't realize that I'd had a colored man's child. When I told her, she just looked at me, didn't say a word, as if it wouldn't sink in. For a couple of days she spoke to me only when it was absolutely necessary and was very formal with me. But after a while she started to come around. I think it was because she brought Lou into the world. And although I say it myself, she really is a gorgeous baby. But Uncle Dai was different. He wouldn't even look at her. As for me, well, as far as he was concerned, I no longer existed. It was as if he'd somehow guessed that Bill's color was linked to Mum's death.

It's awful what's happened to him. He's lost the power of speech, and he's paralyzed down his right side. The doctor says he might get better eventually, but there's no guarantee. I don't think he'll ever be able to do the heavy work on the farm again. So Aunt Rhiannon and I have to do it between us. I've learnt how to shear a sheep, how to milk the cows and drive the horse and cart. Luckily Lou sleeps a lot. We take her around with us in a little basket with a sheet rigged over it as a sunshade and David follows, trying to help.

My aunt keeps saying it'll be all right when Trefor, her son, comes home from the war. Goodness knows when that'll be. I can't stand Trefor anyway. He was horrible to Dilys and me when we were kids.

I try not to think about the future—to be honest, I'm too worn out most of the time to think about anything much. I read the paper in bed sometimes and wonder what Bill's doing. I know he must be in France, but I don't know whether it's possible for him to send letters now. I keep telling myself he's all right—that he won't be involved in the fighting. But it's awful, this silence. Just like when Eddie went away.

With a deep sigh Cathy folded the pages of the letter and slipped them back inside the envelope. *Poor Eva*, she thought. How terrible it must be for her, not even being able to tell Bill he had a daughter. And then there was the guilt about her uncle's stroke, which wasn't going to help ease the blame she already felt for her mother's death. And all that work on the farm so soon after giving birth. Cathy thought about the time Eva had collapsed in the snow at the railway station. If she wasn't careful, she was going to make herself ill.

She sat for a moment staring into space, thinking about Eva and Bill. When Eva went to Wales, Cathy wondered if she might decide to cut him out of her life and make a fresh start, that the guilt she felt about Mary's accident would kill her feelings for him stone dead. But her letters made it clear that was not the case. And now that she had his baby, the desire to be with him must be all the stronger.

Cathy glanced at the clock. Mikey had gone to a friend's house for the day and wouldn't be back for another hour or so. On an impulse she grabbed her bag and made for the door. There was just time to go around to Eva's old house. It was only two days since she'd last checked the mail, but if by some miracle a letter from Bill had arrived in the meantime, Eva needed to know as soon as possible.

~

When Cathy unlocked the front door of her friend's house, the musty smell made her cough. With the weather so hot and the windows shut all the time, the place was like an oven. She glanced at the mat. Nothing. She hesitated on the threshold, not sure what to do. She had intended to go straight back home, but instead she went into each room in the house, opening all the windows. "Let the place breathe a bit," she muttered to herself. She wondered if Eva was going to keep the house now that things had changed so much. It seemed pointless paying rent for the sake of Dilys's occasional trips home on leave.

The doorbell rang and Cathy nearly jumped out of her skin. "Who on earth can that be," she said aloud, peering out of the bedroom window at the street below. Her heart missed a beat when she saw the red bicycle propped against the lamppost. A red bicycle had come to her house the day she received the news of Stuart's death. A red bicycle meant only one thing: a telegram. She ran down the stairs as the bell rang a second time.

"Mrs. Melrose?"

A boy of about fifteen stood in front of her, the soft down on his upper lip glistening in the sunlight.

"Er . . . no." Cathy hesitated. "She's not here at the moment, but I can take it for her."

The boy frowned as if she had suggested something quite improper. "I'm only supposed to hand it over to the person it's addressed to."

"She'll be back soon," Cathy lied, "and she'll be devastated if she finds out there's a telegram and I can't tell her what it's about."

The boy looked her up and down, his lips set in a supercilious curl. *Cheeky little bugger,* she thought, as she smiled beseechingly at him.

"All right then," he said grudgingly. "Sign here."

As soon as she had closed the door on him, she ripped the telegram open. With a cry of disbelief she sank back against the hall table.

"AS 5398 Edward Herbert Melrose recovered alive," the message read. "Arrival in UK to be notified." Cathy's hand shook as she scanned the words again. Eddie was not dead. He was coming back.

The baby. She heard Eva's voice as clearly as if she were standing beside her. *What will he do when he finds out about the baby?*

Part Two

LOUISA

Chapter 16

Eva poured the last pail of milk into the churn and went over to the corner of the cowshed where baby Louisa was fast asleep in her basket. Her long black eyelashes flickered as Eva picked up the basket, but she didn't stir. *Good,* Eva thought. With any luck she'd have time to eat some breakfast before Louisa woke up. It was only half past seven, but Eva had been awake since just after five. She was ravenous and the thought of bacon and eggs made her quicken her step as she made for the door.

Her aunt usually had breakfast ready. Eva trudged across the farmyard sniffing the air. But there was no smell of cooking coming from the kitchen. She peeped around the door and saw Rhiannon sitting at the table, her head in her hands.

"What's the matter?" Eva set the basket down on the slate flagstones and ran across the room. Rhiannon looked up, her cheeks wet with tears. "Oh," she said, glancing at the clock, "I thought you were still milking!" A tear trickled down her face.

Eva sat down beside her, taking her hand. "What's happened? Is it Uncle Dai?" She felt a sudden stab of horror. Surely he couldn't have died in the night?

"No, it's not Dai," her aunt said, blowing her nose. "It's this," she fished a letter from the pocket of her overalls. "It came yesterday." She unfolded the scrap of paper and smoothed it out on the table in front of her, looking at it with an expression of utter despair. "It's from Trefor," she said, fresh tears welling as she looked up at Eva. "He says he's met an Italian girl. Wants to marry her. Says he won't be coming back."

"What?" Eva took the letter, scanning the few paragraphs of her cousin's untidy handwriting. "How can he do that? What about the farm?"

"He says her family has a farm out there, and they want him to help run it." Rhiannon sniffed.

"But what about Uncle Dai? Surely if Trefor knew what had happened, he'd change his mind?"

Rhiannon shook her head. "He already knows, *bach*. I wrote to him the day after Dai had the stroke. He says he's very sorry, but the girl's parents won't let her marry him unless he stays in Italy."

How convenient for him, Eva thought, picturing Trefor's smug face. "Listen, you mustn't worry," she said, sounding much calmer than she felt. "You've still got me: I'm not going anywhere." She was looking at her aunt but seeing Bill. His face hovered between them, his eyes reproachful, accusing. Her dream of being with him in America was slipping further and further away. She turned her head away, glimpsing the fields stretching into the distance beyond the farmhouse door. There were sheep waiting to be sheared, cows that would need milking again this evening, pigs to be fed, as well as machinery to be fixed. How could she possibly leave her aunt to cope with all this alone?

From her basket Lou gave a thin wail, like a hungry kitten. Eva bit her lip as she went to pick her up. *Would Bill ever see her?* The thought made her panic, made her want to gather Lou in her arms and run and run until she found him.

"It's all right," she whispered as she held the baby to her, stroking her soft brown hair. "It's all right." She rocked from one foot to the other, eyes half-closed, chanting the phrase like a prayer. How she wished it was true.

~

Cathy picked up her overnight bag and gave her son a final wave. He was so busy with his friend's Meccano set, he didn't even look up when she called good-bye. She smiled as she walked down the path that divided her house from her neighbor's. At least she wouldn't feel so guilty about leaving him behind. He would probably have loved the idea of a train ride to Wales, and if the circumstances had been different, she would have taken him. But it was too serious a business for a child. She had thought long and hard about how to deliver the bombshell the telegram had contained. Giving Eva the news in person was the only solution, she'd decided. Her presence was unlikely to be much comfort, but she would at least be on hand to offer what support she could.

Cathy looked at her watch. It was going to take most of the day to get to the farm, but before she went to the station, she wanted to pop into Eva's old house just in case there was a letter from Bill. It couldn't be long before Eddie arrived back and Eva was going to have to decide what to do. If there was the slightest chance of some sort of future with Bill, she needed to be able to contact him, and fast.

As she turned the corner, a newsboy shouted the headlines across the street: "Paris liberated! Read all about it!"

She stopped and bought a paper. She had already heard about it on the wireless last night, listened to the cheering, the crowds singing the "Marseillaise." But it would be nice to read about it on the train. Something cheerful to take her mind off what was to come.

She tucked the paper under her arm. Two minutes later she was walking past the Goodyear factory and up the narrow street toward Eva's house. She fumbled in her pocket for the key, cursing as she dropped the newspaper onto the pavement. Eventually she got the key into the lock. It wouldn't turn. She frowned and tried again. She tried the handle, and to her amazement the door opened. Surely she hadn't forgotten to lock it last time?

Her mind was racing as she walked into the hall. What if the house had been burgled? It would be her fault for leaving it unlocked. *Oh no,* she thought, *please, not that. Not on top of everything else . . .*

"Who the hell are you?" The voice gave her such a shock, she let out a yelp of fright. She caught sight of him through the banisters and froze. A gaunt white face with huge hollow eyes staring back at her. A tramp—or a madman? No. He was in uniform. A clean, new-looking uniform. A navy uniform. "Oh . . . Oh my God," she stammered. "Is it . . . are you . . . Eddie?"

"How do you know who I am?" The voice was different. Softer and less aggressive. He sank back onto the stairs as if Cathy's words had winded him.

"The photo in Eva's bedroom . . ." She hesitated, her heart thumping. The sight of him whipped up a crippling cocktail of pity and fear inside her. "I . . . er . . . we worked together on the railway. She got a job after you were sent overseas . . . didn't she say in her letters?"

He stared at the fading flower pattern on the stair carpet, and she noticed a streak of pure white running through his close-cropped black hair. "I never got any letters." His voice was no more than a whisper now. "Where is she? And David? Where's my little boy?"

Cathy took a deep breath. "They've gone to stay with relatives," she said. "A lot's happened while you've been away." Another breath. "Eva's mother died, I'm afraid, in a road accident."

"Mary? Dead?" He looked up, blinking. "So that's why the place is in mothballs." He nodded slowly and slipped a bony hand inside his jacket. "Don't worry," he said, with the flicker of a frown puckering the sallow skin of his forehead. "I know the rest." In his hand was an envelope, ripped open. He leaned forward, passing it to her through the banisters like a prisoner reaching through the bars of a cell. "Go on, read it."

Panic surged as she spotted the US Army stamp at the top of the envelope. It was addressed to E. Melrose. No prefix. He must have found it lying on the mat and thought it was for him. Cathy cursed herself for not finding it first. As she read Bill's words, her insides shriveled.

> *My darling Eva,*
>
> *We are in France, which I guess you will probably already know about from the newspapers. I can't say much more than that, but I want you to know that I'm thinking about you and the baby. I don't know if you've been getting my letters. I guess not, as I haven't heard from you, but I know how bad the mail is now, so maybe you've written me and your letters have gone astray.*
>
> *As I write, I'm wondering if our little boy or girl has been born yet. It's so strange, thinking I might be a dad and not even know it. I met a guy from the Red Cross a few days ago and told him all about it. I gave him your address, and he's going to send some forms through about getting the baby over to the States when he or she is old enough. I realize how tough this is going to be for you, but it seems the only solution for the time being. It's really hard, not being able to talk with you about it . . .*

Cathy glanced up at Eddie. There was a tear coursing down his face. She dropped the letter, almost tripping up the stairs in her clumsy attempt to put a comforting arm around his shoulders. It was like hugging a skeleton. She could feel his bones through the coarse fabric of his uniform.

"It's all right." He wriggled away from her as if she were contaminated. "I just want Eva. I've got to find her. Will you tell me where she is?" Once again he turned his big, round, pleading eyes upon her.

This took her by surprise. "But she's had a baby, Eddie. A little girl. By another man. Surely you can't—"

"Yes, I can," he cut in, his voice calm and even. "It doesn't matter. She thought I was dead. I can't blame her for that . . ." He stared at a blue patch of sky framed by the glass pane in the front door.

"Well, that's a very generous and compassionate thing to say," Cathy began, "but it's not as simple as that, is it? You're talking about taking on someone else's child and she's—"

"It doesn't matter," he cut in. "How old is she, the baby?"

"Just a few weeks. But—"

"So I can be a father to her, can't I?" He was nodding as if he was talking to himself rather than to Cathy. "She won't know any different, will she?"

Cathy made a silent prayer. She felt as if Eva's whole future was now in her hands. If she told Eddie about the baby's color, he might realize how hopeless his plan was and leave Eva alone. But was that what Eva would want? What if Bill never came back from France? Would she want the chance to try again with Eddie? Her head was spinning, trying to second-guess what Eva would want her to say. What if she didn't tell him? Gave him the address and let him find out for himself? *No,* she thought, *that would be inhuman.* Whatever had happened to Eddie while he was away, he had obviously suffered enough.

"Eddie," she said, "why don't you let me get you something to eat? It's a long way away, where Eva's gone, and you're going to need a decent meal inside you before you go looking for her." She smiled at him, trying not to betray her nervousness. She needed time to plan what she was going to say.

"All right," he murmured, a distant look in his eyes.

"If you could set the table for me," she went on, as if it was Mikey she was talking to, "I'll be back in a moment with some food."

She closed the front door firmly behind her and hurried back to her own house. She felt horribly tempted to stay there. He didn't know where she lived, wouldn't be able to find her. The feeling lasted for only a few seconds. She scurried around the kitchen, bundling food into a shopping bag. A tin of soup, some Spam, and a jar of homemade pickle. Some lettuce from the garden and a few slices cut from the hard, gray National Loaf. Tea, milk, and a bit of sugar twisted in brown paper. Not exactly a feast, but by the look of Eddie, it was probably a lot better than he'd been used to.

She concentrated hard as she set off again. She would try to stall until he'd eaten. Bad news never seemed quite so bad on a full stomach. Then she would have to help him come to terms with it. Should she offer to let him stay with her while he got back on his feet? She thought of Mikey. What would he make of having this strange, hollow-eyed man living in the house? Would he be frightened? Perhaps it would be better to leave Eddie where he was. Call in now and then to get him a meal and make sure he was okay. She wondered what he would do, whether he was fit enough for some sort of work. She hoped so, for his sake. It wouldn't do him any good to sit around brooding about what Eva had done.

She stopped short a few yards away from his house. What if her revelation tipped him over the edge and he went off looking for revenge? She mustn't tell him where Eva was until she'd told him about Bill. Perhaps not tell him at all if things went badly.

~

Eddie was sitting at the kitchen table when she let herself in. He had done exactly as he was told. Cutlery, plates, cups, and saucers were laid out neatly and the kettle set on the stove to boil. While they were eating, she steered the subject away from Eva. She asked him about his injuries, hoping that this would fill enough time for them to finish the meal.

But she was unprepared for the effect her question would have. It was as if she had opened the floodgates to a tidal wave of the most harrowing memories. Her soup went cold as she listened, openmouthed, to the horrors he had endured in Burma.

"They took us to the jungle in a truck," he said, his eyes narrowing. "Five days and nights it took to get there. Thirty-five of us, packed in like sardines. Couldn't all sit or lie down at the same time. Then we had to walk along two rivers. Sixteen miles in the dark each night so we wouldn't be seen. Best part of two weeks, that took. One of my pals, Stan, got sick." He paused, staring at his plate. "I had to carry him or the Japs would've shot him." He looked up and Cathy saw that his eyes had filmed over with tears. "I should have let them: probably would've been the kindest thing." He sniffed. "They made us cut logs from the jungle to build a bloody railway from Bangkok to Rangoon. It was so hot we worked naked except for two bits of rag tied round our waist and between our legs."

Eddie stirred his soup with his spoon and broke off a piece of bread, staring at the coarse gray crust. "There wasn't much to eat. Most days it was nothing but a bowl of rice gruel with maybe a slice of onion in it." He grunted. "One bloke found a fig tree, and we ate figs for days.

"The weight was just falling off us," he went on, after taking a bite of bread, "but if you weren't fit for work, you got no food at all. They could see Stan was on his knees, but they told him to dig out this great big tree stump. Four foot across, it was. No one man could shift it on his own. When he collapsed, they strung him up by his arms. Looked like Jesus on the cross." He blinked and looked away. "Three days, they left him. Don't know if he was still alive when they bayoneted him."

In the silence that followed Cathy stared at her soup bowl, well aware that any attempt at sympathy would sound hollow. "How did you survive?" she ventured.

He drew his lips into a tight circle and let out a deep sigh. "I got what they call a tropical ulcer," he said, rolling up his sleeve to reveal a purplish scar the size of an egg just above his elbow. "Lots of blokes got them. Only had to graze yourself on something and it'd turn into an ulcer. I was lucky. Mine wasn't that bad. There were people round me with their flesh all eaten away so you could see the sinews and the bone underneath." He paused and looked at her. "I'm sorry," he said. "I shouldn't be telling you this. No one should have to hear this stuff."

"No," she shook her head. "Go on—it's all right."

"Well, when the ulcer cleared up, they kept me in the hospital tent and made me help." His voice wobbled and he coughed, struggling to contain his emotion. "Ninety-six amputations with a wood saw." He looked at her with brimming eyes. "Only four men survived the shock."

He slid his hand inside his jacket and pulled out a pencil and a sheet of paper. As Cathy watched, he began to scribble grotesque cartoons of men. Some were being tortured, others dying of horrific injuries or disease. And all around were the smiling figures of the Japanese captors. When he looked up, Cathy saw that his face was composed, with no trace of emotion.

"It helps," he said simply, screwing the paper into a tiny ball and tossing it into the bin.

"How did you get away?" Her words sounded loud in the quiet house.

He frowned and sucked in a breath. "We were put on a prison ship when the railway was finished—those who were left, that is."

He sat for a few seconds examining the veins on the mottled backs of his hands. "On the way to Japan we were torpedoed by an Allied sub." He paused again. "Don't remember much about it, really. One minute I was scrubbing the deck, next I was floating about in the ocean, clinging onto a bit of driftwood. Don't know how long I was there: started drinking seawater and that must have sent me a bit crazy. I saw this thing like a telegraph pole sticking up out of the water. It turned out to be the sub that hit us. When it came up, a bunch of Americans climbed out. They pointed a double-barreled shotgun at me and said: 'Who the hell are you?'" He grunted a laugh. "Bit like you, eh? I must have looked a damn sight worse then than I do now."

He pushed his plate away and glanced at the window. "They wrapped me in this beautiful white blanket. I remember how soft it felt, like silk. Couldn't do enough for me, those boys." He shrugged. "And here I am." His eyes searched Cathy's face. "Where's Eva?"

"Eddie, there's something I have to tell you," she said, her stomach lurching. "The baby," she began. "She's . . ." Cathy paused, losing her nerve. Was a man in Eddie's state of mind capable of handling this?

"She's what?" Eddie frowned. "Has she got a birthmark like David? Did Eva tell you how stupid I was about that? Well, don't worry, Cathy; I've grown up. My God, if I'd known then what . . ."

"No," she interrupted, "you don't understand. It's not that." She cleared her throat. "The baby's father—the American soldier . . ." She took a breath. "He's a colored man, Eddie. The baby's colored." She watched his face, expecting anger, disbelief, but he just gave a half smile and nodded slowly. "Don't you see?" she said, floored by his reaction. "You can't bring her up as your own, can you?"

"Of course I can." His tone was matter-of-fact. "Take a look at this." He pulled a letter from his pocket and pushed it across the table. "I wrote it while you were fetching the food." It was addressed to the US Army, Allied Headquarters, France. The flap of the envelope had not been stuck down and she slid the letter out.

Dear Mr. —,

Thank you for offering to take my wife's baby to America via the Red Cross. That will not be necessary as I intend to adopt the little girl and give her my name. I promise you that she will want for nothing and that I will hold no blame against my wife, as she had no way of knowing that I was alive.

Yours sincerely,

Edward Melrose

Cathy stared at the sheet of paper in stunned silence.

"Do you know his surname?" Eddie took it back and produced a pen from inside his jacket. "I need to put it in the letter and on the envelope."

"It's . . . er . . . Willis," she mumbled. "He's in the Quartermaster Corps." She watched as he filled in the blank space on the letter in slow, painstaking script and then did the same on the envelope.

"There," he said, sealing it up. "I'll post it on the way to the station. Which train do I need to catch?"

"She's in Wales." Cathy trotted out the words as if someone else was controlling her mouth. She felt totally out of her depth, incapable of fathoming this man's mind. "She's gone to her uncle and aunt."

"Ah," Eddie said, pushing back the chair. "Better get going then. It's quite a way, that, quite a way. Thanks for the food. You've been very kind."

"Wait a minute!" she sprang to her feet. "Do you think this is wise? Are you sure you know what you're taking on?" She tried to put herself between him and the door.

"Don't try to stop me." His voice was barely more than a whisper, but it frightened her. "I know what I'm doing."

Chapter 17

Eddie didn't make it to the farm that night. He got as far as Aberystwyth, only to be told that the last train to Devil's Bridge had left half an hour ago. So he booked into a little guesthouse across the road from the station and lay on the bed, rehearsing what he was going to say to Eva.

He wondered how she would react once she'd got over the initial shock of seeing him. He got up and peered into the small square of mirror above the washbasin. He looked so different, he wasn't sure she'd even recognize him. It was quite a while before he'd been able to look at himself. After going all those months in the jungle without once seeing his own reflection, he was frightened of what he was going to look like. But Granville, the orderly who had nursed him back to health in the American hospital camp, had made sure it had been done gently. He had washed Eddie, shaved him, and cut his hair before allowing him to look at himself.

It had taken several seconds to comprehend that the death's head staring back from the glass was his. Cheekbones poked out of skin the texture of old leather. The bloodshot eyes had huge dark crescents underneath. And his hair. That was the biggest shock.

Dark brown when he left home, it was now shot through with a wide streak of white.

But even at that moment Granville had managed to make him smile. Removing the mirror with a wry smile, he said, "You know how much Bela Lugosi had to pay those Hollywood makeup artists to make him look like you? Come on, it's time for your cup of blood!"

Over the past couple of months he had grown used to his gaunt face, but he could tell from the way Cathy had reacted and the odd glances from people on the train that other people still found him frightening. He wondered if he should warn Eva before meeting her. Get her to come to Aberystwyth rather than just turning up unannounced at the farm. But what if she was so horrified to discover he was alive, she upped and left without a word? She could disappear, taking David with her, and he might never find her again.

He put on his jacket and went for a walk, trying to think it through. In a couple of minutes he was on the promenade, the waves crashing against the rocks below. The sound and smell of the sea still had a strange effect on him. He was filled with a mixture of panic and euphoria, remembering his helplessness as he drifted in the empty ocean and the joy at the sight of his American rescuers.

He thought of Granville again, of the kindness that had been so hard to accept after the routine inhumanity of captivity. Granville. The memory of those last days in the American hospital camp set off a surge of impotent fury, which led—inexorably—to thoughts of Eva's baby.

He stared at the sun, a red ball sinking into the sea. It was as if all this was meant to be.

~

He was up early the next day, determined to be on the first train to Devil's Bridge. He knew from the stories Eva had told that the farm was not an easy place to get to. The old man at the ticket office looked at him suspiciously when he asked for directions. He said something in Welsh, then disappeared through a door. Eddie waited for a couple of minutes, but he didn't return. There was no one else to ask, so he wandered up the narrow main street until he spotted the village's one and only hotel. For the price of a pot of tea he got the information he needed.

It was a long walk, but with each mile he felt his mood lift. The thought of seeing his little boy again, of making up for the indifference he had shown him when he was a baby, was uppermost in his mind. He felt an almost overpowering urge to shower the child with love. And he would do the same to Eva and her baby, if she would let him.

As he approached the farm, he could hear sheep bleating and someone whistling on the hills up above. But there was no sound coming from the farmyard. He walked up to the front door and lifted the heavy knocker. His mouth was dry. All his carefully rehearsed words had evaporated. The door was opened by a gray-haired woman who looked at him suspiciously. He recognized her from David's christening.

"Mrs. Jenkins?" he asked. "You're Eva's aunt, aren't you?" She looked at him blankly. "It's Eddie." He coughed, his voice catching in his throat. "Eddie Melrose. Eva's husband."

"*Iesu mawr!*" Rhiannon cried out, her hand flying to her mouth.

"I'm sorry: I didn't mean to frighten you. I've only just got back and I . . ." He stopped short as a chubby little boy with blond hair appeared from behind her. "This must be David!" Eddie beamed at the boy and bent down to scoop him up in his arms. David screamed and clung to Rhiannon's legs, shouting words Eddie couldn't understand. Rhiannon scooped him up, placing a protective hand across his head as she held him to her.

"I'm your Daddy, David." Reaching into his bag, Eddie pulled out a teddy bear. "I've brought you a present!"

David twisted his head around and eyed it suspiciously. He looked at Rhiannon, who nodded. In a flash the child reached out and snatched the bear from Eddie's grasp. Clutching the toy to his chest, he buried his head in Rhiannon's shoulder.

"We . . . we . . . thought . . ." Rhiannon stuttered.

"Yes, I know," Eddie said gently. "I'm sorry if I scared you both, but I was so desperate to get here." He could see the confusion in her face. "I know all about the baby," he said. "It's all right—I'm not going to make a scene. Can I come in?"

He followed her into the kitchen and immediately caught sight of the basket where Louisa lay fast asleep. He wanted to go and look at her, but saw David run across and hover over her as if standing guard. He walked toward him and squatted down so that his head was level with the boy's. "Is this your baby?"

David nodded.

"What's her name?"

"Lou," the child mumbled.

"Can I have a look at her? I promise I won't hurt her."

David frowned and looked over to where Rhiannon was standing. Following his gaze, Eddie saw the fear in her eyes.

"Please—you mustn't worry." He smiled. "I don't blame Eva for what happened. She thought I was dead." He reached out, stroking the tiny hand that lay curled up on the knitted blanket. "I'd like to adopt this little one, if Eva will let me."

Rhiannon's mouth gaped. "Adopt her? But she's . . ."

"Yes, I know." He glanced at David, then back at Rhiannon. "It doesn't matter." He straightened up, feeling the ache in his back from bending over. "Where's Eva? I need to talk to her in private, if you don't mind."

"She's out with the sheep at the moment." Rhiannon looked away. Clearly she didn't know what to make of him. "Can I make you a cup of tea while you wait?"

"No, thank you." Eddie made for the door. "I'll go and find her."

Rhiannon followed him through the farmyard, her face creased with worry.

"Please don't upset yourself." Another man would have patted her arm or put a reassuring hand on her shoulder. But he was not the man he had once been. "I'm not angry with Eva. I just want us to be a family again."

~

Eva was counting the sheep when Beth, the younger of the farm's pair of border collies, began barking furiously. Someone was coming. She shaded her eyes against the sun, frowning at the distant figure. It wasn't the right shape or size for her aunt. It looked like a man: a farmhand looking for work, perhaps, or a hiker who had strayed off the path. She whistled at Beth, who had now lost control of the sheep.

"Eva!" The sound of her name carried on the wind.

Who was it? One of the shearers? But they weren't supposed to be coming until next week. She frowned, peering at the approaching man. With the sun behind him, it was impossible to make out any of his features. It wasn't until he shouted her name again that she thought she recognized something in the voice. Beth was barking madly, running around her in circles. Now she could see the uniform, the thin body inside it. The way he walked was just like . . .

"Eva!"

She felt sick, dizzy. Her mind was playing tricks on her. She was seeing his ghost. Her legs turned to melting wax, and she fell with a thud onto the dry, overgrazed turf.

"Eva! Sweetheart!"

The specter hovered over her as she opened her eyes. She closed them again, wishing it away. Cathy had warned her about this. Overdoing it. Spending too long outdoors in the hot sun . . .

"I'm so sorry, darling: I didn't mean to frighten you!"

She felt a hand stroking her forehead. And there was a faint smell of perspiration. Could he be real? She snapped her eyes open, crying out at the sight of him. "Eddie! Oh my God! Eddie!"

She must have passed out again then, because the next thing she remembered was being carried into the farmhouse. She caught a glimpse of her aunt disappearing through the back door with Louisa in her arms and David trailing behind her. She was put down on the couch in the living room and lay there, staring at the ceiling, unable to move. She could hear footsteps and the sound of cups being placed on the low table beside her.

"I've put a drop of brandy in your tea," Eddie said, cradling her head as he slid her into a sitting position, then stepped back and sat down across from her. "I think it'll do you good."

She reached out mechanically for the tea, sipping it down. It burnt her lips, but she didn't feel it. She stared at Eddie, frowning. Her mind would not accept what her senses were telling her. It was like trying to complete a jigsaw puzzle with pieces that didn't fit.

"I should have warned you I was coming," he said, "but I was afraid you'd run away." She studied his face. He looked older. Years older. His eyes looked bigger, but that was because he had lost so much weight. Although the dark shadows beneath them made him look ill, their expression was softer, kinder than she remembered.

"I've seen the baby," he went on. "She's beautiful."

Tears sprang unbidden into Eva's eyes. She opened her mouth, but no words would come out. She looked at Eddie. His eyes were brimming too. She had never seen him cry. He stumbled to his feet and came to her, clinging to her, his tears soaking into her blouse.

"I've missed you so much!" he gasped between his sobs. "I never thought I'd hold you again!"

She felt numb. She stroked his head as if comforting an injured animal. He had seen Louisa. He knew, then. Why wasn't he shouting, raging at her for what she had done? "I . . ." she faltered, her voice hoarse, "I . . . don't understand."

He pulled a handkerchief from his pocket and wiped his face. "I know everything." His voice bore no edge of malice. It was matter-of-fact. "Cathy told me."

"Cathy?" Eva stared at him, bewildered. "You've met Cathy?"

"She came to the house the day I arrived home." He shook his head with a wry smile. "I gave her a hell of a fright."

"And she told you? About . . ." Eva couldn't bring herself to say Bill's name.

"She filled me in on some of the details, yes. I'd already got the gist of what happened from a letter he'd sent to the house."

"A letter?" Eva's heart skipped a beat.

"Yes. He said he was in France and was arranging for the baby to be sent to America by the Red Cross."

"Where is it? The letter?"

"Here." He reached into his jacket pocket. "And this is a copy of the reply I sent him."

Fresh tears filled Eva's eyes as she read Bill's words. When she saw what Eddie had written back, she cried out in shock. "Adopt her? And you sent this letter without even asking me first?" She lashed out at him, beating his chest with her fists. He grabbed her by the wrists, his grip powerful despite his spare frame.

"It's all right!" He relaxed his grip and held her to him, stroking her hair as her body convulsed with sobs. "You're angry, and you're in a state of shock. I understand." He cupped her chin with his hand, making her look at him. "But I want you to promise me something before you decide what you're going to do." He paused, waiting for the tears to subside. "I want you to hear my reasons for doing what I did—for sending that letter."

Eva blinked, fumbling for a handkerchief. Impotent rage gave way to silent determination. Her mind marshaled the facts as she wiped her eyes. Bill was alive. He was making arrangements for Louisa. There was an address to write to. She could find him.

The two letters had fallen onto the carpet. She picked them up, smoothed them out, and laid them side by side on the table. Then, with a deep breath, she sat back, hands clasped together in her lap. The least she could do was hear Eddie out.

Chapter 18

Nothing could have prepared Eva for the horror of what Eddie had to tell her. As he related what had happened after his capture by the Japanese, she got the impression that he was leaving out as much as he was telling, that there were many things he found too harrowing to talk about.

He described how he had clung to life by a thread, drifting for days in the South China Sea after the prison transport ship was torpedoed. She watched his face soften as he talked about the American submarine crew who had rescued him.

"They took me to a hospital camp at their base," he said. "I was in a terrible state. Out of my mind half the time from the seawater I'd drunk and the medication they'd given me for my wounds. I was looked after by an American soldier called Granville. He couldn't do enough for me, Eva. Treated me like royalty." He cleared his throat. Eva could see that he was fighting back tears. "It was terrible, what they did to him."

After everything he'd told her, she was almost afraid to ask what had happened.

"They shot him," Eddie said. "One of his own side shot him, just for talking to a woman."

Eva shook her head, uncomprehending.

"He was a colored man." Eddie looked at her, his eyes brimming. "He hadn't done anything wrong. He was just chatting with one of the nurses—a white woman—at a party they were holding at the base, and someone shot him. No one would own up to it and as far as I know, no one's ever taken the rap."

Eva blinked, her mind flooded with images of that awful, wonderful first night at the Civic Hall. And then this man, this patient, compassionate black soldier, had been shot dead for doing far less than she had done with Bill.

"So you see," she heard Eddie say, "when Cathy told me the baby's father was a colored man, it all seemed to make sense. I felt as if, somehow, it was all meant to be. Louisa's not Granville's baby, but she *could* have been—do you see? He looked after me, and now I can look after her."

Eva nodded mechanically. Put like that, it made perfect sense. Anyone listening to what Eddie had just said would applaud him for such incredible generosity of spirit. But the sentiment, however admirable, lacked one very important consideration. To him, Bill was just another colored soldier. Just a faceless name. Did Eddie think their relationship had been nothing more than a one-night stand? That whatever had happened between them was meaningless now that he was back on the scene?

"I hear what you're saying." She paused, choosing her words carefully. "I can't get over how unselfish you're being: to take on another man's child, it's—"

"It's nothing," he cut in. "I know I'll grow to love her just as much as David, if you'll let me."

"If I'll *let* you?"

"Yes. Obviously it's your decision. I know it's been a terrible shock, seeing me again when you thought I was dead. I don't know what your plans were." He looked down, avoiding her eyes. "Were you planning to marry him when the war's over?"

"I . . ." she hesitated, not knowing how to answer him. In his letter Bill had never mentioned marriage. He had said he missed her. Was that the same? An awful thought occurred to her: What if he had just been buttering her up in the hope of persuading her to send Louisa to the States, with no real intention of sending for her later?

"I . . . we hadn't really made any plans," she stammered. "I . . . need time to think about all this, Eddie. It's been such a shock."

"Of course you do." He reached out his hand, as if to pat her knee, but suddenly withdrew it. "Why don't you go back to Wolverhampton for a couple of days? Talk to Cathy—she seemed a sensible sort of woman. It'll help you get things straight in your mind."

She searched his face. "Wolverhampton?" It seemed like the other side of the world to her now.

"I'll help with the farm, and I'm sure Rhiannon won't mind looking after the children."

"The children?" She had assumed they would be going with her.

Eddie smiled. "I'm sure you could do with a break," he said. "And you didn't think I'd let young David out of my sight so soon, when I've only just got him back, did you? I know he's scared of me, but he'll soon get used to his funny old dad!"

Eva suddenly saw that the choice he was giving her was no real choice at all. If she chose to leave him—chose to go in search of Bill—it would be without David. Even if she sneaked away in the middle of the night, ran off with the children to another town, she would never be able to leave the country without his permission. She would never be able to find Bill, let alone marry him.

"Eva? Are you all right? You look very pale."

She felt sick. "I need some air," she said, rising unsteadily from the couch. "I won't be a minute. Could you make us another pot of tea? Mine's gone cold." She didn't want tea, but it would stop him from following her. She needed to be alone to think things through.

She leaned against the farm gate, weak with emotion. She felt like a caged animal, doomed to be chained forever to this man who was like a stranger to her now. But how could she abandon someone who had endured so much suffering? He had a right to his family, of course he did. It would be utterly heartless to turn him away. Could she be that cruel? Could she let him stay, even though her heart wasn't in it? She heard a cry and turned to see David running up the track toward her, Rhiannon following a few yards behind with Louisa asleep in her arms.

"Mam!" David hurtled into her legs, hugging them tightly. She scooped him up and held him close, tears spilling from her eyes onto his rosy cheeks. "Why you crying, Mam?"

"Oh, I'm just sad because your daddy's been away such a long time." She gulped, trying to compose herself before Rhiannon reached them. "Don't be scared of him, will you? He's been very brave and we've all got to be extra specially nice to him."

David nodded, as if he understood. "Shall we make him a cake?"

"Yes, my love, if you want to." She wiped her face with her fingers, fresh tears running down the back of her hand.

Rhiannon took one look at her and stopped short. "What are you going to do?" she said, her face taut with emotion.

"I . . . don't . . . know." The words were punctuated with sobs.

~

It was late afternoon on the following Friday when Eva's train drew into Wolverhampton station. She fixed her eyes on the magazine on her lap, knowing that the sights and sounds of the place were going to bring painful memories flooding back.

She felt lost without the children, although she'd only been away from them a few hours. She had made Rhiannon promise to have David sleep in her bed and not let him out of her sight while she was away. He had cried when Eva told him she was going away for the weekend, but Eddie had cheered him up by saying he could help him milk the cows.

Over the past few days David had overcome his suspicion of Eddie. Eva could see how good it was for the boy to have a man in his life. Uncle Dai had filled the role temporarily, but he did little more these days than sit sleeping in his chair. David had begun following Eddie around the farm the way he used to follow Dai.

But the atmosphere at the farm had been tense and awkward. Eddie had kept his distance, sleeping in cousin Trefor's old room, and for that she had been grateful. Aunt Rhiannon had made no reference to their sleeping arrangements, but the situation was clearly taking its toll on her, worn out as she already was with the strain of running the farm and coping with a sick husband. Eva knew without asking that her aunt would be delighted if she and Eddie were reunited.

She took a deep breath as she stepped off the train. As she walked toward the exit, she kept her eyes down, praying she wouldn't bump into any of the women from the rail gang. She knew she wouldn't be able to face the inevitable interrogation about where she had been for the past six months.

She managed to get safely outside and hurried along the few streets that separated the station from Cathy's house. It was hard not to remember the many times she had walked these streets with Bill. She was glad she didn't have to go past the Civic Hall, the air-raid shelter, or the restaurant where they'd met that last time. She hoped she could avoid the town center over the next two days. Catching even the briefest glimpse of those places would be too painful to bear. And she would try to avoid going back to the old house. That would be too full of memories of her mother.

Wolverhampton was a place of ghosts, but she needed space to work out what she was going to do. And Cathy was the only person she could talk to, the only person who knew Bill and had witnessed the way things had been between them.

As she turned the corner into the road where Cathy lived, she caught sight of her in the front-room window. Eva ran the last few yards and the door flew open. The two women hugged each other before either of them spoke.

"You look really well!" Cathy sounded surprised. "I was so worried about you, doing all that heavy work on the farm with a new baby to look after—but I think the country air's done you good!"

Eva gave a wry smile. She hadn't eaten much over the past few days, and she thought she looked awful. She must have looked pretty terrible when she left Wolverhampton if Cathy thought she saw an improvement.

"The kettle's just boiled," Cathy said, taking her coat. "Mikey's gone next door for his tea, so we can have a good chat. Are you hungry?"

Eva shook her head. She'd had nothing but a slice of toast for breakfast, but she felt too churned up to eat. She followed Cathy into the kitchen. The last time she had been in this room was the day her mother died. She swallowed hard, determined not to give way to the surge of grief.

"I was on my way to Wales, you know, the day Eddie came back." Cathy glanced at Eva as she reached for the kettle. "I was at your house when the telegram arrived saying he was alive. I wanted to tell you myself because I thought it would be too much of a shock for you to get the news in a letter. I kicked myself afterwards. It must have been a million times worse, him turning up out of the blue like that."

Eva shook her head. "It wasn't your fault. It would have been a shock however I found out about it. I don't suppose it would have made a lot of difference if I'd been warned in advance."

Cathy spooned tea from a silver caddy into a small brown teapot. "How do you feel now that you've had a few days to get used to him being back?"

Eva hesitated before replying. "I don't know. I feel sorry for him most of all. Did he tell you what happened to him?"

Cathy nodded, pouring water onto the leaves. "I don't know how he got through it. He must be incredibly tough."

"Did he tell you about the soldier who looked after him when he was rescued? The one who got shot?"

Cathy's eyes widened as Eva related it. "I couldn't understand how he could be so calm about Bill being . . . you know." She set a cup of tea down in front of Eva. "What did you say, when he suggested adopting Louisa?"

"I didn't know what to say." Eva stared into her teacup, trying to remember how she'd felt as she lay on the couch at the farm listening to Eddie. Although it was only days ago, it felt like an eternity. "I was in a daze at that point. I remember lashing out at him when he showed me the letter he'd sent to Bill. After that, he did all the talking. That's when he suggested I come here to talk things over with you."

"*He* suggested it?"

"Yes. That was another surprise—until I realized what was behind it."

Cathy paused, her teacup on its way to her lips. "What do you mean?"

Eva let out a long breath. "He was giving me a glimpse of what would happen if I didn't agree to take him back." Her fingers traced the curve of the handle of her cup. "I'd told him I needed time to think it through. I'd hardly got the words out when he said yes, I probably needed a break to get over the shock. And in the next breath he said he'd look after the children while I was away. He was smiling at me, but he was deadly serious: said he had no intention of letting David out of his sight when he'd only just seen him again."

"Well, you can't blame him for that, surely?"

"No, of course I don't. But by sending me off to Wolverhampton, alone, he was showing me the consequences of the choice I have to make. He's made it crystal clear that if I try to find Bill, I'll have to leave David behind."

"Oh Eva! He can't do that, can he?"

"He can." Eva buried her head in her hands. "Imagine it, Cathy: even if I ran away and took the children with me, I'd never get them both out of the country. I'd have to get Eddie to divorce me before I could marry Bill, which I doubt he'd do, and even then he'd never give permission for David to go to America."

Cathy nodded slowly. "I hadn't thought of that. I was going to offer to put the three of you up here for a while, if that's what you wanted, but . . ." She gave a hopeless sigh. "What are you going to do?"

Eva pursed her lips. "What would you do in my shoes?"

"Heavens, there are so many unknowns, aren't there? I mean, what about Bill? What do you think he'll do when he gets Eddie's letter?"

"I've thought about that a lot," Eva said. "My first instinct was to write to him straightaway: tell him to ignore what Eddie had said."

"But you didn't?"

"No. It dawned on me that I should wait. See how he reacts. If he really wants me and the baby, he'll put up some sort of fight, won't he?" She raised the teacup from the saucer, then put it down again. "You asked me once if he'd mentioned marriage and I fudged around it, remember?"

Cathy nodded.

"Well, he hasn't. In that last letter all he wrote about was getting the baby over to the States. There was no plan for us, for a future together. I don't even know whether he intended for me to ever see her again."

Cathy reached across to pour more tea into Eva's cup. "So you're going to wait and see what he does? But for how long?"

"That's the problem. The way things are going, they say the war could be over by next spring. I know there's not a lot he can do until then, and I would never have sent Louisa over to the States on her own, anyway." Eva reached for the milk jug, her hand unsteady as she poured a few drops into her cup. "There's only one way we can ever be together, Cathy, and that's for him to come and live in this country."

Cathy looked at her. "Do you think that's possible? I suppose he might be allowed to, but would he want to?"

"That's the question." Eva raked her hair with her fingers. "That's what I've been asking myself over and over again." Her eyes began to blur with tears.

Cathy reached out to put a hand on her arm. "I don't know what to suggest. You're in an impossible position, aren't you?"

Eva nodded. "All I can do is wait."

"And in the meantime?"

"I think I owe it to Eddie to let him get to know David, don't you?"

"Well, that seems only fair after what he's been through." Cathy nodded. "But how will you manage? Will you come back to Wolverhampton?"

"Rhiannon wants us to stay at the farm."

"Is that what you want?"

"I think Eddie would like it. I think he'd see it as a fresh start. If we came back here, there'd be so much explaining to do." She looked away. "I don't mean any offense, Cathy, but I don't think I could bear coming back here to live. Just walking to your house from the station . . . it brought everything back." She swallowed hard, determined not to cry. "Dilys wants to keep the house for now, so if Bill does write . . ." she paused, realizing how desperate she must sound. "Would you mind carrying on collecting the mail for me?"

"Of course I will." Cathy drained her cup. Replacing it in the saucer, she gave Eva a perplexed look.

"What is it?"

"I hardly dare ask. I was wondering what you're going to do if Eddie wants to . . ."

Eva sighed. "God knows. I can't even bear to think about it. I'm hoping he'll accept that I need time to get used to him being back."

"And if he doesn't? How long do you think you can keep that up?"

"As long as possible."

"And then?"

Eva stared at the table. "I suppose I'll do whatever it takes to keep the peace until I know where I stand with Bill. I'm petrified of him running off somewhere with David. I've had nightmares about it."

"Surely he wouldn't do that?"

"How do I know what he might be capable of? He's a different man, Cathy." She shook her head. "If there was only me to consider, I'd just stay at the farm with Dai and Rhiannon and tell him to leave, tell him the marriage was over. But it's not just about me anymore, is it? How could I face David in a few years' time if he found out his daddy had come back from the war and I'd sent him away?"

"And what about Louisa?" Cathy asked. "What will you tell her when she grows up?"

"I'll tell her I loved her father very much," Eva whispered. "Whatever happens, I'll tell her that."

Chapter 19

Cathy stared at the box on her kitchen table. It was neatly wrapped in brown paper and string. Amazing to think it had come all that way in such pristine condition. The stamps gave it a splash of color—three of them, all bearing the Stars and Stripes. Just looking at them made her feel nervous. Was it really possible that Bill had decided to make contact after all this time? There was no sender's address on the packaging. But who else could have sent Eva a parcel from America?

She had collected the box from the post office that afternoon, having called at Eva's old house for what would be the last time. Dilys had been back the previous week to sort out the last of the family's belongings before moving to Holland to marry Anton. Cathy was glad she had chosen to marry quietly in his hometown. A wedding in Wolverhampton would have been hard for Eva; a reminder of what she had wished for with Bill. As it was, the distance provided a convenient excuse for her not to attend the ceremony. And Dilys had not minded. All she seemed to care about was becoming Mrs. Anton Barnhart as swiftly as possible.

The house had looked very strange. All the furniture had gone: some given away, the odd good piece shipped to Holland. Eva hadn't seemed interested in claiming any of it for herself. All that was left was a box of photographs Cathy had promised to send on, and, lying on the mat, a note from the postman saying that he had tried to deliver a parcel the previous day.

She wished there was some way of telephoning Eva. Today was Friday and Cathy knew the post was delivered to the farm on Tuesdays. So if she wrote straightaway, she could let Eva know she was planning to take the parcel to Aberystwyth on her day off next Thursday. She hoped two days' notice would be enough for Eva to cook up some excuse to come and meet her.

She sat down to write the letter, wondering how Eva would react when she received it. In her last few letters she hadn't even mentioned Bill. It must have been so painful for her when first VE-day and then VJ-day came and went with no word from him. She had no way of knowing if he was dead or alive. *In a way*, Cathy thought, *it would have been better for Eva if Bill was dead. Better than knowing he was alive and didn't care.*

Last Christmas Eva had written of her mixed feelings for Eddie. At a time when so many families were feeling the loss of husbands and fathers so keenly, she knew she should be very grateful that he had come home. Cathy got the impression that things had become less strained between them. Eva had said how good Eddie was with both of the children and how much easier things were on the farm now that he had taken on so much of the work. But she had also mentioned how she'd cried when Louisa said her first word, because it was "Dad."

There were still American soldiers serving overseas. Not all had returned home when the hostilities ended. They were needed to rebuild the places they had bombed. Cathy knew that Eva was still clinging to the hope that Bill was one of these; that he was not yet in a position to come looking for her. But in the past few months the impression given by Eva's letters was that she had finally begun to put him out of her mind and pick up the pieces of her life with Eddie.

And now this.

Cathy looked at the parcel, desperately wanting to rip it open, to spare her friend's feelings. What if it was Bill's personal effects, willed to her in the absence of any relatives to claim them?

Her hand reached toward the package, but then she pulled it away. She had no right to interfere. She must take it to Eva unopened, whatever the consequences.

~

The following Thursday was hot and sunny. Mikey was very excited about their day trip to the seaside and was awake before the alarm went off. At nine years old he was only half a head shorter than Cathy. He had his father's blond hair and his mother's skin, which went brown at the merest hint of sun.

They left the house at a quarter to seven to catch the first train to Aberystwyth. They would be there by midmorning, which would give them six hours before getting the train back. That should be enough, Cathy thought, running through the endless possibilities in her head. She settled back in her seat as the train pulled out of the station. Whatever the parcel on her lap contained, it would be good to see Eva again, and good for Mikey to get some sea air.

There was a perceptible buzz among the other passengers. This was the first summer after the war. For the first time in seven years families were able to go on a proper holiday to the seaside. No barbed wire on the beaches, no anti-aircraft guns firing overhead. Cathy felt a sudden stab of longing for Stuart, knowing how much he would have loved larking about in the sea with his son on a day like this.

Eva was waiting on the platform when the train arrived. Cathy gave a little cry of surprise when she caught sight of her. In one arm she was clutching Louisa, who looked adorable in a white lace-trimmed sun bonnet, while David clung shyly to her other hand.

"Is that Auntie Eva?" Mikey put his nose to the window. "Yes, it is! Who's that little boy? Is it David?"

Cathy nodded. Mikey hadn't seen David for more than two years. It was no wonder he didn't recognize him. "And that's Louisa—Auntie Eva's little girl," she said. "Isn't she pretty?"

Mikey wrinkled his nose. He was at the age when any mention of girls made him squirm. "I want to see the sea!" He grabbed his bucket and spade and the bag of sandwiches Cathy had made and opened the door of their compartment. "Come on, Mum!"

As she got to her feet, Cathy had butterflies in her stomach. She needed to get the boys occupied with something before Eva opened the parcel. Going straight to the beach would be a good idea. Mikey could amuse David while she sat with Eva.

As she walked along the platform, Cathy saw Eva's smile wobble. *She must be tied up in knots, poor thing,* Cathy thought as she went to hug her. David was hiding behind his mother's legs, bundled up in a hat and scarf despite the hot weather.

"He's had the croup," Eva explained as they walked out of the station. "I'm hoping the sea air will do him good."

"What did you tell Eddie?"

"The truth," Eva said. "Well, most of it. I said you were coming for a day out at the seaside and wanted to meet up with me. He couldn't have come because he's busy with the shearing."

"Hasn't David grown?" Cathy reached out to ruffle the boy's hair. "And isn't she gorgeous!" She turned to look at Louisa, stroked her cheek, and was rewarded by a dazzling smile. She had been surprised by how light-skinned the child was. Her features were much more like Eva's than Bill's. A small turned-up nose, big hazel eyes, and long dark eyelashes. Her golden-brown hair protruded from under the deep peak of her bonnet in a cascade of ringlets. "Do you think she'd come to me?" Cathy asked.

"You can try." Eva handed her over. "She's got so heavy, she's making my arms ache!" She gave a nervous laugh as she took the parcel from Cathy and peered at the postmark.

"What's that, Mam?" David craned his neck and gave a short rasping cough. "Is it sweets?"

"No, my love." Eva and Cathy exchanged glances. "It's just something Auntie Cathy's brought from the old house. Are you going to show Mikey your flags?"

The boy dug eagerly in his pocket, and before long he and Michael were walking ahead, deep in conversation about the paper flags Eva had bought for them to decorate sand castles.

Louisa didn't cry when Eva handed her over. She seemed fascinated by Cathy's hair, and as they walked along, Cathy amused her by singing "Old MacDonald." The beach was only a short walk from the station, and it wasn't long before the boys were filling their buckets with sand.

"I hardly dare open it," Eva said, fingering the string on the parcel.

"I know. I was desperate to open it myself." Cathy looked at her. "I hope you haven't built up your hopes, too much, Eva. I'm so worried it might be . . . you know."

Eva nodded quickly. "I thought of that too." She untied the string, her fingers trembling. The paper fell away to reveal a box with the words "Benson's Baby Wear" written across it in gold italic script. Eva lifted the lid. Inside was an exquisite pink lace dress with matching bootees and a hat. The label said, "Age 2–3 Years." Beneath it was a handwritten note:

Dear Eva,

This is a little something for our baby girl from her daddy. I don't know the exact date of her birthday, but I wanted you to know that I haven't forgotten.

I hope things are going well for you and your husband. Please thank him from me for what he's doing for our daughter: he's a fine man and I don't blame you for wanting to start over with him.

I'm back in the army now, traveling around. I'm due to be posted overseas soon, but I don't know where yet. I'll write and let you know when I get my new address. It would be terrific if I could have a photograph of her in this little dress, if your husband doesn't mind.

Best wishes to you all,

Bill

For several seconds they sat staring at the piece of paper. When Eva spoke, her voice was tight with emotion. "Cathy, he thinks I *chose* to stay with Eddie!"

Cathy nodded, her mind reeling. "Eddie showed me the letter he sent. Bill wouldn't have known you were in Wales, would he? He would have assumed you and Eddie had already been reunited— that he'd written with your consent on behalf of you both." She was afraid to look at Eva. "What are you going to do?"

Eva's face had gone very pale. "I don't know." She glanced at David, who was jabbing a Welsh flag into a sand castle. "He said he was going to be posted overseas. Suppose they send him to Britain?"

Cathy bit her lip. "It could be anywhere, couldn't it? It could be the other side of the world." She could see what was going through Eva's mind. "You think if he came here, you and he could be together without . . ." Her eyes went to the boys.

Eva gave a quick, almost imperceptible nod, as if she was afraid someone might see her.

"What about Eddie?"

"I don't know!" The tone of her voice made David look up. She put on a smile, which disappeared the moment he started digging again. "Oh Cathy, what am I going to do?" she whispered. "I haven't stopped thinking about Bill since I got your letter." Tears were spilling down her face. "I told myself he didn't care, that I'd just been a bit of fun for him. But now this . . ." She picked up the pink dress, hugging it to her.

Louisa began to wail at the sight of her mother's tears, and Cathy rocked her, putting her other arm around Eva's shoulder. "You've got to try not to read too much into it," she said gently. "I know this sounds hard, but there's no guarantee he'd want you to break up your marriage for him, is there?" She glanced at Louisa, who had stopped crying but was making small, gasping sobs. "She and David are happy with Eddie, aren't they?"

Eva nodded, sniffling and wiping her eyes.

"And you? I thought perhaps you were coming round to the idea of having him back?"

Eva looked at her through red-rimmed eyes. "I suppose I was. We've been getting along pretty well—much better than when we were first married, actually. But then when I think about how it was with Bill . . ." She fiddled with the string in her lap.

David came bounding up to them. "Mam, can I have an ice cream?"

"Of course you can!" Cathy steered him away from Eva. "Let's go and get one while your Mum has a bit of a rest."

"It's all right," Eva blew her nose. "I'll be fine in a minute. I'll come with you." She reached out to take Louisa, and by the time they got to the promenade, the child had fallen asleep in her arms.

As they made their way to the ice-cream cart, Mikey spotted a stand selling hot dogs. "Mum, can I have one of those instead of an ice cream?" he said, sniffing the air.

"Michael Garner! I've made all those sandwiches!"

"Oh please, Mum! I won't ask for any more treats all day—promise!"

"Go on, then!" Cathy raised her eyes to the blue, cloudless sky and then dug in her purse.

Leaving Michael at the hot dog stand, she took David's hand and walked over to the ice-cream cart. Cathy didn't much like the look of the man selling them. She noticed him giving Eva a supercilious look, glancing from her to Louisa and raising an eyebrow. His apron was dirty, and he rinsed the scoop in a rusty-edged pail of water before digging it into the tub of ice cream. But David couldn't wait to get his hands on the enormous cone. He managed to finish it before Michael had got through his hot dog, which was so hot it burned his mouth.

Cathy glanced at Eva as they stood by the railings, watching the crowds on the beach. She had a faraway look in her eyes. It had been a mistake, coming here. Of course, Eva had a right to know that Bill cared about his daughter, just as Louisa would have a right to know, later on, who her real father was. But Cathy couldn't help thinking it would have been better for everyone if that parcel had never reached its destination.

~

Eva and the children didn't wave them off when they left Aberystwyth. The last train to Devil's Bridge left before the one to Wolverhampton, so the good-byes were said at the beach.

"Please don't do anything hasty," Cathy whispered as they parted. "There's no point getting your hopes up unless he's posted over here, is there?"

Eva stared at the sand. "He still doesn't know where I live. If he writes again, I won't know, will I?"

"Would you like me to call on the new people and ask them to send it on?"

Eva hesitated before answering. "Yes," she said. "I would."

"Are you going to tell Eddie? About the parcel, I mean?"

Eva shook her head. "Do you mind if I say the outfit was a present from you?"

Chapter 20

Three weeks after Cathy's visit, Aberystwyth was making headlines in the national press. They called it "typhoid town." Hundreds had gone down with the fever, and one of them was David.

Eva had written to Cathy as soon as he was diagnosed, warning her that a public health official would be contacting them because she and Mikey had been in the town on the day the outbreak was thought to have started. The letter began in a no-nonsense, practical way, giving the bare facts and symptoms to watch out for, but halfway through it took a heartfelt, harrowing turn:

The men from the council came today and took away all David's bedding. They said they had to fumigate the house, because of the risk of the bacteria spreading to the rest of us. They took his books and most of his clothes, saying they would all have to be destroyed. I tried to be brave, but when they took his teddy, I broke down. I wanted to take it to him at the isolation hospital at Tan-y-Bwlch. It's such an awful place. The doctors and nurses wear hooded overalls and a mask when they go into David's room. It must be so frightening for him. I thought if he could just have his teddy, it might make him feel a bit less scared. But they said no.

Eddie and I are allowed to visit, but they won't let us stay. I'm out of my mind with worry. An old lady died at the same hospital yesterday. They say it's because she was weak to start with, and that it doesn't kill healthy people. But David was weak when he caught it. He hadn't really got over the croup. I'm so scared, Cathy. I pray every night that he'll get better, and I'm terrified Lou's going to get it. Please God, you and Michael are all right. I'd never forgive myself if either of you got ill because of coming here. They still don't know what's caused it. They say it's passed on in water or food. I keep going over it in my head, trying to remember what we did and where we went, but I was so worked up that day it's all just a blur . . .

Cathy put the letter down, rubbing her tear-filled eyes with the back of her hand. She could hear Mikey playing in the street outside, and she ran to the window. He was laughing, kicking a ball about with his friends. He looked as strong and healthy as an ox. She reached for the kettle, an automatic reaction, seeking comfort in the warmth of a cup of tea. She gripped the handle so tightly her knuckles turned white. *If I lost him, life wouldn't be worth living.* She slammed the kettle down on the stove, telling herself there was nothing wrong with Mikey. She would go to the doctor's this evening, though, just to make sure. She shivered and hugged her arms to her body, thinking of poor little David all alone in the hospital. Eva must be going through hell.

~

"Come here, love." Eddie heard Eva's sobs and reached out for her in the dark. They were staying at a guesthouse in Aberystwyth, the same one he had stayed at when he came to find her two years earlier. It was the closest they could get to David, and meant they could visit him every day. When Eddie had asked for a twin-bedded room, the landlady had told them a double was all there was. Eva had said nothing. Both of them had climbed into it exhausted, worn down by the worry of seeing their child at death's door.

"It's . . . my . . . fault," Eva stammered as she clung to him.

"Eva," he said gently, "how can it be your fault?"

Her body shuddered with another sob. "I brought him here. To Aberystwyth. If only I'd stayed at home that day, he . . ." Her voice splintered and he felt her tears on his skin.

"It's *not* your fault. Don't ever say that!" He stroked her hair, wishing their being together, so close, had happened for the right reason, for any reason other than this.

~

A week later Cathy caught the early train to Aberystwyth. This time there were no families in the carriages, no day-trippers laden with sandwich boxes and buckets and spades. The bright sunshine piercing the windows lit up empty seats. No one wanted to visit a seaside town where death lurked in the cafés and ice-cream parlors.

Cathy was traveling alone. She and Mikey had been given the all clear, but it would have been foolish to take any risks. And a funeral was no place for a child. She shuddered as the words went through her head. A funeral was no place for a child, living or dead. No parent should ever have to face this. She wondered how on earth Eva and Eddie were going to get through it.

The little chapel on the hillside was packed. Rhiannon was carrying Louisa, just as she had carried David at Eva's mother's funeral. The thought made hot tears spring up in Cathy's eyes. She struggled to fight them back. She must not cry. Eva was managing to stay composed and so must she.

When the tiny coffin was lowered into the ground, Eva seemed to stumble. *If Eddie hadn't caught her,* Cathy thought, *she would have fallen into the grave.* She saw the tenderness in Eddie's eyes as he held on to her. When Eva seemed to regain her composure, he reached out to Rhiannon to take Louisa, who had started to cry. He stood at the graveside, rocking Louisa in one arm and hugging Eva to him with the other.

Cathy couldn't help noticing how much he had changed from the gaunt, frightening man she had seen on the stairs at the old house in Wolverhampton. He had filled out. Not fat, but muscular. His face was tanned and his hair, although still streaked with white, seemed thicker than she remembered it. But it was his eyes that had changed more than anything. The haunted look that had made him so menacing had disappeared, replaced by a soft, gentle expression that even grief could not erase. And Cathy realized with some surprise that this expression was directed as much toward Louisa as Eva.

Watching him again at the wake at the farmhouse, Cathy could detect no bitterness in him. *She* would have been bitter. Only a handful of the hundreds who had contracted typhoid fever had died. She would have raged against heaven if her son had been one of those. And it could so easily have been Michael. They had traced the outbreak to the ice-cream seller on the promenade. A carrier, they said, whose poor hygiene had led to the bacteria being passed to his customers. Michael had nearly had one of those ice creams. She closed her eyes at the horror of it. And if Louisa had been awake, she would almost certainly have had one too. She glanced back at Eddie, who was wiping cake crumbs from Louisa's mouth. How could he not feel resentful that she had lived while his own son had died?

She went over to speak to him. She had held back up to now, fearful that he would blame her for being the cause of David's ill-fated trip to Aberystwyth. But she had to know how things were, whether he really was going to stand by Eva now that the reason for staying together had gone.

"You're very good with her," Cathy said, unable to find the right words to express her sympathy. She had run through a dozen different sentences and every one of them sounded hopelessly inadequate.

"Got to take care of her," Eddie replied in an even voice. "She's all we have."

"I feel dreadful about being the cause of . . ." Cathy stopped, conscious of tears welling up. She blinked them back.

"You mustn't say that," Eddie whispered, glancing over his shoulder. "It's nobody's fault. Even that . . ." he paused, biting his lip. "Even that man, that ice-cream seller, he didn't do it on purpose."

Cathy looked at him, wondering how he could be so forgiving. Eva was very, very lucky, she decided, to have a husband like him. She thought about Bill's letter and wondered what Eva had done with it. She fervently hoped that the one good thing to come out of this tragedy would be a closer bond between Eva and Eddie.

One of the neighbors had offered to take her back to the station, and before she left, she sought out Eva, who had been making endless cups of tea in what seemed to Cathy to be an attempt to avoid having a proper conversation with anyone. Cathy understood this, but she needed to talk to Eva. She had no idea when they would get the opportunity to meet again.

"I've got to go in a minute—I wanted to say good-bye." The words sounded feeble, and Cathy reached out to hug her friend. For a split second she saw Eva hesitate and thought she was going to pull away. But Eva put both arms around her shoulders and held her tight. When they drew apart, she saw tears in Eva's eyes for the first time that day.

"I'll come outside with you," Eva mumbled, turning so that the guests in the living room couldn't see her crying.

In the bright sunshine streaming into the farmyard Cathy could see that grief had already etched new lines on Eva's face. People always looked terrible in bereavement. Cathy had barely recognized her own reflection when Stuart died. But it was not just Eva's face that had changed. When she spoke, it was as if everything she said had been written down and rehearsed. She quoted lines from the Old Testament about the sins of the fathers being visited on the children.

"Eva." Cathy frowned. "You know you mustn't blame yourself for this."

"But it's *my* fault, Cathy!" she hissed. "My fault and *his* fault!"

"His fault?" Cathy thought of the ice-cream seller.

"Yes!" Eva's eyes turned wild. "Don't you see? He tempted me. Before I even met you that day the seed had been sown, just knowing he'd sent that parcel. In my mind I was with him again—and that's why David was taken from me. I'll never forgive myself, or him!"

"Bill?" Cathy breathed. "You're blaming Bill?"

"Don't say that name!" Eva sucked in her lips until they went white. "I'll never speak that name again! Not as long as I live!"

Cathy caught her breath. "But Eva, you're not being fair! Yes, Bill sent the parcel, but I'm the one who brought it to Aberystwyth and I'm the one who bought that wretched ice cream—so if you're going to blame anyone, surely it should be me!"

"You don't see, do you?" Eva was looking through her rather than at her. "What we had, it was wrong—from the very start. First my mother and now . . ." She pulled at a wisp of hair.

"Your mother?" Cathy shook her head. "That was a tragedy, Eva, but to blame Bill—"

"All I know," Eva broke in, "is if it wasn't for him, they'd both be here now."

Cathy blinked in disbelief. "What about little Louisa? Would you rather she'd never been born?"

"It's not her fault." Eva closed her eyes and drew in a breath. "She didn't ask to be born."

"No, she didn't, but one day she's going to want to know who her father is." Cathy reached out to take Eva's arm. "He asked for a photograph of her, remember? Don't you think he at least deserves that?"

"He deserves nothing!" She spat out the words, pulling her arm away. "As far as Louisa's concerned, he doesn't exist. Tell the new people not to bother sending on any letters. If anything comes here, I'll throw it straight on the fire."

Chapter 21

JULY 1954

Louisa was watching her mother. Looking at her long, pale fingers arranging wild roses in a vase. It was a crystal vase. Aunt Rhiannon's best. Louisa studied her mother's face as she carried the flowers to the mantelpiece. It reminded her of a picture in the *Golden Treasury of Children's Literature*. The one about the Little Mermaid walking for the first time. She remembered the words printed beneath it: "'but each step you take,' the Sea Witch said, 'will be like walking on knives.'" Her mother set the vase down next to the photograph of David.

Louisa followed Eva, climbing onto the worn leather arm of the fireside chair to get a better look at what she was doing. The back of her mother's short-cropped head was facing her, but her eyes were reflected in the framed glass of the photo. Louisa saw they were full of tears. Her mother cried often, but shearing time was the worst. And she knew why. That was when "it" happened. The thing she wasn't allowed to talk about.

She knew it had something to do with ice cream because she'd overheard the shearers talking. Heard them whispering David's name. But when she'd asked them what they were talking about, they'd turned away. She'd thought this very odd because the men were usually so friendly. They'd told her she had dancer's legs and hair as soft as candy floss. "Where did you get that hair?" they'd say. "Can we have a bit?" And she would laugh and pat their bald patches. But long afterward their words would echo in her head. Where did her hair come from? Mam's was not like it, nor Dad's.

"Mam," she said slowly, testing the ground. "Why did David have white hair?" She paused, waiting for a reaction, but none came. "Is it because Dad's hair's white?"

Eva turned, a handkerchief held up to her face. "No, silly!" She moved the hanky away, revealing a watery smile. "David didn't have white hair. It was blond. It only looks white because the photo's black and white."

"Oh," Louisa frowned. "What's blond?"

"It's sort of a golden-yellow color." Eva sniffed and wiped her nose again, casting about the room for something to compare it to. "It's like . . ." She glanced at the bookshelf in the corner of the room. "Like Rapunzel in your storybook. Remember the picture where she lets her hair out of the window for the prince to climb up?"

Louisa nodded.

"Well, her hair's blond." Eva's eyes filled up again as she stroked Louisa's brown curls.

"But why did David have blond hair?" A furrow appeared between the fine, feathered crescents of Louisa's eyebrows. "Your hair's auburn, isn't it?"

"Yes, what of it?"

"Well, no one in our family's got blond hair, have they? Dad's got white hair, but you said it used to be brown, like mine, so—"

"Yes, well, everybody's different," Eva said quickly, turning back toward the kitchen. "Now will you go and call Dad and the men for me? Tell them lunch is nearly ready."

Later that week, when the shearing was in full swing and Eva was busy helping the men, Louisa was bored. Aunt Rhiannon and Uncle Dai had both dozed off in their armchairs, so she put on her boots and walked the two miles to the nearest farm. She should have worn her hat. Her mother said she should always wear it in the sun. But she didn't like it because it made her head feel itchy.

The Lewis girls were not her best friends, but it was too hot to walk all the way to the village. Anwen, who was nine, and her teenage sister, Elin, were just as bored as she was. The three girls wandered up the hill behind the farmhouse and lay on their stomachs in the warm grass, making daisy chains; Elin studiously ignored the younger girls as they jabbered away in Welsh.

"Who's got the brownest arms?" Anwen piped up, leaning across so that her elbow touched Louisa's.

Louisa peered at Anwen's plump, tanned skin with its sprinkling of tiny dark hairs before glancing back at her own skinny arm.

"It's Lou: no contest!" Elin's daisy chain was already finished and adorning her head like a coronet. She gave her sister a haughty look.

"No it's not!" Anwen complained. "We're nearly the same, aren't we, Lou?"

"Nearly," Louisa nodded, casting a cautious glance at Elin. "Compare eyes, though: yours are definitely browner than mine." The two girls peered into each other's eyes. "Yours are nearly black!"

"And yours are sort of green-brown, aren't they?" Anwen replied, mollified by this unchallenged victory.

"It's called hazel, stupid," Elin said.

"Wish mine were hazel," Anwen muttered. "Everyone in our family's got dark-brown eyes. It's really boring. What color are your mam and dad's?"

Louisa screwed up her nose as she pictured their faces. "My mam's are sort of gray, I think, and my dad's are dark brown like yours."

"So who do you take after, then?" Anwen propped up her chin with one hand, looking at Louisa curiously.

"She doesn't take after either of them, stupid," Elin hissed, digging her sister in the ribs.

"Oh, yes, I forgot," Anwen said. "I thought you got the brown bit from your dad, but you couldn't have, could you?"

Louisa looked from Anwen to Elin and back again. "What do you mean?"

"Anwen!" Elin kicked her sister on the shin.

"Ow! What was that for?" Anwen glared at her sister, who mouthed something Louisa couldn't make out.

"What did you mean when you said I couldn't have got it from my dad?" she repeated. Anwen looked away, shamefaced.

Elin tutted under her breath. "We're not supposed to say anything," she said, "but Big Mouth went and put her foot in it, didn't she? Come on, An: you've got to tell her now."

Anwen stared at the grass. "He's not your real dad," she mumbled.

"What did you say?" Louisa jumped to her feet, seizing Anwen's shoulders so that her head jerked up. "Tell me what you just said!"

"Your real dad's an American," Anwen said, blushing scarlet as the words came out. "Your aunt Rhiannon told our mam it was a secret."

Louisa dropped the daisy chain, her boots crushing the petals as she pelted down the track. She didn't stop running until she was nearly home, slowing her pace only to dodge out of sight of one of the shearers, who was chasing a stray sheep across the yard. She dived into the kitchen and hid under the table, curling herself into a tight ball. Great sobs shook her little body, the tears making round, dark patches on the pale-blue fabric of her skirt.

"Louisa? Is that you?" Aunt Rhiannon was suddenly peering at her, the embroidered tablecloth hanging around her ears like a veil. "Whatever's the matter, *cariad*?" She pulled a handkerchief from the pocket of her apron. "I thought it was one of the dogs whimpering about under there!"

"Nothing," Louisa mumbled, burying her head and clasping her hands tightly around her knees.

"Well, it doesn't look like nothing!" With a grunt of effort Rhiannon lowered herself to her knees, shuffling slowly and painfully under the table until she was alongside Louisa. "Come on," she said, gently pulling the child's hands apart and lifting her chin to dab her nose and eyes. "What's upset you so much that you have to hide yourself away under here?"

Louisa's eyes brimmed with tears. Her aunt was her friend, her ally. The one she went to when her mother was too sad to talk. But Anwen had said it was Aunt Rhiannon who had told this great big lie. "Why did you tell them he's not my dad?" she blurted out. "You said my real dad's an American—but it's not true, is it?"

Rhiannon's face crumpled. "Who told you?" she whispered.

"Anwen and Elin Lewis," Louisa sniffed, looking at her aunt with growing alarm. "They're telling lies, aren't they?"

"Listen, *bach*," her aunt said, "will you be a brave girl for me? Because I know you *are* a brave girl."

Louisa nodded, mesmerized now by the shock of what her aunt was saying.

"Your mam and dad were going to tell you when you were a bit older." Rhiannon shifted herself into a more comfortable position, bracing herself on her elbows. "Anwen and Elin weren't telling lies. Your real dad *was* an American. A soldier, he was." She glanced up at the rough underside of the table, pressing her lips into a thin line. "A very brave soldier," she said, nodding her head, "who got killed in the war like Huw Morgan's dad."

There was a moment of complete silence as Rhiannon and Louisa looked at each other.

"Was he David's dad as well?"

"No, *bach*."

Louisa frowned as her aunt's eyes welled up. "I don't understand," she said. "David was my brother, wasn't he? So how can we have different dads?" She shuffled sideways toward the pointed edge of the tablecloth. "I'm going to go and ask them," she muttered.

"No!" Her aunt grasped her arm. "Please, Louisa! Not today, of all days!"

"Why not?"

"You know what today is, don't you?" Her aunt looked at her with pleading eyes. Louisa nodded. She knew that today was the anniversary of when "it" happened, and that "it" was the reason she no longer had a brother. Why would nobody tell her what "it" was?

"Promise me you won't say anything to your mam and dad about what the Lewis girls said?" Rhiannon's grip on her arm was beginning to hurt. "It would upset them so much . . ."

She didn't need to say any more. Louisa knew better than to say anything that might set her mother off. "All right," she said, wriggling out of her aunt's grasp, "I promise. But you've got to promise me something in return."

"What?"

"I want to know what happened to David." Louisa's eyes narrowed. "No one ever tells me anything and I'm not a baby!"

Rhiannon looked at Louisa with such a strange face that she wasn't sure if she was about to shout at her or burst into tears. "All right, all right," her aunt sighed, her face sliding back into its normal, calm expression. "Give me a hand getting out from here, and we'll have a nice cup of tea and some cake, and I'll tell you all about it, if that's what you really want."

~

Louisa's cake lay half-eaten on her plate as she sat, stunned, listening to her aunt's story.

"It was the first summer after the war ended," Rhiannon said. "You'd just turned two and your mam took the pair of you to Aberystwyth for the day to meet a friend of hers from Wolverhampton who was having a trip to the seaside. David had had the croup, and she thought the sea air would do him good." She paused to dab her eyes with the same lace-trimmed handkerchief she had offered to Louisa. "It was the ice cream, they said in the end. Hundreds of people got it. It was this one man. Selling it from a cart on the prom, he was. Don't know where he came from. Foreign, probably. Not from round here, anyway. And he'd got it. Hadn't washed his hands properly, the dirty beggar." She paused, shutting her eyes tight to keep in the tears. "They sent David to the isolation hospital at Tan-y-Bwlch. Wouldn't let your mam or dad stay with him, though they begged to."

"Why didn't I catch it?"

"They didn't give you any ice cream. Your mam said you were asleep when they bought it."

"And did everyone die who caught it?"

"Not everyone. Only a handful in the end." Rhiannon gazed out of the window at a shorn sheep that was being chased out of the yard. "It's a funny disease, typhoid. Only seems to catch the weak ones. Maybe if David hadn't had the croup . . ." She blew her nose loudly.

"I don't remember it." Louisa frowned. "I don't remember the sea, or Mam's friend, or anything."

"Well, you wouldn't." Rhiannon sniffed. "You were too young. And your mam and dad haven't been near the place since. Wouldn't go there for love nor money."

"Wouldn't go where, Mrs. J.?" The grinning face of one of the shearers appeared around the kitchen door. "Can I borrow this young lady for a minute or two?" he asked, without waiting for a reply. "We need an extra pair of hands on the gates."

"Off you go," Rhiannon said, putting out a skinny hand to stroke Louisa's cheek. "And remember what you promised!"

~

It was hard, keeping quiet about a secret as big as that. After a week Louisa began to wonder if it would be all right to say something to her parents. Her mother was looking better now. Being outdoors every day with the shearing had done her good. She didn't look nearly as ghostly next to the men as she had before. And after all, she reasoned, Aunt Rhiannon hadn't made her promise *never* to say anything.

On Sunday, during chapel, she caught Elin Lewis giving her sly looks. She was going to have to do something before the end of the summer holidays. She could avoid Elin and Anwen for now, but not when school started. She needed to know more. Something to throw back at the Lewis girls if they started in on her again. She decided to talk to her aunt about it after lunch. Find out if it would be all right to ask her parents a few questions.

She glanced along the pew to where Aunt Rhiannon and Uncle Dai were sitting. Uncle Dai's mouth was lolling open, like it always did when he was trying to say something. Everyone else was singing "All Things Bright and Beautiful," but he just made strange grunting noises. No one looked at him because they were all used to it.

Louisa looked back to the pulpit, but as she did so, she caught a flash of movement out of the corner of her eye. She heard her aunt cry out as Uncle Dai's arm flailed in the air and he collapsed, knocking her sideways. Her head hit one of the wooden pillars holding up the roof.

The organ played on as people in the pews around them scrambled about, the men trying to pull the unconscious Dai off his wife's body. As the notes of the hymn petered out, Louisa caught a glimpse of her aunt's legs, sticking out at strange angles from underneath Uncle Dai's bulging stomach. She stared in shocked fascination as five men, including her dad, counted to three before heaving her uncle back onto the pew. Aunt Rhiannon lay on the hard stone floor like a crumpled rag doll. Her dress was up around her thighs and Louisa could see a suspender peeping out from beneath the fabric. She thought how embarrassed her aunt would be when she found out the whole congregation had seen her like that.

"Don't look, love!" Eva was suddenly beside her daughter, covering her eyes and pulling her away. "Come on," she said, pushing past the people who were crowding the aisle to see what had happened. "We've got to go and fetch the doctor!"

~

The next few days were a blur to Louisa. She spent most of her time sitting in a corner of the kitchen, pretending to read but more interested in watching the comings and goings of the adults. She hardly saw her mother, who was camped out in her aunt's room and refused to leave her bedside for more than a few minutes at a time.

Her father was out looking after the animals and a procession of old ladies from chapel took turns feeding Uncle Dai, who slept in a chair in the parlor nearly all day, waking only to eat a meal. She heard the doctor tell her father that Uncle Dai had had another stroke, but only a mild one. No one would tell her what was wrong with Aunt Rhiannon, but she could tell from their faces that it was bad. On the fourth day she came down to breakfast to find her mother sitting at the kitchen table. She looked pale and tired and her hair was sticking up, as if she hadn't brushed it for days.

"What's the matter, Mam?" As Louisa ran to her, she saw a tear trickle down her mother's face. She stopped in her tracks, as if by instinct. She had learned long since not to ask questions when Mam was like this.

Eva reached out a hand for her. Catching hold of Louisa's arm, she hugged the child to her. "Don't mind me." She sniffed, blowing her nose. "I'm just sad because Aunt Rhiannon's gone to heaven to look after David."

For a long moment Louisa couldn't open her mouth. Her throat went tight, as if she'd swallowed something that wouldn't go down. "Why?" she whispered at last, her voice wobbling. "I wanted her to look after *me*!"

~

Louisa wasn't allowed to go to the funeral. She sat making sandwiches with Mrs. Pugh, one of the elderly women who had been helping to look after Uncle Dai. Mrs. Pugh was very deaf and didn't say much, but she seemed able to slice bread much faster than Louisa could butter it. Soon there was a mountain of bread in front of her so high that she couldn't see out of the kitchen window.

As she reached for more butter, she heard a noise coming from the farmyard. It was a sort of meowing sound, which surprised her, because the sheepdogs rarely let any cat venture inside the gates.

Getting down from her seat, she dodged around the table to the window. Standing in the yard was a woman holding a baby. The baby was making the strange wailing sound, kicking its little legs out under the shawl wrapped around its middle. The woman was looking at the house and, as Louisa watched, a man appeared, leading a horse and cart.

Louisa tugged at Mrs. Pugh's sleeve. "There's someone coming to the door," she said, as loud as she could without shouting. Mrs. Pugh frowned and bent down, cupping her hand to her ear. Before Louisa could repeat the words, there was a loud rap at the kitchen door. Mrs. Pugh appeared not to have heard it, so Louisa went, thinking the funeral must have finished already and this was the first of the guests for the wake.

"Is Mr. Melrose at home?" The man standing on the threshold was taller than anyone she had ever seen. He looked at Louisa in a strange way. The kind of way Elin Lewis had looked at her in chapel. It made her feel frightened.

"He's not here," she blurted out, as Mrs. Pugh came sidling over. "He's gone to a funeral."

"The funeral's today?" The man's expression changed to one of angry confusion. He turned to the woman and the baby and said something in a language that Louisa couldn't understand. "You'd better let us come in and wait," he said to Mrs. Pugh, pushing past without waiting for a reply. "I'm Trefor Jenkins. This is my farm."

Louisa stared at him, her brow furrowed as she worked out who he was. "Are you Uncle Trefor from Italy?" She looked from the man to the woman and her baby.

"That's right," he said, unsmiling. "I'm not really your uncle, though. I'm your mam's cousin." His eyes narrowed as he looked at her with the same curious expression as when she had answered the door. She stood rooted to the spot as he looked her up and down. She felt hot with embarrassment as his eyes lingered on her chest, where two slight contours in her sweater marked the beginnings of breasts. "Yes," he nodded slowly, a sneer curling up his mouth on one side, "and you must be the Yankee nigger's bastard!"

Louisa felt the blood surge from her neck to her face. She didn't have a clue what the words meant, but she could tell by the twisted smile on his face that it was something nasty.

A sudden clatter of hooves in the farmyard distracted him. "Oh, here she comes, your mam." He arched his eyebrows and settled himself into the big farmhouse chair her dad always sat in. "You'd better go and pack your suitcase, miss!"

Chapter 22

AUGUST 1954

It was a bad day to be on a train. Louisa was hot and thirsty and tired of playing I-spy with Eddie. Eva was staring out of the window. She hadn't joined in their game and Louisa wondered if she'd noticed any of the animals, fields, or rivers they were leaving behind.

The train slowed as they pulled into yet another station. "Is this it?" Louisa gasped, jumping up when she saw the sign for Wellington out of the window.

"No, love, not yet. It just begins with the same letter." Eddie patted her shoulder. "Sit down. It won't be long now. Only another couple of stops."

After a few more miles the fields began to give way to squat brick factories with towering soot-blackened chimneys. The stately River Severn with its swans and weeping willows was replaced by mean little canals, dead straight and murky yellow. Smoke hung in the afternoon sky like a gray curtain drawn across the sun.

"Where have the sheep gone?" Louisa demanded, her nose pressed to the window. "And why is everything so dirty?"

Eva bit her lip and fiddled with her bag.

Louisa turned to Eddie. "Why is it, Dad? Why are those big houses so dirty?"

Eddie laughed. "They're not houses, sweetheart, they're factories. Places where people make things."

"But why is everything so black?"

"Ah, well." He chuckled. "This is the Black Country! It's where me and your mother were born."

"The *Black* Country?" Louisa wrinkled her nose and looked at Eva to see if her father was joking. But Eva had closed her eyes and was leaning back against the shabby upholstery.

"That's what they call it, cross my heart." Eddie smiled. "But it's not as bad as it sounds. You'll soon get to like it."

"But there's no grass! And look at those horrible yellow rivers!"

"They're called canals," Eddie said, "and yes, they do look a bit nasty—but there are loads of good things in Wolverhampton. Like the cinema: there's the Odeon, the Savoy, the Gaumont—I can't wait to take you, you'll love it!"

Louisa frowned at him, unconvinced.

"And as soon as I get my first week's wages, I'll take you and your mother into town to buy some new clothes," he went on. "You won't believe it when you see the shops, Lou. I'll take you to Beatties. They've got three floors with everything you can imagine. Dresses, hats, shoes, toys—you name it. We'll have a whale of a time, won't we, Eva?"

Louisa looked at her mother. Her eyes were still closed, but she wasn't asleep. Her fingers were moving, pulling at a bit of loose thread on the strap of her bag.

~

Louisa had never ridden in a car in her life; during the taxi ride from the station she felt like Cinderella on her way to the ball. She perched on the wide leather seat, bewildered by the streets full of shops and the crowds of people. She had never seen so many people. And they looked so strange. So different from the people she was used to. Their clothes, their hair, the brightly painted lips of the women—as far as Louisa was concerned, they might have come from a different planet.

"Where are we going?" she asked, as they left the town center behind and swung into a wide road with tall terraced houses along one side and the huge glass edifice of the Midland Counties Dairy on the other. "Are we going back to your old house, Mam?"

The expression on Eva's face told Louisa she'd said something wrong. Her mother looked as if she was about to say something, but Eddie patted her hand and answered instead.

"No—we're going to a new house!" he beamed at Louisa, who was looking anxiously at her mother. "It's just round the corner from your new school and only ten minutes' walk from the place I'm going to work, so we'll both be able to come home for lunch: that'll be nice, won't it?"

"So I won't have to take an egg to school?"

"No. And you won't have to get up so early either."

Louisa smiled at the prospect of not having to trudge for miles through muddy fields on dark winter mornings to get to the school at Devil's Bridge.

"And there'll be other children living in the street," Eddie went on. "Someone for you to play with without having to walk miles to find them."

The taxi stopped on Sycamore Street—a long, narrow canyon of two-up, two-down terraces. If sycamores had ever graced its gray pavements, there was no evidence of them now. Number thirty-six was decidedly shabbier than its neighbors. The front door and the window overlooking the street were a dull brown, with the odd fleck of maroon showing through where the paint had begun to flake and peel.

"It's not as big as the farmhouse, is it?" Louisa said as they trooped into the narrow hall. "Where's the kitchen?"

"In here." Eddie led her into an L-shaped room at the back of the house.

"Where's the table?" Louisa's eyes ranged over the grease-spattered walls.

"There isn't space for one in this part of the house," he replied, "but we can eat through here." He took her into the front room, where a narrow table was pushed up against a wall. "Look," he said, "you can pull it out to make it bigger."

Louisa looked at its spindly legs and the round white burn marks on its surface. "Can we see my room now?" she said, turning on her heel and darting up the steep stairs.

Eddie found her staring through a narrow sash window at the high brick wall at the end of the yard.

"Do I *have* to have this one?" she asked. "I can't see anything. I used to be able to see the sheep and the rabbits . . ." All she could see was her own reflection in the glass. A sulky face with two stupid, sticking-out pigtails. With a grunt she pulled out the ribbons and slides, raking her hair into a fluffy halo.

"Don't worry," Eddie said, "your mother's going to fix up some nice curtains and a bit of net, and then you won't be able to see that horrible old wall. Here," he dug his hand into his pocket and pulled out a few pennies. "There's a shop at the end of the street. You go and get yourself some sweets while we sort out the bags."

~

Louisa had never chosen sweets for herself before. Her aunt would always bring some back from her monthly trips to Aberystwyth, but as Louisa was not allowed to go with her, she usually ended up with a bag of pear drops, which were Rhiannon's favorite, or a licorice bootlace if money was tight.

As she walked along the street with the coins clasped in her sweaty little hand, she tried to work out how many pear drops or bootlaces she was likely to be able to afford.

The shop seemed dark after the brightness outside. It smelled funny too: like the moldy potatoes she'd once unearthed at the back of the farmhouse larder. As her eyes got used to the gloom, something caught her eye. A whole shelf of chocolate bars. She turned her head to one side to read the wrappers: Cadbury Dairy Milk, Toffee Crisp, Fry's Chocolate Cream. The very name of the last one made her mouth water. As she reached out to pick it from the display, she heard a voice behind her.

"Sorry. We don't serve blacks."

She turned her head, curious to see what was going on, expecting to see a person as dirty as the factories she had seen from the train. But there was no one there. She walked up to the counter and put her money down next to the bar of chocolate.

"You deaf?" A woman with stringy hair and a tight, low-cut top appeared from behind the till. She pushed the coins back at Louisa. "We don't serve niggers," she hissed.

Louisa stared at her. That word again. The same one Uncle Trefor had used. So that's what it meant.

"I am *not* black!" She held the woman's gaze, although she could feel the sting of tears coming. "I wash my hands and face every day—and I have a bath every Sunday!"

"You can wash yourself till kingdom come," the woman sneered, "but you won't get nothing in this shop!"

Angry and bewildered, Louisa opened her mouth, then clamped it shut. Instead of arguing, she snatched the chocolate bar and ran out of the shop, her money left behind on the counter. Her feet pounded on the pavement as she hurtled along the street. Seeing a group of women coming toward her, she dived into an alley. She found herself running along the backs of houses, the air musty with the smell of pigeons, running and running until she left the houses behind and found herself scrambling onto the weed-covered wilderness of a bomb site.

Scuffing her sandals on a half-buried kitchen sink, she stumbled into an old air-raid shelter. She crouched there, panting for breath in its crumbling mouth, watching white fluff drift from the tatty heads of rosebay willow herb. The sun beat down on the concrete walls of the shelter and the rank smell of other kids' wee filled her nostrils as she pulled the wrapper off the chocolate and bit off a big chunk. Her mouth was so dry, it stuck to her tongue. As she tried to chew, the melting white cream ran down the back of her throat, its sticky sweetness making her retch. She spat it out and thrust the bar back into her pocket in disgust.

"Stupid sweets!" she hissed. "Stupid shop!" Turning her head, she shouted into the darkness of the shelter: "I AM NOT BLACK!"

"*Black . . . black . . . black . . . black . . .*" Her voice echoed like a gang of angry ghosts.

"I CAN'T BE A YANKEE NIGGER'S BASTARD!" she screeched, "BECAUSE MY REAL DAD WAS A SOLDIER! AN AMERICAN!"

"*Can! . . . Can! . . . Can! . . . Can!*" The spooks of the shelter teased back.

She ran back up the steps, grabbed a handful of stones, and hurled them at the withered petals of the nearest weeds. Clouds of fluffy seed cases flew into the air, dancing in the sunlight. *Like fairies*, she thought, glaring at them. So delicate. So *white*.

She found a stone with a sharp edge and started scraping it on the shelter wall.

"*Rydwi ddim yn ddu!* I am not black!"

She thought the Welsh version looked much more impressive, so she rubbed the English words out, replacing them with her initials and the date. Then she retraced her steps, stamping hard on all the seed cases that drifted across her path.

~

It was getting dark by the time she found her way back home. She pushed past Eddie when he opened the door, running toward the kitchen as he called after her.

"Lou! Where on earth have you been?" He chased her down the hall. "Your mother's out looking for you!"

She turned on the single tap over the sink, sending water cascading to the floor as she splashed it onto her face.

"Lou? What's the matter?"

She grabbed the hard new bar of soap, rubbing it furiously until suds oozed out between her fingers. "She said I was dirty!" she muttered, a beard of lather slithering down to her chin as she attacked her face.

"What?" Eddie pried the soap from her hands. "Who said that?"

"The woman in the shop!" she yelled. "She said I couldn't buy any chocolate because I was black!"

"She *what*?" Eddie's hands were around her waist, hoisting her onto the draining board.

He wiped her face with a tea towel, cupping her chin in his hand. "Now you tell me again," he said, his voice gruff with anger. "What did she say to you?"

"She called me a nigger, Dad." Louisa snatched the towel from his hand, rubbing the stinging soap out of her eyes. "Uncle Trefor said it too. *The Yankee nigger's bastard*, that's what he called me. It's not true is it? My real dad's an American—I know that." She pushed the towel back at him. "What's a bastard?"

Eddie's head dropped and he clasped his hand to his mouth as if he was afraid of what might come out of it. "Oh God," he mumbled. "Who told you he was American?"

"Anwen Lewis." Louisa was half shocked, half fascinated by the effect her words had had on him. "And Aunt Rhiannon said he was a soldier."

His eyes closed for a moment, and he took a deep breath. "We were going to tell you when you were a bit older," he began.

"I know," Louisa cut in, "Aunt Rhiannon said."

"What else did she say?"

Louisa shrugged. "Nothing much. She said he died in the war like Huw Morgan's dad, and she told me not to tell you and Mam that I knew."

"How long have you known all this?"

"Not very."

Eddie looked at her intently, the skin between his eyebrows puckering into two deep ridges. "It wasn't quite true, what your aunt said."

"What do you mean?"

"When she said he died in the war." Eddie took a breath. "We don't know what actually happened to him."

"Well, if he's not dead, where is he? Why isn't he here?" Louisa felt a lump in her throat.

"He had to go back to America when the war ended, love. Back to his own country."

Louisa turned her head away so that Eddie couldn't see her eyes. "I don't want him to be my dad," she cried out. "Why can't *you* be my real dad?"

He reached out and hugged her to him, and she buried her face in the familiar, smoky scent of his clothes. "You know that I love you just as much, don't you, sweetheart?" he said, stroking her hair. "It doesn't make any difference that I'm not your real dad. I'm real in all the ways that matter."

She nodded, wiping her eyes on her sleeve. "I still don't understand, though," she sniffed. "Why did Uncle Trefor say he was a nigger?"

Eddie sighed. "Because Uncle Trefor's not a very nice man. *Nigger* is a rude word for someone who's got black skin. It's nothing to do with being dirty. It's the way people are born."

"*Black* skin?" Louisa looked at him incredulously.

"Well, not really black." Eddie frowned. "More like very dark brown."

"Like this?" She pulled the sticky remains of the chocolate bar from her pocket.

"Yes." Eddie nodded his head slowly. "Just like that."

"So my real dad was a . . ." she hesitated, "a black man?"

"A colored man, yes. That's what he'd be called. Colored."

Louisa frowned. "But *I* haven't got black skin!" She held the chocolate next to her arm. "My skin's the same color as Anwen Lewis's. Is her real dad a colored man as well?"

"No, love." Eddie pressed his lips together, an anguished expression on his face.

"Then that woman in the sweet shop must be stupid, mustn't she?" Louisa pulled her knees up onto the draining board, rolling down one of her white ankle socks. "Look," she said. "Look at the difference!" She jabbed her finger at her ankle, where the mahogany flesh of her leg gave way to a band of the palest brown. "It's just tanned, isn't it? How could she be so stupid?"

Eddie reached out to stroke her head. He didn't say anything. He didn't need to. Suddenly she twigged what it was that had given her away.

The sound of a key in the door made them both jump. Eddie gave her an anxious look. "Don't say anything to your mother about this, will you, love?" he said. "It's been hard enough for her these past few days."

Louisa nodded, wondering what he meant.

"I'll tell her when things have settled down a bit," he whispered. "Let it be our secret for now, eh? Just tell her you got lost."

~

The following Saturday Eddie took Louisa to a matinee at the cinema. They walked into town, pausing by the Midland Counties Dairy to watch the never-ending procession of milk bottles jiggling past on the conveyor belt. Louisa could see her reflection in the huge plate glass windows. She had stuffed her hair into the wide-brimmed straw hat Aunt Rhiannon had bought her for chapel. Reaching up, she tucked a stray wisp behind her right ear. Then she pulled the sleeves of her blouse as far down her arms as they would go so that her hands were half covered by the white fabric. Instead of ankle socks, she was wearing a knee-high pair and had loosened the drawstring waist of her pink cotton skirt so that it hung an inch or so lower than usual. Luckily her mother had been out shopping when they left the house; otherwise, she might have noticed. Louisa frowned at her reflection. She did look a bit strange and her head itched, but at least she was covered up. That was the important thing.

The cool darkness of the cinema was a relief after the stifling jostle of the streets. She could take her hat off now. No one would see her hair. As she bent down to push the hat under her seat, something brushed against her face: the hem of the usherette's dress as she guided people to their seats. A heady scent of poppies drifted in her wake. The red glow of her torch was like a magic wand pointing the way to a secret world.

Louisa gasped when the pink satin curtains rippled back. She was transfixed by the enormous screen. A box of popcorn lay untouched on her lap as she gazed awestruck at Snow White singing into the wishing well.

~

That night, when she was supposed to be in bed, she stood in front of the strip of mirror on her wardrobe door. She had rolled the long arms of her blouse up past her elbows to look like puffed sleeves and draped her blue bedspread around her waist to make a long skirt. An old black shawl of her aunt's was pinned to look like a bodice and a red ribbon was tied hair-band-style around her head.

Eddie caught sight of her reflection as he walked across the landing. "What are you doing, love?" He gave her a look that hovered between a frown and a smile. "I thought you were asleep."

"Do you like me, Dad?" She glanced at him before staring back into the mirror. "I'm Snow White."

Chapter 23
SEPTEMBER 1954

On the first day at her new school Louisa was mesmerized by what met her eyes as she slid into her seat. It was the back of a neck, nestling in the white collar of a regulation shirt, as snug as a chestnut in its padded case. She couldn't see the girl's face. In fact she only knew it was a girl when the hunched figure raised its head, revealing dozens of tiny plaits caught up with shiny black hair clips.

Louisa fingered her own hair, which her mother had fashioned into long, sausage-like ringlets by winding it in strips of rag the night before. "Who's that?" she whispered to the girl sitting beside her.

"Beverley Samuel," was the hissed reply. "I don't like her. She smells."

"Does she?" Louisa glanced sideways. Sylvia Barker was supposed to be looking after her. But the look in her eyes was like the farm cats back in Wales when a duckling strayed into the yard.

"*They* smell too." Sylvia jerked her head at two children sitting together on the other side of the classroom, both with their heads down, writing in exercise books. "Their dad's got a shop round the corner, but it stinks of curry. I went in once and nearly puked."

Louisa studied the pair carefully. Their skin was lighter than Beverley's: just a little darker than her own. One had a small bun with a white handkerchief twisted over it, and the other had a thin plait with pink ribbon woven into the end; the braid was so long that it snaked over the back of the chair. The one with the bun wore gray school trousers, while the other wore a tunic over what looked like shiny black pajama bottoms.

"Are they girls or boys?" she whispered

"Both," Sylvia hissed. "They're twins: Harjinder and Narinder."

"Where do they come from?"

"Pakistan," Sylvia hissed.

"And what about *her*?" Louisa's eyes fixed on the back of Beverley Samuel's neck.

"Jamaica."

"Oh." Louisa was confused. "Not America?"

Sylvia gave her a patronizing smile. "America? Colored people don't come from America!"

~

When the bell rang for playtime, Louisa found herself shuffling along in a crocodile toward the school yard. As soon as they were out of sight of the teacher, Sylvia vanished. Louisa stood forlornly, bewildered by the screams and yells of so many children. It had been so different at Devil's Bridge. Including herself, there were only sixteen children in the whole school. This playground was a blur of bodies, everyone running and shouting.

At the far end of the yard she spotted Beverley Samuel. She was playing by herself, throwing rubber balls against a high brick wall and catching each one expertly before the next bounced back at her. Louisa wondered if she had any friends.

"Do you want to play?" The voice came from behind her. A small girl in a green dress and a white fluffy cardigan was holding out the wooden handle of a skipping rope. "My name's Gina. What's yours?"

"Louisa—but everyone calls me Lou." She took the handle and stood awkwardly, unsure what Gina had in mind.

"Do you know how to skip backward?" The girl had a strange lilt to her voice: not what Lou's dad called a Black Country accent.

Louisa shook her head. She felt awkward. Everything about the new school was making her feel stupid. She had a sudden urge to drop the rope and run home.

"Want me to teach you?" Gina smiled. It was a proper smile, not a spiteful one like Sylvia's. Her dark eyes crinkled at the corners and dimples appeared in her cheeks. Louisa stood like a statue as Gina wound the rope behind her legs and put the other end in her left hand.

Half an hour later both girls were doubled up with laughter. "Where do you come from?" Louisa asked, panting as she handed over the rope.

"Italy." Gina flicked the rope into a loop and skipped through it. "I've only been here since Easter. What about you?"

"Wales," Louisa replied.

"Is that in England?" Gina asked. "Only I thought you sounded like you came from somewhere else. Like me, I mean."

"Well, it's next door to England," Louisa said, detecting the note of disappointment in Gina's voice. "But my real dad's American."

"Oh! Like Frank Sinatra? My mum's got all his records!"

Louisa hadn't a clue who Gina was talking about, but she nodded eagerly. "Teach me something else," she smiled, picking up the rope.

When the bell rang for the end of playtime, Sylvia reappeared. "Come on," she said, marshaling Louisa into line. As they filed past Gina on their way back to the classroom, Sylvia nudged Louisa's arm. "I wouldn't play with her," she whispered. "She's an eyetie and they eat garlic all the time. Yuck!" She eyed Louisa suspiciously. "You're not Italian, are you?"

"No," Louisa mumbled, "I'm Welsh."

"Is that why you talk so funny?"

A loud scraping of chairs prevented any further conversation. The children scrambled to their feet as the teacher marched into the room. Miss Pudney reminded Louisa of the old ladies from chapel who had come to look after Uncle Dai. Everything about her was gray. Her hair, her eyebrows, and even her legs were gray in their thick woolen stockings.

"Everyone—get changed for PE!" she announced, in the kind of voice a farmer would use to round up straying cows. "Boys: football. Girls: hoops. Not you," she said, looking at Louisa. "Tell your mother she must buy you a pair of navy-blue knickers and black plimsolls for next week."

The word *knickers* produced fits of giggles among the boys as they dived beneath their seats to scrabble about in their bags. Louisa watched as everyone else got ready to go back outside. All except Beverley, who was sitting quite still, her head resting on her hands.

"Beverley Samuel! Why aren't you getting changed?" Miss Pudney barked, a deep line appearing between her whiskery eyebrows. "Don't tell me you've forgotten your PE kit again!"

Beverley said nothing, her head dipping farther forward.

"Have you actually got a PE kit?"

Beverley mumbled something Louisa couldn't make out.

"What did you say?"

"No, Miss." Beverley sounded hoarse and close to tears.

The teacher nodded and cast her eyes over the rest of the class. "Put your hand up," she said in an imperious voice, "if you have a television at home."

Three hands went up on the far side of the classroom.

"Hmm." Miss Pudney's eyebrows arched like a pair of escaping caterpillars. "Now put your hands up if you've got a gramophone."

"What's a gramophone, Miss?" one of the twins piped up.

"A machine that plays records, Harjinder," she replied, enunciating each word slowly and deliberately. "Who has one of those?"

A forest of hands went up this time, including Louisa's and Beverley's.

"Ah, Beverley! You have a gramophone!" A treacherous smile played on the woman's lips as the child nodded eagerly. "Your father has the money for a gramophone and yet he can't afford to buy you a pair of navy knickers and plimsolls? Well, children, what do you think of that?"

Louisa heard the sniggers. She couldn't bear to look.

"Go and stand outside the headmaster's office, Beverley. And you tell your parents you'll be standing there every Monday afternoon until they buy you a PE kit!"

There was a loud scrape as Beverley pushed her chair back. Louisa heard a muffled gulping noise. She glanced sideways. Beverley's face was half-hidden by her arm. As she loped across the room, Louisa saw that the sleeve of her sweater had two dark patches where it had pressed against her eyes. Her shoulders convulsed with sobs.

"Silly nigger," Sylvia muttered under her breath.

~

When the bell rang for the end of school, Louisa hung back, lingering just inside the gates with Beverley Samuel in her sights. A woman in a flowered dress who was as dark-skinned as Beverley waved to her from down the street. Beverley ran to meet her, the flash of a smile transforming her sullen face.

Louisa walked home alone. Her mother had wanted to come and meet her, but she had begged her not to, pretending that it was more grown-up to make the short journey on her own. But that wasn't the reason. Her mother's presence at the school gate would have drawn attention to their differences. Both of them knew that—but neither of them talked about it, the same way that neither of them talked about the reason for her new hairstyle.

Louisa pushed open the kitchen door quietly and went to pour herself a glass of barley water. Balancing it on a tray with some biscuits, she tiptoed into the front room.

"Is that you, Lou?" Eva called from the yard. "Aren't you going to come and tell me about school? It's lovely and sunny."

"I'm too hot, Mam," Louisa called back. It wasn't a lie. She had kept her long-sleeved sweater on all day even though it was as warm as midsummer. But she wasn't just hiding from the sun. She put down her cup and knelt on the hearth rug.

"Frank Sinatra," she whispered, flicking through the dog-eared sleeves of the records that were still in the cardboard box they'd traveled in from Wales. She wanted to know what an American looked like. As she neared the back of the box, her fingers froze. She was staring at the smiling face of a man with skin the color of Beverley's. His short black hair was combed away from his face, lying in shiny waves above his broad, smooth forehead. His lips were parted in a wide smile, and there were faint, curved lines above the sweeping black bows of his eyebrows, giving his eyes a mischievous look. He wore a white shirt with a narrow black tie and a houndstooth-check jacket, beneath which were the words "Nat 'King' Cole."

She slipped the disc out of the sleeve and put it very carefully onto the turntable.

She was not supposed to touch it, but she knew how it worked. As the words on the label spun into a blur, his voice drifted from the Dansette box. Louisa closed her eyes, trying to imagine that he was in the room with her. She listened to the words. Something about love being too hot not to cool down.

"Louisa!"

Her eyes snapped open. Her mother's face, pale and tense, was framed in the doorway. Eva ran to the machine, her hand trembling as she plucked the needle from the record, cutting the voice dead.

"I'm sorry, Mam," Louisa began, "I only put it on because he's colored."

"What?" Eva's head whipped around, the shiny black disc in her hand.

"He's colored. Like my real dad, isn't he?" Louisa bit her lip, studying her mother's face. "Is that what he looks like?"

Eva's legs seemed to buckle under her. She tottered backward into the faded blue armchair under the window. She was shaking her head, her lips opening and shutting like a goldfish but no sound coming out.

"Mam?" Louisa knelt by the chair. "Please don't cry! I just want to know what he was like, that's all."

Eva buried her face in her hands.

"What's his name?" Louisa persisted, her voice dropping to a whisper. "Can't you just tell me that? I promise I won't ask anything else . . ."

"No!" Eva mumbled through her fingers. "I . . . I can't remember . . ." She pressed her hands into the sockets of her eyes, tears coursing down her wrists and dripping onto the flowered cotton of her dress.

"Don't cry, Mam." Louisa pleaded again, "*Please*—don't!"

~

That night, when Louisa was getting into bed, Eddie appeared at the door.

"Where's Mam?" she asked.

"In bed, love. She's too tired to do your hair tonight." He opened the chest of drawers and pulled out a bundle of rags. "I'll have a go if you like, but you'll have to tell me what to do."

"I didn't mean to hurt her feelings, Dad," Louisa said as she took a strip of white muslin and knotted it close to her head. "I only asked her his name." She set her mouth in a hard line. "Anyway, I hate him," she muttered to herself, twisting a lock of hair tightly around the rag. "He must have done something horrible to make her cry like that. I don't want to know anything about him—ever!"

Eddie reached across and stroked her hair. "Tell you what," he said. "Why don't we go into town on Saturday? I'll buy you a new dress, like I promised."

Louisa looked at him. "I'd rather go to the pictures," she said in a small voice.

Eddie laughed. "Are you sure?"

Louisa nodded. "It's my favorite thing in the whole world."

"Okay. How about if we take one of your new classmates?"

Louisa frowned. She thought of Beverley, her shoulders shaking as she sobbed her way out of the classroom; the twins, whose names she struggled to remember; and Sylvia, whose spiteful words had been echoing around in her head all day. "There's no one in my class I really like," she said, "but there is someone at school who's nice. Her name's Gina. She taught me how to skip backward."

"Good." Eddie smiled. "Let's ask her, then, shall we?"

~

Louisa had been warned that the film was going to be nothing like *Snow White*, and it wasn't. This time the people were real. Men in smart suits and long-legged dancing girls in sequined costumes. Eddie had told her that *Scared Stiff* was an American film. She wanted to ask him how it all worked. How moving pictures of people and boats and cars could appear on a flat screen. But she was worried she might miss something.

"Look," Gina said, passing her a toffee. "It's Dean Martin. My mum loves him nearly as much as Frank Sinatra."

"Oh." Louisa squinted at the singer in the tuxedo. Her eyes flitted from the screen to Eddie. He had settled back in his seat, and his eyes were closed. "He looks just like my real dad," she murmured.

"Wow," Gina hissed back. "He's really handsome! You're so lucky!"

"Yes." Louisa's lips curved in a smile that never reached her eyes. "I am, aren't I?"

Chapter 24
December 1961

Louisa loved Saturday nights. In the seven years since the move to Wolverhampton, the only thing that had surpassed the thrill of visiting a cinema was working in one. She loved the fusty, sweet smell of popcorn that hit you when you walked through the doors; the warm, velvety feel of the seats as the darkness descended; and the figure-hugging red uniform—a vast improvement on the navy tunic and shapeless pullover she wore on weekdays.

Her parents hadn't been keen on her applying for the job, but they had been so desperate for her to stay on at school that they'd agreed to the trade-off. She had planned to leave at fifteen, like Gina, and take a secretarial course, but instead she was studying for A-levels in English, history, and geography. She was the only colored girl in the sixth form at Wolverhampton Girls High School, but it didn't matter because nobody knew.

It was a lot of work, fooling them. She took hot irons to her hair every morning and wound it into a tight bun caught up in an invisible net. This and a liberal dose of extrastrong hairspray guarded against any frizz brought on by the weather. And although makeup was strictly forbidden, she had discovered a cream in the chemist's that was meant for teenagers with acne. With a consistency like clotted cream, it gave her skin the desired pallor. As far as her classmates were concerned, she was as white as everyone else. But she kept them at arm's length, all the same. She never felt quite at ease with these girls, who mostly came from comfortable homes in the leafy suburbs. Perhaps it was because she knew she was deceiving them. But she had deceived Gina too, so that couldn't be it. Whatever the reason, she simply didn't belong. She couldn't wait to escape at the end of the week.

On this particular Saturday night the cinema was packed, with only a handful of seats left. She was standing at the back, by the door, when she felt it push open. A couple of latecomers muttered an apology. She flashed her torch over a tangle of arms and legs on the back row. She hated it when people came in halfway through a film. As the couple scrambled to their seats, to moans and curses from the lovers, she turned her attention back to the screen. Rita Moreno was running up the steps to the roof of a tenement building in Manhattan. This was Louisa's favorite part of the film. She had seen it eleven times, but it never failed to thrill.

She slipped into the little alcove where boxes of sweets were stacked from floor to ceiling. There was a hard fold-up chair for the usherettes to sit on, but she pushed it against the wall. A strip of red velvet curtain screened off the alcove, with a mesh square halfway up that allowed whoever was inside to keep an eye on the audience. And the screen.

They were all on the roof now, the Sharks and their girlfriends. Rita Moreno was strutting and swishing the full skirt of her pink taffeta dress. Her pointed satin shoes tapped out "A-mer-i-cah." Louisa had each movement down pat. Her uniform swirling against the sweet boxes, she sang along in the certain knowledge that no one in the audience could hear or see her. Rita Moreno sashayed across the roof, magnificent in her contempt. Stamping her feet. Spitting the words at the light-skinned boys who danced in her wake.

The music faded and Louisa peered through the mesh at the couples on the other side. She recognized several regulars. Boys with the same girls; boys and girls who swapped partners from one week to the next; and one particular boy who seemed to have a different girl every time.

As she watched them necking and fondling each other in the semidarkness, she wondered what it would be like to kiss a boy. In her head it was always the way it was in the films. Sometimes she would lie in bed at night, close her eyes, and try to picture kissing Elvis Presley or Dirk Bogarde. But she couldn't imagine ever being in the back row of the Odeon with a real boy.

When the film ended and the lights went up, she could hear the groans of disappointment from the gropers.

"Lou!" She heard a loud whisper from the other side of the curtain. The voice belonged to Ray, the junior projectionist. She drew back the curtain, blinking in the brightness. Ray was eighteen, taller than her but only just, with large blue eyes smiling eagerly from a face marred by a volcanic spot on the left-hand side of his nose.

"What time are you finishing tonight?" His tone was casual, matter-of-fact. She wondered if his father, who managed the cinema, had sent him down to check up on her.

"Ten o'clock." She frowned. "Why?"

"Oh." He looked at the carpet. "It's only that I'm going over your way later to pick up some stuff for Dad. Thought you might like a lift home."

"Oh . . . er, thanks." Louisa felt herself blushing. "It's okay, though—my dad's coming to meet me." She looked at him and saw that he was blushing too.

"Oh, right." He thrust his hands in his trouser pockets and shrugged. "Another time, maybe?"

"Er, yes," she gulped. "Another time." She watched him as he wove in and out of the crush of people making for the exits. He reminded her of a big puppy, all legs and eyes. She swallowed again and felt her mouth go dry. What was she going to say if he asked her again?

~

Gina coughed as the lid came off the box of Coty's loose powder, sending a small white cloud shooting up her nose. "Oh no! It's gone over the bedspread!"

"It's okay—it'll come off." Louisa leaned across the bed and smacked the cover, sending the powder flying out onto the lino beneath. "Are you sure your sister's not going to mind us using her stuff?" She lay back on the pillow, her face plastered with a layer of foundation.

"She won't find out as long as I put it all back before she gets home." Gina dipped the huge powder puff into the box and dabbed it onto Louisa's forehead, cheeks, and chin. "Right: no looking!" She rummaged in the makeup bag. "Eye shadow next, and then some mascara."

"Gina." Louisa tried not to move her face too much as she spoke. "What do you think of Ray Brandon?"

Through half-closed eyes Louisa saw Gina's mouth split into a grin. "He fancies you! I knew it!"

"He does not!" Louisa raised herself on her elbows, sending the mascara sliding off the bed.

"Oh yes he does!" Gina smirked, bending down to retrieve the mirrored box, which had parted company with the little brush when it hit the floor. "My sister told me!"

Louisa frowned. "Told you what?"

"That Ray Brandon wants to ask you out: he plays football with Donna's boyfriend."

"Well, I don't fancy *him*!" She wasn't sure if she meant it or not. Ray was not like the screen idols she kissed in her fantasies. But since the night he'd asked to take her home, she'd found herself stealing glances at him when she was at work. Once she'd even made an excuse to go up to the projection room, just to check how she felt when he looked at her.

"He's going to the Christmas Ball at the Civic Hall." Gina wiggled her eyebrows suggestively. "What will you do if he asks you for a dance?"

Louisa shrugged, studying her new face in the mirror.

"Could be a bit awkward, couldn't it," Gina said, "with you both working at the same place, I mean."

Louisa's head dropped. "I might not be working there much longer. My parents want me to give it up so I can spend more time studying." She sighed. "They never wanted me to take the job in the first place."

"Really! I've always been dead jealous of you, getting to see all the films." Gina spat on the black cake of mascara and rubbed the brush in it. "What will you do when you finish school?"

"Dad wants me to go to teacher training college."

Gina pulled a face.

"I know. Every time he says it, I get this mental image of myself in thirty years' time looking all gray and woolly like Miss Pudney—remember her?"

"Oh, please! Promise me you won't turn out like her!" Gina applied the mascara brush to Louisa's eyelashes, turning them into spider legs. "What about doing something really glamorous? Acting, maybe. Wish I could do that."

"Hmm," Louisa murmured, trying to keep still. "Don't think I'd be much good at that. I wouldn't mind being a dancer, though. In a film like *West Side Story*."

"Yes, I can just picture you." Gina laughed. "You've got the legs for it—not short and fat like mine!"

Louisa smiled, suddenly transported back to her childhood days at the farm. Dancer's legs. That was what the shearers used to say.

"You'd have to move to London, though," Gina went on. "No chance of doing that round here!"

"Well, that's out, then." Louisa shrugged and smiled, blinking as her eyelashes stuck together. "I couldn't possibly leave my parents."

Gina frowned. "You mean you're going to carry on living with them till you're an old lady? Not get married or anything?"

"No, I don't mean that—not that anyone's ever likely to want to marry me—I mean I couldn't ever live far away from them."

"Why not?"

She closed her mouth momentarily as Gina homed in to apply a coat of sugar-pink to her lips. "I had a brother, but he died." She felt a twinge of guilt at her poker-faced reflection.

"Oh—you never said!" Gina looked embarrassed.

"I don't remember him: I was only two when he died. But my mum's never been the same since, according to my dad. From when I was tiny, he's always said to me: 'You won't ever leave us, will you, Lou, because you're all we've got.'"

"Hmm." Gina dabbed spots of rouge onto Louisa's cheeks. "Well, *my* dad always says you've got to follow your dream." She zipped up the makeup bag. "There! You look fantastic!"

"Do I?" Louisa stared uncertainly into the mirror. "I'll have to wear something with long sleeves: look at my hairy arms!" She stuck out her elbows.

"They're not hairy!" Gina laughed. "Not compared to Donna's anyway—did you know she waxes them as well as her legs?"

Louisa winced. "That sounds painful."

"I don't know why you're always putting yourself down." Gina sat down next to her, the mirror capturing both their faces. "I wish I had your skin," she said. "Look at me—all spotty!"

Louisa frowned. If only Gina knew how much she hated her own skin. *To be spotty was far better*, she thought. *At least the spots would go.*

~

It was snowing outside, and Louisa was alone in the house. Both of her parents were at work. Her mother had recently started a new part-time job at the town library. It had been her father's idea. Her mother would never have had the confidence to apply for it. One of his friends at the office had told him about the vacancy, and he had gone to the library himself and come home with the application form.

The effect on her mother had been amazing. For the first time in years she was animated, talkative. And she was being so much— Louisa struggled to find the right word for what she sensed was happening between her parents—kinder. That was it. Her mum was doing thoughtful things that made Dad happy. Like taking him breakfast in bed on a Sunday morning before she went to church, or rubbing his shoulders when he'd been out with a shovel clearing snow.

Louisa pushed another shilling in the meter and pulled the table as close to the electric fire as she could without incinerating what she was sewing. She glanced at the clock as her foot worked the treadle of the machine. Her mother should be back from town soon.

She eased the pink taffeta under the foot of the machine. It was tricky stuff to sew, but it would be worth it when it was finished. She was copying Rita Moreno's dress for the Christmas Ball. And with her new makeup she was going to have Audrey Hepburn's eyes.

The sound of the doorbell made her slip, the needle almost jabbing her finger. She snapped down the foot and dragged the table away from the fire, worried that the slightest breath of air might blow the precious fabric onto the glowing bars. The bell rang again, followed by a thumping on the door. "I'm coming!" She ran down the hall and turned the handle. Standing in front of her was a tall man in a heavy overcoat, his face half-hidden by a gray woolen scarf. Snowflakes were melting on his black hair.

"Louisa?" His mouth twisted up on one side as his eyes searched her face. She felt a shiver of foreboding, though he looked vaguely familiar.

"Don't you recognize me, girl? I'm your uncle Trefor. From Wales!" He laughed. A short, humorless chuckle. "Aren't you going to invite me in?"

As she took his coat, images flooded her mind. This was the sneering man who had turned up at her aunt's funeral and called her names, then thrown her and her parents out of the farmhouse when his mother was barely cold in her grave.

"I . . . there's no one here," she faltered.

"Well, you can make me a cup of tea, can't you?" He pushed past her into the front room. Reluctantly she shut the door and followed. She saw the smug look as he took in the decor and the furniture, as if the contrast between her home and the farmhouse gave him immense satisfaction.

"No school today, then?" The smile he gave her now was conspiratorial as his eyes traveled up and down her body.

She shook her head, mortified. "Last day was Friday."

"Well, get the kettle on, girl: I've come a long way, you know. And I've brought you something!"

She shuffled wordlessly out of the room, perspiration prickling her skin. The way he had looked at her made her feel dirty. She stayed in the kitchen while the kettle boiled, hoping her parents would be home soon to save her from having to make polite conversation with this horrible man. Then she heard his footsteps coming along the hall.

"The watched pot never boils, Louisa—didn't your mam ever tell you that?" He took something from his jacket pocket and dangled it in front of her. A silver pendant, the shape of a diamond, with a Celtic cross engraved on it and a violet-colored gemstone at its center. "It's an amethyst," he said. "Belonged to your aunt Rhiannon. She wanted you to have it when you were grown up— and you look pretty grown-up to me!"

She didn't like the look in his eyes as he said it.

"Hold still and I'll put it on." He leaned forward, his arms around her neck as he fastened the clasp. She stiffened, feeling his hot breath on her neck. He smelled of sweat and something else. Something sweet and unfamiliar.

"You're very tense, aren't you?" He pulled something else from his pocket. A small bottle of whiskey. "Here! Take a slug of this in your tea, girl! Loosen you up a bit!"

She opened her mouth to say no, but before she could get the word out, he was on her, pressing his lips against hers, shoving her against the cold kitchen wall.

"Yes, you really have grown up, haven't you? Nigger's child!" He pushed his hand up her skirt and she cried out, struggling to push him away. "Oh, playing hard to get, are we? I like that," he leered. "That's nice!"

She tried to scream, but he had his hand over her mouth now. Her head banged against the wall as he pushed her to the floor.

"Now, come on," he hissed. "Don't pretend you don't want it! Like your mother wanted it—from a nigger!"

Chapter 25

The kettle hissed as Trefor pulled away and began buttoning his trousers, oblivious to the sobs that shook Louisa's body. "Come on!" he barked. "Get up! Make the bloody tea!"

She stared at the ceiling, not hearing, not wanting even to look at him. Her limbs felt numb against the cold, hard lino.

"Get up, I said!" He kicked her in the ribs, and she yelped in pain. She struggled to her feet and cowered against the sink, fearful of more blows. "Come on," he snarled, "don't you know how to behave when you have a guest? Teapot! Cups!"

With trembling hands she spooned tea from the caddy and poured boiling water onto the leaves.

"That's better!" He smirked as she set the cup in front of him.

She stiffened as she felt his hand on her behind.

"I want you to give this to your dad," he said, reaching into his jacket pocket. "Your uncle Dai died last month, you know."

She didn't know. He was looking at her as if he expected her sympathy. She looked away, fixing her eyes on the pattern of triangles on the floor.

"This was left in his will." He handed her a piece of paper with numbers written on it and the name of a bank. "It's a check," he said. "Don't suppose you've ever seen one before, have you?"

She stared at it. Her parents' names were written in a delicate script on one line and the words "Five Hundred Pounds Only" below.

"A tidy sum, isn't it?" He looked about him. "Enough to get them out of this dump, anyhow." He took her chin in his hand, forcing her head around. "Aren't you going to thank me? I could have contested it, you know!" His eyes were boring into hers. "And I still might if you breathe a word of this to them!"

She could see his teeth between his lips. They were stained brown and lumps of white like chewed bread were stuck in the gaps where they met the gums.

"Did you hear what I said?" He shouted the words, making her jump. She nodded dumbly. "Right, then!" He drained his cup and banged it down on the draining board. "I'll be off. And remember, not a word!

"Congratulations, young lady!" He looked over his shoulder as he stepped out into the snow. "You've just become the most expensive tart in England!"

~

Louisa was lying huddled under her sheets when she heard the front door open. She froze, thinking he had managed to get back into the house.

"Lou!" It was her mother's voice. "I'm home!"

Louisa leapt out of bed, smoothed her clothes and grabbed a comb from the dressing table. She glanced at her reflection, afraid of the face staring back at her. She had crawled under the covers like a wounded animal when he left and lain there, paralyzed, unable to think or do anything. She felt dirty. His smell was still upon her. And she was terrified that her mother would be able to read what had happened in her face.

She walked unsteadily to the stairs. "Up here," she called. Even her voice sounded different.

"I'm in such a state!" Her mother's short, shrill laugh drifted up the stairs. "I had to wait an hour and a half for the bus! It's absolute chaos in town." A pause and then, "Would you make me a cup of tea, love? I'm chilled to the bone!"

Louisa came down slowly, gripping the banister.

"Are you all right, love?" Eva caught sight of her as she draped her coat over the wooden ball that topped the stair rail. "You look a bit peaky."

"I'm fine," Louisa mumbled, "just a bit of a headache."

"Take an aspirin with your tea—it's all that sewing, you know, that's what's caused it!" Eva followed her into the kitchen and saw the two cups on the draining board, one empty and the other full of cold tea. "Has Gina been round?" She took the full cup and poured its contents down the sink.

"No." Louisa busied herself with the kettle so that her back was to her mother. "Uncle Trefor called." Saying his name made her feel sick. "From Wales. He brought something for you and Dad."

"Trefor!" Eva gasped. "That devil had the cheek to come to our house?"

Louisa turned and saw that her mother's face had turned bright red. "He brought this," she said, opening the kitchen drawer. She grasped a corner of the check between her nails, as if it were contaminated.

"What is it?"

"He said it was a check." Louisa passed it to Eva.

"Five hundred pounds!" Eva put out a hand, bracing herself against the draining board. "Is this some kind of sick joke?"

"He said it was in Uncle Dai's will."

"Will?" Eva blinked. "Dai's dead? When's the funeral? We must go!"

"I think they've probably had it already. Uncle—" She gulped, not wanting to say the loathsome name again. "He said Uncle Dai died last month."

"Last month?" Eva echoed, staring at the piece of paper in her hand. She shook her head slowly. "Oh, it must have grieved Trefor to part with this!" She paced the narrow kitchen, clutching the check to her chest. "Your aunt Rhiannon must have wanted us to have it—that's what it would have been, I bet—but it would all have gone to Dai until . . ." She stopped, looking at Louisa. "How was he? Was he nasty about it?"

Louisa looked away. "He . . . er . . . no, not really," she mumbled, fighting down the sick feeling welling up inside.

"No wonder he didn't hang around!" Eva grunted a laugh. "Bet he couldn't bear the thought of seeing my face when he handed it over!" She disappeared into the hall, returning with her handbag. Unzipping one of its compartments, she slid the check carefully inside. "Wait till your dad sees it! We'll be able to put down a deposit on one of those lovely new houses in Fir Grove!" She beamed at Louisa, "And tomorrow we'll go to Beatties and buy you a whole new outfit! Something really stunning for the Christmas Ball!"

"It's okay, really," Louisa spooned tea into the pot and emptied the steaming kettle over the leaves. "You spend it on yourself and Dad. I don't need any of it, honest." She left Eva standing in the kitchen and went through to the front room. Gathering up the pink taffeta, she slipped it under the foot of the sewing machine and began pumping the treadle. Pumping and pumping, as if its noisy whirring would drive the screaming from her mind.

~

The snow had melted by the night of the Christmas Ball, but it remained bitterly cold. Eva had insisted on buying Louisa a fur wrap to wear over the dress she had made.

"Ooh, that's gorgeous!" Gina said when she came to the house. "It's real, isn't it?" She stroked the soft white fur. "What is it?"

"I . . . er . . . I don't know." It wasn't a lie. She had accepted the gift but had not wanted to know anything about it. Especially not how much it had cost.

"Come on!" Gina tugged her arm. "We'd better get going." She looked Louisa up and down and smiled. "You do realize Ray's going to go completely gooey when he sees you?"

Louisa shrugged and followed Gina out of the house, trying to feel enthusiastic about the evening ahead. Both of them had been looking forward to it for weeks, planning what they were going to wear, and practicing their makeup. But tonight Louisa felt nothing. For the past few days she had been going through the motions of living. Speaking only when she had to. Hiding away in her room. And at night she was afraid to go to sleep. Afraid to close her eyes, because it was then, when everything was quiet, that the images in her head threatened to engulf her. And it was then that she wanted to scream.

When they arrived at the Civic Hall, the band was playing "Take Good Care of My Baby." She wished they'd hurry up and play something faster. Like "Runaway" or "Let's Twist Again," so she could dance herself into oblivion. As the number faded, she caught sight of Ray. He was on the other side of the room talking to Gina's sister and her boyfriend. She had never seen him in a suit before. *It made him look much older*, she thought. And his hair. That was different too. It was swept up in a quiff, which made him look a bit like Eddie Cochran. He turned and, catching sight of her, gave her a little wave. She stood rooted to the spot, arms clamped to her sides. The band struck up again. "Runaround Sue." Ray was coming over.

"He's going to ask you for a dance!" Gina squealed delightedly. "Go on!" She gave Louisa a little push. "Now's your chance!"

"Hello, Lou." He stood awkwardly in front of her, as if his new shoes were a bit too tight. "You look really . . . nice!"

She bit her lip. She didn't feel nice. The fur and the taffeta would have looked lovely on someone else. And the makeup. When she had looked at herself in the mirror, she had seen a clown's face staring back at her. Everything about her felt false.

"Would you like to dance?" Ray was blushing.

"Yes," she said suddenly, grabbing his hand. "I would. Come on!"

All over the dance floor couples were moving energetically to the music, the girls' skirts swinging out as their partners spun them around. Louisa let herself become Ray's puppet, bending and spinning as if her body were made of rubber. Some other girl's ponytail swished against her face like a whip, and a man's shoe crunched her toes as the crowd on the dance floor grew into a crush. But she didn't feel a thing. As one fast number gave way to another, she was aware of nothing but the music. If Ray hadn't offered, she would have danced with anyone who asked her. She needed some other man's face to obliterate the leering, sneering one that hung in the space before her eyes.

They broke off only once, both of them gasping for something to drink. Ray was still at the bar when the slow numbers came on, and Louisa dived into the ladies' room. She dabbed fresh powder onto her face, which was streaked with perspiration. There was a bare patch of skin where she had wiped her forehead with the back of her hand. It looked very dark in the stark fluorescent light over the washbasin. She wondered if Ray had noticed.

When she emerged, Ray was standing at the edge of the dance floor with the drinks, looking self-conscious, as if he thought she'd run out on him.

"Can I take you home after this?" he asked, as they sat down.

She hesitated before replying, looking around for Gina.

"It's okay." Ray grinned. "I'll give Gina a lift too, as long as we drop her off first!"

~

Ray's dad's van smelled of popcorn. Louisa was squashed between Gina and Ray, and every time he changed gear, Ray's hand brushed against her leg. When they reached Gina's house, Louisa felt an overwhelming urge to jump out with her.

"Have fun!" Gina winked at her from the pavement. "Don't do anything I wouldn't do!"

As the door slammed Louisa shivered. She couldn't get out here. How would she explain it to Gina's parents? How would she get home?

"Are you cold?" Ray put his hand on her shoulder. "Do you want my jacket?"

She shook her head. "I'm fine, honest." She felt sick. The way she felt every time Trefor's smell drifted from that dark place in her memory. She took a breath. "Ray?"

He smiled. "What?"

"Could we go somewhere? Not go straight back to my house, I mean?"

"Sure, if that's what you want." He was still smiling, but he looked surprised. "Where d'you want to go?"

"Anywhere you like," she replied, shocked at the way she sounded, but meaning it.

Ten minutes later Ray pulled into an unlit road that quickly turned into a single-track country lane. He swerved suddenly to the right and turned off the engine. Through the windscreen Louisa could just make out a farm gate. Ray reached for her in the darkness, his arm slipping around her shoulders, pulling her to him. She stiffened as she felt his lips on hers.

"Hey," he murmured. "Relax!" He kissed her again. This time she felt his tongue sliding into her mouth. She backed away.

"You haven't done this before, have you?" he whispered. She shook her head violently. "Don't worry," he put his hand on her knee as he came closer. "I won't hurt you. Promise."

She let him kiss her neck but flinched as his mouth slid toward the neckline of her dress. As his hands began fumbling with the zipper, she felt the numbness overwhelming her again. She shouldn't, wouldn't be doing this if it wasn't for . . . She slithered down onto the seat, putting up no resistance when Ray slid his hands inside her bra. She had to blot out that terrible memory. Ray seemed kind. He had told her she looked nice: something no boy had ever said to her before. Now, when she closed her eyes, she would see Ray's face instead of . . .

"Are you sure?" She could hear the uncertainty in his voice as he pushed away the rustling layers of her skirt, pressing himself against her.

"Y . . . yes," she whispered. "I . . . it's okay."

He didn't hurt her the way Trefor had. She had her eyes tight shut and lay motionless as he rocked on top of her. She thought of Elvis in *Blue Hawaii,* but it didn't help.

When it was over, Ray offered her his handkerchief. She wondered whether he was being a gentleman or was just worried about messing up his dad's van.

"Are you all right?" he said, as she smoothed out her dress.

She caught her breath, her throat tight with the threat of tears. "Yes," she mumbled. Perhaps she would be. Perhaps next time it would be better.

Chapter 26

Gina turned the record player up to full volume and grabbed Louisa, who was perched on the edge of the bed. As Sam Cooke belted out "Twistin' the Night Away," Gina shimmied her way down to the floor and back. Louisa watched, stubbing out an imaginary cigarette with the toe of her left shoe, a token attempt to join in.

"Come on, Lou!" Gina shouted. "What's wrong with you? I thought you loved this!" She reached over the bed and turned down the music. "He hasn't broken up with you, has he?"

Louisa shook her head.

"So what's wrong? Come on, tell me! What's up?"

Louisa hunched herself up on the bed and stared at the Cliff Richard poster on Gina's wall. "I think I'm pregnant, Gina."

The music gave way to the slow, rhythmic scratch of the needle in the groove. It was a mournful sound. *No more dancing for you.*

"Say something, for God's sake."

"Oh, Lou—please say you're joking."

"I'm not joking."

"You mean you've actually done it with him?"

"I knew you wouldn't approve. That's why I didn't tell you."

Gina flopped down beside her on the bed. "But I thought you weren't all that keen on him! Why did you let him, Lou?"

"I don't know." She bit her lip. "Maybe I just wanted to know what it was like."

"How many times?"

Louisa shrugged again, staring at the ceiling.

"God, Lou! What are you going to do?"

"I don't know!" Louisa's voice wobbled and broke, tears spilling onto the pink candlewick bedspread.

"You'll have to tell him." Gina put her arm around Louisa. "He'll have to marry you, won't he?"

Louisa didn't reply. She burrowed frantically in her sleeve for a handkerchief.

"Do you want to marry him?"

"If he wants me." Louisa sniffed. "Why not?"

"If *he* wants *you*?" Gina jumped to her feet. "What about what *you* want?"

"Well, let's face it. No one else is going to want me, are they?"

~

A few hours later Louisa was in Ray's dad's van, hurtling along the same country lane he had pulled into that first night. It looked very different in the dying sunlight of a spring evening. There were sheep grazing beyond the fence on one side, hay piled into a rusty metal manger near the gate where Ray had pulled in. It looked so bucolic and innocent until you spotted the shriveled remains of used condoms lying on the muddy grass verge. Why hadn't Ray used one of those?

He was taking her to a fair in one of the nearby fields. She didn't feel like going, but she didn't want to talk either. She hoped the noise and the people would keep her safe: prevent her from giving away what was on her mind. She'd been rehearsing ways to say it for the past three months. Every time she opened her mouth to tell him, she clamped it shut again, terrified of the consequences, of the net that was closing around her.

Ray had just been paid and insisted on taking her on every fairground ride at least twice. As their bumper car lurched into life for the second time, Elvis Presley's latest hit boomed out from the loudspeaker: "I Can't Help Falling in Love with You." Ray sang along, steering with one hand and squeezing her shoulder with the other.

Louisa flinched as another car bashed into them. He was so happy, and she was going to ruin his life. It was all her fault. She was the one who had led him on. He had been willing enough, but she sensed Ray was the type who would have settled for a good-night kiss on the first date. And if they had stuck to that, if they had waited: might she feel differently about him now?

There was a loud bang as a car hit them from behind, sending them crashing into the barrier. Louisa suddenly felt sick. She scrambled out of the car and jumped over the barrier, oblivious to Ray's shouts.

"What did you do that for?" he gasped as he caught up with her a few minutes later. "We still had five minutes left!"

"I don't feel very well," she mumbled. "All those bangs and crashes . . ."

"Oh, I'm sorry, sweetheart!" His round, blue eyes were full of concern. "Do you want to go and sit down somewhere?"

There was nowhere to sit but the grass, so Ray threw his coat down for her. He put his arm around her and held her close. A few yards away the Ferris wheel tumbled and turned, casting spangles of colored light across their faces. Roy Orbison's "Dream Baby" drifted across the field.

"I love you, Lou . . ."

He was nuzzling her hair with his face, and her eyes filled with tears. He had never said that before. She could tell that he was waiting for her to say it back.

"Ray," she began, "there's something I've got to tell you."

~

"Marry her!" Eddie Melrose stared at the gangling teenager standing on the brand-new carpet in his brand-new living room. Ray's face had gone bright red, which made his latest crop of spots even more noticeable. His blond quiff had wilted in the heat from the Melroses' new gas fire. He looked a mess, Louisa knew that, and she felt desperately sorry for him.

Was that how she was always going to feel? Would she ever be able to tell him she loved him and mean it? She had a sudden image of herself in an apron, cooking his dinner. Day after day, year after year. Was that what it was going to be like? A tide of panic rose inside her.

"I'm sorry, son," Eddie said, his face as livid as Ray's, "I can't possibly give you an answer until I've talked to my daughter about it. So if you don't mind . . ." He held open the door and ushered Ray out into the hall. "Stay there, please," he said to Louisa as she tried to follow. "You can come back this evening," he called after Ray. "I'll have an answer for you then." Louisa heard the door slam shut. For a moment the house was absolutely silent.

When Eddie came back into the room, there were beads of sweat on his forehead. "Does your mother know about this?"

"No, Dad." Louisa stared at the swirls on the pristine carpet. The new house. Her parents were so proud of this fresh start. Now she was going to ruin their lives.

"I'm going to ask you a straight question, Lou, and I want a straight answer." She could hear the fear in her father's voice. "Has this . . . this Ray, put you in the family way?"

She nodded, eyes glued to the carpet.

"I'll kill him!" Eddie leapt to his feet. "I'll bloody kill the little bugger!"

"Dad, please!" She ran over to him, trying to take his arm. "It wasn't his fault!"

"What?" He shook her off. "You mean you . . ." He trailed off, unable to put it in words. "Oh God, Lou!" He slumped back into the armchair, which was still in its plastic wrapping. "I thought we'd brought you up better than that!"

"You have! You did!"

The look on his face was too much to bear. But she couldn't tell him, couldn't explain why it had happened. Knowing the truth would tear him apart.

"Please, Dad, don't be cross!" Tears spilled from her eyes. As she rubbed them away, she saw that he was crying too.

"Do you love him?"

"I . . ." she gulped back a sob.

"Because if you don't, you don't have to marry him. You know that, don't you?"

"Wha . . . what are you saying?"

"You could have the baby adopted."

"What?" Her mouth fell open. She was staring straight at him, wondering if he had said the same words to her mother.

"Do you love him?" Eddie repeated.

She nodded once, twice, not trusting herself to speak, knowing it was herself she was trying to convince.

He sighed and wiped his eyes on the sleeve of his shirt. "We'd better tell your mother, then." He put his head in his hands. "God knows what this is going to do to her!"

Louisa followed him to the door. She felt strangely relieved. As if in letting this secret out, she had made up for the months of keeping silent, of watching her parents spend that dirty money.

And now she was going to marry Ray and have his baby. *His* baby. She wouldn't allow herself to believe anything else.

~

"Louisa's got something to tell you," Eddie began as Eva kicked off her shoes and settled down with a cup of tea at the kitchen table.

"I'm getting married, Mam," Louisa mumbled.

"What?"

"I'm getting married to Ray from the Odeon. And we're going to have a baby." The words came tumbling out like a shopping list, breathless and bereft of emotion.

Her mother froze, the teacup halfway between the saucer and her mouth.

"Say something, Mam," Louisa pleaded. "I know it's not what you and Dad wanted, but . . ."

"A baby?" Eva blinked. "You're having a baby?"

"Yes." Louisa held her breath.

"But you're seventeen!" Her mother's eyes ranged wildly around the room.

"I know I need your permission. Ray came round this morning to ask Dad."

Eva's frantic gaze fixed on Eddie. "And you agreed?"

"No, love." His face was anguished. "I told him to come back tonight when we'd had a chance to discuss it."

She turned to Louisa. "What about your exams? You were going to be a teacher!"

"I never said that, Mam. It's what you and Dad wanted. I—"

"Sounds like you've made your mind up already!" Eva cut in. "Does he know? This . . . Ray?"

"Know what? That I'm still at school? Of course he does!"

Her mother's face told her this was not what she meant. Louisa went cold. Had Trefor said something? Had he written to her parents?

"Know what?" she repeated.

Eva hesitated. "About . . . your real father. About him being . . . you know."

Louisa stared at Eva in blank amazement. This was the first time in six years her mother had spoken of him.

"Why on earth would I tell him that?" Louisa's expression was a mixture of defiance and curiosity. "Do *you* want him to know?" She wanted to add: "Because you never wanted *me* to!" But she stopped herself. She didn't want to hurt her mother any more than she'd wanted to hurt her dad.

"I just don't want there to be any . . . you know," Eva paused and gulped her tea. "Any surprises."

Louisa frowned. "What do you mean?"

"Does he realize the baby could be . . ."

"Could be what?"

"Colored." Eva pressed her lips together so that all the blood went out of them. "Dark-skinned, anyway. Darker than you."

"Darker than me?" Louisa's voice bounced off the walls of the kitchen. "How could it be darker than me? Ray's got blond hair and blue eyes!"

"Yes, but it doesn't always work like that," Eva said quietly.

"What do you mean? How do you know?"

Eva let out a long breath. Her eyes were fixed on the table. "When I was pregnant with you, I went to see a doctor," she whispered. "He told me I should put you in a children's home. He said I'd only be storing up misery for myself if I kept you, because the color would come out for generations and generations." She reached for her teacup, cradling it in her hands. "He warned me I might have a light-skinned child who could give birth to a . . ." she faltered, staring into the cup. "To a black baby."

"So why did you keep me, then?" Louisa's lips trembled as the words came out.

"I . . ." Eva's voice broke away and she jumped up, tea slopping over the rim of the cup and staining the tablecloth. "Just tell Ray, will you?"

Louisa heard her mother's footsteps thudding up the stairs. She looked at her father and saw that his face was drained of color. It occurred to her that he had not heard any of this until now.

"What can I do, Dad?" Her voice sounded small, like a child's.

"I don't know, love." Eddie sank into the chair Eva had vacated. "Let's cross one bridge at a time, shall we?"

~

When Ray came at six o'clock, he was not alone. His mother and father were standing on the doorstep with him when Louisa answered the door.

"She looks foreign," Mrs. Brandon said when Ray introduced them. "Is she English?"

Ray looked as embarrassed as Louisa felt. "Don't take any notice of my mum," he whispered. "She's a bit shocked, that's all."

"She's a good little worker, though, Edna!" Ray's father patted Louisa on the head as he handed her his coat. "If she looks after our Ray half as well as the folks that come to the Odeon, he'll be a happy man!"

Louisa showed them into the living room, uncertain how to behave toward her boss now that he was about to become her father-in-law.

"Your wife's not at home?" Mr. Brandon said, after being introduced to Eddie.

"She's not well," Eddie glanced up at the ceiling. "Having a nap."

"I'm not surprised, with all this upset!" Edna Brandon sank into one of the polythene-swathed armchairs, taking in the newly decorated house and its modern furniture. "Very nice, I'm sure," she said, raising one eyebrow. "Just moved in, have you?"

Eddie nodded.

"Where were you before?"

"Sycamore Street."

The eyebrow went up another half inch. "And your Louisa," she pronounced the name as if it were an exotic fruit she'd never heard of. "You adopted her, did you?"

Louisa glanced at Ray. If he was surprised at his mother's question, he didn't show it.

Eddie hesitated, but only for a moment. "Yes, that's right."

"And the parents?"

"Father's an American."

Louisa saw her father giving Ray's mother a conspiratorial look. She wondered what he was up to.

"Oh, I see," Mrs. Brandon nodded slowly.

"One of those Hispanics, I suppose?" Mr. Brandon piped up.

"We don't know much about him," Eddie replied. He stood up and went over to the drinks cabinet, exchanging glances with Louisa. "Now, can I get you both a drink?" He beamed at Ray's parents, "A glass of sherry, Mrs. Brandon? Or would you prefer a Babycham?"

~

Louisa and Ray were married at the end of May, four weeks before her eighteenth birthday.

Wolverhampton Registry Office was gray and unromantic. And the elastic girdle her mother had bought from Beatties underwear department did nothing to stop Louisa's white satin dress from riding up at the front.

"Marry in May, rue the day," Ray's mother muttered as they stood in front of the registrar. With only a few feet of empty space between them, she must have known Louisa would hear it.

"You look beautiful, Lou," Ray said as he kissed her.

Louisa closed her eyes and kissed him back, hoping rockets would explode and violins strike up in her head. But all she could hear was the wail of a police siren in the street outside. "It's going to be all right, Ray, isn't it?" Her lips trembled as she spoke.

"Yes, sweetheart," he hugged her to him. "Of course it is!"

Chapter 27

Louisa was terrified. Not of the pain, although that was bad enough. She was scared of the child that was now fighting its way out of her body.

During the last month of her pregnancy she had had two recurring nightmares. In the first her baby was a miniature version of Trefor. As she reached to pick him up, his tiny hands turned into snakes that wrapped themselves around her throat. In the second dream she gave birth to a child with black skin and no face.

She found the nightmares equally disturbing, forcing her to confront the very things she had tried her utmost to deny. The awful reality was that she had no idea who her baby's father was. She and Ray had had sex three times in the two weeks either side of Christmas. That had to make him a more likely contender than Trefor, didn't it? Besides, she told herself, Trefor was old. He was older than her mother, so he must be at least forty. Men that age didn't father babies, did they?

Her mother's warning that the child might be dark-skinned had eaten away at her. Ray would never believe that a black baby could be his. She hadn't breathed a word of what Eva had suggested. She was too scared of losing him. She could just imagine his parents' reaction if they found out their precious son had married a half-caste, as Ray's dad called one little boy who came to the Saturday morning shows at the Odeon.

Once, when she and Ray had driven into town with his mother, they had passed a black man and a white woman kissing on a street corner. "Look at that!" Edna Brandon had hissed, her nose in the air. "In broad daylight too! Disgusting, I call it!"

Louisa had been unable to resist a long look at the couple, realizing that her mother must have done just that with her real father. She suddenly found herself wondering how they had met, what places they had gone to together. And how she had felt about him.

She had thought about it a lot when she was in bed that night. *But she can't even remember his name,* she reminded herself. With a sinking feeling she came to the conclusion that it couldn't have been anything more than a one-night stand. She had tried to tell herself that it didn't matter. She had a dad. A better one than many real fathers. But no matter how much she tried to convince herself, it hurt her to think that this nameless, faceless man had cared so little about her mother, had used her without a moment's thought of the consequences. In fact, she thought, what he had done made him almost as bad as Trefor.

She was all alone now, in a brightly lit, sparsely furnished hospital side room. The midwife had left her, saying the baby would be ages yet. She gripped the side of the bed as a contraction turned her belly into a tight ball of pain. She wished her mother was with her. Or her dad. Or even Ray. She didn't understand why women were expected to go through something as frightening as this with only strangers for company.

As the pain subsided, she thought of the farmhouse in Wales. Of the bedroom her mother had told her she was born in. The thought of Trefor lying in that big iron bed made her feel sick.

She cried out as another violent contraction racked her body. "Nurse!" she gasped, trying to slide a leg off the high bed. She thumped her fist on the mattress in a bid to get through the fog of pain. "Help me!"

As an irritated face appeared around the door, Louisa slithered onto the hard hospital floor. "Quick, Joyce!" she heard the nurse shout. "I can see the head!"

Seconds later Louisa heard a strange sound. Like a hungry cat unable to get at its food.

"It's a boy!" The midwife's round, shiny face came into view. She was clutching a bundle in a bloodstained towel. "Let's get you back on the bed, and then you can hold him."

All Louisa could see was a slick of black hair poking out of the towel. As she took her son in her arms, she pulled back the folds to reveal an angry little face with eyes tight shut and a mouth pulled wide with the effort of crying. His nose butted her arm as he burrowed into her skin. She stared at his tiny head, so fragile looking but so strong in its sure, instinctive search for her breast.

"Oh God," she said, as she and the midwife exchanged smiles for the first time. "He looks just like me!"

The midwife laughed. "Don't sound so surprised! I'll give you a few minutes, then I'll come and clean him up. Is your husband about?"

Louisa nodded. Ray had told her he wasn't going to leave the hospital, no matter how long she was in labor.

"I'll go and tell him the good news. He can come and see you both at visiting time." She shut the door behind her, and Louisa lay staring at her baby as he tugged at her breast. She felt a rush of euphoria. Relief that he didn't look like Trefor. Relief that his skin was the same pale brown as her own. But it was more than that. To her amazement she realized that what she felt was love. In an instant she knew why her mother had ignored the advice of the doctor all those years ago. Her mother must have felt the way she did now. Prepared to face anything life might throw at her, whatever the consequences, for the sake of this tiny bundle in her arms.

When Ray arrived, his face was half-hidden by an enormous bunch of flowers. He stood awkwardly in the doorway, looking from Louisa to the wooden cot, as if he didn't know which to approach first. Suddenly he darted across the room, pecked her on the cheek and then went straight to the baby, pulling the blanket from his sleeping body.

"What are you doing, Ray?" She felt a stab of fear.

"Counting his fingers and toes," Ray replied without looking up. "It's all right—they're all there!"

She smiled to herself. This wasn't the way it happened in films. Ray was supposed to give her a big hug, call her darling and tell her how clever and beautiful she was. Then he would gaze adoringly at his baby son and say something profound about their lives being complete. Despite the smile, there were tears in her eyes. Because she knew it was never going to be like it was in the films for her and Ray. It had mattered until today: mattered very much. But now she wasn't sure it mattered anymore.

~

The next day her mother was allowed to come and visit.

"Dad'll be along this evening when he's finished work," Eva said as she kissed her daughter and made for the cot. "Oh Lou!" Her voice wobbled as she caught sight of her grandson. "He looks just like . . ." She turned away, pulling a handkerchief from her pocket.

"Like who, Mum?" Louisa raised herself up on her elbow.

Her mother shook her head and blew her nose. Louisa wondered whose face she had seen. Did the baby remind her of David? It seemed unlikely, given that he had been a fair-skinned blond.

Could it be him? Louisa thought. She remembered her nightmare of the faceless baby with black skin.

"His eyes!" Eva mumbled into her handkerchief. "They're . . . they're so . . ." She seemed incapable of finishing the sentence. Shaking her head, she reached out to stroke the baby's hand.

Louisa watched her intently. Her son's eyes were indigo blue, but the midwife had told her they would almost certainly change color during the first year of his life. "Dark brown, I should think," she'd said. "I've brought hundreds of babies into the world and I'm not usually wrong. Very dark brown, I'd say."

"They're so what, Mum? Who does he remind you of?" There, she had asked the question. She held her breath, as if she had just lit the blue touch paper of a firework.

"He's just so beautiful, Lou." Eva turned to her and smiled. That was it: the mask was back in place. There would be no opening up now, no hint of what Louisa so desperately wanted to know. "What are you going to call him?"

"We can't decide," Louisa said. "We're torn between Thomas and Timothy."

"Oh?" Eva looked quickly away, leaning over the baby. "They're both nice names. I do like Thomas, though. Can I hold him?"

Louisa nodded, studying her mother as she walked around the room, cradling the child in her arms. She was talking to him. Whispering something so softly, Louisa couldn't make it out. And suddenly her expression changed to one of such sadness that Louisa felt a lump in her throat. She thought of David: the black-and-white photo of a chubby, smiling little boy clutching a lamb in his arms. Suddenly she understood, for the first time, how the pain of losing a child must be the worst kind of pain imaginable. Was that what was creasing her mother's face with grief now? Or was it some other buried sorrow that Louisa was never going to be allowed to share?

Chapter 28
September 1967

Although autumn was just around the corner, the sun blazed down on the orchard at the back of the high Victorian terrace along Oaklands Road. Louisa watched Tom piling apples in a toy wheelbarrow. "Stay under the tree," she called. "It's too hot in the sun!" She left her chair in the shade of the building and darted across the grass to adjust his hat. "Don't want him to get sunstroke," she said, in answer to Gina's quizzical look.

Despite the heat Louisa was wearing a polo neck sweater and slacks. Gina had given up commenting on her summer wardrobe years ago, apparently satisfied with the explanation that Louisa had sensitive skin. If she had asked why Tom was not allowed to play in the sun, Louisa would have told her he had inherited the same problem. They had been friends for thirteen years, but that first big lie lay between them like a slumbering tiger.

"I don't know how you managed," Gina said, "when he was little, I mean—all those stairs!"

Louisa smiled. It had been hard, bringing up a baby in a second-floor flat. Up and down the narrow staircase with Tom in one arm and a pile of laundry in the other. Baby clothes strung on the line in all weathers because there was nowhere to hang them inside. Once, despairing at ever getting them dry, she had cut up one of her own skirts to pin around his little body. *Gina was lucky*, she thought. She had married a boy who had been a classmate of theirs. They lived in a brand-new council house with a front and back garden of their own, rather than the communal one Louisa and Ray shared with three sets of neighbors. And now Gina had a baby. A three-month-old girl, who was asleep in her pram under the apple tree.

"I should have been sensible, like you, shouldn't I?" Louisa smiled. She couldn't pretend she wasn't envious of Gina, but she didn't regret the way her life had turned out. Tom was her whole world. If things had been different, she wouldn't have had him, and that was unthinkable.

Perhaps Gina sensed they were straying onto dangerous ground because she changed the subject. "How's Tom getting on at school?"

"Oh, fine. He was a bit clingy the first week, but now he runs into the classroom without even looking back." She shrugged. "I think I was more upset about it than he was. I don't know what to do with myself half the time."

"I thought perhaps you and Ray might . . . you know." Gina glanced at the pram.

"Bit difficult when there's a five-year-old in the bed!" There was laughter in Louisa's voice, but she couldn't look Gina in the eye. She wasn't lying. Tom did creep into their bed most nights. And she was glad. It had given her a convenient excuse. She and Ray hadn't made love more than a couple of times in the past year.

"It's really hard when you have kids, isn't it?" Gina shook her head. "My mum and dad have offered to look after Julia for a whole weekend next month so Andy and I can go away together. We're thinking of Blackpool—you know—to see the illuminations." She grinned. "Not that I'm likely to see very much apart from the bedroom ceiling!"

Louisa smiled back, secretly wondering how Gina could be so keen on sex. It was obvious she and Andy were at it whenever the opportunity arose. Gina had had a couple of other boyfriends before he came on the scene and had always confided all the details of her sex life to Louisa. Andy, she said, was the best lover she had ever had. They had taken great delight in having sex in every room of the new house. They'd even sneaked off to bed when Julia was just two weeks old, seizing their chance while Gina's mother was pushing her around the block in the pram.

For Louisa, sex was something to be endured. She knew it made Ray sad that she didn't enjoy it as much as he seemed to, and she knew he would have liked it more often. He never got home from the cinema before ten thirty in the evenings, and she always made sure she was asleep, or pretending to be. The only consolation, as far as she was concerned, was that on the rare occasions they did wake up alone together, it was always over very quickly. She had timed it once, glancing at her watch on the bedside table while his body pressed against her. Thirty-three seconds. She worked out that during their entire marriage that only added up to about ten minutes in total. Not a bad price to pay for having Tom.

It wasn't that she didn't like Ray. She was very fond of him. He was good with Tom and generous with what little money he had to spare. Always bringing home little presents for them both. She had come to the conclusion that passion was something that only happened in films, not real life, and she might have gone on believing it, had it not been for Gina and Andy.

She would have liked to confide in Gina, but she feared that would mean having to explain why she had started seeing Ray in the first place. And that was another secret she wouldn't share with anyone.

"Perhaps that's what you and Ray should do." Gina's voice cut across her thoughts. "You've never had a holiday alone together, have you?"

"Fat chance! We barely survive on Ray's wages as it is."

"What if you were to get a part-time job—now that Tom's at school, I mean?"

Louisa shrugged. "I'd love to, but Ray won't let me. I could do afternoons at the Odeon and still be back in time to collect Tom, but Ray says he won't have any wife of his going out to work." She gave a wry smile. "As if he had a whole harem!"

Gina frowned. "Andy's the same. He couldn't wait for me to get pregnant. I think he was more pleased about me finishing at the office than about becoming a father. He's so jealous. He was always accusing me of fancying someone or other."

"It must have been difficult, with you both working at the same place, though," Louisa said. "I sometimes think that's the real reason Ray doesn't want me to go back."

Gina looked at her. "Do you trust him, Lou?"

Louisa frowned. "Yes, I think so." It had often crossed her mind that Ray might look elsewhere for the pleasures she rationed out to him, but in her heart she couldn't imagine him being unfaithful. He was always telling her how much he loved her, even though she rarely said it back. "Do you trust Andy?"

"Oh, yes," Gina replied, a big grin spreading across her face. "He wouldn't have the energy to chase after anyone else!"

"I'm really glad you're so happy," Louisa said, trying to conceal the wistfulness she felt inside. What Gina and Andy had was how it was supposed to be: just like in the films. But there were other ways of being happy, she reminded herself. She looked over at Tom, who had stuck apple twigs through the band of his sun hat to make antlers and was crawling around the tree on all fours.

"He's a lovely lad," Gina said. "Ray must be really proud of him."

Louisa gave her a Mona Lisa smile. Yes, he was a wonderful child. Good-natured, well behaved, and, although she would never say it out loud, very good-looking. Where did he get it from? Were his looks inherited from that mysterious grandfather? Did his sweet nature come from Ray or from her aunt Rhiannon? She wished she knew.

~

A few weeks later Louisa and Tom were having tea at her parents' house when Eva made a surprise announcement.

"I had a letter this morning from your uncle Trefor," she said, a look of triumph on her face. "He says his wife's left him. Apparently she's taken the daughter and gone back to Italy."

Louisa swallowed hard, the cake she had been eating sticking to the roof of her mouth. The very mention of his name made her insides churn.

"I don't know how she stuck by him for so many years—it's a wonder she married him in the first place," Eva went on. "Anyway, he's had the cheek to ask if he can come to stay with us for Christmas! He says it's lonely on the farm and he needs a break."

"Well, I think we should bury the hatchet, love," Eddie said, reaching across the table for the teapot. "After all, where would we be now if it hadn't been for that money?"

"Yes, but it wasn't *his* money, was it?" Eva snapped. "It was Aunt Rhiannon's. Hers to do what she liked with."

"All the same, it must have been a blow to him." Eddie topped up Louisa's cup before filling his own. "I think he behaved quite well over it—compared to what he was like over the farm, I mean."

Eva frowned. "Trust you to see the good side."

"Have some pity," Eddie said. "How would you like to spend Christmas on your own?"

"Well, it's no more than he deserves!" Eva glanced at Louisa, who avoided her gaze, staring at the tablecloth. "I suppose it's not very Christian, is it, refusing to have him?" Eva paused, waiting for a response. When none came, she said, "It wouldn't be too much trouble for you to have one extra on Boxing Day, would it, Lou?"

"Me?" She reached unsteadily for the milk jug, playing for time, racking her brain for some excuse.

"He wouldn't have to stay the night," Eva said. "I know you haven't got room. He could go back home after lunch."

For a moment Louisa thought she was going to throw up. The very thought of that evil bastard *sleeping* in her house! But how could she refuse to entertain him? If she said no, she would have to explain why she found the idea so abhorrent. It was no use pretending she and Ray had made other plans. Every year of their marriage had followed the same pattern: Christmas with his parents, Boxing Day with hers. A few hours, her mother had said. And everybody else would be there. They could talk to him while she hid in the kitchen. She would only have to spend about half an hour with him while they ate. Perhaps she needn't even do that. She could pretend to be ill. Get everything ready, then take to her bed.

"Okay," she murmured, through gritted teeth.

Chapter 29

On Christmas night Louisa sat in the kitchen making a trifle. Tom and Ray were both asleep, and she had the little transistor radio on low to keep her company. The Four Tops were singing her current favorite, "Walk Away, Renée." Normally she would have been dancing around the kitchen to it. But not tonight.

She was dreading Trefor's visit. Her plan to feign illness had backfired horribly. Ray had been in bed with the flu since Christmas Eve, and her mother had gone down with it too. Eddie had cooked Christmas lunch for Trefor and said he would probably have to stay and look after her mother the next day. Ray was unlikely to be much better either, which meant Louisa would probably have to entertain Trefor single-handedly.

His face superimposed itself on the whipping cream in the bowl in front of her. She wondered what he was doing at this moment, safely ensconced at her parents' house. She was terrified that he might say something to her dad about what had happened on his last visit to Wolverhampton.

She had gone over and over it in her head, trying to figure out why he had decided to come and visit after all these years.

She didn't believe his lame excuse about not wanting to spend Christmas on his own. He was the kind of man who hated other people so much he would probably have welcomed it. So what was his game? She transferred all her hatred of Trefor to the cream, beating it until her elbow ached.

It was midnight when she crept into bed beside Ray. His snoring was made worse by the infection, and she tossed and turned, unable to get to sleep. She wondered if she could use Ray's illness as a last-ditch excuse for not having Trefor over for lunch. Perhaps if she pretended they both had it? *But no*, she thought, then her dad would be stuck with him for a second day.

Louisa sighed in the darkness. Four hours, maximum, he would be at the flat. Surely she could get through four measly hours? She shivered at the memory of what he had achieved in less than ten minutes last time they had met. But it would be different this time, she told herself. Even if Ray was in bed, he would still be within shouting distance. No: Trefor wasn't going to be able to get away with anything this time.

Grabbing her pillow, she tiptoed out of the bedroom and pushed open Tom's door. Untucking the blankets at the foot of the bed, she climbed in, easing Tom's legs aside with her own. He stirred slightly and curled himself up against her feet. She felt herself relax in a way she never could in the bed she shared with Ray.

~

Next morning Louisa frowned at her reflection in the dressing table mirror. She scraped her hair back from her face, winding it into a bun on the back of her head. She secured the stray wisps with clips that were the same shade of brown as her hair, then finished off with a liberal dose of hairspray. Then she tucked a towel into the neck of her cream wool sweater and applied pale foundation, powder, and a touch of rouge to her cheekbones. She wanted to look plain. Plain but smart. Someone who was in control, despite what he had done to her. She zipped up the new suede boots Ray had bought her for Christmas and smoothed down her tan-colored calf-length skirt. Checking her reflection, she added a slick of pale-pink lipstick. Her hands trembled as she applied it.

In the mirror she could see the hump in the sheets where Ray lay, still asleep. She had brought him tea two hours ago, and he had grunted his thanks but dozed off again without even drinking it. She wondered if she should try to wake him. Ask if there was any chance of him getting up for an hour or two. *No*, she thought, *that would be mean.* This was something she was going to have to get through on her own.

She sat waiting in the room that doubled as lounge and diner, watching Tom playing with his new toys. When the bell rang, she jumped, almost knocking a glass off the carefully laid table.

The sight of Trefor's face turned her stomach to ice. It was as if she had stepped back in time. He looked exactly the same. Same overcoat and scarf, same smell of sweat and whiskey as he took them off and handed them to her. She saw his eyes travel down her body as if she were an animal or a car he had just bought, his face twisted in the horrible leer that had haunted her dreams for the past six years.

Wordlessly she led him up the stairs to the flat. She was not going to put on a front, wish him a "Merry Christmas." She held her head up as she opened the door. Although their flat was small, she was proud of the way she had decorated and furnished it. She knew he would be looking the place over with the same smug sneer he had worn when he saw her parents' old home. She turned to him, ready with a well-rehearsed put-down if he dared to make any critical remark. But he wasn't looking at the decor. His eyes were fixed on Tom, who had wandered out into the hall at the sound of the door, a piece of Lego clutched in his hand.

Trefor dropped to his knees in front of the child and put out a hand to stroke his soft brown curls. "Hello, *bach*," he said, his voice totally different from the harsh rasp she remembered. "I'm your uncle Trefor. I've brought you a present."

He slid a brightly colored package from his jacket pocket. Louisa watched Tom's face as he tore it open, saw his eyes widen in amazement as he gazed at the silver replica E-Type Jaguar. Her jaw tightened. It must have cost more than all his other presents put together.

She felt a stab of fear as Tom took Trefor's hand and led him into the lounge to play with the new car. *Why?* The word beat a tattoo in her head as she followed them. She had expected Trefor to show the same contempt for her child that he had shown her. Surely he couldn't . . .

"Not a bad-looking little kid, is he?" Trefor gave her a sly look as Tom disappeared off to the toilet.

Louisa stared at him through narrowed eyes, saying nothing.

"How old is he now? Five?"

She nodded mutely, her stomach lurching.

"You're five, are you, Tom?" Trefor said brightly as the boy came trotting back into the room. "When are you going to be six?"

"August the thirtieth," Tom announced proudly. "Mum says I'm lucky 'cause my birthday's in the holidays so I won't have to go to school!"

"I haven't offered you a drink," Louisa interrupted, rising from her seat on legs that felt like jelly. "We've got sherry—or would you prefer a bottle of beer?" She fought down a sudden urge to scoop Tom up and lock herself in the bathroom.

"No, thanks." Trefor gave her a look that made her feel like the ten-year-old she had been when she first set eyes on him. "I've brought my own." He slipped a whiskey bottle from his jacket pocket and set it on the table.

She backed into the kitchen, one eye on Tom as she pulled the roast joint from the oven. She felt like a robot, her body performing a ridiculous charade while her mind worked frantically. What was Trefor after? Had he come here with the intention of blurting it all out to Ray? Was he out to ruin her life all over again?

When she brought the food to the table, his whiskey bottle was half-empty. She stared at it as she plunked the steaming plate of pork in front of him. She was sure he had drunk more than enough to put him over the government's new drink-drive limit. *Serve him right if the police catch him*, she thought.

She had to force herself to eat, watching Trefor wolfing his down. Her insides were in knots, waiting for what he might come out with. Wondering what she was going to say to Tom if he did. But Trefor spent the entire meal pontificating about the foot-and-mouth outbreak that was sweeping the country. He was very smug about the fact that the disease had not affected livestock in Cardiganshire, and went on and on about how well he was doing since taking over the farm from her parents.

She let it all wash over her, praying that she had misinterpreted his questions about Tom, counting the hours and minutes until he would be gone. She glanced at her son, whose eyes were beginning to droop as he ate. He'd been up so early on Christmas morning, and now it was catching up with him. When she came back from the kitchen with the trifle, he was asleep, his head resting on the table.

"I'll carry him to his bed." Trefor was already on his feet.

"No!" Louisa didn't want him touching Tom, but before she could put down the trifle, he had hoisted the child into his arms and was heading out into the hallway.

"This one, is it?" he said over his shoulder, jerking his head to a door on the right. Louisa nodded, paralyzed by the feeling of nausea at the sight of her son lying limp in Trefor's arms. She wanted to run into the bedroom, pull Tom away from him, but all she could think of was the feeling of being pinned against the wall of her parents' kitchen, the blinding pain as her head hit the wall, and the worse pain that followed . . .

"All tucked in!" Trefor was back in the room, a look of triumph on his face. His eyes became slits as he fixed her with a penetrating look. "He's mine, isn't he?"

"Don't be ridiculous!" she gasped. "Do you think I'd have kept him if he was?" She stared back at him like a mouse gripped by a cat.

Trefor came slowly toward her, a dangerous smile playing on his lips. "Then answer me this: if he's what's-his-name's boy, how come the pair of you have been married nigh on six years and not managed to produce another?"

"I . . . er . . . we can't afford to have another child—not yet, anyway. Not that it's any of your business!" Louisa backed away from him, jabbing her hip on one of the dining chairs.

"I think you're lying," he growled, coming after her. "I want him! He's mine!"

Her body tensed as he grabbed her by the shoulders. His stinking breath was in her face. The bile rose up into her throat.

"We could be good together, you and me. A proper family. You, me, and young Tom." He pulled her to him, pressing his mouth against hers. She lashed out with both arms, making a choking, retching sound that should have been a scream. He grabbed them, pushing her backward.

"What's going on?" Ray appeared in the lounge doorway in his pajamas, blinking the sleep from his eyes. Trefor's arms dropped to his sides. Louisa stared at her husband for a split second before deciding what to do. She mustn't allow Trefor to say anything to Ray. She couldn't tell Ray what he had been trying to do.

"Nothing. Mince pie went down the wrong way." She gave Ray a hundred-watt smile and put her arm around him as she led him back to the bedroom. "Trefor's just going. I'll make you a hot drink. What would you like?"

In his fuddled state Ray seemed to accept what she said and allowed her to tuck him back into bed. On her way back to the lounge she unhooked Trefor's coat and scarf, thrusting them at him as she walked into the room.

"I think you'd better go!" She fought back tears as she stood, rigid with emotion, holding open the door.

"Don't worry—I've got what I came for!" Trefor gave her another sly look as he slid his arms into the shabby gray overcoat. "And I'll be back!" he smirked. "I know what he looks like now—and mark my words, girl, I'll be back for what's mine!"

Louisa blinked, too stunned to reply. She watched him shamble toward his car. A silver E-Type Jaguar. Apart from the mud spattering its sides, it was exactly like the present he had given her son. He revved up the engine and swerved out into the road, narrowly missing a lamppost as he sped off down the hill.

~

The next few weeks took a heavy toll on Louisa. She had never been overweight, but by the end of February she had become painfully thin. Trefor's parting threat preyed constantly on her mind. She would be at the school gates every playtime and at lunchtime, hovering just out of sight of the children, but standing guard, just in case. It had turned bitterly cold at the end of January, but even when snow was falling and icy winds tore at her coat, still she stood at the gates. In the afternoons she arrived a good twenty minutes early, just in case.

One afternoon she set out even earlier than usual. It was Gina's birthday and she wanted to take her some flowers. Gina had commented on the fact that Louisa had lost weight. She had rolled her eyes at the excuse Louisa gave—that she was dieting after pigging out at Christmas. But it had been a couple of weeks since they last met and Gina gasped when Louisa took off her thick woolen coat.

"My God, Lou! What's happened to you? Have you been ill?"

"No, I'm fine!" She sat down at the kitchen table, feeling slightly dizzy as the warmth of the room hit her. "I've just overdone the diet a bit, that's all: don't worry, I've stopped now."

"I should hope so! Look at you!" Gina reached across the table and squeezed the flesh of her arm. "Nothing but skin and bone! What a pair, eh? Me like the side of a house and you like Twiggy!"

Gina had been horrified to discover she was expecting again within months of giving birth to Julia. She was seven months pregnant now and worried constantly about how she was going to cope with two babies under the age of two. Each time they met, Louisa tried to reassure her, but she found it difficult. She knew what hard work a tiny baby was and couldn't imagine how she would manage in Gina's situation.

"How's Andy?" Louisa was trying to get off the subject of her weight.

Gina's face fell. "Don't ask."

"What's happened? Is he giving you a hard time about the baby?"

Gina's lower lip seemed to tremble. But then she gave a bright smile. *Too bright*, Louisa thought. "No, it's not that," she said. "It's nothing. Take no notice of me. It's just that I'm a year older and I feel like a fat frump. I wish we could get dressed up and go dancing!" She huffed out a laugh. "Next year, okay? Promise?"

Louisa nodded, unable to think that far ahead without the now-familiar feeling of dread. Would she still be watching Tom's every move, scared to leave him with anyone else? She glanced at her watch. "I'd better get going: Tom gets out of school in half an hour." As she stood up and reached for her coat, suddenly everything went fuzzy.

"Lou!" Gina sounded as if she were shouting from miles away. "Lou! For God's sake, speak to me!"

She felt something cold and wet on her forehead and opened her eyes to see Gina's worried face inches from her own. She tried to get to her feet. "Tom," she mumbled, "must get Tom."

"You're not going anywhere!" Gina propped a cushion under her head. "Give me the number of the school. I'll phone them and tell them to keep him there for a while until we get hold of Ray."

"No," Louisa moaned. "You can't! You don't understand."

"What's the matter, Lou? You're shaking!"

"If . . . if I'm not there," Louisa stammered, "*he* might get him."

"Who? Who might get him?"

Louisa's body convulsed into near-hysterical sobbing.

Gina bent over her, bewildered by her friend's distress. With some effort she heaved herself up from the floor and lumbered out to the phone in the hall.

"Right," she gasped, out of breath as she returned to the kitchen. "Everything's under control: Ray's collecting Tom, then he's coming here for you."

Louisa was half sitting, half lying on the floor, propped up against the kitchen unit. She had stopped crying and was staring into space.

"And in the meantime," Gina went on, "I'm going to make you some tea and a sandwich, and you're going to tell me all about it."

~

Louisa had never intended to tell a living soul what Trefor had done to her, but once she started, it all came pouring out.

Gina sat in silence, her face mirroring Louisa's as she took it in. "What a bastard!" she said at last. "I'd have bloody well poisoned him if he'd come to my house for lunch! No wonder you've made yourself so ill!"

"You won't say anything to Ray, will you? Promise me, please!"

"Of course I won't." Gina bit her lip. "You know, I never could fathom why you went for him in such a big way. So quickly, I mean." She glanced awkwardly at Louisa. "But I understand it now."

Louisa nodded glumly. "Do you think I'm terrible?"

"No." Gina sighed and reached for the teapot, topping up the mugs. "We all do what we have to, to survive, don't we? It's human nature."

"Doesn't make it right, though, does it?" Louisa drew her mug closer, feeling the comforting warmth of the steam rising up over her face. "Some people would say I deserve to lose Tom, not knowing who his real father is."

"You don't deserve anything of the kind! You're a good mother and you've been a good wife to Ray. No one could say you haven't!"

"Couldn't they?" Louisa suddenly wanted to tell Gina all the rest. Unburden herself about the misery of not loving Ray as she should, of sharing a bed with a man she had never wanted in the way he wanted her. And she wanted to ask Gina what it was like. How it felt to make love. *Real* love. But at that moment the front doorbell rang. Ray had come to take her home.

~

Ray insisted on dropping Tom at his mother's and taking her to a doctor.

"I'm fine, honestly," she said. "Just a bit tired, that's all."

But he wouldn't have it. When the doctor saw her, he insisted on doing some tests.

"It's no wonder you fainted, Mrs. Brandon," he said. "You're pregnant. Only about eight weeks, I'd say, but pregnant, without a doubt."

Louisa blundered out of the consulting room in a daze. She thought she'd missed her period because of the worry over Tom.

"All right?" Ray searched her face.

She nodded, her lips pressed together.

Ray frowned. "What did he say?"

"Oh . . . er . . . nothing much," Louisa faltered. "Just a bit anemic, that's all. He's given me a prescription for iron tablets." She couldn't tell him. Not yet.

~

The next day was Saturday. Tom was due to spend the afternoon at her parents' house, so Ray dropped him off there on his way to work. Normally she would have gone too, just in case Trefor suddenly materialized and tried to snatch Tom. But she was too exhausted to go anywhere.

Alone in the flat, she told herself she must stop being so paranoid. She tried to think about it logically. Why should Trefor want Tom when he couldn't ever be sure the boy was his own flesh and blood? After all, he had a daughter, didn't he? Even if she was living in Italy, she was still his. She told herself those parting words had been nothing more than an idle threat made out of spite.

But it didn't help. Her mind raced ahead, thinking about what would happen when this new baby came along. How could she go to the hospital? She'd worry herself sick over Tom if she was cooped up in that maternity ward. She would have to insist on a home birth this time: it was the only solution.

She felt a wave of nausea and ran to the bathroom, but by the time she got there, it had passed. The effort made her head spin. She hobbled back to the lounge, putting her hand against the wall for support. Then she sank into the armchair, leaned back, and closed her eyes. She had drifted into sleep when the phone rang.

"Louisa, I had to tell you . . ." Eva sounded breathless. "It's Trefor . . ."

"What?" Louisa's mouth went dry. "Where is he? What's he done?"

There was a second's silence at the end of the phone. "He's dead, Lou."

Chapter 30

A postmortem revealed that Trefor had more than three times the permitted alcohol level in his blood when he died. He had gone out in his tractor, still drunk from the night before, and it had overturned with him in it.

"I never liked him in life, so it'd be hypocritical to mourn his death," Eva said when they were discussing whether to go to the funeral. Louisa nodded her agreement. She would have gone if her mother had wanted it. She would gladly have traveled to Wales to see Trefor put in the ground.

"Why did he drink so much, Mam? Was he an alcoholic?" She was incapable of feeling sorry for him, but his death intrigued her in the way a dead bee might fascinate a child who had been stung by it.

"Yes, I think he probably was," Eva replied, a faraway look in her eyes. "He certainly drank a lot at our house at Christmas. Did he do the same at yours?"

Louisa nodded, her eyes fixed on the tablecloth.

"I think he was devastated by the marriage breakup," Eva went on. "He told us he had no idea where his wife and daughter were living. Apparently the family farm in Italy had been sold and they just disappeared without a trace."

"Oh." Louisa ran her finger through a little heap of salt that had spilled on the cloth. "I didn't realize."

"You know, I think he was jealous of us." Eva's eyes narrowed. "He was always so smug, so high-and-mighty. Even as a child he looked down on us. We were always the poor relations in his eyes. But when he came here at Christmas and saw that your dad and I had all the things he didn't—not just a daughter, but a grandson as well—I think it dawned on him that he wasn't the top dog after all."

Louisa felt an icy surge in her stomach. *Was that why he had wanted Tom? Jealousy?*

"He once tried to kiss me."

"What?" Louisa's head jolted upward. "When?"

"I must have been about ten." Eva was staring at the wall above her daughter's head. "He was chasing me and he pulled me onto the ground. Next thing I knew he was on top of me, holding me down, trying to stick his tongue into my mouth." Her face twisted in a grimace.

Louisa gazed at her, incredulous. "What did you do?"

"I bit it. Bit his tongue. He didn't half yelp, filthy little devil!" She shuddered. "I was his *cousin*, for goodness sake!"

"Well done, Mum—that was brave." She would never have believed her mother to be capable of such an act. She had always seemed so . . . fragile. Louisa was on the brink of saying more. But how could she burden her mother with own dreadful secret? What if it had been Trefor's twisted revenge for Eva's rejection of him all those years ago? And why hadn't she fought back the way her mother had?

"Are you all right, love?" Eva's voice brought her back to the present.

"Yes," she lied, "I'm fine."

~

Louisa squeezed Tom's hand as they walked to school. *No more skulking outside the gates,* she thought. No more sleepless nights worrying what devious plans Trefor might be hatching to snatch her precious son. It was over. Now she could start thinking about the future. About the new baby.

She decided she would break the news to Ray after she had dropped Tom off. He had been asleep when she left the flat, but he would probably be up and about by the time she got back. Monday was his day off, so they would have plenty of time to work out what they were going to do. They were going to have to find somewhere bigger to live and that wouldn't be possible on what he was earning at the cinema.

She needed to get a part-time job—at least until the baby was born. If she did that, they'd be able to put some money aside. She would have to try to make him see sense: swallow his pride about her going out to work. Hopefully, by the time the baby came along, he would be used to the idea. Perhaps she could ask her mother and his to take turns babysitting so that she could carry on doing two or three days a week.

At the school gates she kissed Tom good-bye and hurried home. Opening the front door she glanced at the mat. Someone had picked up the post for the three flats and stacked it neatly on the hall table. She checked the pile. Nothing for them. Or perhaps Ray had been down already. She could hear no sound from above as she climbed the stairs. She wondered if he was still in bed.

"Ray?" she called out. "Are you awake?" She went to the kitchen to put the kettle on and found him sitting at the table looking at the mail. "I thought you were asleep," she said, turning on the tap.

He didn't answer.

"I've got something to tell you," she went on, pulling cups from the cupboard, suddenly nervous. "I . . . we're going to have another baby." She held her breath, staring hard at the kettle, waiting for his reaction. But none came. She wheeled around. He was staring at the piece of paper in front of him. "Ray, did you hear what I . . ."

"I heard!" His voice was a low, venomous whisper.

"Ray? What is it? I know it's a shock, but . . ."

"A shock?" He gave a mirthless laugh. "A shock? I'll say it's a shock—but not nearly as much of a shock as *this*!" He thrust the piece of paper under her nose. It was a lawyer's letter. She glanced at the address. Aberystwyth: Trefor's lawyer. Her heart began to pound as her eyes scanned the text: "Dear Mr. and Mrs. Brandon," it said, "I am writing to inform you of the last will and testament of my client, Trefor Geraint Jenkins, deceased. It was his wish that his entire estate pass upon his death to his son, Thomas Edward Brandon . . ."

Louisa's hand flew to her mouth. Ray's eyes were full of hatred. "It's not true, Ray! This is some kind of sick joke! You know what Trefor was like!"

"Oh yes, I know what he was like, all right!" He nodded slowly. "I saw what you were up to at Christmas when you thought I was in bed asleep! And now you come telling me you're pregnant?" He slammed his fist down on the table. "My God, Lou, you might have taken me for a fool once, but I'll be damned if you'll do it a second time!"

"That wasn't what you think!" She tried to take his hand, but he snatched it away. "I hated Trefor! Before I met you, he ruined my life: please, don't let him do it again!"

His lip curled as he looked at her. "What the hell are you talking about?"

She closed her eyes and took a deep breath. "It happened when I was at home on my own at our old house on Sycamore Street . . ." She told him about the day Trefor had arrived with the check. How he had pushed her against the wall and forced himself on her, kicking her like a dog after taking her virginity.

"I don't believe you." The words came out through clenched teeth. "I think you led him on—the way you led me on—and you were doing it again at Christmas!" He shouted the last sentence, his hands balled into fists.

Louisa cringed against the kitchen cupboard. "No, Ray," she whimpered, "I know what it must have looked like! But I was trying to get away from him!"

"You expect me to believe that? I know you, Lou!" he snarled. "I'll never forget how you came on to me in Dad's van that first night." He shook his head and rolled his eyes. "I couldn't believe my luck! What a bloody fool, eh? No wonder you were so keen, you tart!" He grabbed her sweater, pulling the fabric so tight that it dug into the back of her neck. "Couldn't admit to your mum and dad that you'd been knocked up by your own damn uncle, could you? So you went out and screwed the first sucker you clapped eyes on!"

"N . . . n . . . no!" Her whole body was shaking. "P . . . please, Ray! Please! J . . . just let me explain!"

"Oh no! Don't think you're going to talk your way out of this!" He suddenly loosed his grip and she fell backward against the cupboard, knocking her head. She picked herself up, touching her scalp, feeling for blood. She felt sick with fear, just as she had with Trefor in the kitchen at Sycamore Street. But the terror she felt now was not for herself but for her unborn child.

She sidled toward the door, grabbing her coat and bag. He was glaring at her, but he didn't move. She wanted to run, but she was afraid that would trigger some violent reaction. When she got as far as the hallway, she hurtled down the stairs, slamming the front door behind her.

She ran and ran until she was two streets away. Panting for breath, she sank onto a garden wall. She glanced down the road, still afraid. But there was no sign of him. It was very quiet. Not a car or a person in sight. She felt very alone. A sudden surge of hatred for Trefor flared inside her. The fallout from that single, wicked act was going to ruin her life forever.

She opened her handbag and took out her purse. All she had was a couple of shillings left over from the housekeeping money Ray had given her last Friday. She looked at her watch. She had to sort something out before it was time to collect Tom from school. She couldn't take him back to the flat. She had to protect him from what Ray might say or do. Now that he thought Tom was another man's child, there was no knowing what might happen. She had just seen how quickly his love for her had turned to hate. She couldn't bear the thought of Tom having to witness that.

She took a deep breath and got to her feet. She couldn't go to her parents. That would mean telling them about Trefor—something she had vowed she would never do. There was only one place she could go.

~

Gina looked flustered when she answered the door, and for an awful moment Louisa thought she was going to turn her away. She opened her mouth to explain why she needed to come in, but her lips trembled so badly she couldn't speak. Five minutes later she was sitting at Gina's kitchen table, next to a pile of unironed laundry, with a steaming mug of tea in front of her. In sentences punctuated by sobs, Louisa relived what had happened at the flat.

"So he's convinced himself Tom's not his?" Gina said gravely.

Louisa nodded, reaching in her handbag for a tissue.

"And now he thinks this one's Trefor's as well?"

"I thought he was going to hit me." Louisa shook her head. "He had this awful look in his eyes, like he wanted to kill me."

"Oh Lou!" Gina heaved herself out of the chair, one hand cradling her pregnant belly, and waddled around the table to give her a hug. "You can understand how terrible it must be for him, though, can't you?" she said. "If he thinks you've tricked him into taking on a kid that isn't his and now—"

"He thinks I'm trying it again." Louisa finished the sentence for her. "Yes, I know it sounds dreadful, but it's not true." She took a long breath and let it out. "I could never be sure who Tom's father was, but I always *wanted* him to be Ray's." She gazed down at her stomach, still pancake flat beneath her woolen skirt. Yes, she knew exactly when *this* baby had been conceived. It was the second week in January, the night before Tom started back at school. She had been so worried about leaving him, about Trefor trying to snatch him, that she had been awake in the middle of the night, crying. Ray had woken up and asked her what was wrong. She had lied to him. Said she was upset because they hadn't made love for ages. And he had taken her in his arms, only too eager to give her what he thought she wanted.

"But you're never going to be able to prove to Ray that he's the father, are you?" Gina said. "Now that Trefor's dead, there's no way the truth can ever come out. It's your word against Ray's."

"I thought about writing him a letter," Louisa said. "Setting out exactly what happened, so he can take it in without me being there to make him angry." She looked at Gina. "I don't suppose Tom and I could stay here for the night? Just until I sort something out? I'd go to my parents, but I don't want to have to explain things until Ray's calmed down a bit."

Gina looked bewildered.

"The thing is," Louisa explained, "I'm terrified he's going to go round there and tell them. It'd kill them if they ever found out what Trefor did to me. I have to find some way of persuading Ray not to say anything."

"But how can you keep it from them?" Gina frowned. "They're going to want to know why you're arguing. And what about the will? How will you explain why Trefor's left the farm to Tom?"

"I don't know." Louisa's shoulders drooped. She felt worn-out, as if the last ounce of fight had gone out of her. "I can't think any further than today. All I want is to get Tom back safe from school and keep him away from Ray. Will you let us stay? We can both sleep on the sofa."

"Don't be silly—of course you can stay! You can have the spare room. I was decorating it for the new baby, but . . ." she paused, pressing her lips together.

"But what?" Louisa knew that look.

"Oh, nothing!" Gina cocked her head at the pile of laundry on the end of the table. "Just been a bit too busy with the housework, that's all."

"Well, I can help with that," Louisa said. She was desperate to do anything to take her mind off what the future might hold.

"Okay—but you'd better let me feed you first: I don't want you passing out on me again!"

Louisa gave her a wobbly smile. "Please don't be so nice to me," she said. "You'll make me start crying again."

Later on, when they were folding clean sheets to stack in the airing cupboard, Gina said, "Would you go back to him? If he accepts what happened, I mean."

Louisa thought for a moment. "I don't know," she said slowly. "For Tom's sake, yes, I think I would."

"But not for your sake?"

Louisa shook her head. "It's not just about me, though, is it? I've got to think of what's best for Tom and the baby. I know I should try if he gives me the chance." She swept back a stray lock of hair. "After all, Ray's done nothing to deserve this."

~

Later that afternoon she wrote a letter to Ray, intending to push it through the door on her way to Tom's school. In it she tried to

explain how the trauma of being raped had made her plunge head-
long into a relationship with him—the first and only boyfriend she
had ever had. She wanted to make it clear that she had genuinely
cared for him, not just used him, and she told him that as far as
she and Tom were concerned, he was the boy's one and only father.
But when she read it back, she couldn't help seeing herself through
Ray's eyes. He was never going to be able to forgive and forget.
How could she bring a new baby into an atmosphere weighted
with suspicion and mistrust?

She ended the letter with a request to meet him on neutral
ground to talk things over. She suggested Woolworth's café at
eleven o'clock the following morning. It was big enough for them
to be able to talk without being overheard, and she would feel safer
with all those people around.

She had scribbled a postscript about the fact she wasn't staying
with her parents and asked him not to go there. "Whatever you
think of me, they had nothing to do with it and they know nothing
about it," she wrote. "Please don't tell them. I'm asking you for their
sakes, not mine."

When she turned the corner into Oaklands Road, her heart
missed a beat. There was a police car outside the flat. One of the
neighbors was talking to a uniformed officer. As she drew nearer,
he caught sight of her and his face fell.

"Bob?" She ran to the elderly man, who lived in the flat below.
"What's happened? What's going on?"

He glanced at the policeman, biting his lip.

"Mrs. Brandon?" The officer took her arm and turned to the
neighbor. "Could we use your flat for a few moments, sir?"

Bob nodded, leading the way.

"Will someone please tell me what's going on?" Louisa's voice
was shrill with fear. "Where's Ray?"

"I think you should sit down, Mrs. Brandon," the policeman said. "I'm afraid I have some very bad news: your husband has taken an overdose."

"An overdose?" She echoed, unable to take it in.

"I don't think he meant to do it, love," Bob reached out hesitantly, patting her arm. "He phoned 999, but it was too late. He died on the way to the hospital."

Chapter 31

Louisa felt an unbearable heaviness in the silence of her parents' front room. She was sitting with her father, but neither of them had spoken a word since Eva and Tom left the room. The only sound came from the creaking of the floorboards overhead as Eva moved about the spare bedroom, trying to settle the child for the night. Louisa knew her dad was waiting for her to explain. Clearly he was desperate to know why Ray had taken his life but afraid to ask. She wondered what she was going to tell him.

She wanted to save her parents from more pain, more worry than they were already facing. They had been so wonderful with Tom, shielding him from her grief and finding the right words when she had been at a loss to explain where his daddy had gone. They had even managed to deal with Ray's mother, who, hysterical with shock, had stood screaming at the front door, demanding to know what Louisa had done to drive her son to suicide.

A little voice inside Louisa's head whispered that the truth must come out. If she didn't tell them, someone else would. There would be an inquest. The police would want to know why Ray had taken an overdose, even if he hadn't really meant to kill himself.

She would have to tell them about the lawyer's letter. About Trefor. She would have to stand up in court and spell out what had happened, in front of her parents and his.

She could hardly bear the thought of it. The Brandons would want to tear her limb from limb—and who could blame them? Because of her, Ray was dead and Tom was fatherless. Could she possibly have made things any worse?

"I know it's hard for you, Lou," Eddie began, his voice breaking into her thoughts. "But it might help to talk about it."

"I know, Dad," she nodded, fighting back tears. "I don't know if I can, though."

He reached across and took her hand. "Just tell me one thing, will you?"

She looked at him with fear in her eyes. Did he know already? Had Trefor's lawyer written to her parents as well?

"I'm not here to judge you," he said, "I just need to know: Is there someone else?"

"God, no, Dad!" Louisa gasped. "Is that what you're all thinking? I've *never* been unfaithful to Ray!"

"It's not what your mother and me are thinking, love: it's Ray's mother. She said he phoned her before he took the pills. Said something about Tom . . ." he shifted in his seat, huffing out a breath. "There's no easy way of saying it, Lou: he told her Tom wasn't his. Is it true?"

"Oh, Dad," she whispered, her whole body beginning to tremble. "What have I done?" She fell forward into his arms, and he rocked her like a child as the whole story came tumbling out.

"Why on earth didn't you tell us?" She felt the muscles of his jaw clench. "Jesus Christ! It's a good job that bastard's already dead—I'd have bloody well killed him with my own hands!" He propped her up, gripping her shoulders as he searched her face. "Do you think Tom really could be his child?" The anguish in his eyes pierced her heart. He loved that little boy so much. Just as he had loved her all these years.

"No, Dad," she shook her head slowly, deliberately. "Trefor wanted to believe it: his wife and daughter had left him and he was desperate for a son to inherit the farm. But Tom's not his child. He's Ray's, without a doubt."

Lying bitch! She heard Ray's voice as clearly as if he'd been there in the room.

Eddie's face relaxed slightly. "Thank God for small mercies," he breathed. "Poor Ray! It's all Trefor's fault—bloody monster!"

"What are we going to tell Mam?" Louisa whispered. "This would just about finish her off."

Eddie nodded, his face grave. "We need to get her away," he said.

"What, you mean go on holiday somewhere?"

"For now, yes. We'll tell her Ray had a breakdown when you told him there was another baby on the way. That he was worried about money."

"But what about Ray's mother? What if Mam asks me about that?"

"She doesn't know," Eddie replied. "She left me to deal with his mother while she got Tom out of earshot."

"There'll be an inquest, though, won't there? It's all going to come out then. And even if she keeps away, it's bound to be in the newspaper."

Eddie considered for a moment before replying. "We might have to think about moving for good, then. For your sake as well as for hers." He looked at her. "Can you imagine what it's going to be like if you carry on living round here? Once it gets in the *Express & Star,* there'll never be an end to it. Tom's going to get it at school—and the new baby, once he or she is old enough to understand. People can be very cruel."

Louisa could imagine it only too well. It was going to be tough enough bringing up two children on her own without their lives being blighted by malicious gossip.

"I'll have to get a job somewhere else," Eddie said. "Perhaps I could get a transfer to the London office. It'll be expensive, though, living there: I don't think we'd be able to afford to buy a house . . ." He paused, seeing Louisa's face change.

"The farm! What about the farm, Dad? It's Tom's now, isn't it?"

He frowned. "Could you bear to go there? It being Trefor's, I mean?"

"I don't have any memories of him in the place—not really," she said, looking at the space above his head as she conjured up scenes from her childhood. "I was happy there, mostly," she said. "I didn't want to leave—did you?"

"No—I loved it on the farm. I never wanted to go back to working in an office after that, but . . ." He gave her a wry smile. "Hey, we could sell this place and maybe build a little bungalow on the land: that way you'd have your own place, but we'd be there to help if you needed us." His face turned serious again. "We should go soon, you know: if we're going to keep this from your mother."

"What about the inquest? I'll have to give evidence, won't I?"

"You and I could come back for that while your mother looks after Tom. She wouldn't want to go to something like that: it'd only remind her of . . . you know . . ." He glanced at David's photograph on the mantelpiece.

Louisa bit her lip. "Isn't it going to be upsetting for both of you, though? Moving back there, I mean?"

"We'd be a lot more upset if you and Tom moved away without us. And I don't see how you can stay put, do you?"

Louisa shook her head. "There's nothing for me here now, Dad. I've made such a mess of my life."

He crooked his finger under her chin, lifting her face to meet his eyes. "Listen, Lou: none of this is your fault. No one could blame you for running into Ray's arms after what Trefor did to you. The farm's your passport to a new life—which is the least that bastard owes you!"

~

The funeral was arranged for the following Monday. Louisa had not put up any resistance when Ray's parents telephoned her father to say that they wanted to take charge of things. They had not asked her to choose a hymn or a reading. She only knew where and when the service was being held because of a notice in the obituary column of the newspaper.

"I wouldn't go if I was you," Eddie said when he pointed it out.

"Not go? How can I not go? I was his wife, for God's sake!"

"I know, love, but you know what his mother was like last week—ranting and screaming: Do you really want to put yourself through that again?"

Louisa let out a long breath. "I'd feel so guilty if I didn't go: heaven knows I feel guilty enough already."

"Don't you think you'd feel even worse if the whole thing turned into a shouting match?" Eddie stroked her hair. "I know you only want to do what's right, but in this case I think the right thing is to stay away."

~

On the day Ray was cremated, Louisa went to visit Gina. She took a long time to answer the door, calling from the top of the stairs that she was coming. At nearly eight months into her pregnancy she was having to do everything in slow motion.

"I've come to say good-bye." Louisa was struggling to keep her voice from quavering. "We're moving to Wales—to the farm."

"Oh Lou!" Gina clutched the edge of the kitchen table. "What am I going to do without you?"

Louisa gave her a wobbly smile. "I'm going to miss you like mad too. But you'll be fine. You've got Andy and Julia, and soon there'll be the new baby."

Gina made a small, strangled sound and a tear trickled down her plump cheek.

"What's the matter?" Louisa darted to her side, wrapping her arms around her. "Gina? What have I said?"

"I . . . d . . . didn't want to tell you," Gina sobbed. "It's not f . . . fair: you've got far too much on your p . . . plate."

"Tell me what? Please, Gina, what's happened?"

"I . . . it's Andy," she faltered.

"Andy?"

Gina nodded, scrabbling in the sleeve of her cardigan for a tissue. "He's been . . ." Her body shuddered with a great sob as she sank into a chair.

"What?" Louisa knelt on the floor, searching her face.

"He's been having an affair." Gina gulped for air.

"Oh Gina! Are you sure?"

Gina closed her eyes, her head shaking as she tried to nod. "He's got her pregnant. Her baby's due three months after mine."

"Oh my God! No!" Louisa gasped, shaking her head. "You were so happy! How *could* he?"

"What am I going to do?" Gina whimpered.

"Where is he? Has he gone to this . . . this woman?"

Gina shook her head.

"Is he planning to?"

"He says he doesn't know what to do. He's confused!" She gave a bitter chuckle. "He says he still loves me, but he loves her too."

"And what about you?"

"I hate him! I want to kill him! I have nightmares where I hit him and my fist misses his face."

Louisa reached for her hand. "Listen," she said, "you don't have to put up with this, you know."

Gina looked up, her face red and tear-stained. "What am I supposed to do? Kick him out? How can I, in this state? How would we eat, let alone pay the rent?"

"You could come and live with me on the farm in Wales." Louisa spoke slowly and softly, thinking aloud. "There'd be no rent to pay. We could help each other with the children and work with my dad on the farm."

The ghost of something like a smile crossed her friend's face. "Are you serious?"

"Absolutely serious." There was a lump in her throat, but her voice was steady. "I've made a terrible mess of my life, Gina. I'll never forgive myself for what I did to Ray. Let me do one bit of good, will you?"

Chapter 32

Gina's baby boy, Jonathan, was born four weeks after they arrived at the farm. Five months later, Louisa gave birth to a girl. She called her Rhiannon, after her aunt.

Rhiannon took everyone by surprise—especially Gina. A few days after the birth, when she and Louisa were sitting outside in the warm autumn sunshine with their babies, Gina asked the question Louisa had been dreading.

"Tell me to mind my own business if you like," she began, "but I have to ask. Is she really Ray's?"

Louisa searched the hazy hills beyond the fields where the sheep grazed. "Yes, she is." She took a long breath, her eyes fixing on Gina's. "Her skin color comes from me, not her father. I should have told you years ago, but I was afraid."

"From you?" Gina's confusion was palpable.

"Do you remember, when we were kids, I told you my father was American?"

Gina nodded. "You said he looked like Dean Martin."

"I know." Louisa dropped her head. "I'm sorry, but that was a lie: I was afraid you wouldn't want to be my friend if I told you the truth."

"So your father wasn't an American?"

"Yes, he was: a black American."

In the silence between them all that could be heard was the bleating of the sheep and the distant bark of a dog from the farm down the valley.

"But you . . . you . . . don't look . . ." Gina faltered.

"I know," Louisa said. "I wanted you to think I was like you, with a dad who was Italian or Spanish-looking. Ray's parents thought he was Puerto Rican. People jumped to their own conclusions and I let them, as long as they never guessed I was a . . ." She bit her lip. "A half-caste."

Gina blinked. "So your mother . . . ?" She gave an apologetic shrug.

Louisa gave a short, hollow laugh. "She had a wartime romance with a black GI. Except you couldn't really call it a romance."

"What do you mean?"

"I think it was probably a one-night stand." She closed her eyes, summoning the faceless man who still haunted her dreams. "She can't even remember his name."

"Oh Lou!" Gina reached for her shoulder and squeezed it. "Are you sure? How do you know?"

Louisa told her about the incident, more than a decade ago, when she had played the Nat "King" Cole record. She described her mother's hysterical reaction and the blank look when she had asked her father's name. "He must have been a real user," she muttered. "Probably got her drunk at some dance and shoved her into an alley for a quick knee-trembler." She gave a quick, dismissive shake of her head. "You know I love her, Gina, but how could she have got herself into a situation like that? When I was a kid, I used to feel angry that she wouldn't tell me about him, but now I realize it's no wonder she clammed up. She's too ashamed to talk about what happened!"

Gina frowned. "You told me a while back you had a brother who died . . ."

Louisa nodded.

"Was he . . . I mean, was your mum married before? Before you came along?"

"Yes," Louisa rolled her eyes. "To my dad. He was fighting in the war, and he came home to find me!"

Gina stared at her, openmouthed.

"Incredible, isn't it? I've often wondered why he adopted me, but I daren't ask. I couldn't bear to upset him."

"He's a lovely man, your dad." Gina's sympathetic face was streaked with confusion.

"I think it must have been a lot easier for him when we were living here," Louisa said, glancing toward the farm. "We were hidden away from the big bad world. No one in these villages had ever seen a black person. I suppose I blended in pretty well. Of course, it all changed when we moved to Wolverhampton." She related the incident of the woman in the corner shop who had refused to sell her chocolate.

Gina clicked her tongue. "We used to get abuse sometimes for being Italian—but nothing as bad as that."

"Do you remember Beverley Samuel? The way the teachers treated her?"

Gina nodded.

"So do you see why I didn't want anyone to know?"

Gina nodded, a wry smile on her face. "I suppose it also explains your weird dress sense!"

"I know." She shrugged. "It's mad isn't it? In this heat too!" She tugged at the neck of her sweater. "But I've always done it— ever since that bloody woman called me a nigger. The clothes, the makeup . . . all these years I've been trying to fool people into thinking I'm white. And now this little one's come along and blown my cover!" She traced the outline of Rhiannon's splayed fingers.

"She's beautiful, Lou."

A surge of desolation rose inside her. She swallowed once, twice, unable to reply.

"Can you imagine what poor Ray would have said if he'd lived to see her?" Gina went on. "He'd never have believed she was his."

Louisa shook her head, fighting down tears.

"That's one thing I don't understand." Gina leaned toward her, stroking Rhiannon's mahogany skin. "I mean, Tom—he's like you: sort of Italian-looking . . ." Her eyes searched Louisa's.

"You're wondering how he and I can be like that and Rhiannon so dark?"

Gina nodded. She listened in fascination as Louisa repeated the warning Eva had given her when she was pregnant with Tom.

"God, Lou, you must have been terrified when you gave birth to him—what would you have told Ray?"

"I was in such a state over what Trefor had done, I was just living one day at a time." She blinked as the images jostled for space in her head. "I used to have terrible nightmares," she murmured. "First I'd dream the baby looked like Trefor, and the next thing I'd dream it had black skin but no face."

"I don't know how you stayed sane."

"Looking back, I don't know either. It was like some sort of survival instinct kicked in. All I knew was that I wasn't going to let anyone take Tom away from me."

"Is that what your mum and dad wanted?"

"Dad did suggest that at first. It's the only time he's ever made me angry. I couldn't help wondering if he'd asked my mother to give me up—when he first got back from the war, I mean."

"Well, whatever happened then, it's obvious he dotes on you now—and he absolutely idolizes Tom." Gina searched her face.

"Have they said anything about Rhiannon? Made any comments about her color?"

"Not really." Louisa frowned. "Dad cried when he saw her, but it was because he was happy, that's all. Mum was a bit quiet. There were tears in her eyes too. I don't know what she was thinking. I didn't want to ask. I've always been so afraid of upsetting her."

"What about Tom? What are you going to say if he starts asking questions?"

Louisa thought for a moment. She couldn't help remembering the day she had first started quizzing her own mother, asking about the color of David's hair in the photo on the mantelpiece. "I don't know," she sighed. "I suppose I just don't want to think about it."

"Don't you think this is the ideal opportunity to make a fresh start?" Gina said. "Stop pretending and just be yourself? Why don't you take off that hat and sweater and let yourself get a bit of sun?"

"Oh no—I couldn't do that!" She pulled her sleeves down over her wrists. "Tom's just started at a new school—imagine how much harder it'll be if the other kids find out his mother's black!"

"So what are you going to do?" Gina demanded. "Hide Rhiannon away like some guilty secret?"

"No, of course not!" Louisa's face flushed. "It'd be pretty difficult in a small community like this—and the midwife knows already." Rhiannon whimpered in her sleep, and Louisa stroked her wispy black hair. "No, I'm not going to hide her away—but I'm not going to be parading her outside the school gates either. I'll explain things to Tom when he's older. I think six is a bit young, don't you?"

Gina nodded. "You know what people are going to think, though, don't you? That Tom and Rhiannon have different fathers: that it's *you* who's had an affair with a black man."

"Not necessarily." Louisa shrugged. "They might think Rhiannon's adopted." She kicked out at a clump of hay that had blown across the yard. "Anyway, they can think what they like. It's only seven months since Tom lost his dad. Can you imagine how confused he's going to be if his mother suddenly transforms herself into a different person? Dark skin, Afro hairstyle—and in a place like this?"

"I guess you're right," Gina sighed. "But it's like a time bomb, isn't it? Ticking away all the while, and if you're not careful, it's going to blow up in your face."

Part Three
FATHER UNKNOWN

Chapter 33

The battered Land Rover bounced over the rutted farm track and onto the road that led to Aberystwyth. Louisa was at the wheel, Gina in the passenger seat, and Jonathan and Rhiannon squeezed into the back alongside the boxes of eggs destined for the market.

The radio crackled into life a mile and a half into the journey. Reception was still pretty useless at the farm, so trips like this provided a rare chance to hear the latest hits. As Louisa steered around a hairpin bend, four voices were singing along to "Crocodile Rock."

"How come you two know the words to this?" she called over her shoulder.

"Tom taught us," Rhiannon lisped from behind her.

"She maked up a dance to it," Jonathan chimed in.

Louisa and Gina laughed. Rhiannon had been dancing since almost before she could walk. At four years old she had already learned how to put on records by herself. Her current favorite was Louisa's T. Rex album. Louisa often stood hidden behind the door, just watching her. She seemed to have a natural grace, a sense of rhythm that no one had taught her.

Sometimes the sight of Rhiannon dancing made her feel wistful for the days of swishing around the cinema in her usherette's uniform, dreaming of being Rita Moreno. But mostly it made her think about her father. Her real father. Her mother had never shown any interest in dancing, and Ray certainly wasn't a dancer, so this must come from the mysterious American. The more she watched, the more she wondered. *What was he like? Who was he? And where was he now?*

~

When they arrived at the market, Gina set up the stall while Louisa took the children down to the beach. They always took turns running the stall, and it wasn't difficult to keep the kids amused. They went to the beach if the weather was fine, the penny arcade if it was raining. *It wouldn't be for much longer, though*, Louisa thought, as she watched Jonathan burying Rhiannon's legs in the gritty sand. In September both children would be at school with Gina's eldest girl, Julia. And Tom would be going to the comprehensive school in Aberystwyth.

She smiled to herself. It would be strange, to be without them for the whole day. She would be twenty-nine in six weeks' time, but apart from a few months when Tom started school in Wolverhampton, she hadn't really had a free day for eleven years. Her mother and father helped where they could, but Louisa didn't like to ask too often. Her dad worked long hours on the farm, and her mother hadn't been so mobile since developing arthritis two years ago.

Gina had offered to have all the children once in a while to give her a break. She said she felt guilty because she went to stay with her parents in Wolverhampton over the school holidays and was able to do what she liked for a whole week. But Louisa hadn't bothered taking her up on it. Where would she go, on her own?

And besides, she was quite contented with her life. With two sets of children, a hundred sheep, thirty chickens, and fourteen cows there wasn't time to be bored.

An angry yell nudged her brain back into gear. Jonathan had covered Rhiannon's whole body in sand and was now shoveling it over her face. Before Louisa could reach them, Rhiannon had leapt up. In one swift movement she grabbed the spade from Jonathan and hurled it into the sea.

"Rhiannon!" Louisa shouted as Jonathan burst into tears. "That was naughty!"

"He throwed sand on me!" Rhiannon stood her ground, hands on her hips, staring at Jonathan defiantly.

"Well, you were both naughty," Louisa said, trying to suppress the urge to grin at her daughter's fighting spirit. "Come on!" She put on her no-nonsense voice. "Let's wash you both off and get back to the stall. Do you know how many extra eggs we'll have to sell to buy a new spade?"

"About twenty hundred!" Jonathan sniffed.

"Silly!" Rhiannon glared at him. "About . . . two boxes?" She looked at Louisa, who nodded. "Granddad'll buy them," she announced, a triumphant look on her face. "He likes omelets!" Louisa tried not to laugh as she shepherded them back to the stall.

"You'll never guess what," Gina whispered as the children ducked under the awning.

"What?" Louisa gave her a puzzled grin.

"See those guys over there?"

Louisa shaded her eyes from the sunlight. A few yards away was a stall selling beads, incense, and alpaca sweaters. "The hippies?"

Gina nodded. "They've invited us to a party!"

Louisa's eyebrows arched. They came from the farm down the valley. The one Anwen and Elin Lewis had occupied when she was a child. Now it was a sort of commune. No one was quite sure how many people lived there. There had been rumors at the village school of all kinds of wild goings-on; drugs, orgies, devil worship. But the men and women Louisa had seen at the market all looked pretty harmless.

"It's next Saturday night." Gina's eyes glittered with excitement. "Quentin said we could stay the night if we wanted!"

"*Quentin?*" Louisa raised her eyes skyward.

"Yes—the one with the earring—gorgeous, isn't he? Looks just like David Essex!"

Louisa laughed. "I take it you want to go to this party, then?"

"Don't you?"

"Well, I suppose we could . . ." Louisa hesitated. She hadn't been to a party in years. "What would we wear?" She glanced down at the stout boots, faded jeans, and lumberjack shirt that had become her uniform over the past four years.

"Lou! I'm sure we can find something! And anyway, you don't have to worry." Gina laughed. "You'd look sexy in a potato sack!"

~

"Are we supposed to be taking something to drink?" Louisa picked up a bottle of the elderflower wine her dad had made the previous summer. It was the only alcohol they had in the house, and pretty deadly.

"Don't fret." Gina grinned. "It'll be fine! They'll probably be too out of it to notice what we bring."

"I hope we're not heading off to some seedy psychedelic love-in."

Gina shrugged, inspecting herself in the hall mirror. "Well, there might be some pot on offer, I suppose, but who cares? Let's just enjoy ourselves for once, eh? Let our hair down a bit."

Louisa caught her own reflection as she reached for her jacket. She looked very different from the girl who had arrived at the farm four years ago. Her hair was short now, a little pot of wax giving her sleek waves. A hairdresser in Aberystwyth had encouraged her to abandon the nightly ritual of putting it in rollers, saying the new style showed off her high cheekbones. She was still very careful about her skin, but since she had started taking Rhiannon to market with her, she had become less self-conscious. They got the odd curious look, especially when she was walking along the street hand in hand with both Jonathan and Rhiannon, but by and large people seemed to accept her. Her ability to speak Welsh helped. Although she hadn't spoken the language for fourteen years, it had soon come back to her and the locals respected her for it.

She smoothed down the top Gina had lent her. It was a sleeveless red halter neck, and she felt naked in it. Gina had assured her she looked fine, but she wasn't sure she was going to have the courage to take her jacket off at the party.

They parked the Land Rover where the track ended and walked across the field to Pant-yr-Allt farm. They could hear music, and when they reached the front door, it was half-open. The smell of patchouli and cannabis hung heavy in the air as they ventured in.

"Hi, people!" Quentin appeared in a doorway. He was wearing a purple kaftan over jeans, with a multicolored woven headband flattening his dark hair. "You come bearing gifts!" He staggered slightly as he took the bottle from Louisa's hand. "But you must try some of the stuff we've made." He ushered them into the kitchen, which looked very different from the way Louisa remembered it. Bunches of dried herbs hung from a wooden rack overhead, and bottles and jars in every color of the rainbow were ranged on shelves that lined three of the walls from floor to ceiling. "It's punch," Quentin murmured, slurring his words slightly.

Louisa glanced at Gina.

"Go on, try some!" He dipped a ladle into the enormous metal bowl, sending slices of apple and orange bobbing madly in the livid liquid. "It's homemade wine and fruit grown in the orchard," he went on, slopping the punch into two tall glasses. "Got a great kick to it!"

In the living room people were already dancing. Louisa recognized a few from the school and the market. She and Gina perched on the arms of a threadbare sofa, sipping their drinks.

"It's not bad, actually, is it?" Gina said, taking a bigger swallow, which left the glass half-empty. "Not nearly as strong as your dad's wine!"

Louisa laughed. It was nice. In fact it hardly tasted like alcohol at all: more like fruit juice. She fished a slice of apple from the glass and bit into it. "Quentin seems very friendly." She gave Gina a sly look.

"Well, he *is* pretty irresistible, isn't he—even in that kaftan!"

They had a fit of the giggles and a few minutes later Quentin was back to top up their glasses. "Told you you'd like it," he said as Louisa finished her second glass. She smiled at him. Gina was right. He did look like David Essex. He had the same eyes.

"Will you dance with me, beautiful lady with the eggs?" He was on his feet, holding out his hand to her. She recognized the music. It was Derek and the Dominoes. "Layla." She hadn't danced in front of anyone but Gina and the kids since . . . well, she couldn't really remember. She looked around, but Gina had disappeared. "Come on," Quentin coaxed.

"Okay—why not?" she heard herself saying. Slipping off her jacket, she let Quentin lead her onto the floor.

"You're quite a mover, aren't you?" He brushed her ear with his lips as he spoke.

She smiled back at him. It felt good to dance. She felt relaxed. A little bit tipsy. But it was all right. These people were nice. She would have to tell the other mums at the school that they'd got them all wrong.

"Do you like this?" The record had finished and the strains of a slow number drifted across the smoky room. It was Gladys Knight and the Pips. "Help Me Make It Through the Night." Quentin reached out to her, pulling her gently to him. She could smell the patchouli, stronger than ever, on his clothes, in his hair. The scent was exotic and alluring. She felt a sudden rush of excitement at the feel of his skin against hers.

When the song ended, he led her outside into the twilight. They sat against the wheel of an old wooden plough, and he fished something from his pocket. "This is really good stuff," he said, lighting the spliff and taking a long drag. He passed it to her. "Have you ever tried this before, beautiful egg-lady?"

"My name's Louisa." She grinned, not so drunk that she didn't feel embarrassed by his ham-fisted flattery.

"Louisa . . ." He said her name as if trying it on for size. "Well, Louisa, I think you're going to like this—it'll make you feel really mellow."

She took the spliff from his outstretched hand and stared at it. It was hard to focus. She knew she shouldn't do this. This was a drug. A bad thing. But these people were doing it, and they were so nice, so harmless.

"It's like a cigarette," Quentin explained. "Just take a drag and hold it down as long as you can."

She put it between her lips. It felt huge, awkward. She had only ever smoked one cigarette. When she had started her Saturday job at the cinema, another usherette had offered her one, and she had decided she must try it. It had made her feel so queasy she had never been tempted again.

"Go on," Quentin urged.

She breathed in. The effect was even more alarming than the cigarette had been. Her throat and her eyes burned, and she thought she was going to be sick. "I'm sorry," she wheezed, handing the spliff back. "I'm not very good at this, am I?"

"That's cool," Quentin replied, spitting on his fingers and squeezing the smoking end before replacing it in the pocket of his kaftan. "Come on." He pulled her to her feet. "There's something I want to show you."

He led her back into the house and up the stairs. They passed Gina, who waved drunkenly at them before sticking her tongue back into the mouth of a man Louisa recognized as Quentin's partner at the market stall. She almost tripped up the last step. Her glass tipped sideways, dribbling the dregs of her drink onto the worn carpet.

"It's this way." Quentin led her into a dimly lit bedroom. "Look," he said, sliding his hand under her chin and tilting her head toward the ceiling. She could see an enormous wheel painted in lots of different colors, with strange symbols marked on it. "You can see it better from here." He guided her to the bed. "If you lie on your back and look up, you can make out all the signs."

"Signs?" she said, her own voice strange and distant.

"It's the zodiac," he replied, slipping his arm under her shoulders as they lay gazing at the ceiling. "What star sign are you?"

"Er . . . Gemini," she mumbled. The circle seemed to be spinning.

"Well, that's perfect," he whispered, his mouth brushing her face. "You're the same as me. We're twin souls, Louisa." His fingers pulled at the halter fastening of her top. The fabric fell away, revealing her naked breasts. She gasped, suddenly aware of what was happening.

"Quentin, no!" she hissed.

"Come on!" He was on top of her now, his fingers pinching her nipples as he thrust his tongue into her mouth.

"Ow! You're hurting me!" The pain brought her mind into sharp focus. He was fumbling with the zipper of her jeans now, pulling them down. "No!" With a shout she brought up her knee, knocking him sideways off the bed.

"Bitch!" he yelled, a look of confusion on his face. "I thought you wanted it! You were coming on to me!"

"I was *not!*" Her hands shook as she refastened her top.

"Oh, I get it!" Quentin stumbled toward her, tripped on a rug, and lunged at her as he fell onto the bed. "Wrong color, am I?" He gave her a stupid grin.

She stared at him. What the hell did he mean by that?

"I've seen that little kid of yours. Daddy a big black man, huh? Screwed you and did a runner? Is that what you like? Big black men? Well, honey, I'll show you big. Get this!" He started unzipping his trousers. In one quick movement Louisa shoved him off the bed and ran for the door as he lay sprawled on the floor. She tore down the stairs, clinging to the banister rail for fear of losing her balance. Her head was still spinning. No sign of Gina. The front door was open. A couple of people were leaning against the wall next to it, smoking a joint. She dodged past them and ran out into the cool night air.

Stumbling across the pitch-black field, she somehow managed to find her way back to the Land Rover. She fumbled in her pocket for the keys and let herself in, crawling over the seats to the back. There were sacks on the floor and one of Rhiannon's old jackets. Curling up in a ball, she hugged the coat to her, sobbing as she inhaled its familiar, innocent scent.

In the field outside sheep nibbled at the grass sticking out from under the wheels and foxes called to each other in the still night air. And the Land Rover creaked gently with her sobs, until at last she cried herself to sleep.

~

Louisa was woken by the sound of someone banging on the window. Gray morning light filtered into the back of the Land Rover. She blinked as she realized where she was. Then her heart thumped against her ribs. *Was it him?*

"Lou! You in there?" It was Gina's voice. Louisa fumbled with the door.

"Oh, thank goodness! I was really worried about you!" Gina's smile vanished when she caught sight of Louisa's face. "My God! You look terrible! What the hell happened?"

"Can we just get away from here?" Louisa's voice was croaky, and her eyes were sore from crying.

Gina nodded. "Not home, though, eh? Don't want your parents seeing you just yet. How about the Milk Bar in town? I think it's open on Sundays."

Louisa glanced down at her clothes. The red shiny top was spattered with drops of Quentin's lethal punch. And the button on her jeans was gone, a wisp of cotton marking the place where it had been. Her tongue felt thick and dry, and there was a bitter, charred taste in her mouth. "I don't want anyone to see me like this," she mumbled.

"We'll go in the back entrance," Gina said, "where the toilets are. You can get cleaned up a bit before we go into the café."

"Okay." Louisa scrambled out of the back of the vehicle and walked around to the driver's side, wincing with every movement.

Half an hour later they were nursing steaming mugs of black coffee.

"I thought you liked him." Gina frowned. "I saw you dancing with him and I thought, well, you know . . ."

"I suppose I did fancy him a bit." Louisa sniffed. "But he was horrible! I mean, we hadn't even kissed or anything and he was on top of me, pulling my clothes off. Like an animal! Like . . ." She bit her lip.

"Like Trefor?"

Louisa squeezed her eyes shut. "It was . . ." She shook her head. "I don't know: like I was seventeen again and he was there, holding me down, hurting me. He was so angry—said I'd been leading him on!" Her eyes snapped open. "What is it with me, Gina? What do I *do* that makes men act like that? Do I *look* easy?"

"Of course you don't!" Gina rubbed her shoulder. "Listen, it's him, not you. You were just unlucky. What a bastard—and he seemed so nice!"

"Perhaps he would have been. With you, I mean. I know you fancied him. When he asked me to dance, I looked for you—but you'd gone."

"I know." Gina gave a wry smile. "I got off with his mate, Jeremy, instead."

"The one I saw you kissing on the stairs?"

"Yes."

"And did you . . . you know?"

Gina sucked in a breath. "Do you think I'm terrible?"

The shake of Louisa's head was so quick that anyone watching would have missed it. She took a gulp of coffee. "Was it . . ." she whispered, "was it good?"

Gina stared into the steam spiraling from her mug. "Yes. It was fantastic," she breathed. "Better than Andy!"

"I . . . I'm really pleased for you." Louisa made herself smile. "Are you going to see him again?"

"I hope so. We haven't arranged anything definite, but I'll see him at the market." A flash of concern crossed her face. "That's going to be terrible for you, though, isn't it?"

Louisa shrugged. "Not really. I can handle it. Quentin's the one who should be embarrassed, not me." She almost convinced herself, but beneath the bravado she knew it was going to be awful, having to stand just yards away from him week after week, with Rhiannon a tangible reminder of the horrible things he had said.

She wanted to erase the whole sordid episode from her memory, but his words were etched inside her head. Quentin had accused her of doing exactly what her mother must have done. Imagining that seedy one-night stand made her feel physically sick. *No wonder men treat you like a tart,* Quentin's voice whispered. *Like mother, like daughter . . .*

Chapter 34

On the way to Aberystwyth market the following week Louisa steeled herself. She had decided that the only way to cope was to blank Quentin out, pretend the party had never happened. If he said anything to her, or made any snide remarks about Rhiannon, she would simply ignore him.

When they pulled up in the square and began unloading eggs, she shot a quick glance at Quentin's stall. To her surprise and relief he wasn't there. He was still missing the following week and discreet inquiries by Gina revealed that he had left the commune to go traveling in India.

Over the next few weeks Louisa wrestled with the negative thoughts he had stirred up. She told herself that she was *not* like her mother. That Eva had lost control—probably after a few too many drinks—in the same way she might have lost control with Quentin at the party. But she hadn't. She hadn't had a one-night stand like her mother had with the American soldier.

She tried to push thoughts of her mother's casual liaison out of her mind, but every so often Quentin's words would float up from her subconscious. The assumption he had made about Rhiannon became a nagging worry. What was going to happen when she started school? Would she be teased because of her color? Would she come home wanting to know why her skin was different from Tom's? Louisa agonized over what, if anything, to say to her daughter. It would be easiest to cross her fingers and say nothing, in the hope that Rhiannon would simply be accepted by the other kids. But her conscience told her this was blind optimism. She could still remember how it had felt, that day in the sweet shop, to be called black. Nearly twenty years and the wound was still raw. She would rather die than let Rhiannon go through something like that. But how was she going to explain it all to a child who was not yet five years old?

In the end it was Tom who forced her to confront the past. He came home one afternoon and announced that his school project was to draw up a family tree. "Mr. Roberts said to go back as far as your great-grandparents," he said. "And to bring photos if we've got any. Have we?"

His request struck her like a punch in the stomach. "Er . . . I'm not sure." She sat down heavily at the kitchen table. Great-grandparents? She didn't even know the name of his grandfather. She had already told him a white lie to explain why he never saw Ray's parents. Was she going to lie to him again? "I'll go and have a word with Nan and Granddad," she said, trying to sound calm. "I'll ask them what photos they've got. Have a sandwich and we'll talk about it a bit later, eh?"

"Okay." Tom shrugged and went to fetch peanut butter from the cupboard.

Half an hour later, when he was out in the barn feeding an orphaned lamb, Louisa told Gina what had happened. "What am I going to tell him?" she groaned.

"The truth, I guess," Gina said. "Has he never asked questions before? About Rhiannon, I mean?"

"Only once." Louisa pursed her lips. "He asked why her skin was a darker brown than his and mine."

"And what did you tell him?"

"I said it was just the way she'd turned out. Like the way some sheep give birth to a white lamb one year and a black lamb the next."

"Hmm." Gina smiled. "It seems quite logical when you put it that way."

"But now I've got to spell out what really happened, haven't I?" Louisa sighed. "I've already told him Ray's parents live in Australia. I can't lie to him again."

"Australia?"

"Well, it was either that or tell him they'd died: How else was I supposed to explain why they suddenly disappeared from his life?"

Gina nodded. "Yes, I see what you mean."

"The thing is," Louisa went on, "if I tell him Eddie's not actually his granddad, he's going to want to know who his real grandfather is. How on earth do I explain why I don't even know his name?"

Gina shook her head, glancing out at the farmyard where Jonathan, Julia, and Rhiannon were playing tag. "Well, it certainly won't be easy—but it's got to come out sometime, Lou. Like I said before, it's a time bomb. It's got to go off sooner or later. Better get it over with, I'd say. Tom's old enough to understand, I think."

"Old enough to understand that his grandmother had a baby by a man who didn't hang around long enough to tell her his name?"

"Are you sure that's what happened?"

"How else do you explain why she can't remember it?" Louisa grimaced. "You don't have to be Sherlock Holmes to work it out, do you? I imagine they met at a dance where it was too noisy to talk properly, nipped outside for a quickie, and then he legged it back to his barracks. End of story."

"Okay, so your mum says she can't remember." Gina frowned. "But that doesn't mean she *really* can't, does it?"

"What are you saying?"

"What if she's just . . . well, I don't know—sort of blotted it out because she finds it too upsetting to think about?"

"Upsetting? You mean . . ." Louisa stopped short. It suddenly occurred to her that she might have got it all wrong: that Eva could have been the victim of a rape. It was a horrifying thought, but if it was true, she could no more blame her mother for what happened than she could blame herself for what Trefor had done.

As she turned the idea over, words of Eddie's drifted into her mind. Words spoken when she had been sitting sobbing on the draining board in the kitchen of the house on Sycamore Street: *It wasn't quite true, what your aunt said . . . when she said he died in the war. We don't know what happened to him.*

"What?" Gina was staring at her.

"Just remembering something my dad said when I was a kid." There was a faraway look in Louisa's eyes. "He said my real father didn't die in the war—how would he have known that?"

"Why don't you ask him? If your mum won't talk about it, maybe he will."

"I couldn't!" Louisa bit her lip. "It'd really upset him if I dragged all that up again—it was bad enough when I was a kid."

"But if you explain that it's for Tom's sake." Gina persisted. "He'd do anything for that boy."

"I know." Louisa nodded. "But doesn't that make it emotional blackmail?"

"Of course it doesn't! If he knows more than he's let on, he owes it to you to spill the beans. After all, none of it's your fault, is it?"

～

Gina volunteered to see to the children's supper while Louisa went to find Eddie. He was in the top field, mending a fence. She trudged along the track toward him, her heart in her boots. She watched his ready smile dissolve as she explained about Tom's project.

"You know the last thing I want is to upset you and Mam by bringing it all up again." She put her hand on his shoulder. "But I don't know what to tell him."

Eddie shifted his weight onto a fence post, as if suddenly weary. "I knew it'd all have to come out someday." He shook his head. "As soon as I set eyes on little Rhiannon, I thought, that's it: we won't be able to bury our heads in the sand much longer." He looked at her. "We should have sat you down and told you properly years ago."

"But you didn't." Louisa bit her lip. She hoped she hadn't made it sound like an accusation. "Was it because you were so upset about David?"

He nodded. "Partly, I suppose, yes. Your mother's never really been the same since we lost him. I think she blamed herself."

Louisa frowned. "Why?"

"She never really explained it exactly." He paused to wipe a bead of perspiration from his forehead. "She suddenly went very religious. Kept talking about the wages of sin, stuff like that."

"You mean she blamed David's death on . . ." Louisa faltered. It was like walking on eggshells.

"On the affair? Yes, I think she did." Eddie was staring at the muddy tracks his boots had made in the grass.

"Affair?" She stared at him. "She had an *affair*?"

"Well, yes." He gave her a puzzled look. "You knew about that, though, didn't you? We talked about him that time when you were little . . ."

"You told me he was black, and that you didn't know what had happened to him," Louisa said, her voice rising. "But you didn't tell me it was an affair!"

His eyes were uncomprehending. "But what else could it have been?"

"But I . . . I . . ." she stammered. "When she said she didn't know his name . . . I thought it was . . ." She couldn't say it.

"What?"

"A one-night stand!" she blurted out. "I didn't know what to think!" Hot tears stung her eyes. "For all I knew she could have been raped!" She buried her face in the coarse fabric of his jacket, and he wrapped his arms around her.

"I'm so sorry, Lou! We should have told you . . . I had no idea . . ."

"Please," she whispered, gulping back her tears, "just tell me the truth, Dad. Tell me what really happened."

"Well, I don't think I'll ever know that myself," he said, stroking her hair. "But I'll tell you what I do know." He took a long breath. "His surname was Willis, and she called him Bill."

"Do you know anything else?"

Eddie shook his head. "Not much. He was in the Quartermaster Corps. He was in France when you were born."

"And did he know about me?"

"Oh yes." Eddie cleared his throat, and for a moment she thought he was going to break down. "He knew your mother was pregnant," he went on. "He'd been trying to arrange for the Red Cross to take you over to the States when you were born."

Louisa stared at him, incredulous. "He wanted to take me to the States? You mean he and Mum were going to run off together?"

"I don't know what they were planning, love." He blinked and looked away. "She thought I was dead, you see. I'd been missing for two years. A prisoner of war . . ." He gave a heavy sigh.

"Oh God, Dad—I had no idea . . ." It was all so different from the pictures in her head. Her mother had had a serious affair; she had almost certainly been in love with this man. So why had she lied? Why had she pretended she couldn't remember his name? Louisa glanced at Eddie. There was so much she wanted to ask him, but the strange, distracted look in his eyes made her afraid to push him any further. How could he have kept all this bottled up for so many years?

"I'll tell you about the time I spent in Burma one day." He gave her a wry smile, suddenly himself again. "I'm sorry I can't tell you any more about your . . ." he hesitated for a split second, "about your father. That's all I know. But there is one other person who could probably tell you more."

"You mean Aunt Dilys?" Louisa had only met her mother's younger sister twice. It had occurred to her before that the aunt who had moved to Holland after the war might have known her real father, but she had never dared ask.

"No, not her—she was away in the forces when you were born, so I don't think she'd know much about him. Anyway, you know what she's like. If you were to start asking her questions, she'd be straight on the phone to your mother." He gave her a look that she understood instantly. It was the look he always used to convey that whatever they were talking about was to be kept from Eva. "No," he went on, "there's someone else. A woman by the name of Cathy Garner. She was very close to your mother during the war. She knew your real dad."

"Oh!" Louisa's mouth dropped open. She felt overwhelmed by the thought that the faceless man who had haunted her for almost two decades might suddenly become real.

"Her address is still in your mother's book," he went on, "although I don't know if she's still in Wolverhampton. We never saw her when we were living there."

"Why not?" Louisa asked the question automatically. She was only half listening, her mind still reeling with the implications of what Eddie had said.

"She and your mother lost touch. The last time I saw her was at David's funeral. She carried on sending Christmas and birthday cards for a couple of years after that, but your mother never wrote back." He shrugged. "She's probably moved on by now, but it might be worth a try."

Louisa suddenly felt sick. "I . . . I don't know if I want to."

Eddie took her arm and began walking back along the track. "It's up to you, love," he said gently, "but whatever you decide is fine by me. I want you to understand that."

~

The following Saturday Louisa was on her way to Wolverhampton. Only Gina and Eddie knew where she was going. Her mother and the children thought she was off to Shrewsbury to pick up a part for the tractor. Gina had made her pack an overnight bag.

"Why?" Louisa had protested. "She's either going to be there or she's not." She had no intention of spending the night in Wolverhampton. She hadn't wanted to go there at all. There were too many bad memories. But trying to contact her mother's friend by phone had proved fruitless.

"What if she's out?" Gina had argued. "What if some relative opens the door and tells you to come back later?" She had scribbled her mother's phone number on the back of the Wolverhampton map. "If you get stuck, give her a ring."

Now that she was on her way, Louisa wondered if she was doing the right thing. Ever since Eddie had given her that tantalizing glimpse of what had really happened between her mother and the American soldier, she had been desperate to find out more. The resentment and anger she had felt toward the man all these years had been swept away. *He wanted me*, she murmured. Just saying those few words felt like a betrayal of Eddie. She should have said something back when he gave her his blessing; spelled out what she felt inside—that no matter what happened, he would always be her father—but she was too distracted to give him that reassurance.

The idea of trying to find her real father filled her with a mixture of excitement and dread. He was almost certain to have married and had another family. What if he didn't want to be found? She wasn't sure she could handle that.

It had been difficult, trying to explain things to Tom, but his reaction had surprised her. Instead of asking awkward questions, he'd jumped out of his chair with excitement. "Does he live near Disneyland?" he'd yelled. "Can we go and visit him?" She'd had to admit that she didn't know where he lived at the moment but was going to try to find out. He had accepted this without a word, but getting him to promise not to say anything to his grandma had been tricky.

Louisa knew that if she did manage to trace her real father, she was going to have to tell Eva. But there was no point upsetting her unnecessarily. She would worry about that if and when she managed to track down Cathy Garner. So she had given Tom an excuse that was as near the truth as she could make it: that Nan and his real granddad had been friends once but had had an argument, and Nan would be upset if she knew they were trying to get back in touch with him.

Even as she'd said the words, she had wondered how it had really ended. She decided something pretty awful must have happened for her mother to want to blot him out of her memory as if he had never existed. But what? She felt a flash of anger. What could be terrible enough to make a woman want her child to think she was the product of a meaningless sexual encounter?

Her head was buzzing with questions when, just after eleven o'clock in the morning, she drove into Wolverhampton. It looked very different from the way she remembered it. Huge new roads had been constructed around the town center in the years since she had left. She pulled into a pub parking lot to consult her map. The address Eddie had given her was on the other side of town from where they had lived. She set off slowly along the wide new highway, following signs that led north. Her heart was thudding in her chest, a combination of the anxiety she felt about what might lie ahead and fear of getting lost on the scarily unfamiliar road system. She was glad she didn't have to drive through the town itself: past the cinema where she and Ray had met, and the cafés and pubs where they had done their courting.

Twenty minutes later she stopped again. She had just passed the enormous Goodyear tire factory, which Eddie had told her to look out for. She was only a couple of streets away from the one she was looking for, and soon she was cruising past a row of houses searching for number thirty-six. Her mother must have walked along this street dozens of times. She tried to picture her. She would have been several years younger than Louisa was now. She wondered if her mother had come here when she was pregnant. What Cathy Garner's reaction had been when she found out her friend was going to have a black man's baby. Louisa would never forget how it had felt to confess to her father that she was carrying an illegitimate baby. How much worse must it have been for her mother?

She caught sight of the number she was looking for and pulled up sharply. The house was much smarter than its neighbors. The windows and doors looked freshly painted, and the brickwork had been sandblasted to remove the grime that dulled the walls of the houses on either side. There were rosebushes in the tiny front garden, and the delicate lilac flowers of a wisteria framed the front door. Louisa sat for a moment, perspiration beading her forehead, trying to pluck up the courage to go and ring the bell.

She looked at her reflection in the rearview mirror, gave herself a silent warning about not building up her hopes too much. There was every chance that Cathy Garner had disappeared without a trace. Directory Enquiries had said there was no Catherine Garner listed in the Wolverhampton phone book. When she had persisted, asking if there was a number listed for that address, the woman had told her that there was, but it was withheld from the public directory. She had refused to tell Louisa the name of the current occupant.

She climbed out of the Land Rover and took a deep breath. The scent of the roses filled her nostrils. She could hear the sound of children laughing and shouting farther up the street, and somewhere a dog was barking. As she stood there, tense and nervous, all the sounds, smells, and colors around her seemed to intensify. The sun came out from behind a cloud, giving the brickwork of number thirty-six a warm glow. She pushed open the little garden gate and walked purposefully up the path.

The bell sounded inside the house as she rang it, a melodic series of notes that triggered no other sounds that she could detect. She held her breath. Then she rang again. This time she heard something. The sound of heavy footsteps hurrying downstairs. Then she saw a blur of colors through the frosted glass panel of the door. Suddenly a tall, blond man with a tanned face was standing in front of her.

"I'm . . . er . . . looking for a Mrs. Garner," Louisa stammered. "Mrs. Cathy Garner. Does she live here?"

"No, she doesn't." The man eyed her curiously. "She hasn't lived here for a long time. What do you want her for?"

"Oh, I'm . . ." Louisa faltered, crushed by his words. "She and my mother were friends during the war. I'm trying to trace a relative, and I thought she might be able to help me." She searched his face, thinking how foolish she must sound. "Have you any idea where she's gone?"

"What was your mother's name?" he said, his eyes narrowing.

"Eva." Louisa blinked as a ray of sunlight reflected off the door into her eyes. "Eva Melrose."

"Oh," he said, a flicker of recognition transforming his face. "You're not . . ." He was staring at her hard. "Are you Louisa?"

She gazed back at him, perplexed. "How . . . how do you know who I am? Who are you?"

He smiled, holding out his hand to her. "I'm Michael Garner. Cathy's son."

Chapter 35

Louisa followed Michael Garner into the house. She didn't often meet men who towered over her, but he did. *He must be at least six foot four*, she thought. His short blond hair gave way to a muscular golden-brown neck. The color of his skin was emphasized by the white T-shirt he wore with his jeans. One sleeve of the T-shirt was fraying at the edge, and there was a smear of something like paint across the fabric covering his left shoulder blade. She wondered how old he was. He looked midthirties. How had he recognized her? She was sure she had never seen him before.

"Take a seat," he said, leading her into the living room. The furniture was very modern, quite unlike anything they had at the farmhouse. A brown corduroy sofa with a cane frame stood behind a large, glass-topped coffee table. By the French windows was a huge wicker armchair with a circular back and brown and orange cushions. A wall unit in pale wood held a vast record collection and half a dozen silver-framed photos. The largest was a black-and-white wedding photo, showing a pretty, round-faced woman in a plain satin dress gazing into the eyes of a much longer-haired Michael. Beside it was a color picture of a smiling teenage girl.

"Have you come all the way from Wales?" Michael asked.

Louisa nodded, her brow furrowed. How did he know where she lived?

"Have you eaten? I was just about to make myself some soup and toast—would you like some?"

"Oh, I don't want to intrude if you're having lunch. I could come back later . . ." Louisa felt a sudden, unaccountable shyness. It was his eyes. They were the same blue as his jeans and crinkled at the edges when he smiled. There was something disarming about them, and she looked away.

"No, it's no trouble." He grinned, shrugging. "To be honest I'm glad of an excuse to stop—I've been wallpapering the bathroom all morning, and I hate decorating!" He disappeared around the door. "Is minestrone alright?" he called from the kitchen.

"Yes—lovely," she called back. While she waited, she studied the photographs on the shelf. On closer inspection she saw that they were all of the same three people: Michael, his wife, and the girl—their daughter, presumably. She wondered where his wife was, what she would say if she came back to find a strange woman eating lunch with her husband.

They ate in the kitchen, which had a large table laid with raffia mats and a pottery vase filled with roses from the garden. He told her that Monica, his wife, was away at a Girl Guide camp with their daughter, whose name was Heather.

"Monica's an Akela," he said. "Daft title, isn't it? But she's always been very keen on the Guides. Couldn't wait for Heather to be old enough to join. Do you have kids, Louisa?"

She nodded. "Yes, two. A boy and a girl. Tom's ten and Rhiannon's four."

"That's nice," he said, and she thought she caught a wistful look in his eye, but it lasted only a split second. "I came to visit you in Wales, once," he said, "but you wouldn't remember: you were only a baby."

"Oh." She rested her spoon against the side of her bowl. "I was wondering how you recognized me."

"Mum took me on the train. I must have been about nine or ten. We met up with your mother in Aberystwyth . . ." He paused, glancing down at the table. "You were there . . . and your brother." He looked her straight in the eyes. "I'm so sorry about what happened to him. He was a great little kid—it must have been awful for your family."

"Yes, it was." Louisa nodded. "I don't really remember him, which is sad. It affected my mother really badly . . ." She hesitated, biting her lip. "That's partly why I've come here. Mum never talks about the past. She won't talk about my real father at all." She looked away, a blush rising to her cheeks. She suddenly felt naked under his gaze, realizing he might know more about her than she knew herself.

Michael pushed his bowl aside. "Mum told me something about what happened to your mother. I remember asking her about you when I was—I don't know—thirteen or fourteen. She was writing Christmas cards, and she crossed your mum's name off the list. I asked her why, and she told me she and your mum used to be very close friends, but so many sad things had happened to your mum when she was younger, she probably didn't want to be reminded of them by getting cards from people she knew back then."

He rested his elbow on the table and rubbed his forehead with the tips of his fingers. "I asked her what the bad things were, and she gave me what I think was a pretty honest account. She was always very straight with me as a kid." He paused, glancing into her eyes for a second, as if weighing his words. "She told me about your real father being a black GI." The words were spoken evenly. Louisa detected no hint of prejudice. "She told me how hard it was for him and your mum to be together," he went on. "Evidently he was a great dancer. She said they met at one of the forces' balls they used to have at the Civic Hall—and some white bloke flattened him just for dancing with her."

Louisa leaned forward, her soup forgotten. "What else did she tell you? Did she say where he came from? What happened to him after the war?"

Michael shook his head. "I'm sorry, I don't think I can tell you much else—but I'm sure she could."

A flash of confusion crossed Louisa's face. She had assumed Cathy was dead. Michael saw her expression and gave a sheepish grin. "Sorry, I should've told you earlier—Mum moved to the Cotswolds. She married a man she met on holiday there. He owns a hotel, so she let me have this place."

"Could I . . . I mean, would it be possible to talk to her on the phone?" Louisa's heart was beating so hard, she felt as if her ribs would burst.

"I think we can do better than that." He laughed. "Grab your coat—I'll run you down there!"

~

Before they left, Louisa asked if she could use the bathroom. She smiled when she saw the state it was in. Two walls covered in paper, and the others bare plaster. She had protested when he offered to drive her to Cathy's, but he had waved away her objections, saying there'd still be plenty of time to finish the decorating before his wife and daughter got back.

Coming out of the bathroom, Louisa couldn't help noticing the bedrooms. Their doors were wide open. The walls of the first were completely covered with posters of the Osmonds: *Heather's room*, she thought, smiling. Next to it was a larger room with a double bed, the covers rumpled and a pair of jeans lying in a heap on the floor. The dressing table was bare, apart from a comb and a bottle of aftershave. Two guitars were propped on stands beside it. The remaining room had a single bed and was fussily decorated in pinks and lilacs. She assumed this was the guest room, but then she noticed a pink lacy nightdress draped across a chair by the single bed. On the floor beside it were matching satin slippers. Scent bottles and makeup cluttered the dressing table, along with half a dozen bottles of tablets. *Odd*, Louisa thought. It looked very much lived-in, but by whom?

Michael didn't talk about his family as they drove past the factories and canals, heading southwest. He wanted to know all about her life: what it was like to live on a farm, and how she had come to the decision to start searching for her father.

Soon they were driving through a rural landscape whose contours were less rugged and dramatic than Wales but no less beautiful. The journey had passed quickly. She felt she had talked far too much about herself. She wanted to know more about him. Tentatively she admitted glimpsing the guitars in the bedroom.

He told her about his double life as an engineer at Goodyear's by day and a bass player with a local band by night. "We're not quite in the same league as Slade." He grinned. "But it's a good laugh—keeps me in beer money!"

"What kind of music do you play?" She glanced at his hand as he changed gear. He wasn't wearing a wedding ring.

"Oh, you know, Stones, Jimi Hendrix, all kinds, really."

"Who's your favorite?"

He laughed. "That's a tough one. From the past, it'd have to be Jimi. At the moment, I'd say T. Rex. Have you heard 'Twentieth Century Boy'?"

She nodded. "I keep meaning to buy it—we can't pick up the radio at the farm because it's so remote. The only time I get to hear it is when I'm driving."

"What about your husband?" he asked. "What kind of thing is he into?"

His eyes flickered with surprise when she told him she was a widow. But there were no probing questions. He seemed to accept that she didn't want to explain how her husband had met his death at such an early age. She talked instead about living in Wolverhampton as a child, about the shock of the racism she had encountered, and the lengths she had gone to hide her color. She had never talked to anyone but Gina about this before. Why was she telling him? She paused, glancing at his profile as he scanned the road ahead. It was because he knew all about her already. She had no need to hide anything, no need to pretend she was someone she wasn't. With this man she could be herself.

He pulled in by a picture-postcard building with stonewalls the color of honey and a stream, with its own wooden bridge, running through the grounds. "Welcome to the Boatman's Arms." He smiled. "Shall we go and find my mum?"

If Cathy Garner was surprised at the identity of her son's guest, she didn't show it. She was tiny beside Michael, her graying hair swept up in a bun. She wore a camel-colored cashmere sweater with a knee-length black skirt and black patent leather pumps. When Louisa went to shake her hand, she pulled her into a hug. "I had a feeling you might come looking for me one day," she said. "I'm so glad you found Mikey."

She led them both into a small sitting room overlooking the stream. In the corner was a cream damask ottoman, from which she took a leather-bound photograph album. "This is me and your mother in our railway days." She smiled, handing Louisa the open album. "Although you'd hardly recognize us in that getup! That's Eva, with the cap."

Louisa stared at the black-and-white photo of women with spades ranged along a stretch of railway line. The baggy clothes and the peaked cap couldn't conceal her mother's stunning good looks. Her face was bright and free of the worry lines that marked it so deeply now. Long tendrils of hair had escaped from the cap, giving some hint of what it must have been like before the short, unflattering style her mother had worn for as long as Louisa could remember. It seemed almost unbelievable that she had done such hard, physical work when nowadays she found it difficult to climb the farmhouse stairs.

A tray of tea and cakes was brought into the room by a young girl in a striped apron. "Thank you, Sheila," Cathy said. "Now, Louisa," she went on, turning a page of the album. "This is the one you'll want to see."

Louisa's mouth went dry. Dressed in a US Army uniform, with his arm around her smiling mother, was a tall, athletic-looking young man with the face of an Egyptian pharaoh. The sunlight had caught his high cheekbones and his huge dark eyes—which were just like Tom's—twinkled with mischief.

"You've got his smile." Cathy's voice seemed to come from a hundred miles away. "As soon as I saw you, I thought: oh, yes, that's Bill's girl."

Louisa blinked back the tears welling up. "I . . . I've always wondered what he looked like," she stammered, "and now that I've seen him . . . it's so . . . I'm sorry!" She fumbled for a tissue, suddenly aware of Michael's hand on her arm.

"It's okay," he said. "It was bound to be a shock. Here, drink this." He handed her a cup of tea. "Sugar?"

She shook her head. "It *is* a shock." She sniffed. Turning to Cathy, she said, "Mum would never talk about him. For years and years I've tried to push him out of my mind. She told me she couldn't remember his name . . ." she faltered, struggling against the tidal wave of emotion his face had unleashed. "You can imagine what I thought: I had no idea he even knew I existed, until a few days ago."

Cathy pressed her lips together as if she was uncertain how much more to reveal. "There was a reason for your mother's silence, you know," she said gently. "I can still see her face, the way she looked at me after your brother's funeral." She looked down at her teacup, a frown wrinkling her high forehead. "She blamed herself for his death, you see. Not directly, you understand—it was the typhoid epidemic that killed him, poor little mite." She paused for a moment, then met Louisa's eyes with the same direct gaze as her son. "The reason she blamed herself was because if she hadn't been to Aberystwyth to meet us that day, David would never have contracted the disease."

Louisa frowned. "But that was just chance, surely?"

"Yes, you're right of course, but that wasn't the way Eva saw it. She'd come to meet Mikey and me because I was taking her a parcel that had arrived at her old house in Wolverhampton. It was from Bill."

Louisa's eyes widened. "He was still in touch with her after the war ended?"

"Not exactly, no. She lost track of him after he was sent to France for the D-day landings." Cathy told her the story of Eddie's sudden, unexpected return, of his letter to Bill and Eva's attempt to rebuild her life after the war. "So when she got that parcel, with a little outfit he'd sent for your birthday, it set it all off again. He said he'd rejoined the army and was about to be posted abroad. She was fired up by the idea that he might be sent back to this country. That was the only way they could have been together, you see."

Louisa listened in shocked silence as Cathy explained the terrible dilemma Eva had faced on Eddie's return. "She had to choose between Bill and your brother," she said. "If she'd tried to follow him to the States, she would've had to leave David behind, you see." She shook her head. "I don't know if he's ever told you, but your dad—Eddie, I mean—went through a terrible time during the war. All he wanted was to get his family back. He would never have agreed to your mother taking David to the States."

"Did my . . ." Louisa hesitated. She couldn't say the word *father*. "Did Bill want her to go?"

"That was the other thing." Cathy let out a long breath. "She didn't really know what was in his mind because he was whisked off so quickly. He wanted to do the right thing by you, which was why he'd been trying to arrange for the Red Cross to take you to his aunt in Chicago. But Eva said he never actually mentioned marriage." She paused, her face creased with concern, and Louisa saw that she was searching for a way of softening the harsh reality of what had happened. "He was very young," Cathy went on. "Your mum was only twenty-one when they met, and he was a few months younger, if I remember rightly. And although they both believed Eddie was dead, marriage would have been out of the question until his death was officially confirmed at the end of the war."

Louisa stared at the photograph album in her lap. Her mother looked radiantly happy. Was she already pregnant when it was taken? She wondered how long the affair had lasted, how her mother had come to give birth at the farmhouse in Wales instead of in Wolverhampton, and why Bill hadn't fought harder to get her over to America. There were so many questions hammering inside her head, but one was more insistent than the rest. "You say he wanted to send me to his aunt in Chicago," she said, struggling to keep her voice steady. "Is that where he came from?"

Cathy shook her head. "No, he was from New Orleans. In Louisiana."

This brought a small, bewildered sound from Louisa: something between a gasp and a sob.

"You didn't know how you came by your name, then?" Cathy bit her lip. "Well, he couldn't send you home to his mother because of the race laws. There were strict rules in the southern states about black and white people intermarrying. He knew you'd be treated as an outcast if he sent you there."

"But it was different in Chicago?"

"Yes. He told your mother that his aunt had raised five children of her own and would be prepared to take you on until the war ended."

"Do you know her name?" Louisa felt her heartbeat quicken.

"I think it was Millie." Cathy frowned. "I never knew her surname, I'm afraid."

"And what about Bill? Dad said his last name was Willis."

"Yes, that's right." Cathy nodded. "But Bill wasn't his real first name. Your mum said he wouldn't tell her his real name. I think he was embarrassed about it."

"What? Oh no!" Louisa's hand flew to her mouth. "How am I going to find him without a first name?" She glanced from Cathy to Michael, then back again. "What about the parcel he sent after the war? Did it have an address on it?"

"No, it didn't. He said he'd write with his new address when he knew where the army was going to post him." Cathy explained how Bill had never known about Eva's move to Wales, that any further mail would have gone to the old house in Wolverhampton, which had changed hands. "At first she wanted me to ask the new people to forward any letters he sent," Cathy said, "but David died before I'd had a chance to go round there. She made it very clear then that she wanted nothing more to do with Bill. You see, she blamed him for David's death as much as she blamed herself."

Louisa blinked away new tears. If only she'd known all this. If only her mother had confided in her. But how could she? How could she have let on that Bill had been the love of her life? The man she wanted to marry. And that Louisa's beloved dad was the second best she had been compelled to put up with?

"You must understand, Louisa: she was very much in love with him." Cathy's voice was almost a whisper. Louisa saw that there were tears in her eyes too. "Before your brother died, when Eddie had just come back from the war, she came to my house in Wolverhampton. We talked it all through. She knew that going to the States was going to be impossible for her. I asked her then what she was going to tell you when you grew up." Cathy blinked. "I remember her exact words. She said: I'll tell her I loved her father very much."

Chapter 36

"Would you like me to go and organize some supper?" Michael's voice startled Louisa. She'd been so wrapped up in Cathy's story of the romance between Bill and her mother that she had lost all track of time.

"Oh, it's half past six!" She jumped to her feet. "I should be getting back!"

"Wouldn't you like to stay the night, dear?" Cathy said. "It seems a shame, you having to rush off."

Louisa looked at Michael.

"Okay by me," he said. "We can drive back first thing in the morning if you like."

She hesitated a moment before replying. She hadn't intended to be away overnight, but there was still so much she wanted to ask. The children would be fine without her for just one night, and Gina would cook up some excuse for her being held up. "I'd love to stay." She smiled. "If you're sure I'm not putting you to any trouble. You've both been so kind."

Gina was almost speechless with excitement when Louisa phoned a few minutes later. "So, some hunky bloke drives you to a posh hotel," she spluttered, "and then invites you to stay the night . . ."

"Don't get carried away." Louisa laughed. "He's married with a teenage daughter. Luckily for me they were away for the weekend—otherwise I probably wouldn't have got to meet his mum."

"Hmm. Well, don't do anything I wouldn't do." Gina giggled.

Louisa gave a wry smile as she replaced the receiver. *Just like Gina*, she thought. Couldn't get it into her head that the only man she was interested in finding was Bill.

~

During the evening meal Cathy related everything else she could remember about Bill and Eva's time together. Louisa's eyes widened when she described what had happened to Bill's friend Jimmy.

"Your father knew the girl was lying," Cathy said. "He'd seen them together several times, and from what he said, she'd been more than willing. She cried rape when she found out she was pregnant. You see, she was terrified of admitting to her parents that she'd had an affair with a colored man."

"And they hanged him for it?" Louisa glanced at Michael, who looked every bit as incredulous as she was.

Cathy nodded. "It made the headlines. He was the first man ever to hang in this country for the crime of rape. But he wasn't the last."

"There were others?"

"Yes. All American servicemen. Most of them black, I believe." Cathy frowned. "You have to understand that attitudes were very different then. Most people in this country had never set eyes on a colored person until the Americans arrived. There were all sorts of stupid rumors going round. I remember a girl at work telling us that black men had tails like monkeys." She made a face. "I think most of the rumors were started deliberately by the US Army: they wanted British people to keep their distance from the black GIs, I suppose because they thought any mixing would make them more resentful of the segregation back home. Your father was punched to the ground by a white American soldier the first night he met your mum—and all they were doing was dancing."

Louisa blinked. This was almost unimaginable. Her mother, dancing. Her mother a rebel who flouted social taboos. And her father—the man whose face she didn't have to imagine anymore—he was brave enough to risk a beating for the chance to dance with her.

"Your mum couldn't abide racism. She told me she couldn't bear to hear people picked on just because of their appearance." Cathy pressed her lips together. Once again Louisa got the feeling she was working out just how much she should say. "It was because of David, your brother," she went on. "When he was born, he had a birthmark on his face. It faded quite quickly, but your mum never forgot how cruel people were about it."

Louisa considered this for a moment. She couldn't square this image of her mother as a feisty, fearless young woman with the nervous, introverted person she had grown up with. "Was Mum already pregnant with me when my father's friend was hanged?" she asked. It had occurred to her that Eva could have tried exactly the same trick as Jimmy's girlfriend. To say she had been raped would have deflected the blame when Eddie came home from the war.

"Yes, she was about four months' pregnant, I think. She was on her way to tell Bill about it the night Jimmy was arrested, but when all that blew up, she realized it would be too much for him to take. In the end she waited until she was about five or six months gone."

Cathy described how Eva had collapsed in the snow at the railway station after trying to hide her pregnancy. "She hadn't told anyone: not even her own family. You see, when Mary—your grandmother—read in the papers about Jimmy's girlfriend being pregnant, she was absolutely scathing about it. She made her views very clear to your mum, saying no one would want the baby and it'd probably end up in a children's home. Eva was too terrified to tell her that she was in the same boat." Cathy drew in a breath. She opened her mouth as if about to say something else, then closed it again.

The scenes Cathy conjured seemed as real to Louisa as images on a cinema screen. They triggered a barrage of questions. How had she concealed the pregnancy? Had she really believed she had a future with Bill? Did Bill know that she was married with a child?

"Not at first," Cathy said, when she voiced this last question. "She did tell him later, though."

Louisa's face fell.

"I know that makes her sound bad, but you mustn't judge her too harshly. It's hard for your generation to understand how things were during the war. None of us knew if we had any kind of future. When you think you could be dead this time next year, next month, next week even, you just live for the moment." She reached for the coffeepot and topped up their cups. "When your mother met Bill, she wasn't looking for romance. She only agreed to go out that night because I talked her into it. Bill quite literally whisked her off her feet."

Louisa sipped her coffee, trying to picture the Civic Hall as it would have been that night. The men in uniform, the young women desperate for a bit of excitement to distract them from the nightmare of war. She remembered that Christmas Ball she had gone to at seventeen, desperate to dance away her own nightmare. How she had danced with Ray, seduced him, in a hopeless attempt to blot Trefor's face from her mind. But it was not the same. She had never felt what Cathy was describing. That burning desire. That obsessive longing. That unstoppable passion blitzing every obstacle in its path.

~

It was half past nine when they finally got up from the table. Cathy excused herself, saying she had a party of guests due to arrive early the next morning. "Why don't you show Louisa around the village?" she said to Michael.

It was still light outside, and Michael took Louisa down the road to a place where another wooden bridge led across the stream into woodland. "There's not much to see in the village." He smiled. "Shall we have a quick walk and then go for last orders at the pub? The other pub, I mean?"

Louisa chuckled. "I suppose it must be strange, drinking in your mother's bar," she said, following him along a path bordered by tall cow parsley and red campions.

"It is." He grinned at her over his shoulder. "I have to be on my best behavior in front of the staff. And the guests are . . . well, suffice it to say I once made the mistake of bringing the lads down here to play a gig."

"Didn't go down well?"

Michael winced. "I think Mum's clientele are more into Andy Williams than Mick Jagger. Since then I've always done my drinking at the Nag's Head."

They walked on in silence for a few minutes. There was no sound other than the warbling of roosting birds and the distant murmur of the stream. The scent of honeysuckle and wild garlic drifted in the air, and for a second she closed her eyes, drinking in the peace. Her mind was a jumble of emotions. She was both thrilled and shattered by what she had learned from Cathy. And all the time new questions were popping up in her head.

"Oh!"

Michael had stopped suddenly, and she had bumped right into him.

"Sorry," he said, "we've come to a stile. It's getting dark, isn't it? We should have turned back sooner."

"No, it's . . . it was my fault." She couldn't get the words out properly. The touch of his hand on her arm had sent an electric shock through her entire body. She could feel his breath on her neck and suddenly she wanted to reach out and pull him to her, feel his arms wrap themselves around her body. "Y . . . yes," she mumbled. "You're right." She stepped backward, away from him. "We'd better head back."

As she followed him back along the path, she felt as if her limbs were on fire. Her mouth was so dry, she could barely swallow. The power of it terrified her. And all he had done was touch her arm.

~

The Nag's Head was crowded, but they managed to find a couple of stools next to a table that was little more than a shelf protruding from one side of the enormous fireplace.

"It's a shame Mum doesn't know your father's address, isn't it?" Michael said, setting down two glasses of cider.

Louisa nodded, shifting her stool as he sat down beside her. The feelings he had stirred up made her feel guilty and confused. She mustn't allow their bodies to touch again. As she sipped her drink, her forehead puckered. "What would you do?" she asked, staring into her glass. "If it was your father, I mean?"

"I think I'd try the American Embassy." He put his half-empty glass back on the table. "There's got to be a list of World War Two servicemen who came to this country." He paused, rubbing his chin. "Without knowing his first name, though, it could be tough."

"I suppose Willis is a fairly common name. I wonder how many there'd be in a place like New Orleans?"

"Could be hundreds." He thought for a moment. "The newspapers might be your best bet, you know. Mum said Jimmy's hanging made the headlines. What if your father's name got a mention—if he had to give evidence at the court martial, say?"

"I suppose it's worth a try." She looked at him. His blue eyes sparkled in the firelight. "How would I go about it?"

"I'll do it if you like. They keep old copies of the *Express & Star* in the town library. I could pop in next week sometime."

"Are you sure?" She found herself wishing he wasn't so nice.

"Absolutely." He grinned. "I quite like the idea of playing detective."

~

That night Louisa lay awake for a long time. Cathy had given her a lovely room overlooking the stream. She had opened the window before climbing into bed, hoping the water's gentle rhythm would lull her to sleep, but there was too much going on in her head.

She went over and over it, piecing together all the precious glimpses Cathy had revealed. In a few short hours the chief mystery of her life had been solved. She had seen his face, found out where he came from, and understood the true nature of his relationship with her mother. But now there were new puzzles. Her dad must have known the depth of his wife's feelings for Bill. So why had he been prepared to adopt his rival's child?

It began to dawn on Louisa that, as a baby, she may have been little more than a bargaining chip. *If you want David, Lou comes too!* She could almost hear her mother hissing those words, full of bitterness at having to choose between her lover and her son. Was that why Eddie had adopted her?

But he must have grown to love her, mustn't he? Otherwise he would have upped and left when David died. A depressing thought occurred to her. She was a substitute. Like a dog someone buys when they lose a partner and can't bear to live alone. Eddie only loved her because he no longer had David. The wrong child had died.

The thought of this made the tears she had been fighting back all day flow freely onto the pillow. Suddenly she felt very alone. She wished she was at home and could creep into Rhiannon's bed for company.

It was almost dawn when she fell into a fitful sleep. She dreamed of Bill, no longer the faceless stranger who had haunted her for so long, but the handsome young soldier in the photograph. He was leading her down the aisle of the big church in Aberystwyth. She was in the dress she had worn to marry Ray, but when she looked toward the altar rail, the man waiting for her was Michael.

~

She woke up in a sweat, her heart pounding. Someone was knocking on the door.

"Are you awake, Louisa?" It was Michael's voice. "I've brought you some breakfast."

She jumped out of bed, grabbing the soft, white terry-cloth robe Cathy had laid out for her. She opened the door and peered around it, revealing only her head. Michael was dressed. He looked as if he'd been up and about for ages.

"Thank you." She took the tray of tea and toast. "What time is it? Have I overslept?"

"It's ten past nine." He gave her a smile that made her insides slide like melted butter. "Sorry to wake you, but I thought you'd want to be getting back."

"Oh . . . yes." She felt flustered, cross with herself. "I'll be as quick as I can."

When she got into his car, the radio was on and she was glad of it. Her head was still muddled with the images of the night before. She needed time on her own to get things straight. Michael seemed to sense that she didn't want to talk. Apart from a polite inquiry about whether she minded Radio One, he said nothing until they were approaching Wolverhampton.

"Will you write down your telephone number so I can let you know if I find anything in the paper? There's a pad and pen in the glove compartment, I think."

"Oh yes. Okay." She found the pad and scribbled it down. Should she ask for his number? She wanted to, but wasn't sure it was a sensible thing to do. If she had it, she knew she would be tempted to phone him on some pretext, just to hear his voice. *No, she thought, if he finds anything, he'll phone me.* If not, there's no reason to contact him again. The implication of this hit her like a slap in the face. Then the image from her dream flashed into her mind's eye. Michael standing at the altar rail, smiling as she reached for his hand. *He's married,* she reminded herself. *Forget him!*

There was an awkward moment when they arrived at Michael's house. He walked with her the short distance to where the Land Rover was parked. They said good-bye, and she went to shake his hand as he went to give her a hug. She ended up jabbing him in the chest with her fingers. He laughed it off, saying he hoped they'd meet again one day.

She drove off with an empty feeling inside. *Of course he hadn't meant it,* she told herself. *He was just being polite.* She reached across to the passenger seat and flipped her bag open. She felt inside until her fingers found what she was looking for. The photograph of Bill that Cathy had given her. She propped it on the dashboard and smiled. *I'll find you,* she whispered. *If it takes the rest of my life, I'll find you!*

Chapter 37

The next day Louisa went up to the top field, alone except for Mattie, one of the sheepdogs. Gina was the only person she had talked to so far about the events of the weekend. Eddie had called in to see her soon after she'd got back from Wolverhampton, but she had fobbed him off with short, noncommittal answers when he'd asked how the trip had gone. She despised herself for being so mean to him, but she felt overwhelmed with what she had learned from Cathy. She would talk to him, but not yet.

She had shown the photograph of Bill to Gina but not to the children. She wanted to have a copy made for Tom to take to school and get the original framed to hang in the living room. But then Eva would see it. Should she hide it away in her bedroom, then, just to spare her mother's feelings?

As she trudged around the field inspecting the fences Eddie had checked just days before, she realized that she was sick and tired of pretending, of hiding things away. She had been doing it all her adult life. Was she going to make her own children do the same? Send them tiptoeing around their grandmother the way she had done, keeping things from her for fear of making her cry? *No,* she thought, *this has got to stop.* She felt very sorry for the way her mother's life had turned out, but she mustn't let its legacy hurt her children.

She decided she would show them both the photograph that evening and tell them as much of the truth as they were old enough to understand. And her mother would just have to accept it. *It had been thirty years ago*, she reminded herself. Thirty years since her mother's romance with Bill. Surely that was enough time to get over someone?

Then her brother's face drifted into her head. David had died more than a quarter of a century ago—but was the death of a child something a parent could ever get over? She tried to imagine how she would feel if anything happened to Tom or Rhiannon. She could still remember the terror she had felt when Trefor threatened to snatch her son. What if he had succeeded? Taken her boy away? Would she ever have been able to forgive him? Of course she wouldn't: and was that so very different from the blame her mother had assigned to Bill?

He, unlike Trefor, had meant no deliberate harm, but she could understand how her mother's mind would have twisted with grief. For years after David's death, her mother had made the tortuous journey to chapel twice a day on Sundays. When they moved to Wolverhampton, she had joined the Congregational church around the corner from the house on Sycamore Street. She still went to chapel now that they were back at Devil's Bridge, although not as often. Was it because of her arthritis or something else? Perhaps the heartache had loosened its grip and she didn't feel such a need for religion anymore.

Louisa wondered what it was like inside her mother's head. What she really felt about Eddie. On the face of it, her parents seemed quite contented with each other. Was this because, over the years, her mother had come to realize that Eddie was the right one after all? That Bill had been some hopeless romantic fantasy that probably wouldn't have worked out?

She knew she was going to have to talk to her mother before she showed Bill's photo to the children. She would have to tell her about finding Cathy and explain why she needed to bring everything out in the open. But first she would have to warn her dad. He was the one who would have to cope with most of the fallout. And she must do everything in her power to reassure him of his place in her heart.

She found him ferrying bales of straw with the tractor. She waved him down and climbed into the cab beside him. He poured her tea from his thermos and listened in silence as she told him all that had happened over the weekend. She hesitated only when she came to the part about her mother having to choose between Bill and David.

"Don't worry: I know." He had sensed what she was holding back. "I was very selfish, wasn't I?" He blinked to banish the tears brightening his eyes. "I came back from the war very hard, very determined to cling onto what was left."

Now it was her turn to listen. An expression of horrified fascination crept over her as he relived the nightmare of his time in Burma. When he described what had happened to Granville, the black orderly who had nursed him back to health, the tears that had been welling up spilled down her face.

"You see, when I came back and found you, it all seemed to make sense," he said, patting her hand. "It was as if you were Granville's child. He'd saved me, and now I could take care of you."

"Oh Dad!" she wailed, reaching out for him. "I thought you only adopted me because you had no choice: that you had to take me to get David . . ."

"Oh God, Lou, did you really think that? Didn't you realize how much I love you?"

"Yes . . . yes, of course I did!" She fumbled in her pocket for a tissue. "But when I found out what happened from Cathy I thought . . . well, I just didn't know what to think anymore!"

"I have been selfish, haven't I?" He looked at her, his eyes full of regret. "I remember when you were a kid, when you first found out about him, I was so jealous."

She wiped away a tear. "Jealous?"

"Yes. I could have told you so much more, back then. Put you right when you said you hated him. But I wanted you to hate him. I was so afraid he'd take you away from me."

Louisa stared at him, incredulous. "But how could he? He couldn't have found us anymore than we could've found him!"

"I don't mean it in that way." He sighed. "I thought if you knew more about him, you might become obsessed with the idea of finding him, that you wouldn't want me for a dad anymore."

"Oh you!" She hugged him tight. "How could you *ever* think that? You'll always be my dad: even if I manage to find him, it'll never change things between us!"

"Will you forgive me, then," he whispered, "for not telling you things I should have told you when you were little?"

"There's nothing to forgive." She squeezed his hand. "I don't think anyone would ever blame you for holding things back. I'm sure I'd have done exactly the same in your shoes. The difference for me, though, is Rhiannon. I'm not just doing this for my sake: she needs to understand where she comes from."

He nodded. "Maybe it's time for all of us."

Louisa wondered if her mother really appreciated what a fantastic thing her dad had done, taking on another man's child and loving her as if she was his own flesh and blood. *Well*, she thought, *I'm about to find out.*

~

As Louisa made her way along the rutted track that led to her parents' bungalow, her boots kicked up a billowing trail of dust. The air was still and heavy. Leaden clouds had turned the sunlight a treacherous yellow-gray. Her stomach did an involuntary flip as she rehearsed what she was going to say. She told herself it was for the best. But she was frightened of the effect her words were going to have. Her mother had been bottling all this up for more than half her life. How was she going to react when she found out Louisa had gone searching for Cathy behind her back? That her daughter knew secrets she thought were dead and buried?

"Hello, love." Eva looked up from her knitting as Louisa pushed open the door. "I'm doing this for Rhiannon when she starts school." She held up one side of a navy-blue woolen cardigan. "D'you think it'll be all right?"

"Oh . . . yes." Louisa stared at her for a moment, knocked off-balance. Eva's short wavy hair was quite white at the front and the temples. Only from the back was it possible to tell that she had once been a redhead. The lines on her face deepened as she bent over her knitting, gravity accentuating the bags under her wide gray eyes. Her knuckles were knobbly with arthritis. Louisa knew knitting was an effort for her, which made what she was about to do seem even more heartless.

"Mum," she said, "I need to talk to you. It's about Tom." Eva looked up, the lines on her face twitching into an expression of alarm. "It's okay—nothing's wrong. Shall I make us a cup of tea?"

In the kitchen Louisa took a deep breath. She mustn't lose her nerve now. She had to face her mother, not let her find out by accident. Once the children had seen Bill's photo, it wouldn't be fair to expect them to keep quiet about him. They'd be sure to say something next time she came to the farmhouse and that would be a much greater shock than doing it this way.

"Mum," she began, setting down the teacup on the table at her mother's elbow. "There's something Tom's been asked to do for school."

Eva listened, still knitting, as Louisa began to explain. When Bill's name was mentioned, the needles suddenly stopped clicking.

"I'm sorry I went behind your back, but I just had to know the truth." Louisa searched her mother's face, willing her to understand. "If I hadn't managed to find your friend Cathy, I'd have let it drop. But I did." She held her breath. Her mother was looking at her as if she'd put a knife into her stomach. "She told me everything," she whispered. "I don't blame you for not wanting me to know about him, Mum. I understand how upset you must have been." She swallowed hard. "But I have to tell the children the truth about where they came from. You do see that, don't you?"

Eva nodded, staring past Louisa at the twisting garlands of honeysuckle on the wallpaper. Her lips moved as if she was about to speak, but she said nothing. Outside there was a rumble of thunder.

"Cathy gave me a photograph." Louisa held her breath. Watching her mother's face was like walking on broken glass. "I don't suppose you'll want to see it, but I wanted to give a copy to Tom for his project. Is that all right?" No response. "I wanted to warn you in case you caught sight of it at our house."

Still Eva said nothing. Still she stared at the wall. A tear oozed from the corner of her left eye and slid down her bare, unmade-up cheek. A blue vein pulsed at her temple, and perspiration glistened on her forehead like frost on a furrowed field.

"Mum?" Louisa's mouth went dry. "Mum?" She leaned forward, put her hand on her mother's shoulder. "Are you okay, Mum? Here, have a sip of your tea." She took the cup and brought it to Eva's lips, tilting it for her mother to drink. And, like a child, Eva drank, her hands locked in her lap. There was a flash of lightning. Rain lashed against the window as the storm passed overhead.

"I'm all right now," Eva murmured, draining the cup. "It was the shock, that's all." She seemed to be saying it to herself. "I'll be all right as long as I don't see his face. You do understand, don't you?" She looked at Louisa, her own face twisted with fear. "I can't see him. I can't even bear the smell of oranges, you know."

"Oranges?" Louisa felt a stab of alarm. What was she talking about? *God*, she thought, *she's had a stroke or something.*

"Don't you remember?" Eva went on in a whisper. "I could never have them in the house. Not even satsumas at Christmas. You asked me to buy some once. We had a row about it in the greengrocer's."

Louisa bit her lip, her eyes frantically scanning her mother's face. "N . . . no," she faltered, "I . . . don't remember."

"They reminded me of him, you see." Eva's forehead puckered and her mouth went into a tight circle. "He always smelled of oranges. It was the oil he put in his hair. To make him look more European—that's what he said."

"Oh, Mum!" Louisa hugged her, overcome with relief. She was all right—she was remembering! "You know the last thing I want to do is upset you by making it all come back," she said gently, "but if there's anything—anything else you could tell me about him . . ." She smiled at her mother through a film of tears. "I was so confused when I was growing up: I imagined all kinds of things, you know. It would be so good to know the—"

"I expect you want to find him?" Eva cut in, her voice calm, even. Louisa was startled by it. When her eyes cleared, she saw that the mask was back in place. "I'm sorry," Eva went on, "there's nothing more I can add to what Cathy's already told you." She paused and her lips twitched slightly, as if she was fighting to keep control. "Will you promise me something?" The hand she placed on Louisa's was shaking. "If you find him, you won't bring him here, will you?"

~

Louisa trudged back along the muddy track and kicked off her boots, slumping into one of the kitchen chairs. She felt emotionally drained and somehow cheated. She took Bill's photograph from her pocket. Her mother had kept him under wraps for so long— was it really surprising she had refused to open up? She stared at the smiling faces in the picture. *It was almost as if Mum was happy someone else had done her dirty work for her,* Louisa thought bitterly.

The sound of the telephone made her jump to her feet. She slid the photo back into her shirt pocket, instinctively guilty about leaving it lying around. When she heard the voice at the end of the phone, she caught her breath. It was Michael.

"I don't want to get your hopes up, but I've found something that might be of help," he said. "I got hold of the newspaper report of the hanging. It didn't mention your father, but it did mention the name of the army chaplain attached to the Quartermaster Corps. There's a good chance he'd have information about your father."

"Oh! Do you . . . would he . . ." Louisa stammered, too excited to get the words out. "Would he still be alive?"

"I think so. There's a photo, and he looks quite young. His name's Father Diarmuid Corrigan. I don't reckon it'd be too hard to track him down. Shall I start making a few inquiries?"

"Are you sure? I mean, I should do it myself, shouldn't I?" Her mind was reeling, wondering where to start.

"Well, it's up to you, of course, but I really don't mind. I'm going on a business trip to the States next month—I could put a few feelers out then, if you like."

"Would you?" She wanted to reach down the phone and hug him.

Chapter 38

It took Michael three months to track down Father Corrigan. He had retired from the army and was running a Catholic mission in India. Michael tried contacting him by phone, only to be told the priest had gone on a fund-raising tour in America. But the week before Christmas Louisa received the call she'd been waiting for.

"I finally got him!" Michael sounded almost as excited as she was. "He remembers your father and he knows his first name: it's Wilbur."

"Wilbur?" It was a name she would never have guessed. In all the long nights she'd lain awake reeling off possible names like the princess in Rumpelstiltskin, that one had never occurred to her.

"I know," Michael chuckled down the phone, "Wilbur Willis: not surprising he got called Bill, is it?"

"Did he remember anything else about him?"

"Nothing that's going to help you much, I'm afraid. He hasn't seen him since the Quartermaster Corps sailed into New York at the end of the war. He said some very nice things about him, though."

"Like what?"

"Well, he said how determined he'd been that you'd be looked after, and wouldn't grow up without a father the way he had."

"Oh." Louisa stared at the receiver. So he'd been brought up by a single parent. A woman on her own, like herself.

"He said he was very upset when he got a letter from your dad saying he was going to adopt you. He went to Father Corrigan for advice about what to do."

"And what did he say?"

"He told him that because your mother was married and not a widow, there was nothing he could do. Even though he was your real father, he wouldn't have had any legal right to claim you."

"So he couldn't have sent me to the States?"

"No. He wouldn't have been allowed to."

"I see." Louisa's stomach was in knots. She pulled a stool up to the phone and sank down onto it. *So that was why he didn't put up a fight*, she thought. She wondered how he must have felt, knowing he had a daughter he was never likely to see.

"Evidently he didn't even know your name," Michael went on. "He showed Father Corrigan the letter your stepdad sent. All it said was that you were a girl."

Louisa felt the sting of tears. "Isn't that sad?" she whispered. "I didn't know his name and he didn't know mine."

"What are you going to do now?" she heard Michael say.

She took a breath. "Well, I've got an initial now, so I can contact the American Embassy, can't I?"

"Will you let me know how you get on?"

"Of course I will!" Did he really think she was going to cut him off after all he'd done for her? "Actually," she said, "I'd really like to thank you properly." She paused, suddenly shy about what she was about to suggest. "I don't suppose you're ever in this neck of the woods, are you? I'd like to take you out for a meal or something." She heard him take a breath. "Your wife and daughter too, of course."

"That might be a bit tricky."

There was an awkward silence. Clearly she'd put him on the spot. She wondered why but didn't dare ask. "I'm sorry," she said. "Probably a stupid idea. Never mind."

"No—it's not that. I'd really like to come down. In fact one of my mates in the band has a holiday cottage not far from you. He's always offering to let me stay there."

"Oh? Where is it?"

"A place called Ynyslas. Just north of Aberystwyth. He says it's very wild and beautiful. Just miles of sand dunes and salt marshes."

"Yes, I know it." Louisa smiled. She and Gina often took the children there in summer. Even at the height of the season you could escape from the crowds on its vast, sandy beach.

"Perhaps I'll come down in the spring," he said. "It'd probably just be me and Heather, though—it's not really Monica's scene."

This struck Louisa as odd. She remembered Michael saying his wife liked to go camping. Why would a woman like that not want to spend time in a seaside cottage?

"That'd be great," she said, realizing with a pang of guilt that she was really glad Monica wouldn't be coming. When she hung up, she raced to the cupboard where she kept stationery and dashed off a letter to the American Embassy. She had written it in her head a hundred times. All she needed to add was that precious first name.

~

Over the Christmas holidays she tried to put the letter out of her thoughts, knowing that it would probably be weeks before she received a reply. But it was difficult to keep her mind from running on, imagining the possibility of finding her father, of meeting him for the first time.

She told Eddie what had happened, and he warned her not to get too excited. He pointed out that if Bill had made a career in the army, he probably would have been sent to Korea or Vietnam. Louisa knew what he was saying. She had already told herself that Bill could be dead. But in her heart she couldn't believe it.

Two days after posting the letter to the embassy, she went to see Rhiannon in the school Nativity play. Although she was one of the youngest children there, she'd been given a starring role. Dressed as a snowflake, she had to dance up the aisle of the chapel and sing a solo in Welsh. Louisa's heart was pounding as she watched, wondering if her daughter would be overcome with last-minute nerves. But she needn't have worried. There were gasps from the audience as Rhiannon glided past, graceful as a swan in her lacy white outfit. And when she opened her mouth to sing, the big voice that emerged from her little body filled the whole chapel. Louisa sat there with tears in her eyes. She had been fearful for her daughter, worried about racist comments from the other parents. But all she could hear were whispers of admiration. She found herself remembering Michael's words about her father. *Evidently he was a great dancer. How wonderful*, she thought, *if one day he could see his granddaughter dance.*

~

On the fifth of January a letter arrived from the embassy informing her that all records of American servicemen sent to Britain during the 1940s had been destroyed in a fire. "Records are available only from nineteen-sixty onward," the letter read. "There is no Wilbur Willis listed in existing US Army recruitment files whose date of birth would have enabled service during World War Two."

Louisa stared at the letter, bewildered, all her hopes and dreams shattered in a few short lines. Her first instinct was to phone Michael. He would know what to do.

A female voice answered. Heather? Or Monica?

"Er, could I speak to Michael Garner, please?" She wondered if either of them would know who she was.

"Hold on a moment, please. I'll just get him." The voice was self-consciously polite. *Heather,* Louisa thought. His wife would have been sure to ask for a name.

It was a couple of minutes before Michael picked up the phone. He sounded flustered when he heard her voice and gasped in disappointment when she told him her news.

"Don't worry," he said. "I'll get onto the chap in our American office. He's the one who helped me track down Father Corrigan. He might have some ideas."

They chatted for a few minutes, and when she put the phone down, she felt more optimistic. Michael had told her he'd booked a week at his friend's cottage. He and his daughter were coming for Whitsun week at the end of May. She glanced at the calendar on the wall. Was it too much to hope that Michael might have found her father by then?

~

As the weeks rolled by, her hopes began to fade. Michael's American colleague had drawn a blank. The only thing he could suggest was a genealogy service run by the Mormon Church in Utah.

"He said they have records of everyone in America, and you could write to them and request a list of all the Willises," Michael said when he phoned.

"What do you think?" She tried not to sound disappointed. "It'd be like looking for a needle in a haystack, wouldn't it?"

"It is a long shot." She heard him take a breath. "I think it's worth a try, though. They'd be listed on a state-by-state basis, so if you get hold of the list, you'd be able to see how many W. Willises there are in the two states we know he had connections with. It might not be too horrendous. If it's under a hundred, say, we could start sending out letters."

"But he could be living anywhere, couldn't he?"

There was a pause. "I'm sorry—it's not much good. But I've run out of ideas."

She wondered if he was losing patience with her.

"I'm . . . really looking forward to our trip to Wales." He sounded tentative. "Do you still want to meet up?"

"Of course I do!" She bit her lip. "Listen, whatever happens— whether I find him or not—I'll always be grateful for the way you've tried to help. I hope you realize that."

"Okay," he said. "So are you going to send off for that list?"

"Yes." She smiled. "And if it rains when you come on holiday, you can help me go through it!"

~

But by the end of May the list hadn't arrived. And it didn't rain. Whitsun week was so hot that the first thing Michael and his daughter did when they arrived at the cottage was to run down to the sea and jump in. He laughed as he told Louisa about it. She had driven to Ynyslas the next day with Tom and Rhiannon, who were both hot and sticky and only too happy to be whisked off for a paddle by Heather.

"How old is she?" Louisa asked, as they spread blankets in a little hollow in the dunes.

"Fifteen." Michael grinned. "Going on twenty-five!"

"She does look a lot older." Louisa took a flask of iced coffee from her bag and offered him a cup. "What's she planning to do when she leaves school?"

"She wants to be a doctor."

"Wow."

"She's about to sit for her O-levels. I don't know who's more nervous: her or me!" He pulled off his shirt, and Louisa felt a familiar surge in her stomach, the same sensation as when she'd bumped into him at the stile in the woods. That was nearly a year ago. This morning, in the mirror, she'd told herself very sternly that Michael was a friend. That he could never be anything else. So why was she feeling like this?

She looked away, uncomfortable in the heat. Her long-sleeved top was creased from the journey, and her jeans felt as if they'd been toasted in front of a fire. A floppy sunhat shaded her face.

"Aren't you a bit warm?" Michael eyed her curiously, sipping his coffee.

"Yes, I am," she said with a wry smile. "I know it's stupid—but I can't help it." She told him how covering up in the sun had become a way of life since the taunts she'd received as a child in Wolverhampton.

Michael's face creased with sympathy. "That's awful. Like—like a phobia?"

She nodded.

"But what about Tom and Rhiannon? You haven't covered them up."

"I used to: especially Tom," she said. "When Rhiannon was born, I realized it was pointless, but I still couldn't bring myself to change the way I dressed myself." She shrugged. "I got it into my head that people would treat me better if I was light-skinned—and I can't seem to shift it."

"But you're with *me* today." He gave her a puzzled smile. "I know all about it—about your father and everything. So how could it possibly matter?"

"I don't know. I can't explain it." She looked away. His blue eyes were melting her insides.

"Well," he said, draining his cup. "I'm going for a swim. You coming?"

"I . . . er . . . haven't brought a swimsuit."

"So?" Before she could say another word, he had scooped her up and was running down the sand dunes with her in his arms. She yelled and laughed, pummeling him with her fists, but he didn't stop—not even when they reached the water's edge.

She gasped as he plunged her into the sea. "Michael!" she spluttered. "You're crazy! Look at me!" She held out her arms, her sleeves hanging like bats' wings. He gave her a sheepish look, and she burst out laughing.

"You'll have to take them off, now, won't you?" He grinned. "Don't worry—Heather's got shorts and T-shirts that'll probably fit you." He ducked as she lunged at him and missed, falling flat on her face in the water.

An hour later she was back on the blanket in the dunes, feeling very self-conscious in Heather's high-cut white shorts and halter-neck top. Michael had stayed in the sea while she went to change. Now she could see him coming up the beach. She draped a towel over her legs.

"You decent?" he called.

"As I'll ever be." She grimaced. "Where are the kids?"

"Heather's taken them to get an ice cream—is that okay? I thought we could eat later."

She nodded as he sat down beside her. She could smell his skin. A mixture of seawater and sun lotion. He settled onto his back and closed his eyes. When she was sure he wasn't looking, she let her gaze travel the length of his body. His legs and torso were almost as tanned as his face. Blond hairs glistened on his chest. Ray's was the only other man's body she had studied this close. His skin had tanned easily too, but they had never had the money to go to the seaside. He'd always had a mark on his neck and arms where his collar and shirtsleeves had been. The memory of Ray triggered a wave of regret. Sometimes she felt guilty just for being alive.

Louisa took a deep breath of the salty air. The sun felt good on her skin, and the brightness of the day seemed to defy depressing thoughts. She let the towel slide from her legs as she lay back. *Today would be a new beginning*, she decided. *No more hiding. No more pretending to be white.* She closed her eyes. All she could hear was the distant lapping of the waves and the sweet, high call of a bird in the reedy grass behind the dunes. She was drifting into sleep when she thought she heard Michael whisper her name.

"Louisa?" The sound came from somewhere above her head. "Can I kiss you?"

Her eyes were still closed when his lips touched hers. She wanted to believe it was a dream, because then it would be all right. But the electric surge as his skin slid over her body was beyond anything her sleeping mind could have conjured. She knew it was wrong, but she let him go on kissing her until she thought her body would melt into the sand.

"I've wanted to do that for such a long time," he murmured. "Since the first second I saw you."

She opened her eyes, momentarily dazzled by the sun. "Michael," she began, "we mustn't . . ."

"I know." He kissed her again, and she sank back onto the blanket.

"No!" She struggled out from under him. She felt dizzy, sick. What an idiot she was! The wet clothes, the ice creams—he'd set the whole thing up! It was like Quentin: the same thing all over again—except this time she had wanted it as much as Michael obviously did.

"You must think I'm a real pushover!" She grabbed the towel and jumped to her feet.

"No! Look—I'm sorry!" He took her arm as she gathered up her things. "God, I've ruined everything, now, haven't I?"

"There's nothing *to* ruin!" she yelled. "You're *married*, Michael!"

"Am I?" He sank back onto the blanket, a defeated expression on his face.

Louisa frowned, knocked off-balance by his words.

"*Yes*, Monica and I are still married. And *yes*, we live under the same roof." He huffed out a breath. "Would it make any difference if I told you we hadn't slept together for three years? That we're only staying together until Heather gets to university?"

"Michael, please don't insult me with rubbish like that!" She began to walk away. "Why can't you just be honest," she threw back over her shoulder. "You want to have an affair with me? Well, I'm sorry—it was nice being your friend, but I *don't* want to be your holiday romance!"

"I'm not lying to you, Louisa!" He ran after her and reached out, turning her around and gazing into her eyes. "It might sound like a cliché, but it happens to be true!"

A memory of the upstairs of his house flashed into her mind. That fussy pink and lilac bedroom with the lacy nightgown and slippers, the dressing table strewn with makeup and tablets. And the bigger, double-bedded room, with the guitars and the solitary bottle of aftershave.

"Why?" Her eyes searched his face. "Why would you do that?"

"The usual reasons." His hands dropped to his sides, and he stared at the sand. "We married too young. Monica was pregnant at eighteen. We drifted apart, and she ended up having an affair."

"*She* did?"

"Yes. She was going to leave me. Had her bags all packed. But he changed his mind at the last minute. Left her high and dry."

"And you took her back?"

"In a manner of speaking, yes. Neither of us could afford to move out. We'd just bought the house from Mum's old landlord and nearly bankrupted ourselves in the process. So we came to an agreement. We'd live in it until Heather left home, then sell up and go our separate ways."

"Does Heather know?"

"God, no." He dug his toes into the pale sand. "I couldn't live with myself if I thought I'd ruined her chances of doing well at school."

Louisa's eyes narrowed. "So how do you explain the fact that you're sleeping in separate rooms?"

He gave a hollow laugh. "She thinks it's because I snore."

Louisa frowned. It sounded plausible and she had seen the evidence with her own eyes. "So how do you cope?" she asked. "Do you both see other people?"

"I think she's got a new boyfriend now," he said. "She's very discreet about it. Never spends a whole night away from home."

"And you?" She held her breath.

"No."

"Oh, come on! You play in a band—you must have had offers."

He shrugged. "One or two, I suppose. But it never seemed worth the hassle. Things were complicated enough already."

"And they're not now?" She gave him a wry smile.

"Listen, Lou, I know this is going to sound corny as hell, but I've never felt like this about anyone else."

Louisa blinked. What was she supposed to do now? He was staring at her with those fathomless eyes, and all she could think about was how it had felt to kiss him.

"Mum!"

She whipped her head around. The children were running up the beach toward them.

~

Tom wanted everyone to play French cricket, so she and Michael spent a strange couple of hours acting as if nothing had happened. They went back to the cottage for lunch, and then Heather asked if she could take the kids to the playground.

"Are you sure you want to?" Louisa asked her. She couldn't help wondering if this was something Michael had put her up to.

"Yes," she said, with a grin exactly like her father's. "If they weren't around, I'd have no excuse not to be studying: that's why he's brought me here, haven't you, Dad? Get me away from my friends, so I won't be distracted!"

"She's a lovely girl," Louisa said, watching them disappear up the path.

"I hear what you're saying." Michael pursed his lips. "Yes, I agree: it's a shame about Monica and me. But we passed the point of no return a long time ago." He reached for her hand across the table. "Do you understand how I feel about you? I'm not interested in some meaningless fling, you know." He traced a line from the tip of her index finger to her wrist. "Do you remember that time in the woods when you bumped into me? I wanted to kiss you then. When we said good-bye, I wanted to run down the road after you. I wanted to phone you the minute you got home. I've spent all these months wondering what it would be like to hold you, to be with you . . ."

Listening to him, realizing they had both felt exactly the same from the very start, something clicked inside her head. Without a word she got up, walked around the table and sat on his lap. Taking his head in her hands, she kissed him, dizzy at the sensation of his lips on hers. "I want you so much," she whispered. "I've never wanted anyone as much as I want you."

Chapter 39

Two weeks later, on the eve of her thirtieth birthday, Louisa walked into the most luxurious bedroom she had ever seen.

It had been Michael's idea to spend their first night together here. In the cottage at the beach they had done little more than kiss, afraid of being discovered by the children. But now she was afraid for a different reason. Since that hot afternoon in the dunes she had thought about little else but making love to him. Now, in the conspiratorial glamour of this hotel bedroom, she was nervous. She felt her stomach ice up at the memory of the other times. The robotic fumblings with Ray that had made her feel numb and dirty. And the pain and shame of Trefor's brutal rape.

She went over to the window. Below her couples were walking along Aberystwyth's promenade, some hand in hand. Gina's words buzzed inside her head. *He's taking you to a hotel? For a dirty weekend?* Despite Louisa's explanation, she'd been skeptical. *How can you be so sure he's telling the truth?* Gina said it reminded her of what had happened to her: for all she knew, Andy could have spun his girlfriend a line like that.

Knowing that Gina had a point didn't make it any easier. All Louisa knew was that she was deeply, hopelessly in love.

"I've been useless at work the past few days." She felt his breath on her neck as he came up behind her, sliding his arms around her waist. "Couldn't stop thinking about you." The ice in her stomach melted. Her pulse raced at the warmth of his hands through the thin fabric of her dress.

"Michael," she began, turning to face him. "I . . . I haven't . . ." She didn't know how to explain. She wanted to warn him, ask him to give her time. She was afraid of being a disappointment to him.

He put his finger up to her lips, stroking them softly. Then he was kissing her, paralyzing her with desire. He picked her up, lifted her onto the bed, and began unbuttoning her dress. A sob shook her body.

"Oh, Louisa! Darling! What's the matter?"

Lying together, side by side on top of the covers, as the sun slid into the sea, she told him all about Trefor. All about Ray. He reached out for her, stroking her hair.

"I'm sorry," he whispered. "I shouldn't have just assumed . . . We don't have to . . ." She heard him take a breath. "We can just go to sleep." His fingers, massaging her scalp, sent ripples of heat along her spine.

"No." She touched his face, letting her hand slide down to his chest. She undid one button of his shirt, then another, burying her face in the earthy warmth of his chest. She could feel his tongue on the back of her neck, tracing a path of fire over her bare shoulders. She pulled off his shirt, then wriggled out of her dress. His mouth hovered over her breasts, his hands sliding over the skin of her belly.

"Are you sure this is what you want?" His eyes were indigo pools in the twilight.

"Yes," she murmured, "I want to know . . . how it feels. To *really* make love."

The sea whispered through the open window as they shed the last of their clothes. She felt the warm, urgent tautness of him against her. A shiver of fear spread icy tentacles over her skin, but his mouth was on her neck, his hot breath and the flicker of his tongue melting her again. Her body arched with desire, shuddering as his wet fingers slid down her belly. She wondered if he could hear the noise her heart was making. She could feel her blood pumping, rainbows shooting behind her eyes. And then he was inside her. She could hear herself crying out like a wild animal. *Who was she, this woman? This new creature he had made?*

~

Louisa lost count of the number of times they made love that night. Each time they closed their eyes, their limbs entwined, the slightest movement, the merest touch, would set them both on fire again.

At eleven o'clock the next morning they were woken by the cleaner knocking on the door. Having missed breakfast, they settled for alfresco bacon sandwiches from a kiosk on the promenade. Later they swam, Louisa in a bikini this time. Her skin was the darkest it had ever been. When she had seen her reflection after that first day at Ynyslas, she was shocked at the transformation. But as she'd gazed at her new face in the mirror, fragments of ancient summers had drifted into her mind, making her smile. This was the face of those carefree childhood days before the move to Wolverhampton.

Now, on the beach, she was aware of curious stares. Some of the looks they were attracting were downright hostile. She pulled her towel around her shoulders, determined not to let it get to her.

"I've got us tickets to see a band tonight," Michael said, as they sat hand in hand, watching the waves.

"A band? In *Aberystwyth*?"

353

"Don't look so surprised—they do come here, you know."

"Who are we seeing?"

He arched his eyebrows. "It's a surprise."

"Oh?" She snapped the elastic of his trunks playfully. "Where, then?"

"The Arts Center. Ever been there?"

She shook her head. "It's on the university campus, isn't it? I thought it was just for the students."

"No: anyone can go. So come on!" He winked as he pulled her onto her feet. "We've only got about five hours before it starts—do you think they'll have finished cleaning the room yet?"

~

They made love in the shower before falling exhausted into bed, waking just forty minutes before the concert was due to start.

Louisa shrieked at the sight of her hair in the mirror. "Hell, look at me! I can't go out looking like this!"

"Yes you can." Michael slipped his arms around her waist, kissing her neck. "You look gorgeous." He stretched. "Don't know about you, but I'm famished. What shall we do about food?"

She fed him fish and chips from the wrapper as they drove up the hill. "Are you sure we'll be allowed in?" She felt suddenly nervous, self-conscious.

"Of course we will!" He plucked another chip from the newspaper in her lap. "You're going to love it: believe me!"

Louisa spotted the poster as they turned off the road. "Hot Chocolate! Is *that* who we're going to see?"

Michael nodded. "You said you liked them." He shot her a worried glance. "You did, didn't you? I didn't dream it?"

She leaned across the car and kissed him.

They got to their seats with less than a minute to spare. The auditorium was packed. Louisa looked around in amazement at the black people in the audience. She had had no idea there were people like herself living in Aberystwyth. She had certainly never seen any on her weekly trips to the market.

Michael had followed her eyes. "I think they're probably students," he said. "I guess the university brings in people from all over the world."

She reached for his hand as the lights went down. "Thank you so much for bringing me here," she whispered.

～

On Sunday evening they climbed to the top of Constitution Hill to watch the sunset over Cardigan Bay.

"Are you happy?" Michael asked, nuzzling her neck.

"What do you think?" she beamed back at him.

"Can you bear it? Waiting, I mean." He looked at her with fear in his eyes. "I don't want to lose you, Louisa."

"Two years." She shrugged. "What's two years?" She kissed the tip of his nose. "I've waited nearly half my life to feel the way you've made me feel these past few days."

～

Before their next weekend together Louisa received a heavy package with a higgledy-piggledy line of American stamps. She gasped as she unfurled the reams of paper inside.

Michael was incredulous when she phoned him with the news. "A hundred and fifty thousand Willises?"

"One hundred and fifty-one thousand, four hundred and eighty-two, to be exact," she said. "I've started writing down the addresses of the ones with the initial *W* and the zip code for Louisiana. I've got two hundred already!"

"What are you going to do?"

"Get writing, I guess. I'll start with the ones who live in New Orleans, and if nothing comes of that, I'll try the rest of the state." She took a breath. "Don't know what I'll do after that."

"Don't they give some idea what age these people are?"

"No," Louisa sighed, "I phoned them this morning to ask. They said if I had a date and place of birth, they could do a search. But I don't even know what year he was born, let alone the date."

"I bet your mother knows when his birthday was."

"Yes, I'm sure she does. But after what happened last time, I daren't push it any further. I'm quite scared of her having a stroke or something—she got so worked up about him."

"I can understand how you feel, but writing all those letters—it'll take you forever!" She heard him click his tongue against his teeth. "There *has* to be someone still living in New Orleans who remembers him, who could help us narrow it down a bit."

"But how would we find them?"

"I've been thinking about that," he replied. "When I was over there, I noticed that all the different cities seem to have their own TV stations. What if we got in touch with the one for New Orleans and asked if they could put out some kind of appeal?"

"Do you think they would?" Louisa couldn't imagine any television producer being interested in something as mundane as tracking down a relative.

"Well, there's no harm in asking, is there? If you could let me have a copy of Bill's photo and write down everything you know, I'll find out the name of the local station. We can send it off when I come down, if you like."

Louisa smiled as she replaced the receiver. She was touched by his enthusiasm for her search for Bill. It was as if the whole thing excited him as much as it did her. *Why was that?* she wondered. *Was it because he had never really known his own father?*

~

The next few months were a roller coaster of highs and lows. The day after she sent off the first batch of letters, she had a call from a TV reporter in New Orleans. He wanted to know if she had any photos of herself and the children to show alongside the one of her father. He explained that his station was doing a feature on war babies to coincide with the next anniversary of Pearl Harbor.

"We'll have to be careful how we put your story across," he said. "Don't want to ruffle any feathers—if he's got a wife and family, I mean."

"Oh." Louisa frowned at the phone. "I hadn't thought of that. How will you do it?"

"I think we'll take the line that the men we're featuring may not have known their wartime sweethearts were pregnant. That lets them off the hook with their current families, doesn't it?"

"Well, yes," she said, considering the implications. "I suppose that would be the best thing—even though it's not strictly true."

"You know what they say." He chuckled. "Never let the facts get in the way of a good story!"

~

During the weeks after the program aired, Louisa was in a state of permanent tension, waiting for a letter, perhaps even a phone call from New Orleans. But there was nothing. In the end she phoned the TV station herself. The journalist said he was sorry, but the appeal had brought no response. The following week the photos she had sent with such optimism returned in the mail.

She clung to the hope that the letters she was writing to all the W. Willises in Louisiana would bear fruit. But by the summer of the following year she had sent nearly three hundred, and all she'd had back were a few polite nos and a hoax letter from a man who said he was sure he was her father, despite being unable to recall her mother's name, and asking her to send return tickets to the UK as soon as possible.

When Michael came down to the cottage with Heather in August, she felt the strain beginning to tell. They had to pretend nothing was going on between them, so apart from visiting for the day with Tom and Rhiannon, she hardly saw him.

Christmas had been awful too. She had spent the whole day thinking about him sitting down to lunch with Monica, opening presents with Monica, when he should have been with her. They had managed to spend New Year's Eve together, but only because Heather had been invited to a party and wouldn't be around.

Louisa liked Heather, but she found it increasingly difficult not to feel jealous of the hold she had on Michael. He had become very defensive when she'd tried to explain. His words echoed in her memory: *You know I love you, Lou! Do you think I like living like this?*

He had begged her to be patient, reminding her that this time next year everything would be different. As if she needed reminding. She was counting the days.

~

A few weeks after Michael's visit, Gina announced she was moving in with Jeremy. They had been seeing each other off and on ever since the party at the commune. Jeremy had ditched the hippie lifestyle to set up his own sawmill business at a farm farther down the valley.

"I'm really happy for you," Louisa said, as she watched Gina pack the last of her things. There were tears in her eyes, but no twinge of envy this time. No wishing she had what Gina had. Because she already had it. Well, almost.

"Are you sure you're going to be okay?" Gina took her hand. "I worry about you, you know."

"I've got Michael, haven't I?" Louisa smiled through her tears.

Gina looked away. "Are you sure about him, Lou? I know I'm a cynic, but do you really think he's going to leave her when the time comes?"

"Yes!"

Gina didn't smile back. "Have you told your parents about him?"

"Well, not exactly: Dad knows."

"What did you tell him?"

"I said I was seeing someone who's separated but not divorced yet. He doesn't know it's Cathy's son."

"And you didn't mention Heather? Or the fact that he's still living with his wife?"

Louisa shook her head. "I told him Michael has a grown-up daughter." She looked up, a frown creasing her forehead. "I didn't want to worry him, Gina."

"Doesn't that tell you something?"

"What?"

"You're lying for him already." Gina pressed her lips together. "You shouldn't have to do that, Lou—you deserve better!"

Louisa stared at the sun-faded pattern on the rug by Gina's bed. "I know it's not ideal," she murmured, "but in a few months things are going to be different. I love him, Gina. And he loves me. He's just trying to do what's right."

~

On Louisa's birthday the following year, Gina's words were ringing in her ears. During the intervening months, she had kept herself frantically busy, sending off hundreds more letters to America. She had written to every single W. Willis in the state of Louisiana, and now she had moved on to addresses in Illinois. She told herself that Chicago was the place. With its more liberal laws, he would have been bound to head there, especially if he was as close to his aunt as Cathy had suggested. Michael had been worried when she'd said this. She knew he thought she was becoming obsessed. That perhaps the time had come to admit defeat.

Now she was sitting in the restaurant of the Aberystwyth hotel where they'd spent their first night together. She was watching the sunset, waiting for him to arrive. It was going to be the last birthday they would have to celebrate in this cloak-and-dagger way. This time next year they would be together. Maybe even married.

She looked at her watch. He was twenty minutes late. Perhaps his car had broken down. *Please God*, she thought, *not an accident*.

What if he's stood you up?

The voice in her head was Gina's. *No, he wouldn't do that. Would he?* She tried to recall the last conversation they had had. He had been uptight when she phoned because Heather was in the middle of her exams. He was worried for her. Louisa told herself that was only natural, that it wasn't surprising he didn't want to talk about the future when he had so much on his mind.

What if he's just stringing you along? Gina's voice again. *He'll keep coming up with excuses, Lou—just wait and see. He wants the best of both worlds.*

Another quarter of an hour went by. The waiter was looking at her. She saw him whisper something to the manager. Then a woman appeared, the hotel receptionist, heading for her table.

"Mrs. Brandon?"

Steel fingers squeezed Louisa's heart.

"There's someone on the telephone for you."

The walk from the table to the hotel reception seemed to take forever.

"Louisa?" Relief swept over her when she heard Michael's voice. "I'm sorry, darling, I'm not going to be able to make it."

"What's happened?" She felt dizzy and sick to her stomach. Gina was right. He was standing her up. On her *birthday*.

"It's Heather." He lowered his voice to a whisper. "She's in a terrible state."

"Wha . . . what? Why?" Her voice sounded distant, as if it belonged to someone else.

There was silence at the other end of the phone. Then she heard a door close. "You know she was taking her last exam today?"

"Er . . . yes," she mumbled, "was she ill or something?" She held her breath. This was shaping up to be the most pathetic of excuses.

"No, no—she was fine. But when she got home, she found a note from her mother. Monica's gone, Lou. She's moved out."

Chapter 40

Monica's abrupt departure had initially struck Louisa as absolutely heartless. How could she have left that note, knowing Heather would be the first to find it? But as the weeks went by, she came to realize that in leaving when she did, Monica had ultimately done her daughter a favor. Although distraught that her mother had moved in with another man, Heather at least had the whole summer to come to terms with it.

She and Louisa had some long chats at the cottage during August. Louisa was grateful that Heather didn't seem to hold her responsible for what had happened. On the contrary, she seemed appreciative of Louisa being there for her dad. She told her that her biggest worry had been that he would be all alone when she went off to university.

And so, on Midsummer's Day 1977, the week after his divorce came through, Louisa and Michael were married. It was a quiet ceremony at Aberystwyth's tiny registry office. Gina and Jeremy were witnesses, and the only others present were Heather, Tom, and Rhiannon—who was a bridesmaid.

Louisa and Michael had agonized over just who should be there. They couldn't have asked her parents without having Cathy there too. But how would Eva react in that situation? In the end they had decided to keep things simple. They would save the explanations for after they were married and—hopefully—bring everyone together at some point in the future.

The beach was just yards from the entrance to the County Hall, and after posing for a few photos, Michael picked Louisa up and ran across to the water's edge.

"No!" she squealed, clutching up the skirt of her cream silk dress as he pretended to throw her in.

"I wouldn't dare!" He grinned. "Just thought I'd remind you of how it all started!" He gave her a long, lingering kiss. "Well, Mrs. Garner," he whispered, "you've finally made an honest man of me."

They celebrated with lunch at the hotel they always thought of as theirs, then drove back to the farm.

"Is Michael coming to live at our house now?" Rhiannon asked as they chugged up the track.

"Sort of, yes." Louisa and Michael exchanged glances. "He's got his own house just a little way away from the farm, and he's going to take turns staying there and with us."

"Why?" Rhiannon's forehead wrinkled beneath the circlet of pink rosebuds in her hair. "I thought when people got married, they had to live together."

"Well, it's a bit different for us . . ." Louisa hesitated, not sure how to explain.

"It's because of my new job, Rhiannon," Michael said. "Did I tell you about it? It's a really noisy job: lots of people singing and playing instruments very loudly—I couldn't do that at your farm, could I? I might scare the sheep!"

Rhiannon giggled, apparently satisfied by this explanation. Louisa reached across and squeezed his hand. The reality was far too complicated for an eight-year-old to understand: the fact that the farm was really Tom's, and that the barn down the valley that Michael had converted into a recording studio came with a house they would move into when Tom was old enough to run things by himself.

Later that afternoon there was more explaining to do. She went alone to find her parents because she wasn't sure what her mother was going to say when she broke the news. If there was going to be a scene, she'd rather Michael wasn't a witness to it.

She told her father first. He was outside chopping logs. "You look nice, love." He straightened up, wiping his brow. "Going somewhere special?"

"Been somewhere, actually, Dad." Now that the moment had come, she felt ashamed. She held out her left hand so that he could see the new gold wedding band. "Michael and I got married this morning." She watched his face melt as tears blurred her eyes. "I wanted to tell you, but I was worried about what Mum would say."

He gazed at her, speechless. "Why?" he said at last. "Why be worried? She'd have been happy for you—you know she would."

"There's something I didn't tell you about him, Dad." She glanced at the logs, then back at his face. "Michael's Cathy Garner's son. We met when I went looking for her."

"Oh, I see." He sank down on an ax-bitten tree stump, a far-away look in his eyes. "It's been a long time, Lou. Couldn't you have given her a chance?"

"What do you mean?"

"To put the past behind her. For your sake."

"But Dad," Louisa bit her lip. "You know what she was like when I told her about meeting Cathy: I thought she was going to have a heart attack or something! Can't you see why I did it?"

"Yes, I do understand." He reached for her hand. "I'm sorry: I suppose I just feel a bit cheated. Come on—let's go and find your mum."

To Louisa's surprise, her mother reacted in almost exactly the same way. She blinked when she saw the ring, then shaded her eyes against the sun to take a long look at her daughter's wedding dress.

"I would have liked to see you marry." She gave Louisa a reproachful look. "I don't know why you thought I wouldn't want to see Cathy." She tilted her head, as if weighing something up. "I always liked Michael. Such a nice, polite little boy. Where have you hidden him?"

Louisa marched back up the track to fetch him, dust flying as her dress swished against her legs. "I give up with her!" She burst through the farmhouse door. Michael and the children looked up from their game of Monopoly. "She's like the flipping Sphinx!" Louisa shook her head. "Whatever I say, I never seem to get it right!"

Later that evening, when the awkwardness of the introductions was over and they were alone together, she finally felt able to relax. It seemed strange, snuggling up to Michael in the big iron bed she had slept in on her own for so long.

"I'm so happy," she whispered.

"Me too." He nuzzled her ear.

"Shall I let you in on a secret?"

"What?"

"I dreamed I'd marry you the first day we met." She told him of the strange image that had come to her while she slept at his mother's hotel—of Bill walking her down the aisle of the church in Aberystwyth, and him standing at the altar rail waiting for her. "It's so weird," she said, "because he *did* lead me to you, didn't he? If I hadn't been searching for him, we'd never have met."

He kissed her softly. "What a shame we haven't been able to find him."

"I know. Bet he'd be delighted about playing Cupid!"

If he's alive.

The words popped unbidden into her head. Lately she'd become despondent about the letter writing. She hadn't sent any for several weeks. In her heart she was beginning to believe he was dead. The melancholy mood that crept over her every time she thought of him began to descend once again. But she willed it away. Nothing was going to spoil their wedding night. Not even a ghost.

~

In the months that followed Louisa led a schizophrenic but happy existence as part-time farmer and part-time rock band hostess. Michael's studio began to attract big-name bands that found the remote Welsh hills the perfect place to put an album together. While they spent the day in the barn, she would prepare nightly feasts in the main house. For the first time she'd felt truly comfortable in her skin.

At first she had stayed in the kitchen, shy about mixing in such stellar company. With Michael she felt comfortable, but with strangers—especially men—her old phobia about her appearance sometimes threatened to overtake her again. But an unexpected request from the lead singer of one of the bands brought her well and truly out of her shell. He told Michael she had the perfect look for the cover of the album they were putting together. Would Louisa consider it? They didn't want her in makeup or fancy clothes—just a natural pose with the Welsh countryside in the background. The photographer was already there, taking shots of the band, so she didn't have long to think about it.

"Are they crazy?" She stared at Michael, flabbergasted, when he relayed the request. "Why on earth would they want *me*?"

"Because you're gorgeous, sexy, beautiful . . . Do I have to go on?" He grinned.

..._.

..

"Well, they must all need their eyes tested." She gave him a crooked smile. "They're not going to make me look stupid, are they? They're not going to superimpose a cow flying over my head or something like that?"

"No, you daft woman!" He pulled her to him and kissed her slowly. "It'll be stunning—trust me."

And he was right. "My God," she gasped, as she unwrapped the framed cover the band had sent.

"You're a star, Lou," Michael whispered, nuzzling her ear. "How does it feel?"

"Very weird." She smiled. "But good."

~

Just before Christmas she arrived back home after a stint at Michael's place to find a letter waiting for her. The sight of the American stamps set her heart pounding. It was postmarked New Orleans. She stared at it. It had been nearly three years since she'd sent a letter there. She ripped it open. A compliment slip from the TV station that had featured her story was stapled to a handwritten letter.

To the lady searching for her father:
My name is Cora-Mae Parker. I should have written you a long time ago, but the truth is I didn't want to. You see, I was married to the man you're looking for . . .

Louisa clutched the letter to her chest. *Married to him?* She sat down, resting her hands on the table in a vain attempt to stop them shaking.

The marriage didn't last. Things were very bitter between us. I married again and had children, but when I saw his face on the television, it stirred up all the bad memories. I guess I held back out of spite.

Then, last month, my eldest girl gave birth to a little boy. My first grandchild. When I held that baby in my arms, I got to thinking about the picture of you and your children they showed on TV. I thought how terrible it would be if my little grandson grew up not knowing who I was. I told myself—Bill has a right to know that he has grandchildren.

So what can I tell you about him? We met in the late thirties when we both worked in a drugstore downtown. He went back in the army when the war ended, but in the fifties he came back home to New Orleans. We were married in April 1956, but it didn't last much past our first anniversary. He never said, but I think he was still in love with your mama. He told me her name was Eva, and that he had a little girl whose name he never knew. You might not believe this, but I was jealous of you. He talked about you all the time.

Just after our divorce, his mama died. Bill and Martha, his sister, decided to start a new life in Detroit. It was 1958, as I recall. Martha wrote me for a couple years after that. Said Bill was doing pretty well, but we lost touch when they moved apartments.

I'm sorry I can't tell you any more than that. Please don't write me back or try to call me on the phone—my husband doesn't know I've done this and I don't think he'd be too pleased if he found out.

~

It took Louisa less than a week to write to the fifty-two W. Willises in Detroit. Ten days later her heart flipped when the postman delivered a thick envelope with the familiar Stars and Stripes stamps. Inside was a Christmas card. Beneath the verse in careful, copperplate writing were the words: *I'm the one.*

She dropped to the floor, her legs suddenly too weak to support her. Beside her on the hall rug was a tightly folded letter that had dropped out when she opened the envelope.

My dear daughter,
Words can't express how thrilled I was to receive your letter . . .

The spidery script blurred as her eyes welled up. Holding the letter in one hand and a sodden tissue in the other, she managed to read the words she had longed to hear. He had never given up hope of finding her, even when his letters to her mother were returned unopened. He had been posted to a base in the south of England in 1955 and had come to Wolverhampton, driving around the streets in the hope of catching sight of her. And now that she had found him, he couldn't wait to hear her voice.

That night, with Michael by her side, she dialed the number Bill had scribbled beside his signature. As the phone rang, she reached for the tumbler of vodka and orange juice she had beside her to calm her nerves. She took a big swallow. The ringing stopped.

"Bill Willis."

His voice was deep and gravelly. The American accent threw her. She stared at the phone for a second, unable to speak. Of *course* he was going to have an American accent. She took a deep breath. But it wasn't the accent. Suddenly, after all these years of searching, he was real. And she wasn't sure she could handle it. She shot Michael a desperate glance, and he took the receiver from her. After a few sentences of explanation he passed the phone back.

Louisa's hand shook as she put it to her ear. "Hello . . . yes, it's Louisa. I . . . I'm sorry . . . it's just that I can't quite believe it!"

"You'd better believe it," the voice replied. "It's your dad!"

Chapter 41

On the way to the airport Louisa studied the photograph that had arrived in the mail just two days ago. In the three decades since his romance with her mum, Bill's face had filled out and the short, slicked hair had become a gray-tinged mane drawn back into a ponytail. It had been a shock to see how he looked now after carrying the image of the youthful GI in her head for so long.

Time had not been kind to Bill or her mother, she thought. His smile was the same, though. And the dark-brown eyes shone with an intensity the old black-and-white snap hadn't picked up.

"Do you think you're going to recognize him?" Michael glanced at her as they turned off the road.

"I hope so. He said he'd be wearing a black leather jacket with a yellow rose in the buttonhole." Just describing him made her heart skip a beat. She looked at her watch. His plane was due to land in half an hour. *Half an hour!* She had been speaking to him once a week for the past two months, but until she could touch him, put her arms around him, part of her would not believe he was real.

She pulled a packet of mints from her handbag, her mouth dry. Despite their long conversations, she felt she still knew very little about him. He had told her that he lived alone and had not remarried after splitting up with Cora-Mae. That had surprised her. She'd expected him to have at least one other child—but apparently there were none. The only blood relatives he had spoken of were his sister, Martha, and her two teenage boys. Louisa wasn't sure whether she felt disappointed or relieved. To have discovered a half sister or half brother would have been thrilling—but what if they had resented her?

She had to admit she was glad there was no stepmother on the scene. That could have made things very awkward. A wife would have probably wanted to come with him. Louisa smiled. She was going to have him all to herself.

Michael dropped her outside "Arrivals" and went to park the car. She hurried to the big black information boards, frowning as letters and numbers jumbled before her eyes, reassembling into places and times. With a gasp she registered the fact that his plane had landed, that he was already somewhere in the building. She dodged past knots of tourists to where a cluster of people stood craning their necks. Some were holding boards with names on them. She should have thought of that. A trickle of weary-looking people came through the gates pushing trolleys. British tourists, she decided, looking at their sunburned faces. Definitely not from the Detroit flight. She jumped as she felt someone touch her arm. It was Michael.

"Hey, calm down!" He took her hand and squeezed it tight. "Any sign of him?"

She shook her head. Then something caught her eye. A ponytail, thin and curly, resting on the collar of a black leather jacket. The man was bending over his luggage.

"Michael!" she hissed. "Is that him?"

They watched the man straighten up. He turned slightly. There was something yellow on his lapel.

"Bill!" Louisa called out his name, waving frantically. His head whipped around. And suddenly she was running toward him, oblivious of the wall of people on either side, running into his outstretched arms.

They clung to each other, her face pressed against his shoulder, her eyes closed, the scent of warm leather mingling with the perfume of the rose in his buttonhole. She felt his chest rise and fall. They were both fighting back tears. She drew away, suddenly aware that she was crushing the rose, realizing even as she did so that it didn't matter. She felt embarrassed, awkward. He was a stranger, but he was her father.

They held each other at arm's length, looking each other over. He was tall. Much taller than her. Her eyes were level with the knot of his tie. A strange tie: black with a pattern of tiny white crosses. As he released her, a thin gold cross on a long chain slipped from behind the tie. He saw her eyes flick to it and smiled. An apologetic smile.

"Yeah." He grimaced. "It's *Reverend* Bill Willis—I didn't tell you because it puts some people off."

"Oh no!" Michael smiled as he reached forward to shake his hand. "I married a vicar's daughter!"

They all laughed, the ice broken.

"Just look at you . . ." Bill shook his head as he gazed at Louisa. "I can't tell you how . . ." His eyes were brimming. "And Eva? How is she?"

Louisa and Michael exchanged glances.

"We'll catch up on everything when we get back, shall we?" Michael reached for Bill's suitcase. "Tom and Rhiannon are desperate to meet you: they'll be counting the minutes!"

Louisa could feel the adrenaline pumping as she climbed into the back of the car. It was so wonderful to have him sitting here beside her. But she dreaded having to tell him that her mother wouldn't see him. How would he take it? She told herself that as a man of religion, he should be forgiving. Was that too much to expect?

She frowned as she fastened her seat belt. His revelation about being a reverend perplexed her. He had told her he worked in a hospital. Why had he told an out-and-out lie?

"I'm sorry if I misled you," he said, as if reading her mind, "but I wasn't lying. I'm a chaplain at Harper University Hospital."

She was relieved by this explanation and felt her body relax a little. Still, she was intimidated by the cross, which glinted in the sun as he fastened his seat belt. She had so looked forward to this day, and the days that lay ahead, visualizing the long chats they would have, filling each other in on all the missing years. But how could she open up to a minister of religion? He wasn't going to approve of Michael when he found out he'd had to get a divorce before he could marry her. She felt her heart sink. He wasn't going to approve of *her* either.

Bill produced a wallet full of photographs and began passing them to her to look at as Michael pulled away from the airport. She studied them gratefully. They could talk about his family instead of hers on the long journey home. The photos were mainly of her aunt Martha and her cousins, Marvin and Leroy. Louisa was struck by the resemblance between Martha and Rhiannon. She said as much to Bill, who beamed and produced another photo of his sister as a child. Louisa gasped. It was like looking at Rhiannon's twin.

She told him how worried she'd been about her daughter starting school, and how people had assumed her children had different fathers. She didn't explain that Michael wasn't their dad. She needed time to think how she was going to break that to him.

Bill gave her a look of such sadness she thought he was going to break down. "I thought about that a lot, you know, after you were born," he said. "I worried so much about how people would treat you, being half-black and half-white." He pursed his lips. "Do you remember I told you on the telephone about the time I was based in England after the war, when I came looking for you in Wolverhampton?"

She nodded.

"It was 1955—eleven years since the last time I was in Britain— and boy, what a difference. You should have seen the faces when I came cruising along the street. They looked at me as if I was some- thing they'd stepped in. I realized then things had gotten as bad as back home in Louisiana. And I thought of you growing up in that place, going to school and all, and I said to myself, I did wrong letting her stay: she would have been better off in Chicago."

Louisa's eyes filled with tears. She could hardly bear to think of him searching for her, driving around the streets on the other side of town with no idea she was sitting in a classroom just five miles away.

"It was okay until I was ten years old," she said, swallowing her tears. "It sounds crazy, I know, but I actually grew up thinking I was white."

She told him about the move from Devil's Bridge to Wolverhampton, of the shock of being refused service in the cor- ner shop. Slowly, hesitantly, she began to tell him about the shame she had felt about her color and the lengths she had gone to, to make herself white. But each word was carefully chosen. This was an edited version of her life.

He had pulled a large white handkerchief from his pocket, and she noticed he was blowing his nose a lot. She realized he was hid- ing too, not wanting her to see him cry.

When they got to Michael's, the atmosphere lifted. Gina was waiting there with Tom and Rhiannon, who jumped on Bill the minute he got out of the car. Having only ever known one grand- dad, the children were incredibly excited to acquire another— especially Rhiannon, who made him roll up his sleeve so that they could compare arms, proudly announcing they were the same color.

After lunch Michael went to show Bill the studio while Louisa washed up. They were gone a long time, and when she'd finished tidying up, she slumped into a chair, overwhelmed by an inexplicable feeling of depression. Bill and Michael seemed to be getting along so well. And he was obviously smitten by the children. She felt like the odd one out, and she wanted to cry at the unfairness of it. This was supposed to have been her big day. She knew her feelings were utterly childish, but she couldn't seem to shake them off. When Michael slipped into the kitchen, he found her sobbing into a tissue.

"I feel so stupid!" she sniffed, her shoulders shaking as he hugged her to him. "It was so exciting when I first saw him: when he showed me those photos, it was like the missing pieces of a jigsaw falling into place. But I can't *talk* to him, Michael! I'm not sure he even *likes* me!"

"Of course he does!" Michael shook his head. "You saw his face at the airport—he looked like he'd just scooped the jackpot!"

"B . . . but . . . he . . . doesn't know anything about me." She sobbed. "And when he does, he'll be ashamed of me—I know he will!"

Michael held her shoulders, fixing her with his eyes. "He will *not* be ashamed of you! How can you say that? What on earth have you got to be ashamed about?"

"My whole life," she mumbled. "How can I ever explain about Ray? About Trefor? About you, even?"

"Listen, Lou, he may be a reverend, but he's not some prude. You should have seen him in the studio! I played a couple of Stones numbers, and he was on his feet, dancing with the kids. He's really into the music, you know." He squeezed her shoulders. "And anyone who appreciates my playing can't be all bad!"

She gave him a wan smile.

"I think you're being too hard on yourself and on him," he went on. "It's bound to be an anticlimax at first, isn't it? You've built him up so much in your head. You've got to give him a chance—give yourselves time to get to know each other."

~

Later that afternoon Michael took the children back to the farmhouse. Bill was going to be sleeping at Michael's place—to keep him well away from Eva and Eddie. The idea was that Louisa would stay behind at the barn so that she could spend some time alone with him. But as she waved the others off, she was overtaken by a feeling of dread. She didn't know how she was going to get through the hours that lay ahead.

"Michael sure is a nice guy," Bill said as the Jeep disappeared up the track. "You been together long?" He smiled as her face tensed. "The kids don't call him Dad, do they? And they told me he was taking them home."

"Sorry." She plaited her fingers, eyes fixed on her hands. "I should have been straight with you. Michael's my second husband. My first husband committed suicide ten years ago because of . . ." She took a breath. "Because of something in my past he found out about." She paused, expecting an interrogation. But Bill said nothing. She looked up. His face was unreadable.

"I met Michael when I started looking for you." She hesitated again. "He was . . . he's divorced. We have separate homes because the farm is really Tom's—or will be in a few years' time when he turns eighteen. He . . . it's complicated." She held her breath, watching his face. A look of sadness clouded his eyes.

"That must have been hard on you, losing your first husband so young." He reached out and took her hand. "How did you manage, with the kids?"

Instead of replying, she burst into tears. Tears of relief that he wasn't judging her and tears of pain as the pent-up memories came flooding back. "I'm so afraid of telling you about my life," she sobbed. "I so wanted you to like me! To love me! But if you knew the truth . . ."

"You tell me just as much or as little as you want to," he whispered. "It won't make any difference to the way I feel about you: you're my daughter!" He hugged her to him, and she felt his own tears against her skin. "But I'll tell you something else, Louisa: when you hear about *my* life, I don't guess anything you've done will seem so bad."

~

The light was fading, but she was too wrapped up in what he was telling her to think of switching on the lights.

"I was thirty-two when I left the army. I realized it was about time I settled down. Didn't have much idea what I was gonna do, so I went back to New Orleans. Ended up waiting tables in a restaurant downtown. It wasn't long after that I hooked up with Cora-Mae." He shrugged. "Got hitched too quick. She wanted kids right away; I didn't." A frown creased his forehead. "Never felt I had a right to. It tore me apart, thinking I'd done just what my daddy did to me."

Louisa nodded slowly. "Michael's mum told me that you and Martha had lost contact with your dad."

"I was three years old when he walked out on us. Martha was no more than a baby. Never set eyes on him again. I don't even know if he's dead or alive."

She saw the haunted expression in his eyes and wondered if he had dreamed of his father the way she had dreamed of him.

"It hurt real bad, growing up with no daddy." He tapped his chest. "I never would let on, though. Kept it all inside. But all the time Cora-Mae was talking about babies, I felt like yelling at her. In the end I told her about you. I said, 'Look, Cora-Mae, somewhere, on some street thousands of miles away, a little piece of me is walking around. A little girl who wouldn't know me if she passed right by me. How can I go having another one till I've found the one I already have?'" He shook his head. "It got so she was sick of hearing it. We used to fight all the time." A wry smile turned up the corners of his mouth. "Sure seems strange that it's her I have to thank for you finding me!"

Louisa smiled back. "She's a grandmother now—did you know?"

"Is she?" He folded his arms and leaned back in his chair. "I'm glad. She deserved better."

Louisa watched his eyes cloud over again. *Why did he have such a low opinion of himself? Surely it wasn't all due to being an absent father?*

"What happened when you got to Detroit?" she asked.

He huffed out a laugh. "Not much, first off. Me and Martha thought we were headed for the promised land. I was sick of the way black folks were treated in the South. I suppose traveling like I did with the army made me realize I didn't have to put up with that kind of stuff—that not everyone had us down as the scum of the earth." He paused, examining the veins on the backs of his hands. "It didn't make much difference when we arrived, though. Still couldn't get anything better than waiting tables. But at least I was serving black folks alongside the whites." He looked at her, his eyes twinkling. "Sounds crazy, I know, but I used to do this little act, where me and one of the waitresses would break into a dance routine in between serving the food. And one night this black guy—real flash—comes in the restaurant and calls me over. Says he manages a band and needs someone to teach them how to move. Turns out to be Berry Gordy—you heard of him?"

"*The* Berry Gordy?" Louisa gasped. "From Tamla-Motown?"

"Uh-huh." Bill smiled, but his eyes had lost their shine. "It was nineteen fifty-nine, and he was just starting out. It was great for me—he was always signing new acts, mostly young kids straight off the streets. I was one of a bunch of people working out the routines, teaching them how to dress, how to hold themselves, that kind of thing."

Louisa's eyes widened. "So you must have known loads of really famous people?"

"Yeah, I did meet a few." He dropped his eyes, studying the backs of his hands again.

"Come on—tell me!"

"Well, there was the Four Tops—I knew them pretty well, the Supremes, and Smokey Robinson . . ." He shrugged.

"Wow! You must have had an amazing time!"

"Well, yes, I guess so." The tone of his voice suggested otherwise. "The problem was it all went to my head. It was the kind of job where girls would be coming on to me all the time—not because they saw me as anything special, you understand: they thought I could get them a break." He let out a breath. "It was pretty hard to resist. I'm sure not proud of how I was back then. And the whole thing just backfired on me, which served me right."

"What happened?"

"Well, I was getting invited to all these parties and one of the girls I met turned me onto drugs. I started smoking pot, then a couple weeks later I got into cocaine."

She stared at him, fumbling for the right words. "Is that what you meant when you said your life had been bad?"

He nodded. "I lost everything, Lou. Lost my job at Hitsville, lost my apartment. Martha tried to help me, but I froze her out. By the end of sixty-five I was sleeping on the streets. I got a job washing dishes, but soon as I got paid, I'd be after my next fix. Only food I had was leftovers from the kitchen." He gave her a crooked smile. "You think I look rough now, you should have seen me back then!"

"But you kicked the drugs?"

"Only because I was forced to. I got caught trying to steal a pair of shoes from Walmart. They put me in a rehab program, and while I was there I . . ." He hesitated, shaking his head. "I suppose you could call it a vision." His eyes flickered from side to side as he stared at the wall. "I don't know if it was withdrawal from the drugs or what, but I saw this evil-looking man with flames licking around him right there on the grass in front of me. And then I heard a voice. *You have a choice, Bill. Me or the devil.* That's what I heard."

Louisa didn't know what to say. She hadn't been to church since she was ten years old. She glanced at him awkwardly. "Is that why . . . you became a minister?"

He nodded. "It probably sounds strange to you—it does to most folks—but to me it was very real. And powerful. I'd tried so many times before to kick the drugs—I'd been living on the streets close on five years—but when I woke up the next morning, that crazy urge had gone away."

"So how long have you been working at the hospital?"

"Coming up on four years."

She looked at him, wondering how best to say what she was dying to know. "And since you . . . got back on your feet, you haven't . . . you know, *met* anyone?"

"No ma'am!" He smiled. "I don't drink, I don't do drugs, and I don't . . ." He arched his eyebrows.

"Oh!" She looked at her feet, embarrassed at what she'd made him almost say.

"Reckon I'm bad news, far as ladies go." He grunted a laugh. "I got a dog for company now. He ain't complained about me yet!"

Louisa laughed. But the inward delight she took in his resolution to stay single made her feel guilty. "Do you really think you'll never meet anyone else?"

"I doubt it." His eyes took on a wistful look. She wondered if he was thinking of her mother. *Was that the real reason he would never marry again?*

"There's something I have to ask you," she began. "Do you still have feelings for . . ." She paused, unable to say it.

"For your mama?" He drew his lips into a tight circle. "I thought that was coming." He blew out a breath. "It's been so many years, but yes, I still have wonderful memories of the time we spent together. Truth is I never met a woman like her, before or since."

Louisa's stomach lurched. This was what she'd been dreading. "It means a lot to me that you cared so much for her," she said, her voice a hoarse whisper. "The trouble is, though, I don't think she can bear the idea of seeing you again."

There was a moment of silence. Then he said, "Well, I guess I can understand that. Sure is a pity, though. I would have liked to see her again." He looked straight at her, catching the fear in her eyes. "For old times' sake, you understand. Nothing more. I would have liked to meet your other dad too. I'd like the chance to shake him by the hand, tell him what a good job he did, raising you."

Louisa blinked back tears, wondering how Eddie would react to that. She had told him Bill was coming, reassuring him that he would be kept well away from the farm. She hadn't known what to do about telling her mother. She knew it would be unfair to expect Tom and Rhiannon to keep quiet about it. In the end Eddie had offered to tell Eva after she and Michael had left for the airport.

Louisa bit her lip. It was almost as if Eddie was on Bill's side. How could he be so understanding? She wondered if he had any idea that David's death had been directly linked to Bill's actions, wondered if her mother had ever told him the real reason for her visit to Aberystwyth that fateful day.

As if he'd read her mind, Bill took her hand in his. "I don't expect him to want to see me any more than your mother does. But I'd be grateful if you could pass on what I just said."

She nodded. "You don't mind me not calling you Dad, do you? It's just that it takes a bit of getting used to . . ."

"Of course I don't!"

"My . . . my other dad, well, he's never blamed you for what happened. But Mam . . ." she trailed off with a shrug.

"I guess she hasn't forgiven me for messing up her life?"

Louisa shook her head. "But it's not what you think. She doesn't blame you for me being born, anyway. It's what happened afterwards that really turned her against you."

"Afterwards?"

She watched his face crumple as she pieced the story together. "Cathy said it was the first time Mam had heard from you since before the war ended," she explained. "She was all wound up because she'd been trying to make a go of things with my dad—but she was still in love with you, I think. Cathy said Mam was hoping you were going to be posted to Britain. She said it was the only way you and she could be together, because my dad would never have let her take David to the States."

He blinked, grief etched in the lines around his eyes.

"I'm so sorry I had to tell you." She pulled her lips in over her teeth. "I had to make you understand why she's so against you. I think that when David died, she wanted to . . . just wipe you out of her memory." She swallowed, her eyes pooling. "She told me she couldn't even remember your name."

Both of them were crying now. Bill wrapped his arms around her, and they clung together in the dark.

"It wasn't your fault," she whispered. "But do you see why I have to keep you away from her?"

She felt him nod his head. "Don't you worry," he murmured. "I'll stay away."

Chapter 42

Michael and the children arrived in time for breakfast the next morning. Rhiannon said she'd been awake since five o'clock, too excited to go back to sleep.

"Will you come and see me at the Eisteddfod, Granddad?" she said, taking Bill's hand and dancing him around the kitchen.

"The *what*?" Bill gave her a puzzled grin and turned to Louisa.

"It's an arts festival we have in Wales," she said, casting a worried glance at Michael. "She's got through to the county finals."

"I'm singing a song in Welsh and doing a solo dance routine," Rhiannon beamed. "You'll still be here next Saturday, won't you?" She had no idea, of course, of the implications of this invitation.

Bill and Louisa exchanged glances. "Well, I'd love to come and see you, honey." He smiled. "But I'm not sure Americans are allowed. We'll have to get your mama to ask. Tell you what, though." He picked her up by the waist and twirled her around. "I'd like to see you practice—could we use the studio, Michael?"

They all filed across to the barn.

"What's she dancing to?" Bill asked.

"It's an instrumental track," Michael replied. "We had a heck of a job finding something. They have very strict rules: no English lyrics allowed, only Welsh. It's a Cozy Powell number. You heard of him?"

"Not 'Dance with the Devil'?" Bill's eyes clouded.

"That's the one." Michael smiled. "It's all drums—very fast!"

"What is it, Dad?" Louisa bit her lip as she realized what she'd called him.

He looked up and smiled. "Oh, nothing serious." He shook his head slowly. "I remember, first time I heard that number, it reminded me of something me and your mama used to dance to: 'Drum Boogie,' it was called. We used to jitterbug to it in the air-raid shelter."

"What's a jitterbug, Granddad?" Rhiannon piped up. "Will you show me?"

"Sure I will, honey." He smiled at the child through a film of tears.

"Are you crying, Granddad?"

"Aw, no—it's just these old worn-out eyes of mine . . ." He took her hands in his. "You ready?"

Rhiannon squealed with delight as he twirled her around and flipped her over his head.

"What are we going to do?" Louisa whispered to Michael as Bill and Rhiannon careered around the studio. "We can't let him *and* Mam and Dad go."

"I know." Michael nodded. "It seems mean, though, keeping him away. It means so much to him that she's inherited his talent. When's he going to get another chance to see her perform in public?"

Louisa frowned. "You're right—but how do I explain that to them? They're proud of her too—and they're so much looking forward to it."

"Don't you think this might be a good opportunity to try and get your mother to bury the hatchet?"

She sighed. If only it was that simple.

~

At lunchtime Louisa went back to the farm with the children while Michael took Bill to the local pub.

Eddie was busy milking when she found him.

"How did Mam take it?" she asked, as they sat down together on an old wooden bench in the cowshed.

Eddie shrugged. "She said she'd been expecting it. Said she was surprised he hadn't come sooner."

"What?" Louisa gasped. "Didn't she have any idea how hard it was, trying to find him? It's certainly no thanks to her that we did!"

"Try not to be too hard on her, Lou. She says things she doesn't mean when she's had a shock—you know that."

Louisa nodded. "I'm sorry—it's just been so stressful, the last few days—and now Rhiannon's gone and invited him to the Eisteddfod and I don't know what to do!" She caught her breath, close to tears.

Eddie patted her arm, rubbing his forehead with his other hand. "Well, it's only natural that he'd want to go. *I* don't mind him being there, but as for your mother . . ."

"Oh Dad!" She hugged him. "How can you be so . . ." She struggled for the right word. Unselfish? Kind? Forgiving? He was all those things. Things that had made her wish a hundred times that she was *his* child, not her mother's. "I . . . I don't know how to say this," she faltered.

"What?"

"Aren't you afraid that if she . . . you know?" Her words hung in the air like the motes of dust floating in the afternoon sunshine.

Eddie stared at the rough floor of the cowshed, rolling a piece of straw with the sole of his shoe. "Not really." His voice was quiet but steady. "It was a long time ago, Lou. People change."

Yes, she thought, *they do.* Her mother had been just twenty-one when she met Bill. Louisa shuddered at the memory of herself at that age. What had changed her? Time—and the love of a good man. Was it the same for her mother? Eddie had been there for Eva through all the grief and the good times the past thirty years had brought. And Bill had not. In that moment something occurred to Louisa. That it would have been so much easier for Bill to find her mother than for her to find him.

If he had wanted to.

He knew her surname, the place she had once worked. Yes, he had searched the streets of Eva's old neighborhood. But he had told her it was her, Louisa, he was hoping to find. Perhaps he had never truly loved Eva the way she had loved him—and deep down, her mother knew it.

She looked at Eddie's profile, lit up by the sun slanting through the window. "What would you do if you were me?"

He drew in a breath. "I'd go and see your mother. Tell her what you've just told me: that it's Rhiannon who's asked him. Maybe that'll make a difference."

"And if it doesn't?"

"Then it's up to you. She's your daughter—you're the one who has to decide who goes."

~

Louisa chewed over Eddie's words as she made her way to the bungalow. What if her mother refused point-blank to be in the same room as Bill, which she almost certainly would? What if Eddie decided to go alone? Would it be fair to let the two men meet? To let Eddie shake hands with Bill, not knowing the awful secret of David's death? Should she tell Eddie like she'd told Bill? Could it possibly be right to rake up all that misery again? Eddie didn't deserve that. Better to let sleeping dogs lie.

Eva was in the kitchen making a sponge cake. She looked up, a sieve full of flour frozen in midair. Her eyes said it all. Reproachful, disappointed, and . . . scared. *Yes,* Louisa thought, *there was real fear in her eyes. Had she expected her daughter to come waltzing into the house with her long-lost lover in tow?*

"Mam?"

The sieve clattered noisily onto the mixing bowl. "You've not brought him, then?"

"No! Of course I haven't!" Louisa was fighting to stay calm. "I promised I wouldn't, didn't I?"

Eva set her lips in a thin line. "How is he?" The question was addressed to the table.

"Okay." Louisa took a breath. "He's not had an easy life, but he's picked himself up. He's gone into the church."

"Oh." Eva traced a river in the powdering of flour that had escaped the sides of the bowl. "The church." She sounded like an echo.

"I told him you didn't want to see him—but Rhiannon wants him to go to the Eisteddfod." She paused. Her mother's finger was still moving through the flour. "Did you hear what I said, Mum?"

"Yes, I heard." Eva's voice was little more than a whisper. "Let him go, then. There'll be other chances for us to see her. She's such a bright little thing—she's bound to win more competitions."

"Oh Mam!" Louisa didn't know whether to hug her or shout at her. "But you were so looking forward to it!"

"I know." Still Eva didn't look up. "But like I said, there'll be other times." There was a puff of white as a tear dropped onto the table.

Louisa stepped across the floor. She lifted her hand. It hovered in midair. Why was it so hard to touch her? "You don't have to stay away, Mam. I was hoping . . . for Rhiannon's sake—"

"No!" her mother cut in. "Please don't ask me. You know I . . ." she faltered, "I can never . . ."

"Forgive him?" Louisa's hand found her mother's shoulder. "I know, Mam. I know what happened with David, and I don't blame you for feeling the way you do. But it wasn't Bill's fault—not really, was it? Why can't you let it go?"

"Don't look at me like that," Eva whimpered.

"Like what?"

"Like my mother!" Eva's lower lip began to tremble. "When she . . ."

"When she what?"

"She was right." Tears coursed down Eva's face as she stared past Louisa, her head nodding, then shaking in denial. "We never should have . . . and God punished me for it."

Louisa took her mother by both shoulders, bending at the knees so that her eyes were level with Eva's. "Listen to me, Mam! Bill believes in God, but I don't think even *he* would buy anything as cruel as that!" Her voice seemed to ricochet around the tiny kitchen. Her mother burrowed in her pocket, her hand leaving floury trails on the fabric of her dress. She lifted a handkerchief to her eyes. "I'm sorry, Mam, I didn't mean to shout." Louisa tried to regulate her voice, but she felt like screaming. Didn't her mother realize how it made *her* feel, going on about Bill like that? *As if she wished I'd never been born,* she thought bitterly.

She glanced at her mother's tear-streaked face. "Maybe it's not Bill," she said slowly. "Maybe it's yourself you need to forgive."

~

The day before the Eisteddfod Louisa saw Tom off to school and set to work on Rhiannon's costume. She had a boxful of sequins to sew onto the pale-pink leotard, and she knew it was going to take her most of the morning. Rhiannon had been given the day off school to practice and was already in the studio perfecting her moves with Bill.

As Louisa threaded the silver disks onto the needle and jabbed it into the fabric, she thought about her mother, wondering what really lay behind the brick wall she had built in her mind to keep Bill out. Was there more to it than just guilt? Was she afraid that if she saw even a photograph, it would bring all the old feelings flooding back? Eddie had seemed confident that it was all in the past, but how could he be so sure?

Louisa held up the costume to the light. This time tomorrow Rhiannon would be dancing in it. She tried to imagine how it would be if her mother, Eddie, and Bill were all there to watch. Despite Eva's words, Louisa couldn't stop hoping it might happen. She realized it was something she longed for above anything else. It was as if one final piece of the jigsaw was still missing. Her mother's refusal to have anything to do with Bill was almost physically painful to her. The more she thought about it, the more it felt like a denial of her very existence.

Michael pushed open the door and set a mug of tea down in front of her. "Rhiannon's going to look fantastic in that." He rubbed her shoulders. "Have you told her about your parents?"

"No, not yet." Louisa pursed her lips. "Dad said the best thing would be if we tell her afterwards. Say Nan's had one of her turns, and they couldn't get there. He thought it might upset her if she knew they weren't going."

Michael nodded. "I think Bill feels really guilty about it."

"Well, he shouldn't—not really. What Mum said is true—there probably will be other chances for them to see her, won't there?" She couldn't tell Michael how she really felt. She was afraid he'd take matters into his own hands. Go to her mother and try persuading her himself. *No*, she thought, *this is something no one can talk her into doing. There's something she's not telling me. Might never tell me. Like I've got things I'll never tell her. And I'm just going to have to accept it.*

Neither Louisa nor Michael heard Rhiannon tiptoeing off down the hall. She had come into the house for a drink and, hearing her name, had listened at the door. Her nine-year-old face was like thunder as she trudged back to the studio, kicking at the tender heads of crocuses sprouting along the path. She stopped at the entrance, planning what she was going to say. Forcing her mouth into a smile, she went inside, where Bill was rewinding the tape.

"Granddad, I'm a bit fed up of rehearsing—could we go for a walk instead?"

"Sure." Bill looked up and smiled. "Reckon you've had all the practice you need: you could do this routine in your sleep!"

"Good!" She took his hand. "I want to show you the countryside around here. Stuff you can't really see from the car. Do you like long walks?"

He gave her a conspiratorial wink. "Long as we can take some candy: keep our strength up."

"Okay—I'll go and get some."

"And tell your mama where we're going," he called after her.

～

An hour later Bill and Rhiannon stopped at a stile to share the packet of Maltesers she had stuffed into her pocket.

"Where are we now?" he asked, panting from the effort of the climb.

"Up there's Bryn Llwyd," she said, popping three sweets into her mouth without stopping to draw breath. "It means Gray Hill in Welsh."

"Well, it sure doesn't look gray!" Bill wiped a trickle of perspiration from his forehead. The spring sunshine had broken through the high cloud, lighting up the emerald boughs of the pine trees that lay a few yards ahead of them.

Rhiannon looked at him, a frown wrinkling the soft brown skin between her eyebrows.

"What is it, honey?"

"I'm really thirsty, Granddad. I should have brought something to drink." She looked about her. There was a small white bungalow a hundred yards or so up the hill, nestled in front of the thick margin of pine trees. Rhiannon let her eyes rest on it for a moment. "Do you think if we went and knocked on the door of that house, they might give us a drink of water?"

He shrugged. "I don't suppose there's any harm in asking."

As they trudged toward the bungalow, Rhiannon's heart began to hammer in her chest. She knew very well this was wrong. But she would do it. She had to.

Her eyes darted around as they walked up the path to the front door. The Land Rover was parked at the end of the track. She swallowed hard. What if her other granddad was at home? She hadn't counted on that. Would there be a fight? She glanced at the porch and saw with relief that Eddie's big work boots were missing from the shoe rack. Raising her hand, she knocked on the blue-painted door.

Eva was a long time getting to the door. They heard her slow footsteps and the tap of her stick on the tiles as she approached. She blinked as the sunlight caught her eyes.

"Rhiannon?" She raised her free hand to her forehead to shield her eyes. Then she caught sight of the figure standing in the shadow of the porch. The hand fell to her mouth.

"Eva?" Bill's face was as pained and confused as hers was. He turned to Rhiannon, who instinctively grabbed her grandmother's arm. But Eva brushed her aside, struggling back down the hallway.

"No!" Eva cried out, her free hand flailing backward, as if she was fending off flies. "I told your mother! I can't!"

Bill sank onto the porch step, his head in his hands. Rhiannon glanced from him to the receding figure of her grandmother. She followed her into the house. Eva was slumped in an armchair, staring out of the window at the sheep grazing the hummocky field down the valley.

"Why can't you be friends with him, Nan?" Rhiannon whispered the words, but her tone was steely. "He told me how you used to dance together in the air-raid shelter. What fun you had." She sniffed hard, fighting back the tears that stung the back of her eyes. "Why do you hate him so much?"

Eva answered her with silence, her lips a tight, straight line and her expression blank.

"*Why* Nan?"

"You . . . you're too young to understand." Eva's voice was like the hiss of a snake about to strike.

"I'm not a baby!" Rhiannon cried out, indignant.

"I know that." Eva stared at her swollen knuckles. "I'll tell you when you're a bit older."

"That's no good!" Rhiannon's voice rose. "I want you to be friends now! I want *both* of you to see me tomorrow!"

"I'm sorry." The words came out through clenched teeth. "I just can't. Now will you take him away?"

"I know why you hate him." Rhiannon's voice was quieter now, but it had a sinister edge. "It's because he's a black man, isn't it? You're ashamed of him, aren't you?"

"No!" Eva's face tipped upward. "It's not *that*!"

"Yes it is!" Rhiannon's eyes had an odd look. A mixture of triumph and fear. "And I remind you of him, don't I? I bet you wish I'd never been born!"

"No! That's not true!"

"It is!" She stared straight into Eva's eyes. "Well, don't worry—you won't have to come to the Eisteddfod because I won't be there! You'll never have to see me again!"

Rhiannon shot out of the room as her grandmother struggled out of her chair. By the time Eva got to the hall, Rhiannon was running past Bill, who had been wandering distractedly around the garden.

"Hey! Where you going?" he called as she hurtled over the fence.

"The falls!" she yelled, without looking back.

Within seconds she had disappeared from his view. Then Bill saw Eva framed in the doorway, stick in hand. He leapt onto the porch. She turned away as if he was an evil spirit.

"What did you say to her?" He took her face in both his hands, forcing her to look at him. "Where's she gone?" He searched her face. "The falls? Where's that?" He saw a flicker of fear in her eyes. His hands fell to her shoulders. "Eva! Talk to me!"

"Please, God, no!" She was looking through him like someone in a trance. "Not my little angel! Not there!"

"We have to find her!" Bill grabbed her arm, pulling her toward the path. "You show me the way!"

"I . . . I can't!" Eva's lips quivered as she glanced down at her legs.

"Can we get there by road?"

"Y . . . yes," she stammered, "b . . . but I . . . can't drive!"

"Well, I can!"

She gave a small, strangled cry as he picked her up in his arms and ran with her to the Land Rover.

～

Louisa stood up and stretched. Her shoulders were stiff from sewing. She wandered through to the kitchen to make herself a coffee.

"Michael!" she called. "Want a drink?" No reply. He must be in the studio with the others. As she picked up the kettle, she caught sight of a scribbled note propped against the tea caddy.

Dear Mum and Michael, I've taken Granddad Bill to make friends with Nan. See you later, love R.

"Oh my God!" Louisa grabbed Michael's keys from the hook on the wall and ran from the kitchen. She had to find them. Stop them. As she revved the Jeep's engine, she wondered whose idea this had been. Not Bill's surely? He had promised to keep away. She sped up the track to the road, a spray of mud shooting out in her wake.

~

"Which way?" Bill looked at Eva as they reached the main road.

"That way." She pointed right. "It leads straight down to the bridge."

"And that's where the falls are?"

Eva nodded. "Her father . . ." she trailed off, shaking her head like a dog shedding water.

"What about him?" Glancing sideways, Bill saw that her face had lost what little color it had.

"He . . . took his life."

"Louisa told me." Bill swallowed hard. As his eyes flicked back to the road, he caught the flash of a tear coursing down Eva's cheek.

"Don't worry." He reached over and patted her hand. "We'll find her!"

She gave a great gasp, sobs convulsing her body. "I . . . I'm s . . . so sorry," she breathed. "All these years I . . . I—"

"No!" He thumped the dashboard, anguish in his eyes. "*I'm* sorry. I know why you felt that way: Lou told me—about losing your son."

As he went to change gear, he felt her hand find his.

~

Louisa drove toward the bridge, her eyes scanning the fields on either side of the road. Which way would they have gone? And how long ago had they set off? Perhaps they were already there? Her insides froze as she pictured the scene. Her mother opening the door to Bill. The shock would be too much. She pictured her mother collapsing. A stroke. A heart attack. "Please, no!" she said aloud.

As she drove across the bridge something caught her eye. A flash of red. By the barrier above the falls. Rhiannon's anorak? She pulled in at the side of the road and jumped out. Running back, she shaded her eyes, searching the steep, muddy bank that dropped away to the raging torrent below. Yes! It *was* Rhiannon! But where was Bill? And why was Rhiannon leaning over the barrier, looking down?

"Rhiannon!" Louisa shouted her daughter's name, but a truck sped past, drowning her out. Then a Land Rover. She stared at the license plate. *Their* Land Rover. She saw it pull in on the other side of the bridge. As she ran toward it, she saw Bill leap out of the driver's seat. She opened her mouth to call his name, but the sound died on her lips as she saw what he was doing. He was lifting her mother out of the passenger seat. Carrying her to the edge of the falls.

"Rhiannon!" He was shouting over the furious noise of the water. "Rhiannon! Look!" Louisa stared in utter amazement as her mother craned her neck to kiss Bill on the cheek.

~

Bill waved from the Land Rover as Rhiannon scrambled into the Jeep beside her mother. He glanced at Eva, who was fumbling with her seat belt. When she raised her head, her eyes were brimming.

"Please don't cry, honey—she's safe now." For a moment it was as if time had stood still. He was standing in a snowy street in his army uniform, staring at her swollen stomach, telling her every-thing would be all right.

"Thank you." Eva's voice was little more than a whisper. "You saved her. What I said before: I didn't mean . . ." She paused, hold-ing back tears.

"It's okay," he said. "You don't have to explain."

"I . . . I just want you to know I . . . I don't regret it. You and me." She bit her lip. "I turned it into a terrible burden all those years ago. Blaming you, blaming myself; really, it was so . . . destructive. What happened . . . it was nobody's fault—I should have seen that."

He took her hand in both of his. "I guess things never turn out the way you expect them to," he said. "But so much good has come out of the sadness. We made something pretty special, didn't we?"

~

"I shouldn't have done it, should I?" Rhiannon was sitting in her pajamas, a mug of hot chocolate steaming on the bedside table.

Louisa sat down beside her, slipping her arm around her daughter's shoulders. "You shouldn't have run away, no," she said, "and I want you to promise me you'll never go anywhere near that bridge on your own again." She paused, feeling the warmth of Rhiannon's face against her skin as the child nodded her head. "But taking Granddad Bill to see Nan—that was something I should have done days ago."

Rhiannon sat back in bed, a puzzled look in her eyes. "But I thought . . ."

"I know." Louisa smiled. "But I was wrong. I thought that if I left things alone, Nan would sort it out for herself, change her mind about things. But I realize now it would never have hap-pened. What she was feeling inside would have just eaten away at her like a maggot in an apple." She cupped Rhiannon's chin in her hand. "What you did was like holding up a mirror. Suddenly she was seeing herself through your eyes, and she didn't like what she saw."

Rhiannon frowned. "So everything's all right?"

Louisa nodded, hugging her tight. *Yes*, she thought, *sometimes shock tactics are the only way*. She smiled inside as she remembered the day Michael had thrown her into the sea. What would she be like now if she hadn't conquered her phobia about her skin? And what if she had kept up that pretense until she was her mother's age? What kind of paranoid, self-obsessed creature might she have become?

"What about Granddad Eddie?" Rhiannon piped up suddenly. "What's he going to say?"

Louisa thought for a moment before replying. "Well . . . I think he'll be pleased."

"Pleased? That Nan kissed Granddad Bill?"

"No." Louisa ruffled her daughter's damp hair. "But he wouldn't mind them having that sort of kiss, anyway. What I mean is I think he'll be pleased that she's stopped being so sad."

~

The Eisteddfod was a seething mass of anxious-looking parents, grandparents, aunts, and uncles. Louisa scanned the faces for Eva and Eddie. Nothing had been said since the previous evening. No phone calls exchanged. Eva had been exhausted by the day's events, and Louisa hadn't wanted to push things any further just yet. She wandered up and down the foyer. No sign of either of them. People were starting to file into the hall.

"Come on," Michael said, catching her arm. "We'd better get seats."

They settled into a row near the front of the hall with Bill sitting between them. Louisa looked over her shoulder a few times, but it was impossible to see much behind her as the seats began to fill up.

When the MC walked onto the stage, everyone fell silent. Bill glanced at her, his eyebrows like question marks. She shrugged, wondering what was going through his mind. Had she misread the situation yesterday? Was that kiss the reason her parents hadn't turned up? She forced the thought firmly to the back of her mind.

The MC spoke Welsh. Bill and Michael wore faces of puzzled concentration as each category was announced. "Solo singing next," Louisa whispered.

Rhiannon was the third of seven performers. Louisa's gaze moved from her daughter to Bill, enjoying the sight of him, so obviously moved by her singing. She came in second, and he grumbled loudly, saying she was clearly the best and the judges must be prejudiced. Louisa had to shush him as the MC walked onstage to announce the next category.

"She's dancing next—hope she's had time to change!" Louisa's stomach was in knots.

As the first few drumbeats sounded, Rhiannon hurtled across the stage, starting her routine with a series of backflips that drew spontaneous applause from the audience. Louisa hoped the noise wouldn't put her off.

It didn't. She won first prize.

"That's my girl!" Bill thwacked his hands together. Louisa had to grab his arm to stop him from leaping up as Rhiannon received her medal. There was a loud whistle from the back of the hall. Twisting her head, she caught her breath. It was Eddie. He was standing just inside the door, holding her mother's hand. And Eva was cheering, dabbing her eyes with a handkerchief.

"Bill!" she whispered. "Look!"

As the applause subsided, Bill rose without a word and, taking her hand, led her down the long aisle, past the sea of curious faces. She saw her mother, eyes shining, her arm around Eddie's waist now, holding him very close.

As Louisa drew nearer, Bill's fingers squeezed hers. A feeling of lightness filled her whole being. For the first time she could remember, she felt proud of her mother. It no longer mattered whose daughter she really was. She belonged in equal measure to all three of them.

The last thing she saw was Bill holding out his hand to Eddie. Two pink palms meeting. The other colors blurring in a film of tears.

Acknowledgments

In the two years preceding the D-day landings, approximately 130,000 black GIs were stationed in the United Kingdom. It is estimated that between 700 and 1,000 babies were born in Britain during the Second World War as a result of relationships between British women and black American servicemen.

Although this book is a work of fiction, it was inspired by interviews with a number of these so-called brown babies. I am grateful for the honesty with which this material was given, and I respect the wishes of those concerned for their anonymity to be preserved.

The places described in the story are all real. As a child growing up in Wolverhampton I witnessed some of the racial bigotry, which was, unfortunately, common at that time. Later I moved to the coast of Wales, near Aberystwyth, where I live now. I am grateful to my Welsh friend Janet Thomas, whose guidance and encouragement have played a key role in my development as a writer.

Special thanks also to Christina Henry de Tessan for her editorial advice and to Jodi Warshaw and the team at Amazon Publishing.

This book began life as a self-published novel and was "spotted," thanks to Amazon's Breakthrough Novel Award. I would like to thank my daughter, Isabella, and my son, Deri, for their creative and technical input, without which this would not have happened.

About the Author

Lindsay Ashford grew up in Wolverhampton, UK. She was the first woman to graduate from Queens' College, Cambridge, in its 550-year history. After earning her degree in criminology, Ashford worked as a reporter for the BBC and a freelance journalist for a number of national magazines and newspapers. She has four children and currently lives in a house overlooking the sea on the west coast of Wales.